# BEEFCAKE

# BEEFCAKE

## The Hotties Of Haven, Book 2

Jenna Jacob

**BEEFCAKE**
The Hotties Of Haven, Book 2
Jenna Jacob
Published by Jenna Jacob
Copyright 2018, Dream Words, LLC
Edited by: Blue Otter Editing, LLC
ISBN 978-1-7325731-9-2

This is a work of fiction. Names, places, characters and incidents are the product of the author's imagination and are fictitious. Any resemblance to actual persons, living or dead, events or establishments is solely coincidental.

Noble Grayson loves to drown women in pleasure…but he loves his freedom more. When an old high school friend asks him to be the best man at his wedding, Noble jumps at the chance to spend a wild weekend in Sin City. But after a night of ecstasy with a beautiful stranger, Noble soon learns that what happens in Vegas doesn't always stay in Vegas.

Before Ivy Addison can leave scandal behind and settle down in tiny Haven, Texas she first has to survive her sister's wedding. But when the sexy cowboy across the hall rescues her from frustration—in more ways than one—Ivy throws caution to the wind and spends one night of spine-bending splendor that changes her life…forever.

Once Noble returns to Haven, his memories of the green-eyed vixen extinguish all interest in other females. He's still reeling when a cryptic phone call leads him to the new bakery in town—where he gets the surprise of his life. Will he figure out that he needs Ivy more than he needs bachelorhood before she puts the fire out between them for good?

*Beefcake is dedicated to you, the amazingly supportive readers who have bravely followed me into the unchartered waters of steamy contemporary romance.*
*I hope you're having as much fun reading the hopes, heartbreaks, and happily ever after's found in*
*The Hotties Of Haven*
*that I am writing about those sexy as sin*
*Grayson brothers.*

*A love and gratitude filled THANK YOU to Shannon, Rachel, Amy, Shelley, Pearl, Brea, Trisha, Vicki, Rhonda, and Brandon. I couldn't pull this off without the hours and hours you spend helping mold the movie in my mind, the advice, direction, and compassion you give me. You all own a very special place in my heart.*
*And as always,*
*Thank You, Sean…*
*My love.*
*My rock.*
*My inspiration.*
*My life.*

# CHAPTER ONE

"STOP BEATIN' IT like it owes you money, and get out of the shower. You've been in there for thirty minutes. I'm going to be late!"

Noble Grayson exhaled a low curse and gripped his throbbing erection tighter. Closing his eyes, he stroked faster. Blocking out his brother, he filled his mind with visions of Trudy Hanover. The pretty blonde had moved to town a week ago and currently held the number one spot in Noble's spank bank. Though he'd plundered her hot pussy two nights ago, he was eager to fuck her again. Trudy wasn't exactly skilled in the bedroom, but her surgically enhanced DDDs and willingness to try all kinds of kinky things made up for it. The memory of squeezing his dick into her tight little asshole had his balls churning and muscles straining.

Noble fisted faster as his orgasm crested.

"And make sure you wash off the walls this time, you sick fuck!" Nate snarled, pounding on the bathroom door once again.

Noble's climax stalled.

Biting back a snarl, he worked his cock with punishing strokes and focused on how he'd scraped his tongue over Trudy's hard nipples…the way her glossy red lips parted as she screamed out her orgasm while clamping down around his cock.

The rising roar in his ears drowned out the steady thrum of the water pelting his body. As he hammered his cock with a vengeance, his balls drew tight, and his legs quivered. Noble bit his lips together and issued a muffled grunt as thick ropes of come surged into the spray of water.

"For the love of… Squirt your sauce and get out already," Nate barked, fiercely banging on the door like a sledgehammer.

"Use the other bathroom, dick-breath," Noble rasped out.

"Dad's in there, dropping a deuce."

*Figures.*

"Keep your tampon in. I'll be out in a minute."

A shiver slid up Noble's spine. "Christ, can't a guy cop a damn nut in peace around here?" he grumbled, squeezing out the last of his self-indulgence.

He couldn't fault Nate for spazzing out like a hooker who'd missed her period. Noble would be flipping his shit if he were bringing a girl home to meet the family. Thankfully, he was far smarter than his pussy-whipped twin. Noble had no intention of ever getting *that* involved with any girl. But then Gina Scott—owner of the Hangover, Haven's only bar—wasn't a girl, she was a woman…a woman twelve years Nate's senior.

Noble turned off the water and grabbed a bath towel. As he dried the water from his body, he wondered what would shock their mom more tonight: discovering that Nate—the self-proclaimed virgin of the family—had given his cherry to Gina when they started bumping fuzzies six months ago, or finding out she possessed a four-letter-word vocabulary so colorful a sailor would blush.

He grinned, wondering if their mom would threaten to wash Gina's mouth out with soap like she still did with him and his five brothers. No doubt about it, dinner tonight was going to be damn interesting.

While Noble wanted to be sympathetic to Nate's plight, he couldn't. It was too entertaining watching the stupid bastard working himself up with worry and freaking the fuck out. Of course, there was no need for so much angst. His family, especially his mom, Nola, and dad, Norman, would welcome Gina with open arms. Not out of pity over her recent brush with death, four days ago, but because Nate loved her enough to risk his own life to save her.

Gina's abduction had sent an unsettling pall through the normally quiet town of Haven, and even more so within the Grayson clan. It was a shock to discover town bully Victor LaCroix wasn't just a bastard but a cold-blooded murderer. The crazy prick had been nursing a grudge against Gina after she'd kicked his sorry ass out of her bar. His anger had festered for six long months. In the wee hours of the night a few days ago, he'd snuck into the bar and attacked Gina. Victor had then knocked her out with chloroform, hauled her to his filthy trailer on the outskirts of town, and tied her to what Nate had described as a vile, come-and-sweat-stained mattress. Victor had planned to torture Gina, eventually kill her, and bury her in a grave next to the wife he'd claimed left him years ago. The asshat was batshit crazy beyond all reasonable doubt.

Nate had elicited help from Emmett Hill—World War II veteran and Haven's official Bigfoot hunter. After the two men had subdued LaCroix, Nate freed Gina and comforted her while Emmett held Victor at gunpoint until Sheriff Jasper Straub arrived.

Older brother Sawyer had mentioned something about Nate getting in several solid punches of Grayson payback, but Noble hadn't wormed the details out of his twin yet.

LaCroix, the warped fuck-nut, was now sitting in the county jail awaiting trial. The prick was lucky he was behind bars and not in a vault at the morgue.

Shoving his anger aside, Noble cinched the towel around his waist and gathered up his clothes before opening the bathroom door.

Nate stood in the portal, pinning him with a seething glare.

"I remembered to hose off the walls, but you might want to rinse the soap."

Nate rolled his eyes in disgust. "Get out, you sick fuck."

"Since you're running late and all, I'll be happy to drive into town and pick Gina up for you."

"You stay the fuck away from her! I wouldn't *be* running late if you hadn't raced into the bathroom ahead of me, dick-face."

"You have the same face I do, bro." Damn, it was almost too easy to rattle Nate's cage tonight. "I was only trying to help."

"Shove your *help*, come-stain," Nate snarled, pushing past him and slamming the door in his face.

A chuckle rolled off Noble's lips as he strolled down to his bedroom.

Forty minutes later, the entire Grayson clan—mom, dad, six brothers, two sisters-in-law, and the guest of honor, Gina—sat at the dinner table. The poor woman was sporting a hell of a black eye. A rainbow of colors mottled her cheekbone and blended across one whole side of her face.

Anxiety, thick and palpable, was pinging off Nate as Gina nervously relayed the horrific details of her kidnapping.

"I still can't wrap my head around that level of evil. And none of us had a clue it was living right under our noses," Nola tsked. "Victor was never a friendly man, but a murderer? It boggles the mind."

Gina nodded as she took a sip of water. As she placed the glass down on the table, she gave a furtive tug on her sleeves to cover the angry red rope burns and thick scabs that marred her wrists.

"He's definitely a sick and twisted soul, but I still think Haven is a wonderful town. Everyone has been so kind. They've been bringing me food or simply stopping in to check and see if I need anything. Even Reverend Thompson stopped in yesterday to tell me his whole congregation was praying for me. It's a bit overwhelming, really. I never had a clue so many people actually cared."

She flashed a demure smile Nate's way. He responded with an encouraging wink.

"And I've monopolized the conversation long enough. Tell me about the ranch," Gina coaxed. "Everyone sings praises about Camp Melody and the amazing work you do for those poor children."

Norman's face glowed with pride and his chest expanded as he set his fork down and drew in a deep breath.

Noble slid a sidelong glance at Gina. He had to hand it to her. She'd seamlessly shifted the focus off herself and her ordeal.

It was a relief that the stabbing shards of anxiety, courtesy of Nate, and the throbbing pulses of concern, also courtesy of his twin, thrumming beneath Noble's skin had lessened. Like most twins, he and his brother were emotionally hardwired to one another. What one felt, they both felt.

The distress plaguing his brother would likely be around for a while. Yesterday, Nate had left Gina briefly and returned to the ranch to pick up some clean clothes. The minute he'd pulled into the driveway, Noble nearly doubled over beneath the weight of his brother's worry. He'd followed Nate into the house and plopped down on his brother's bed while he packed.

Noble had sent him a pointed stare, and in his mind, he'd simply stated, *You're not leaving until you tell me what's bothering you.*

*Fuck. I should have expected this,* Nate had replied without vocalizing a single syllable. "Sorry, man." Nate had exhaled heavily, then walked to the door and closed it.

"What's wrong?" Noble's voice had been teeming with concern.

"It's Gina. She's barely eating, hardly sleeping, and her mood swings…" He'd let out a long, low whistle. "They're like nothing I've ever seen before. One minute she's clinging to me, all weepy and shit; the next she's screaming at me to leave her alone and not touch her. I-I think she's losing her damn mind. I've invited her to join us for dinner tomorrow night. I'm hoping that if I surround her with my love, and the love of our family, it might coax the old, feisty, sassy-as-hell Gina out of hiding."

"I think you need to get her some help. That's classic PTSD and you know it."

"I do." Nate had nodded. "I'm planning to broach that conversation with her soon."

"It's a labor of love," his dad began now, drawing Noble from his thoughts. "I started the camp in honor of my sister, Melody. She was born with a rare blood and bone disorder. Unfortunately, she died of a lung infection when she was seventeen…"

Noble could recite this story by rote, but then so could his brothers. They'd grown up working alongside a staff of nurses, counselors, and cooks to provide sick and terminally ill children a week-long vacation from hospitals, tests, and fixating on their uncertain futures. Even his sisters-in-law, April and Brea, were now on the payroll.

He'd never held down any other job, nor did he want to. Noble reaped an enormous amount of satisfaction from the guests' giggles and smiles. Of course, heartache and sorrow were part of the package as well. Some never had the chance to return to camp again…at least not in body. But he and his family made sure their spirits continued to thrive and light the hearts of those left behind.

While their oldest brother, Ned, and his wife, April, touted the joy they gained working with the kids, second-oldest brother, Sawyer, and his new bride, Brea—still in honeymoon mode—exchanged heated stares. Even Nate had stopped freaking out long enough to toss his two cents into the conversation.

Younger brother Nash didn't say a word, of course. The dumb shit still hadn't managed to pull his head out of his ass or dust off the funk he'd been wallowing in, making everyone around him miserable. Noble wanted to smack some sense into the stubborn mule for breaking up months ago with his high-school sweetheart, Megan. But stubbornness was the dominant strand that held all the Grayson brothers' DNA together.

Norris, the youngest of the bunch, was quiet as well. After shoveling down his dinner, he asked to be excused. Evidently, killing insurgents on his gaming console held more appeal than hanging out with the family.

"Who's tending the bar for you, tonight, Gina?" Ned asked.

A prickly discomfort crawled across her face before she

dropped her lashes. "Gretchen Kingman."

That bombshell had Noble rearing back as if he'd been sucker-punched. His eyes grew wide as he scoffed. "You left one of the linoleum sisters in charge of your bar? Make sure you disinfect the place when you get back. God only knows what—"

"Noble Franklin Grayson!" his mother chided harshly.

"What? Everybody knows what kinky bedroom games Gretchen, Sylvia, and Annette play." Noble slid a knowing smirk at Sawyer, who'd suddenly taken profound interest in the crumbs left on his dessert plate.

Before Brea had come into his life, Sawyer regularly got his freak on with the wild and willing trio. Gretchen, Sylvia, and Annette held the dubious title of the linoleum sisters because they were so easy to lay.

"Gretchen is the only person I know who has any experience bartending."

"From the gossip around town, she's experienced in a whole lot of things," Ned said with a chuckle.

"Yes, well…tending bar is one of them. She used to work at a big club in Dallas while earning her dental hygienist's degree." Gina scowled. Worry was written all over her face. "Maybe I should head back to the bar in case she's having any trouble."

"Remember to bleach that sucker good. God only knows what…or rather *who* she's been doing on it," Noble cautioned, flashing Gina a crooked grin.

She opened her mouth, probably to volley some colorful four-letter word his way but quickly snapped her jaws shut. After she politely thanked the family for a "lovely dinner," Nate led her out the front door.

Instantly, an awkward silence enveloped the room. Norman absently tapped his thumb on the table, staring off, deep in thought. His mom, lost in her own ponderings, absently traced her fingertips through the condensation on the side of her iced tea glass.

Nash, wearing a usual mask of disdain, raised his eyes to the ceiling as if seeking divine intervention. Or maybe Mr. Angst was simply waiting for a bolt of lightning to come crashing through the roof. It was hard to tell.

Sawyer and Ned exchanged some odd kind of communication, consisting of quirked-up lips and arched brows, with their respective spouses.

All the while the tension grew increasingly thick.

The prickly undercurrent had Noble wondering if his assessment of the family accepting Gina had been way off base.

Whatever was going on, he found it deeply disturbing.

Finally, his dad leaned back in his chair, stretched his arms high over his head before lowering them, and locked his fingers behind his neck. "Gina seems like a…nice girl. Clearly, Nate is smitten with—"

"Oh, Norman. Just…hush." Nola's voice held an unusually sharp edge. She skimmed a glance over the table, scooted back in her chair, and stood. "You all go to the family room and relax. I'll clean up these dishes."

As she reached for a plate, Sawyer placed his hand over hers. "You don't approve of Gina…? You think she's too old for Nate, don't you?"

She blinked at him as if her son had suddenly turned clairvoyant. Quickly banking her surprise, Nola shrugged. "Who am I to judge?"

"You never do. That's why I'm asking." Sawyer sent her a concerned stare.

"Clearly, he feels responsible for what happened to her, though I'm not entirely sure why. And since she has no family, he's taken on the onus of helping her. It just seems…I don't know…sudden."

"Sudden?" Nash scoffed. "He's been banging Gina's brains out for the past six months, Ma."

Nola blanched.

Sawyer pinned Nash with a seething glare.

Noble, who was sitting beside the big-mouthed idiot, simply

smacked him upside the head. "Way to go, ace."

"What?" Nash gaped. "I thought it was common knowledge among the family."

"I certainly didn't know," Nola bit out tersely.

"Settle down, Momma," Norman softly soothed. "He's a grown man. We don't know how he feels about her. It could be nothing more than him sowing some wild oats."

Nola jerked her hand from Sawyer and raised an open palm, flashing Norman the international *don't say another word* sign.

Noble cleared his throat before he nipped this whole judgmental clusterfuck in the bud. "It's more than sowing wild oats, and we all know it. Yes, Gina is older. So what? Age is just a number. And yes, she owns a bar. That doesn't make her trash. You're forgetting the only important part in all this. She makes Nate happy. That's got to count for something."

"It does, and I want him to be happy. It's just that…I'm worried," Nola confessed.

"About?"

"Everything," she said with a sigh. "You all might be grown men, but to me, you'll always be my babies. I'll never stop worrying about any of you."

Her voice cracked, adding a whole new layer of tension to the room.

"I understand that. But you're going to need to use a chainsaw to cut the apron strings, Ma. In case you didn't notice…they're in love."

"In love?" Nola gasped as if he'd up and slapped her.

Noble had said far too much. He hadn't meant to share Nate's personal feelings with the whole family. It was time to steer this conversation in a new direction…lighten up the mood, and then find a way to leave the room. "I'm impressed. Gina didn't drop a single f-bomb all night. If that isn't love, I don't know what is."

Sawyer shot him a seething glare. Obviously his brother's sense of humor was locked away in Brea's purse…along with his balls. But then marriage always changed a man.

"You have *no idea* what love is," Sawyer spat. "You're too scared to find out. That's why you spend your life hopping from one bed to the next."

"Scared?" Noble scoffed. "I'm not scared. I'm smart. And who the hell are you to lecture me? You weren't a damn choirboy before Brea took pity on your sorry ass and married you. The whole town knows you used to spend nearly every weekend getting freaky with the linol—"

"Don't you have someplace to go?" Sawyer interrupted, shooting daggers at him.

"As a matter of fact I do." Noble dragged his cell phone from the back pocket of his jeans and started scrolling through his endless list of female contacts. "I wonder which damsel I need to rescue from hours of dreaded horniness tonight."

Nola scowled as she gathered up the dirty dishes. "You knock up one of those damsels, and my shotgun's gonna be aimed at your crotch while you watch her walk down the aisle in a pretty white dress. I won't tolerate any son of mine giving me illegitimate grandchildren."

Noble scoffed. "Oh, yeah? What are you going to do if I knock 'em all up at the same time?"

"Take a switch to your ass for being horny *and* careless."

Noble grinned and stood before easing in beside his mom. He wrapped an arm around her waist and planted a kiss on the top of her head. "Relax, Ma. I'm not an idiot. I never rescue the damsels without wrapping my anaconda in latex."

"Jesus, bro," Sawyer groaned. "We just fuckin' ate."

Nola spun on her heel and slapped one hand on her hip. "You know better than to curse like that in my house."

"Sorry," Sawyer mumbled. Closing his eyes, he pinched the bridge of his nose.

"Sorry-lookin'," Noble and his brothers replied in unison.

Every since grade school, if one had to apologize for something, the others collectively poked back with the insult; *sorry-*

*lookin.*

Completely unamused, as always, Nola shook her head and leveled an unhappy stare at Noble.

"Relax, Ma. And keep your shotgun locked up. I'm *never* getting married."

"I'll put it up when you start keeping your junk in your pants. One of these days you're going to mess up and be forced to say *I do* to someone you don't even love."

"That'll never fucking happen."

Nola snatched up a wooden spoon and swatted him on the butt, reminding him to watch his language.

Noble grinned and wiggled his ass. "Oooh, harder, Mommy. Spank me harder."

The whole room erupted in laughter.

"Where did you *come* from, you sick freak?" Ned asked, still laughing.

"Same place you did." Noble smirked. "From between my momma's—"

"Hush!" Nola barked. "Get out of here, you perverted little heathen."

"Whoa, wait," Norman called out, still chuckling. "Before you go out and impregnate half the town, what day are you leaving for Vegas? I need to set up the schedule for next week."

"Thursday," Noble replied. "I fly out of Dallas at one o'clock."

"Got it." Norman nodded.

"I still can't believe little Harvey Hays is getting married." Nola shook her head.

"I can't believe any woman would *want* that weasely son of a—"

"Neville Sawyer Grayson, I'm not going to tell you again to watch your mouth," Nola warned, raising the spoon.

"What? It's the truth. You remember what he was like growing up, don't you? Harvey Hays was an obnoxious little bitch," Sawyer grumbled.

Noble bristled. "Hey! He and I were friends back in the day."

"You were his *only* friend back in the day. How long's it been since you've seen him, talked to him? Six? Seven years? Did you ever stop and wonder why the Soy House Coffee King of Seattle invited *you* to be best man at his wedding?"

"Because Noble's still his *only* friend," Ned said with a snort.

"Kiss my ass!" Being forced to defend his old pal pissed Noble off. "You two don't know a damn—"

"Easy, boys," Norman interrupted in the same conciliatory tone he'd used to diffuse their arguments since they were kids. "Obviously, Harvey still feels a strong bond of friendship with Noble and wanted him to be his best man."

Feeling vindicated, Noble flashed Sawyer a triumphant grin. "Thanks, Dad."

"What do you know about the girl he's marrying?" Norman asked.

"Not much. I know her name is Celina and that she owns the crystal and herb store next door to Harvey's coffee shop."

"Crystals? You mean like rocks and shit?" Ned scoffed.

"I don't know. I guess." Noble shrugged. "Harvey said she sells metaphysical stuff…whatever that means. I know she grew up in Texas, and like Harvey, she moved out to Seattle after high school. That's where they met."

"Sounds like kismet. But if Celina's roots are here, why on earth are they tying the knot in Las Vegas?" Nola wrinkled her nose. "I don't like the idea of you going to a place called Sin City."

"I'm a big boy, Ma. I'll be extra careful. I promise."

"Right!" Sawyer scoffed. "You'll be like a kid in a candy store."

*Damn straight!* If the bachelor party Harvey planned turned out to be true—party bus, open bar, and strippers—this trip was going to be off the chain. Before he could reply, his cell phone pinged. Noble glanced at the screen and smiled.

*Trudy: I'm naked and lonely.*

His pulse doubled.

*Hell yes!*

After he quickly tapped out a reply that he was on his way, Noble hurried to the sliding glass door. "I'd love to stay and chat, but the fair maidens of Haven need me to work my magic on them. See y'all in the morning."

"Just keep your wand covered, Mr. Wizard," his mom called out.

Laughing, Noble closed the door, raced across the wooden deck, and jogged to his truck. He fired up the engine while placing a call to his lonely, naked damsel. After engaging the speakerphone option, he laid the device on his thigh and turned onto the gravel drive.

Trudy answered in a low, sultry purr that had his blood pumping and his cock stiffening. "I'm on my way, sweet cheeks. Start warming yourself up. I want you nice and ready when I get there."

"What do you want me to do, lover boy?"

"Spread your legs…spread them nice and wide," he instructed as the truck bounced along the uneven ground.

"They already are."

"Wide enough that I can wedge my shoulders between them and dive tongue-first into your dripping cunt?"

Trudy let out a mournful groan. "Uh-huh."

"Good. Slide your fingers down there and play with your clit. Don't come before I get there. Understood?"

"Oh, my hands are cold."

"Not for long. Once you touch your hot pussy, they'll warm right up. I'll have you even hotter soon."

His cock leapt, eager and ready. When the truck tires grabbed hold of the blacktop at the end of the drive, Noble adjusted his dick off the teeth of his gnawing zipper and turned toward town.

"Rub it hard, baby. Get it all nice and swollen for me."

"Mmm," she moaned. "It's slippery and achy."

"I'll make it all better real soon. Keep playing with it, but don't come. I wanna be there to feel and watch you explode." The pressure inside his jeans made the mile-and-a-half trek to Haven painful as hell.

Her little whimper of understanding slammed from the base of his balls all the way to the tip of his weeping shaft.

Noble sucked in a deep breath. "Dip your fingers inside your pussy for me."

"Noble…hurry," she mewled.

"I am. Believe me, I am." He pressed on the gas pedal, hoping Jasper wasn't running any speed traps tonight. "You wet?"

"Dripping," she moaned.

Saliva pooled in Noble's mouth. "Fuck!"

"What's wrong?"

"Just anxious to get to you."

"How close are you, stud muffin?"

"Close."

He was close, all right…close to shooting a load of choad-nectar in his fucking jeans. Dialing back his demand, he thought about his trip to Vegas instead of pounding Trudy's hungry pussy. When Noble reached Haven, he sped through the side streets and slammed on the brakes in her driveway.

"Your front door better be unlocked," he barked impatiently.

"It's as wide open as my legs, lover boy," she panted. "Hurry, Noble. I-I'm ready to c-come."

"No! Take your hands off your pussy…now!"

She exhaled a long-suffering moan that made him grin.

"I'm going to be inside your house and inside you in less than a minute."

Noble ended the call, killed the engine, and yanked open the glove box. After grabbing a stack of condoms, he bolted from the truck and raced into the house. He kicked the door closed behind him before hauling ass down the hall to Trudy's bedroom.

He found the nymph breathless and splayed out naked on her bed. Her face was wrinkled in desperation as she writhed on the mattress. A greedy smile tugged his lips as he watched her pluck her berry-hard nipples straining toward the ceiling fan.

Out of patience, Noble strode to the dresser and pulled down a couple of silk scarves before he tore his clothes off. In two long strides, he ate up the distance to the bed and skimmed a stare up and down her squirming body. "You waited for me, didn't you?"

"Yes, but it was hard," Trudy whimpered as she longingly stared at his erection.

Noble wrapped a fist around his cock and stroked up and down as he climbed onto the mattress by her head. Trudy licked her lips as a glistening bead of pre-come slid from the crest and over his knuckles. "Harder than this?"

He slapped the wet tip to her mouth and she immediately parted her lips and swallowed him down her throat. The woman could suck the red off a barn, but he didn't want oral, he wanted pussy.

When he pulled his cock away, Trudy whined pathetically. He simply smirked and wrapped the scarves around her wrists and tied them to the decorative wooden spools on the headboard.

He was a laid-back, go-with-the-flow kind of guy until it came to sex. Then he was a complete control freak. Trudy had embraced his kinky side the last time he'd tied her to the bed. In fact, she'd nearly lost her damn mind. After teasing her with his fingers and mouth, he'd shoved his fat dick inside her. She'd nearly squeezed his cock off. He couldn't wait to feel her narrow tunnel clamping around him again.

If he didn't get inside her soon, he was going to roar. But Noble hadn't earned his esteemed reputation with the ladies by rushing the deed, and he wasn't going to risk tarnishing it now.

Prowling onto the bed, between Trudy's legs, he dipped his head and dragged his tongue over her center. In no time, he'd coaxed her to two powerful orgasms and his cock was screaming for relief. Noble quickly sheathed himself, hoisted Trudy's legs over his shoulders, and slammed balls deep into her pussy. With a low growl, he began pumping in and out of her hot walls as sweat dripped off his brow.

"That's it, stud. Fuck me hard, like a wild bull," Trudy cried out.

Noble picked up the pace and pounded her pussy until the familiar swell of release rolled up his body. "Come with me," he grunted.

Trudy tossed back her head and let out a scream that nearly perforated his eardrums as she clamped around him. Noble pushed through her contracting tissue, grunted, and filled the condom. Again, it wasn't the best sex he'd ever had, but it definitely took the edge off.

Long minutes later, after their breathing evened out, he slid from inside her. Before disposing of the condom, he untied her wrists. On his way back to the bed, Noble longingly glanced at his jeans and T-shirt heaped on the floor. He enjoyed fucking, but the postcoital snuggling most women *expected* frightened him. While he never made promises to any of his bed-bunnies, he always feared one of them might confuse their good times as something more. He was definitely not in the market for a girlfriend or, god forbid, a *wife*. He didn't do relationships…ever.

Clenching his jaw, he forced himself to join Trudy in the bed.

To his relief, she rolled over and snagged her cigarettes off the nightstand as if he wasn't there.

"Thanks for the screaming good time again, lover boy." She lit up and then exhaled a thick fog of smoke. "Unfortunately, I won't be able to bang your brains out for a while."

"You leaving town or something?"

"Or something," she repeated with a humorless snort. "No. My fiancé, Calvin, arrives in the morning and is moving in with me. He's taking over Dr. Hubbard's dental practice."

*Fiancé? What the fuck?*

The air in his lungs froze.

She had to be kidding, right?

"Y-your fiancé?"

"Yeah."

Noble slept around. Okay, he slept around a *lot*, but never with another man's woman. He could forgive Trudy for using him but not for manipulating him to break the one cardinal rule he held sacred: *Never poach another man's girl*. Anger careened through him faster than the orgasm he'd just achieved.

"Did you purposely forget to mention the fact that you were engaged, or did it simply slip your mind?"

His incredulous tone made her bristle. She sent him a scowl. "Don't go getting all butt hurt or sanctimonious on me. It's no big deal." She took another drag off her smoke and shrugged. "At least not to me."

"I already gathered that."

"Wow. I didn't take you for someone with a conscience."

Her insult stung. "And why's that?"

"Well, all the girls in town talk about how good you are in bed. I figured a big, bad-assed man-whore like you wouldn't give a shit who he's fucking."

In two seconds flat she'd made him feel like a piece of gum being scraped off the sole of her shoe. He didn't like it.

"If I'm wrong"—*she was*—"then…sorry. You didn't know, so there's nothing to feel guilty about."

But he did, because in Noble's book, ignorance didn't equal innocence. He clenched his jaw tighter and mentally counted to ten, working to contain his anger. It wasn't working.

He pinned her with a glare. "Let me get this straight. You moved to town, kept your engagement quiet, and sought me out to play with until Calvin showed up?"

Inside, Noble was ready to blow a fucking gasket, but somehow he'd managed to keep his voice low and controlled.

Trudy shrugged. "What Calvin doesn't know won't hurt him. I mean…it's not my fault the man has a dick the size of a toddler or shoots off in like five seconds. I just wanted to spend some time with a stud who had a big cock and stamina before I have to live a life of sexual frustration."

Shock pinged through him like a speeding bullet. "If he's such a shitty lover, why are you marrying the man?"

"Because Calvin fits into my long-term plans, all right? Don't judge me," she snapped defensively.

*Plans?* Noble didn't want to know what plans the morally corrupt bitch had up her sleeve.

"Trust me, lover boy, if Calvin's pathetic pencil was as big and talented as your massive hose, I wouldn't let anyone else near my pussy." Trudy's voice took on that familiar slow, seductive timbre that had snagged Noble's attention the first time they'd met outside the post office. She dragged her hot pink acrylic fingernails through the dark spattering of hair on his chest while batting her fake eyelashes at him. "The wedding isn't for a couple of months because Calvin is going to be busy setting up his practice. If we're careful, you and I could hook up once a week and keep having fun, without him ever finding out."

Her proposition made Noble's stomach twist.

"Are you for fucking real?" he barked, brushing her hand off him. "Haven is a small town. No one keeps a secret here. No way could we carry on an affair under Calvin's nose." Not that he'd even want to. "We might as well strip naked and fuck in the middle of Main Street. Gossip is its own goddamn food pyramid around here. You should already be worried. Your neighbors have seen my truck parked in your driveway twice now. It won't be long before Calvin hears that I've been sticking my dick in *his* woman."

"What? You mean…someone might tell him?" Trudy blanched.

"There's no *might* about it."

"B-but they don't know you were here for sex. I mean…you could have come by to…I don't know…fix my sink."

"Sure," Noble said with a humorless laugh. "And Calvin's going hear all about how the big, bad-assed man-whore of Haven was here *laying pipe*."

"Oh, god. The neighbors won't put it like that, will they?"

The last thread of Noble's patience snapped. Anger seared his veins. After launching off the bed, he jerked his clothes on.

"Maybe not, but since the whole town knows my reputation, you might want to start trying to save yours. Oh, and you won't ever be banging my beast again. Don't call me. Don't text me. Hell, if you see me on the street, don't even bother talking to me. Got it? Or I'll tell Calvin what a cheating, skank-assed bitch you are myself."

Shock and outrage flashed like lightning across her face as Trudy sat up. "You son of a bitch. Are you threatening me?"

An evil smile stretched across his mouth. "No, darlin', that there was a promise. I don't threaten women, nor do I lie to them, either. My momma raised me better…which is far more than I can say about yours. Good luck with your marriage, 'cause you are definitely going to need it."

Shaking his head in disbelief, Noble turned and stormed out of her room. As he hurried down the hall, Trudy let out a high-pitched scream, followed by a string of obscenities. Noble slammed the door behind him, hurried to his truck, and peeled out of her driveway in a cloud of smoke and burning rubber.

Cursing under his breath, Noble headed to the Hangover. He needed a drink—several in fact—to burn away the caustic guilt scorching his veins.

"Engaged! Son of a bitch," he snarled. "People wonder why I won't find a good girl and settle down? Because of women like Trudy…the deceitful slut…that's why."

Still seething, he pulled to a jarring halt in front of the bar. After killing the engine, he climbed out, pocketed his keys, and jogged inside.

# CHAPTER TWO

Ivy Addison was clinging to her omnipotent southern charm by a thread. Her mother, Janice—who'd drilled the importance of *proper behavior* into Ivy's head since she was a fetus—would not be proud. Unfortunately, at the moment, she felt like a rabid mountain lion instead of the sweet and retiring woman her mother expected her to be.

As Ivy held the phone to her ear, she closed her eyes and rubbed her forehead with her fingertips. "No, Alma. We've discussed this a hundred times. I do not want a local construction crew doing the renovations. I've already given Rick Hastings a hefty deposit to start work on the shop, Monday morning at eight o'clock sharp."

And if she could keep her meddling landlady, Alma Anderson, out of the mix, Rick and his crew might actually succeed and transform the defunct clothing boutique into the classic bakery Ivy had always envisioned owning.

"Oh, I remember, dear," Alma assured. "Just checking to make sure you haven't changed your mind is all."

"Thank you, but I rarely ever change my mind. All I need you to do is drop the key off to Rick at eight on Monday morning so he can start the work. As soon as this wedding is over, I plan to load up my things in Dallas and move into the apartment above the shop." Ivy wished she could do that right this minute.

"Of course, dear. I'll deliver them to him, myself."

"Thank you. I'm sorry to impose on your time, but if my sister had only learned to plan ahead, I wouldn't have to beg this favor."

"Oh, it's no trouble," Alma assured. "Love can't be planned. Why, when I was getting ready to marry Mr. Anderson, I was as nervous as a moth in a bug zapper. I'll take care of everything. You just keep your sister calm," Alma instructed and ended the call.

*Keep Celina calm?* There weren't enough sedatives on the planet for that. The past few days before the wedding, Ivy's usually sweet, docile sister had turned into a bitchy, temper-tantrum-throwing diva. In turn, Ivy's attitude had grown into a jungle of resentment.

Instead of overseeing the fabrication of her new bakery, she had to hold her surly sister's hand while Celina prepared to marry the biggest misogynistic pig on the planet. Ivy had met her future brother-in-law twice. She couldn't find a single redeeming quality about the man. Why her sister wanted to marry him was beyond Ivy's comprehension. Celina was stunningly gorgeous. She could have men falling all over themselves by simply flashing a shy, southern belle smile. Instead, she'd picked Harvey Hays, a loudmouthed, egocentric, prematurely balding, overweight, waddling troll.

Seriously. What the hell did Celina see in him?

Even if Harvey was a multi-billionaire who could lick his damn eyebrows and had a twelve-inch cock in his boxers, Ivy wouldn't give that slime bag a second glance.

But then she hadn't given *any* man a second glance in…forever. Sadly, the only hot and sweaty time she'd had lately was at the gym. She hadn't had a good workout between the sheets since Jesus wore diapers.

She glanced at the clock and blanched. *Oh, hell! I'm late…again.*

Frantically, Ivy grabbed her purse and raced out the door. Weaving through the traffic like a maniac, she pushed the beat-up truck she'd had since high school for all it was worth. Obscenities that would make her mother stroke out and die slid off her tongue. Twenty minutes later, Ivy skidded to a stop in front of the bridal store, turned off the engine, and grabbed her purse before she raced toward the shop. She gripped the handle of the door, sucked in a fortifying breath, and stepped inside.

"She's always late. I swear to god, she'll be late for her own funeral." Celina's agitated voice scraped Ivy's flesh like razor blades.

"Relax, darling," Janice, their mom replied in a soothing tone.

"I'm here. I'm here," Ivy announced frantically.

"Finally," Celina huffed.

"I'm sorry. I was on the phone with my landlord, trying to get everything set up before we fly out in the morning."

"I wish you'd put as much time and attention into my wedding as you do that stupid bakery," Celina bit out hatefully. "Honestly, throwing all your settlement money on a business that'll be bankrupt in a year is the stupidest thing you've ever done."

The mere mention of the settlement awarded her nine months ago stunned Ivy like a slap to the face. Memories of her former boss, Eugene McMillian—CEO and president of Fiduciary Freedom Investment Corporation—sent humiliation and rage pinging through her. Ivy swallowed the bile rising in the back of her throat, balled up her fists, and clenched her jaw as she worked to shove memories of the man out of her head.

She pinned her sister with a glare. "Listen here, bridezilla, I've taken all the spoiled-brat diva bullshit I can from you. Take a pill and chill your shit, or better yet, hop a plane to Aruba and elope. But don't ever mention that settlement to me again. Got it?"

A flash of regret flitted over her sister's face, but Celina quickly banked it by sliding a brittle, condescending smile in place. "Fine, but you have no room to talk about attitudes. Yours is ten times worse than mine these days. I'm not being a diva. I'm simply trying to save you time, money, and heartache. Your bakery won't ever see a lick of profit and we both know it."

"Says the woman whose business is drowning in debt?"

"My sales might be a little low." Celina tossed her nose in the air. "It's natural for a new business to run in the red in the beginning."

"In the *beginning*? You've been trying to make a profit for *five* years! Mom and Dad are bleeding money left and right to help cover your lease."

"That isn't a proper subject to discuss in pub—"

"Not anymore, they're not," Celina spat, interrupting their mother. "After Harvey and I get back from our honeymoon, I'm closing my shop. He wants to start a family right away. I won't have time to run Jaded Jasmine once I'm a mother, so get off my nipples."

"You're the one who started tugging mine first!" Ivy screeched.

"Girls!" their mother hissed, shooting them both an angry scowl. "Stop your ridiculous squabbling. Immediately. You're causing a scene."

Ivy rolled her eyes and waited for her mom to launch into her favorite lecture about how proper southern ladies should never cause a scene. It was pointless to remind Janice that she was anything but a proper southern lady. Her mother was rattled and stressed out enough…they all three were.

"Oh, Mom! Stick a sock in it, will you?" Celina bit out. "I'm not in the mood to hear any of your pompous lectures right now. I have enough on my plate, thank you very much."

"Then stop acting like a couple of hissing, spitting cats. Honestly, I raised you both better."

Ivy sucked in a deep breath and sought her Zen. It was a pointless exercise. All semblances of peace and serenity had packed their bag nine months ago and hopped a shuttle to the moon.

She'd have to deal with her cranky sister and anal-retentive mother as best she could for the next seven days. After that, she could pour all her energy into the bakery. Then maybe one day, she'd get brave, let her guard down, and give dating a try again.

"All right," Janice breathed out on a heavy sigh. "Everyone

just relax. Let's all head back to the dressing room so you can try on your bridesmaid dress again and see how the alterations on Celina's dress turned out."

On the outside Ivy smiled, but inside she cringed. The bridesmaid dress her sister had picked out was a ghastly combination of green and purple. Of course, it could have been worse. She could have chosen the colors orange and black for her late-October wedding.

*Gag me!*

"I swear to all that's holy, if they've fucked my dress up, heads are going to roll!"

"Watch your language, Celina," Janice spat before raising her head to the heavens. "Lord, please give me strength."

"Oh, Mother! Do you have to be so over-dramatic all the time?" Celina growled before turning and stomping away.

Ivy and her mom shared a look of exasperation. "You hold her, I'll beat the crap out of her."

"You're on," Janice replied without batting an eye. "But wait until we get her in the dressing room. We don't want to cause—"

"A scene. Yeah. I know, Mom," Ivy drawled. "We wouldn't want to do that."

"Certainly not." Her mom's face softened as she cupped Ivy's cheek. "At least one of my girls has paid attention to the things I've been saying all these years."

When Janice turned and started toward the dressing room, Ivy shook her head.

*Yeah, I listened, Mom. But that didn't stop me from bringing a shitload of embarrassment down on the family, now did it?*

The inky memories Ivy had staved off earlier plowed through her in an icy wave of revulsion. Like fragments of glass, sharp and wicked, the image sliced at the scars she'd worked so hard to heal. She could still feel the weight of Eugene McMillian's fat body pinning her to the wall. Feel his hand squeeze her wrists as he restrained them high over her head. Feel his other hand slide up her skirt to jab at her pussy while his eel-like tongue wiggled down her throat. She'd struggled and twisted as she tried to fight off the vile pig's assault. Thankfully, she'd managed to break free before she'd driven her knee between his fat, stumpy legs. When he'd dropped to the carpet, red-faced and gasping for air, Ivy ran…ran from his office…ran for her life. Tears had streamed down her face while his contemptible scream, *You bitch* had chased her down the hall.

Mentally slamming the horrific ordeal beneath a wall of lead, Ivy forced the acidic residue from her veins and sucked in a deep breath.

Digging up the past was poisonous.

Justice had been served.

Dwelling on Eugene McMillian and the ensuing trial served no purpose.

She was on a new path, making a fresh start…reinventing herself. And soon she'd be building the life she'd always wanted.

"Ivy, darling…what's keeping you?" her mother called out.

Skimming a glance over the wedding dresses drenched in tulle, sequins, and lace, Ivy shook her head.

"Nothing, Mom. I'm coming," she hollered back.

Thankfully, the alterations were completed perfectly, but even more impressive was that Celina actually smiled. Ivy had to admit her little sister looked like a princess. Too bad she'd be standing at the altar next to a pig shoved in a tux. She wished there was a way to talk some sense into her sister, but Ivy feared it was too damn late.

The next morning, bright and early, she and her family loaded their luggage and drove to the airport. As Ivy stood in line with her mom and sister to get coffee before boarding their flight, the young woman behind the counter studied her intently.

"I know who you are." The employee smirked. "You're that woman who sued—"

"Please," Ivy interrupted harshly. "Can you just fix our coffee? I'd rather not discuss that…here."

The young woman blushed and nodded. "Sorry."

Ivy trembled with anger for being recognized yet again. Janice simply jerked her chin in the air, like she'd done during the trial. It was her mother's silent reminder to keep a stiff upper lip.

Yes, Ivy knew how to build walls around her. She'd grown lax in these past months following the media circus that had consumed her. The publicity had been beyond brutal. Ivy's name and face had been plastered all over the Internet, newspaper, and every television station in the Dallas-Fort Worth metroplex. It was major news that the out-of-work bakery shop worker was taking on a powerful, mega-millionaire philanthropist like Eugene McMillian.

Ivy couldn't step outside her door, couldn't go to the store or the cleaners without a microphone or camera being shoved in her face. Even her old boss, who'd reopened the bakery, didn't want to her back due to all the adverse publicity.

She'd hidden in her apartment for months. Then one day her father had knocked on her door. He'd helped Ivy pack her things and then moved her back to the safety of her childhood home. Each morning she'd wake surrounded by the joyful memories of her past, but then the oily drama of the trial would sluice through her veins and coat her flesh.

Nothing had prepared Ivy for the repugnant and emotionally crippling venom spewed during the trial. McMillian's attorney had tried to paint Ivy as a scheming extortionist who had attempted to seduce his client in order to get rich by blackmailing him. Thankfully, Margaret Neill had had the foresight to interview every woman who'd left his company. Out of the forty-five women who no longer worked for the prick, twelve had agreed to testify. As it turned out, McMillian had offered each one of them the same vacant title of senior vice-president, the same six-figure salary, and the same penthouse apartment. But Ivy had been the only woman McMillian had touched inappropriately.

The jury had been quick to unanimously side with Ivy, awarding her a massive settlement. Unfortunately, no amount of money could have assuaged the humiliation and degradation she'd endured. Or the embarrassment she'd felt while recounting the details of her hideous encounter with Eugene McMillian, while a slew of reporters and a courtroom chocked with strangers hung on her every word.

Even after the news crews had left to chase their next sensational story, Ivy remained reclusive and withdrawn. Then one day, she'd ventured out of the house to retrieve the mail and looked up. The sun had warmed her face and the sound of children's laughter echoed in her ears. She'd stood, mesmerized, watching them run and giggle and play. It then had dawned on her that locking herself away wasn't really living…it was merely existing.

With her wounds still weeping, Ivy had vowed to rejoin the human race.

Her coveted culinary degree wasn't getting her anywhere while she remained in hiding. So she'd started researching. She'd spent hours and hours online, learning how to start her own business. Desperate to leave Dallas and the inky film that still clung to her flesh, she'd scoped out small towns. Towns that were far enough way to provide anonymity from the trial but still close enough she wouldn't be cut off from her family. They were her lifeline and had kept her sane during the trial. Even her mother hadn't let the slanderous comments send her cowering. Janice had simply lifted her head and projected a regal strength.

In her heart, Ivy knew that their love had kept her from falling into an even deeper depression than the one she'd struggled to claw free from.

Standing at the coffee counter in the airport, Ivy leaned over and kissed her mom on the cheek. "Thank you."

"For what, love?"

"For everything." A genuine smile tugged Ivy's lips.

The flight from Dallas to Las Vegas was uneventful except for her dad, Jeff, teasing his three girls unmercifully. Between laughs, Ivy paused and stared at her family. They might be dysfunctional as hell, but they were hers. Even after all the emotional hell she'd gone through, she was blessed in ways she'd never imagined.

After landing, they retrieved their luggage and boarded a shuttle to the hotel. There was a palpable energy filling the air in Las Vegas. As Ivy stared out the window, taking in all the decadence and growing anxious to explore the hotels and shops, Celina tapped on her cell phone, grinning excitedly.

"Harvey's already here and checked in to our suite. Oh, my god. I can't wait to see him again."

"You've only been apart five days," Janice reminded with a tight smile.

"It's five days too long, Mother." Celina rolled her eyes.

Ivy groaned inwardly. Bridezilla had come out of hiding again. *Joy!*

"I'm going to invite him to come to dinner with us tonight, Daddy."

"You sure he doesn't have any other plans?"

"Of course not. His best man isn't arriving until tomorrow. Unless you don't want to be around—"

"I didn't say that pumpkin," Jeff interrupted. "Ask him if he can join us. I'll call the restaurant and add him to the reservation."

As Celina dropped her head and began texting, Ivy caught the silent, less-than-thrilled look her parents exchanged. Evidently all the votes were in, against the pompous groom-to-be. Holidays from now on were sure to be oh such fun. Ivy nearly rolled her eyes at the thought.

When their hotel came into view, Celina squealed. "Oh, my god! I can't believe I'm actually getting married here. Ever since I saw that movie...oh, what's it called..."

"The Hangover?" Ivy prompted.

"Yes! Oh, my god. Look at that fountain," Celina screamed, pointing out the window as the shuttle came to a stop. "This place is gorgeous."

Ivy couldn't disagree. The Roman architecture and marble

statues were breathtaking, but after they'd gathered their luggage and stepped inside, she was swept away by more jaw-dropping opulence. While her dad handled checking them in, Ivy studied the map the front desk clerk had handed them.

"They've got a whole city in this place. Look." She held the map out to Celina. "They have stores and restaurants down this way. Oh, I feel a shopping spree coming on."

"Knock yourself out." Celina giggled. "I'm going to spend some pre-wedding quality time with my man."

Ivy's stomach tilted. "Well then…you knock yourself out little sister."

"Oh, I plan on knocking a whole lot out. This wedding has been so damn stressful I'm about to lose my damn mind."

*Trust me. We all are.*

Instead of voicing her feelings, Ivy simply smiled.

"Here's the card key to your room," her dad said, pressing the plastic rectangle into her palm. "Do you want me to help you get settled in?"

"No, Dad. I'm good. You and Mom go on up to your room. I'll be fine."

"All right. We'll meet down here at seven and grab a cab to take us to dinner."

"Don't be late," her mom stressed, giving both Ivy and Celina a stern look. "And text Dad if Harvey will be joining us."

"Will do." Celina grinned as she headed toward the elevator, dragging her suitcase behind her.

"What are we doing here?" Janice asked, worry lining her face.

"Having a wedding, unfortunately," Ivy sympathized.

"Knock it off, you two," Jeff admonished. "The last thing Celina is going to need in the future is you two touting her with *I told you so*. I'm not thrilled, either, but we're here to support her, like we did—"

"With me. Yeah, I know, Dad," Ivy said grimly. "I'll see you both in a little bit."

As she headed in the same direction her sister had moments earlier, Ivy mentally scraped the sickly residue of memories Eugene McMillian constantly conjured. After taking the elevator to the twenty-second floor, Ivy exited and strode down a long, lush hallway until she found her room.

She slid the card into the reader but the light remained red. It took her two more tries until a green light suddenly began to blink and the lock snicked. She shoved the door open and smiled. The room was posh and huge, especially the bed. She released her suitcase and kicked off her shoes. Then, acting like a kid, she ran and jumped on the mattress. Giggling, Ivy flopped onto the soft padding and let the comfort envelop her before she grabbed the map from her purse and began plotting her shopping excursion for tomorrow.

At seven o'clock, she was freshly showered and properly prepared for dinner with her family. As she carefully made her way across the lobby on a pair of hot red stilettos that matched her dress and lipstick, she caught sight of her folks. But she didn't see Celina anywhere. Ivy was glad she wouldn't be the one getting the familiar, *proper southern girls are always prompt* lecture from their mom.

"At least I'm not the one late *this* time," Ivy chuckled as she sidled up between her parents.

"Your sister isn't coming to dinner with us," Janice announced, clearly perturbed.

"Why not?"

"Harvey has a tummy ache. Celina is staying in to take care of him. Honestly, he's a grown man capable of calling room service and ordering some chicken soup, for crying out loud. This was our last night together as just the family." Her voice cracked and she quickly clenched her jaw.

"Oh, Mom, I'm sorry." Ivy sighed.

"Easy now, Momma," Jeff cooed softly as he wrapped the woman in his arms. "We'll go out anyway and have a lovely dinner. It will be all right."

Janice nodded and quickly pulled herself together.

The three of them made the best of a bad situation, and in the end, they really did have a lovely dinner. The upscale steak house had a killer view of the massive fountain in front of the restaurant. Ivy almost forgot to eat, she was so entranced by the beautiful dancing water and colorful flashing lights.

When they returned to their hotel, she said good night to her parents, then walked toward the shopping area to scope it out. Though Ivy was stuffed from dinner, she couldn't keep from stopping and buying a slice of peanut butter cheesecake and taking it back to her room.

Relaxing on the bed she flipped on the television and found the Food Channel. As she watched teams vying to be the cupcake champions, Ivy nibbled the decadent cheesecake.

# CHAPTER THREE

THE TWO-HOUR RIDE to Dallas beside his brooding brother had been mostly silent. Noble waved goodbye, slung his duffle bag over his shoulder, and then strolled into the airport terminal. After placing his bag on the security belt, he watched it disappear inside the X-ray machine before stepping up to have his body scanned. An hour later, he was buckled in his seat on the airplane, next to a sweet old lady named Kitty.

"You going to Vegas for work or pleasure?" she asked.

"Pleasure. An old pal from high school is getting married."

"I'm going for pleasure, too. I'm being inducted into the AVA Hall of Fame," she announced with a big, proud smile.

Noble had no idea what that was, so he simply returned a polite smile and nodded while he studied her more closely. The woman was dressed in stylish clothes, though she wore more makeup than most her age The diamonds twinkling off her fingers, wrist, and neck spoke of wealth. She might be a famous philanthropist. Still, the words *AVA Hall of Fame* rolled through his brain as he worked out the acronym. Maybe it stood for the Athletic Veterans Association. He could be sitting next to a gold medal winner from one of the early modern Olympic games.

"You don't know what the AVA is, do you, sugar?" she asked with a pronounced southern drawl.

"No, ma'am, I can't say as I do."

"It's the Adult Video Awards."

Noble's smile slid from his lips. *Adult movies? Was she talking...porn?*

"I can't believe a big, strappin' hunk like you hasn't heard of the AVA," she mused, sadly. "But nowadays, it's all too easy to find such things on the Internet. Surely, you watch them while you're"—she dropped a glance at his crotch—"you know…spanking your meat-monkey?"

Noble nearly choked on his tongue. He'd rather die, buckled to his seat in a fiery airplane crash, than discuss his masturbation preference with the old girl.

"It's a pity that all the video stores went belly-up. No one sees my movies anymore and it's a darn shame. I mean, I spent my whole life taking it every which way but inside out." Kitty leaned in closer and whispered, "Double penetration was always one of my favorites."

The visuals flashing through Noble's brain weren't only wrong but nauseating.

"Oh, those were the best of times. I still do some oldster porn now and then." Kitty scrunched her face and shoulders like an excited child. "I just love giving my all. Though most of my co-stars have to pop Viagra like they're M&Ms, it's still fun."

Hands down this flight was going to be the most awkward and psychologically damaging three hours of his life.

"My screen name is Syndee Suckem," Kitty stated proudly. "Maybe you've heard of me?"

She flashed him a hopeful smile full of perfectly aligned dentures.

As he shook his head, the twisted half of his brain was dying to ask if she kept them in or took them out while working. But then he could feel his junk shrinking up inside him, as the other half of his mind cried, *Dude! What the fuck is wrong with you?*

"That's a shame," Kitty tsked. "You should rent one of my movies, handsome. I guarantee you'll like what you see. I might be old, but I'm still flexible."

He sent her a painfully polite smile as he shoved visions of wet gums, wrinkled, saggy boobs, and scraggly gray pussy hair out of his head.

"While I'm in town, I'm also going to visit my daughter,

Karen," Kitty announced, changing the subject—*thank you, god!* "She's a blackjack dealer and mother of four who's divorcing her third scumbag alcoholic husband."

"That's a shame."

"It is." Kitty nodded. "I wish she was more like her brother. My sweet boy, Kyle, is a genius, and he's so damn handsome. He could have been in movies, like me."

As the plane taxied down the runway, the old woman prattled on about her golden boy, Kyle, while sprinkling in disparaging comments about her not-so-smart daughter. Noble obliged her with nods and smiles long after the plane lifted into the air while Kitty regaled him with every photo on her cell phone. While none were work related—*thank fuck*—there were plenty of pictures of the old gal wearing barely a stitch, with her body bent in lewd, sexually suggestive poses.

No amount of bleach would ever scrub the images from his eyes or his brain.

But when Kitty started describing—in great detail—the oozing, pustule ass boils her late husband suffered at the nursing home, Noble had to swallow back the bile rising in his throat and quickly excused himself.

After working his way to the back of the plane, he found all the lavatories full. He couldn't find the willpower to return to his seat and listen to more of Kitty's disturbing stories, so Noble decided to loiter outside the bathroom door. While a middle-aged flight attendant busily checked supplies on the drink cart, he turned on his charm. Three and a half minutes later, she pressed her number, scribbled on a piece of paper, into his palm.

After using the facilities, he squandered several more minutes sweet-taking the fight attendant, before reluctantly returning to his seat. To his delight, Noble found Kitty fast asleep. Thankfully, the old porn star snored the rest of the way to Vegas.

When they landed and the cabin doors opened, Noble grabbed his duffle bag, bid farewell to Kitty, and sprinted off the plane. He stepped outside, and the carbon monoxide fumes pouring from the string of taxis sucked the air from his lungs.

Noble gaped up at the palm trees before snagging a cab to take him to his hotel.

Peering out the window, he felt as if he'd landed on a distant planet. Huge, elaborate hotels soared into the bright blue sky, while on the ground, bumper-to-bumper traffic crawled at a snail's pace as hordes of people strolled up and down the busy sidewalks of the strip.

*You're definitely not in Texas anymore.*

His eyes grew even wider when the cab pulled into a circular drive and came to a stop beside an ornate marble fountain. Grecian urns and statues were situated throughout the meticulously manicured landscaping. Noble paid the cabbie, grabbed his bag, and climbed out of the car.

As the taxi drove away, Noble stood slack-jawed as he took in the white marble columns and intricately carved sculptures tucked in arched alcoves lining the front of the hotel. He stood mesmerized by the beauty before him, ignoring the people coming and going around him until someone bumped his shoulder, jostling him from his trance.

He entered the lobby and simply stared. Beneath his feet, huge circular patterns of inlaid marble swept the floor. Noble paused to take in the large fountain of three sleekly carved Roman goddesses—with perky nipples exposed—standing shoulder to shoulder in a semicircle, surrounded in a dome of gold and marble. Dragging his eyes from the beauties, he drank in massive Roman paintings and even more sculpted statues that lined the curved walls. The ceiling above him was dotted with enormous chandeliers that cast a golden glow over several recessed cupolas.

Noble knew exactly how Alice had felt when she'd tumbled down the rabbit hole. He yanked out his cell phone and started snapping photos. Even if he found the words to describe the grandeur of this hotel, his family would never believe him. Best to have proof.

"Grayson!"

Jerking toward the sound of his name, he peered across the lobby and spotted a bald man waddling his way. Noble blinked in disbelief when he realized his old friend Harvey was beneath all those layers of…weight.

*Christ, what the hell happened to him?*

"Harv." Noble banked his shock and wrapped the large man in a brotherly hug. His hands sank into gelatinous flesh as he clapped Harvey on the back. "You look…you look great, man."

"Right. Liar," Harvey growled. "I'm a hundred pounds overweight." More like two hundred, but Noble kept that observation to himself. "My hair keeps sliding off my head into my ears and down my back. I can't see my dick anymore. I've turned into my fucking old man."

He had. But again, Noble wasn't going to confirm that claim. He simply chuckled.

"But you, you lucky prick. You haven't changed one damn bit. What the fuck? You should be falling apart like me. Prick."

"Dude! We've only been out of school seven years."

"Yeah, well stress is an evil bitch that does ugly things to a man. I'm not complaining, owning my own business is great, but it takes a toll. I'll gladly carry a few extra pounds around my waist and shed like a fucking husky in July to live out my dreams. None of those dickless pricks back home had the courage to grow a pair and try to accomplish all I have."

Harvey's insult stung, but Noble let it slide. There wasn't any use getting riled up about an opinion.

"Looks like you're living a stress-free life. I guess you're still living at home…still being your old man's bitch and sweating your nuts off with his camp thing, right?"

This time, Noble bristled. But instead of following through with the knee-jerk reaction to slam his fist in the prick's jaw, Noble simply clenched his fist, and shook his head. "I'm not his *bitch*. I work hard to earn my paycheck, man."

"Yeah, yeah. Sure, sure. Sorry, didn't mean it as an insult. But, Christ, bro…living at home with Mommy and Daddy must be hell on your sex life. You must not get laid but once or twice a year."

Harvey's caustic laughter was as offensive as his taunting.

"Try three or four times a week," Noble bit out, barely containing his anger. "A real man who possesses the right skills doesn't need a bed to get the job done."

Harvey threw back his head and laughed. "You would know. You've been perfecting those *skills* since we were freshmen."

"Yes, I have."

"Good to know you're still chasing pussy. It got boring as hell to me," Harvey stated, curling his lip in revulsion. "It'll be a welcome relief to pound my meat into one girl from now on. Maybe one day you'll find a snatch so sweet you'll want to slap on the ball and chain, too. Hell, it might even be one of the fine ladies I lined up for us. At least you won't worry about waking up the folks tonight while you're banging bitches."

Damn! When had his old friend's opinion of women turned so…degrading?

*Harvey Hays was an obnoxious little bitch.* Sawyer's words rolled through his head.

Had Harvey always been so condescending and rude? Noble wasn't sure. Maybe he'd worn rose-colored glasses back in high school. If he had, they were definitely off now. Unfortunately, it was too late for him to tell the man to go fuck himself and head back home. Noble would simply have to suck it up and make the best of a bad situation. Besides, it was only for a few days.

"Look, I have to run upstairs and check on the little woman-to-be…maybe knock a little off, yanno?" Harvey grabbed his cock and grinned. "Meet me down here around five and we'll grab some dinner before climbing aboard the party bus. I can't wait to raise hell like we used to. Man, wait till you see the whores I bought for us tonight."

*Whores? He bought…?*

"You lined up hookers? I thought you said they were strippers."

"Strippers…hookers, what's the difference? As long as they spread their legs for us, that's all that matters…am I right?" Harvey's grin was down right lecherous.

The thought of *paying* a woman to have sex with him immediately turned Noble off. He'd never had a girlfriend, per say, but he at least *knew* the women he slept with. The excitement he'd felt about this trip was totally scrubbed from his system; dread had now taken its place. "I thought one-night stands bored you."

"They do. But before I'm locked in the marriage cage for the rest of my life, I want some kinky memories to think about while plowing my wife."

*Jesus Christ! Why marry the poor girl at all?*

Too bad Harvey and Trudy were marrying different people. Those two would be perfect for one another, since neither had an ounce of respect for their future spouses. Maybe they were simply getting married out of convenience. Talk about a death sentence.

While Noble had zero desire to ever tie the knot, he'd never marry for anything other than love. And he certainly wouldn't treat his bride like a blow-up doll. No, he'd treat her like a queen.

"The hookers I hired are smokin'-hot, but they were pretty cheap. So, I'm not really sure how clean they are, but as long as we've got condoms, it won't matter."

Noble's stomach pitched. *Fuck that!* He had no intention of flying home with a dozen STDs oozing from his dick.

"Fuck, I can't wait," Harvey continued, grinning like an idiot. "My bachelor party is going to be such an epic orgy, I'll still be remembering it when I'm eighty."

*Orgy?* The unholy visual of Harvey—*naked*—driving his little trouser worm into some skanky hooker made Noble want to hurl.

He had to extricate himself from this debacle of a bachelor party, and fast.

"Sorry, bro, I'm going to have to take a rain check on the hookers. See, I've got a sweet gal back home who took such good care of me before I left, the skin hasn't grown back yet."

Noble didn't like to lie, but if it kept him herpes free, he'd lie his damn ass off.

"Sucked the skin right off, huh?"

Noble nodded.

"What's her name?" Harvey pressed.

"Trudy Hanover."

"She must be new in town,"

"Yeah. She moved in a few weeks ago." Noble nodded. "She's sexy as fuck. Got the biggest, sweetest titties you've ever wrapped your lips around. And an ass so fine it'd make an onion cry."

"Damn, man. You just described my Celina."

"Seriously?" Noble didn't believe that line of bullshit for a second, but it gave him the opening he needed. "Then why the hell are you going to risk catching crotch crickets, or worse, by fucking some hooker? Passing a family of crabs to your bride on her wedding night makes for a damn ugly honeymoon."

Harvey blanched. "Shit. I didn't think about that. Maybe I should cancel the hookers. I mean, since you're not going to give the beef injection to any of them…"

"Yeah. I'd cancel if I were you. Just to be on the safe side. Besides, if Celina's like Trudy"—*save yourself and eat a bullet now*—"you're gonna need all the stamina you got for the wedding night."

"I sure am. But…I'm keeping the party bus. We'll just go hit some strip clubs, buy some lap dances, and get fuuuuucked up!"

"I like that plan." He did only because he wouldn't get gonorrhea from a lap dance.

Nate watched his old friend waddle away and realized that the camaraderie they'd once shared was long gone. He couldn't stand the pompous, egotistical man Harvey had become…or maybe had always been. Swallowing the disappointment staining his tongue, Noble ambled to the front desk and retrieved his card key.

While he waited for the elevator, a sunburned teen argued with his mom about leaving the pool. The ungrateful little prick didn't stop whining all the way up to the twenty-second floor, where Noble happily exited the lift. Grateful he'd never be a dad or have to deal with the caustic attitude of a pubescent teen, he rounded the corner to search for his room.

Focusing on the numbers, he was halfway down the hall before he noticed a petite woman with a curvaceous hourglass figure. He suddenly itched to wrap his fingers around her narrow waist and skim a palm to her full breasts or sink into the thick mop of strawberry-blonde hair spilling down her back in big, fluffy curls. A mound of shopping bags and a couple of pink boxes lay at her feet as she angrily shuttled her card key in and out of the reader.

"Oh, come on, you miserable piece of..." she grumbled in a husky voice that made his dick stir as she slammed the card into the lock again.

Noble darted his gaze between the room numbers and the woman as he continued striding her way. To his delight, his room was directly across from hers.

*Kismet.* Or so his mom would say.

A wicked smile tugged his lips as he watched the sinfully sexy damsel in distress. If he was lucky, he might have this sweet little creature beneath him and screaming his name long before he had to meet up with Harvey.

"Need some help, ma'am?" Noble smiled, setting his duffle bag on the carpet next to her packages.

The woman snapped her head his direction, sending her pale curls swirling from her face. As she latched her shimmering green eyes framed in thick, dark lashes up at him, the air froze in Noble's lungs.

He dragged an awe-struck gaze over the delicate contours of her face, pausing at her plump lips. The urge to slant his mouth over hers and taste all that sweet honey rode him hard. He was helpless to harness his primitive impulses, and his cock grew thick and hard beneath his zipper. He clenched his jaw and inhaled slowly, struggling to keep from pressing her up against the uncooperative door, peeling off her pretty pink shorts, and driving balls deep inside her right now.

"Did you just call me ma'am?" Her voice was low and sultry and sent his blood surging like lava.

Unsure if he could speak yet, Noble swallowed tightly and nodded.

"Are you a good southern boy or something?"

He cleared his throat as a slow smile spread across his lips. "Well, I am southern, and I'm good at a lot of things." He leaned in closer, inhaling the scent of clean soap and ripe peaches. "But I excel especially well at others."

Her eyes flared briefly and she sucked in a barely audible gasp before her wet, pink tongue peeked from between her lips. She lightly licked them and swallowed as tightly as he'd done a moment ago.

Turning her attention back to the door, she pulled the card key free and waved it in the air. "I don't think this thing works. I should probably go down to the front desk and get another."

The breathy tone of her voice was even sexier than the first time she'd spoken. Noble wanted to spend hours and hours listening to her sultry hoarse moans and whimpers as he made her scream and shatter over and over again.

She locked her hypnotic jade-colored eyes on his once more and he bit back a groan as his jeans grew exponentially tighter. He wanted this woman…ached for her in ways he'd never felt before. Quickly dragging his eyes off hers, Noble glanced at her left hand.

*No ring. Thank fuck.*

Unwilling to let what would undoubtedly be the thrill of a lifetime pass him by, he flashed her one of his most seductive smiles and stepped in closer. Even a blind man couldn't have missed the tiny tremor skipping through her or the way her nipples pebbled under her white cotton shirt.

Tossing up a mental fist pump, Noble was elated that the earthquake of attraction rocking the ground beneath his feet wasn't one-sided.

After dropping his gaze to the packages on the floor, he lifted his head and arched his brows. "Looks like you bought out all the stores."

The throaty chuckle rolling off her lips and the megawatt smile lighting up her face nearly stopped his heart.

"I left a couple of thongs back at Victoria's Secret, but I don't think they're your size."

Her sassy retort intrigued him. Oh, he wanted to know this woman in every carnal way. Wanted to spend hours sweating and thrusting in mutual pleasure for sure, but there was something about this girl that made him want even more. He wanted to peel her open inside and out, wanted to know every morsel about her past, her present, and her future. Blindsided by the notion, he quickly shoved it aside. He had no desire to start dissecting these strange and unfamiliar emotions, for fear of what he might find.

*Calm down. Don't do anything stupid, just keep flirting,* a little voice in his head prompted.

"That's okay. I'm not a fan of wearing thongs anyway."

Her eyes widened in surprise and a brilliant smile stretched over her succulent lips. He'd both surprised and delighted her. *Score!*

"How come?"

He sent her a playful smirk. "Well, the little string separates and strangles the twins something fierce. You ever tried bailing hay wearing those things? It's not fun. You're always stopping to rearrange your junk. Makes it impossible to get any real work done."

Her tinkling laughter fluttered over him like a springtime breeze and warmed his flesh like the hot summer sun.

"I've never baled hay, with or without a thong. But it sounds…painful."

He leaned in close, lips barely brushing the shell of her ear. Dragging in another breath of her intoxicating scent, he dropped his voice to a feathery whisper. "Excruciating."

She trembled and swallowed audibly before easing back and

extending her hand. "I'm Ivy."

Noble stared at the delicate fingers she offered, fighting the urge to haul her into his arms and kiss her breathless. Instead, he swallowed her hand in his calloused paw and gently squeezed. A tingling static charge surged up his arm.

Ivy gasped, obviously shocked by the crazy sensation, too, before she tried to snatch her hand back. But Noble didn't let her go. He held on tight, locked his gaze to her smoldering green eyes, and lifted his other hand. He skimmed the pad of his thumb over her lips, memorizing the soft, warm texture.

Unable to stop himself, he rested his thumb on her chin and brushed a whisper of a kiss across her mouth. Like sparklers, slivers of energy sputtered over his lips. He'd never experienced such a strange sensation, but he liked it…liked it a lot.

Still lost in her eyes, he inched back and released her hand. "Noble."

"Are you?" she playfully asked.

"I am," he murmured. "Especially when I'm tumbling you into ecstasy, darlin'."

He didn't miss the flash of lust that skipped across her eyes or the pulse point at her neck that picked up and hammered in time with each pulsating throb of his cock. As he eased in close to her mouth once more, the scent of succulent peaches surrounded him, stronger this time.

Suddenly, Ivy flinched backward, quickly banking her arousal and lifting her chin defiantly. "Not when, cowboy… *if*. *If* I let you tumble me to ecstasy. But don't go getting your hopes up. Cocky men turn me off."

"No they don't. You're just saying that so I won't think you're a slutty girl. Trust me, I don't…not for a single second," he whispered as he pressed his hungry erection against her soft hip. Her eyes flared. Her lips parted. A beautiful pink blush crawled up her chest and stained her cheeks. "I know you're not easy, and I also know that if I want the chance to drown you in pleasure—which I desperately do—I'll have to work hard to earn that honor. Work real damn *hard*." Emphasizing the last word, Noble rolled his hips, letting her feel every thick, hard inch wedged in his jeans.

Ivy shuddered and pulled back.

Before he could blink, she'd slapped on a look that screamed *hands off*.

Suddenly worried she might decide to knee him, Noble stepped back, ready to cover his junk.

He was quickly learning that city girls weren't anything like the ones back home.

He'd have to find a different tactic in order to seduce this fiery temptress. Thankfully, he'd been blessed—or cursed, depending on the situation—with a healthy strand of the stubborn Grayson DNA. He'd find a way to drag this saucy spitfire beneath him. But first he had to figure a way over or under the wall she'd unexpectedly constructed. He had no idea why she'd gone from a soft, pliant sex kitten to a brittle ice queen, but he aimed to find out.

A sickening thought popped in his head. He lifted his chin and pinned her with a suspicious stare. "You're not in Vegas to get married, are you?"

"Me?" She choked on a gasp before vigorously shaking her head. "Not in this lifetime. Are you?"

"Absolutely not," he adamantly replied.

As if she sensed a kindred spirit, her lips twitched, fighting a smile. With a nod, she tried unlocking her door again. The light stayed red and Ivy issued a tiny huff of frustration.

"Here, let me help you."

"It's okay. I'll get it open…eventually."

"How do you expect me to live up to my name if you won't let me help you?"

"Okay, Noble. I'll let you be *noble* and give it a try."

When she started to lift her hand away, he reached over and cupped his fingers around hers. Once again, that crazy tingle slid up his arm.

"See, it's all in the way you do it. You slide it in slowly…then ease it down…all the way down…nice and deep." The sexual innuendo rolled off his tongue, thick and hoarse, while carnal images of the woman now trembling against his chest filled his brain.

Noble slowly dragged the card back out of the reader, and the green light began to flicker. He gripped the handle, pinning her between him and the door, and drank in the feel of her lush, warm body before turning the knob and pushing the door open.

She sent him a surprised smile over her shoulder. "You did it!"

Ivy hurried into the room while Noble watched the sensual sway of her hips. His grandpa Grayson would say that Ivy had a swing so fine he'd like to park it on his front porch. Noble wanted to park Ivy's ass, all right…park it in the middle of his bed and drag about twelve hours of orgasms from her sinful body.

Somehow, someway, he was going to charm this city girl out of her clothes.

Bending, he gathered up her packages, snagged his duffle bag, and followed her into the room.

# CHAPTER FOUR

Ivy sensed Noble behind her, not so much by the sound of rustling packages but by from the strange and unsettling sexual current connecting them. The attraction she felt toward the man sent warning bells and buzzers clanging in her head. The shiver of wanton desire sliding up her spine was another red flag.

She had to put some space between her and the drop-dead gorgeous cowboy before she did something stupid, like strip off her clothes and jump his sexy bones. Since he'd opened his mouth and that deep, rich voice melted over her skin, she'd been waiting to spontaneously combust. And when he brushed his soft but firm lips to hers, the puddle in her panties grew into a fucking river. She was dripping wet and every cell in her body was screaming for release. That one kiss alone told her that Noble was a skilled lover who'd leave her spineless, sated, and in a damn coma if she'd let him.

*Do it. Good god, the only thing that's touched your vajayjay for months is your vibrator—which you left at home, by the way.*

Ivy didn't need the little voice in her head reminding her how long she'd gone without a lover. Hell, McMillian was the last man to kiss her, and that wasn't even a kiss…it was an assault. She'd sworn off all men after that.

At least until now.

*Come on! What are you waiting for? You're in Vegas, baby! What happens in Vegas stays in Vegas. Remember? Besides, it's not like you're ever going to see him again.*

She also didn't need her riotous hormones encouraging her to bed the sexy beast.

The spark he'd effortlessly ignited inside her was already burning out of control. It was taking all the willpower she possessed not to beg him to strip her naked and extinguish the flames.

As Noble placed her packages on the bed, she stared at his big, capable hands. God, what would those long fingers feel like sliding in and out of her slick core? How many orgasms could he drag out of her before he whipped out that massive slab of beef, bulging beautifully beneath his jeans, and started to, *slide it in slowly…then ease it down…all the way down…nice and deep?*.

She wanted…no, she *needed* a long night of sex, badly.

Disregarding her begging hormones, Ivy tried to curb her hunger. She didn't want a one-night stand. Only desperate, horny women fucked men they barely knew.

*Uh, news flash, sweetheart—you are desperate and horny,* her conscience taunted.

Yes, but she'd never had meaningless sex with a man for fear she'd feel like a whore…like she had when she'd raced out of McMillian's office. The mental anguish assailing her after his attack had been brutal. She'd fought too hard to set herself up for another fall, even with a man as scrumptious as Noble…Noble what?

Lord, she didn't even know the man's last name.

He glanced over his shoulder, capturing her gaze.

Oh, but he was so tempting…beautiful…arousing…

*And a total fucking stranger,* she inwardly reminded her eager libido.

"It's a cryin' shame."

"What?"

"That a sexy little woman like you has to sleep all alone in that big ol' bed."

She felt a blush warm her cheeks. "No. It's actually a good thing. I sleep like a Weed eater…tossing and turning all over the place."

He stood and raked a slow gaze up her body. "Oh, darlin', I

would love to make you prove that."

The thick sexual undercurrent sizzling through the air arced like lightning.

Ivy bit her lips together to keep from extending the offer. As Noble moved in close to brush a strand of hair away from her cheek, her resolve melted like butter.

"Christ, you're beautiful."

His hot breath fluttered over her lips while his stare fixed on her mouth. Oh, hell. He was going to do more than just kiss her. The throbbing of her clit sped up, keeping time with her tripling heartbeat.

Fissures of lust laid waste to her fears.

Yet, from somewhere deep in her brain, a fragment of sanity surfaced.

She was in a strange town and in a strange hotel room with a sensual Roman god she knew nothing about—who could be a freaking serial killer. He was in her room. It was already possible for him to rape her, then kill her and toss her body in a dumpster behind any of the glitzy casinos along the strip. They'd never find her dead body.

When had she turned into such a stupid, reckless woman?

Ivy knew the answer to that…the second he'd offered his help unlocking her door.

Before she could ask him to leave and put an end to this insanity, Noble brushed a ghost of a kiss over her lips, then skimmed them again with the same whispery touch before feathering each corner of her mouth.

Okay, so maybe he wasn't a crazed, murdering rapist after all. She knew those kinds of monsters took their victims by force.

When he pressed a tender kiss at the center of her lips, Ivy's whole body shook. Not out of fear, but with an awakening of the desire she'd forced into hibernation so long ago.

Her nipples stiffened like marbles.

Need, wet and slick, slid from between her swollen folds.

Her throbbing clit ached with desire so brutal she wanted to howl.

Lust, primal and ravenous, uncoiled from deep in her belly.

When Noble placed his palm at the small of her back and pulled her against his solid chest, heat enveloped her like a long-lost blanket.

And when he rocked his steely erection, wedging it between her legs, all logic and reason fell silent.

With an impatient whimper, Ivy threw her arms around his neck and kissed him hard. She inhaled his masculine scent—a combination of sweet grass, sandalwood, and summer sun—as she feasted on his sultry mouth. The first kiss had excited her cells This one set her soul on fire.

Spellbound, she parted when Noble swiped his slippery tongue over the seam of her lips. Ivy was lost in sensual sensory overload with the glide and pull of his soft suction.

*Mercy!*

She'd never been with a man who kissed so erotically or passionately, or one who made her dizzy and sent a host of naughty lurid fantasies clawing through her brain. The man had skills she hadn't even known existed.

Noble deepened the kiss. Every cell in her body ignited like a mile-long string of firecrackers. Melting against his rugged body, Ivy tossed all her reservations about one-night stands straight out the window. Consequences be damned, she'd deal with the aftermath later. She had to fuck this tongue-talented cowboy before the weekend was over if only to experience all the magical skills he possessed between the sheets.

Losing herself in his kiss, Ivy gave back as good as Noble gave.

After several long, pulse-thundering minutes, he slowly eased from her lips. Ivy's head was spinning, her body throbbing…shaking. A whimper of carnal distress slid off her tongue.

"I know, darlin'," he said sympathetically. "But I have to leave before I do something that'll contradict my given name."

*No! No! Contradict it all you want. Please! You can't just leave me like this!*

"I won't tell if you don't." Without thinking, she'd put the bold statement out there.

"Oh, I never kiss and tell. Don't worry, pretty lady, we're not finished here…not by a long shot."

*Thank god!*

"I have to meet an old friend of mine shortly. But I'll be back later tonight."

Ivy blinked, suddenly remembering she'd promised to take Celina out for an impromptu bachelorette party. "I-I have a family thing I have to attend tonight myself. Maybe we could have a drink…if it's not too late when we both get back. I've got a bottle of wine in the fridge."

The crooked smile Noble flashed had her toes curling.

"I'd love to share a glass of wine with the sexiest woman on the planet. I'll tap on your door when I get back…if it's not too late."

"It doesn't matter what time. It won't be too late," she blurted out, uncaring how desperate it made her sound.

"Excellent. I'll see you later then. Oh, and if you need anything…don't hesitate to let me know. My room is right across the hall."

He cupped her cheeks and pillaged her mouth with another spine-bending, sensual kiss. After pulling away with a low growl, Noble turned and walked out the door, leaving Ivy's lips tingling, her core blazing, and head spinning. A pitiful whimper rolled off her tongue as she stood staring at the door, wondering how a total stranger had completely turned her world upside down.

Her body was humming with need, and even her cotton T-shirt felt like sandpaper against her sensitized flesh. Ivy issued a frustrated sigh and stripped off her shirt and bra, tossing them to the floor as she strode to the bathroom. After turning on the shower, she peeled off her yoga pants and thong, noting both were saturated. She pressed a hand to her mound and drew back glistening fingers.

*Damn!*

She was dripping like a leaky faucet.

And what the hell was up with that? She'd spent months with various boyfriends who hadn't put her in a puddle the way Noble had, and she'd only known him fifteen damn minutes.

The way her body responded to the man confused her. She couldn't pinpoint a reason for the forceful animal attraction she felt for Noble, but it was there. Oh, man…it was there…a strong, dangerous, and totally reckless yearning. But none of the scary reasons to avoid him erased the lust bubbling inside her.

Lifting her head, Ivy stared at her reflection in the mirror. Her eyes were smoky and dilated, her lips, red and swollen, her breasts engorged, and her erect nipples were a darker peach color. The needy woman looked foreign. Ivy didn't know where she'd come from. Bewildered, she shook her head and stepped into the steaming spray of water.

She worked to rub the crazy attraction from her skin while trying to calm the demand still pumping through her veins, but couldn't. If she didn't get her libido under control, it was going to be a long, frustrating night hanging out with her sister.

Unable to douse the flames still licking her soul, Ivy stepped out of the shower and dried off. Deciding that obsessing about a man she'd just met was pointless, she forced herself to focus on the wedding. She tried to wrap her head around the reasons Celina was marrying a dick like Harvey but couldn't come up with a single rational answer. Her sister had always been impulsive to a fault, but…damn. This wedding had catastrophe written all over it.

If…no, *when* Celina's marriage fell apart, Ivy would be there to help pick up the pieces and move on. That's what family did. When the shit had hit the fan with McMillian, the Addison clan rallied around Ivy and propped her up through every humiliating, embarrassing minute. Even Janice—bless her sweet southern heart—tried to bolster Ivy's confidence. Unwilling to let the woman who'd given her life down, Ivy had done as her mother instructed. She'd lifted her chin and displayed all the mock self-confidence she could muster during the trial. The scars were still red and raw but healing, but worst of all, Ivy wasn't the same woman she'd once been. She hated McMillian for stealing such precious pieces of her soul.

"Don't start getting your ass all comfy on the pity pot," Ivy warned her reflection in the mirror as she brushed on a light layer of mascara. "Let it go. Move on. Live the life you want. Be strong. Be happy…yadda, yadda, yadda."

The verbal balm she'd drilled into her head during those crushing days had served its purpose. She rarely had to indulge in giving herself pep talks anymore. But some days it still helped to smooth out some of the rough edges. Of courses a long, hot, sweaty night with Noble might do more than take care of her rough edges. He might polish her up like a shiny new diamond.

"A man isn't going to fix you," she drawled out loud.

No, but his kisses still tingled on her lips as visions of him plowing her lady garden sent shivers crawling up her spine.

"Oh, stop it," she chided her reflection. "You don't have time to take a cold shower."

As she painted a light pink gloss over her lips, the phone beside the bed rang. With her heart slamming against her ribs, she raced from the bathroom. She lunged across the bed and plucked up the receiver, praying she'd hear Noble's deep, buttery-soft voice on the other end.

"Hello?" She cringed at her breathless tone.

"Ivy?" Celina asked. "Are you okay? You sound weird."

*Shit!*

She cleared her throat. "Yeah…yeah. I'm fine," she lied as disappointment bled from her system.

"I'm all put together and ready to party the night away. How about you?"

"Give me five and I'll meet you in the lobby, kay?"

"I'm already here. Harvey wanted to introduce me to his best man before our rehearsal dinner tomorrow night. Listen, I…um, I didn't tell Harv that we were hitting the male strip show tonight, so be a doll and don't say anything. All right? The last thing I want is him losing his shit and leaving me standing all alone at the altar."

*If only it could be that easy.*

"He's not going to leave you at the altar. Stop. I won't say a word, but you do know that he and his best man are probably going to hit *numerous* strip clubs tonight, too, right?"

"Not if he wants to consummate our marriage Saturday night!" Celina screeched.

"Whoa. Settle down, tiger. What's good for the goose is good for—"

"Not even. Male strippers don't give lap dances, do they?"

"How would I know? I've never been to a strip club before."

"Come down when you can. I'm going to have a little come-to-Jesus meeting with my future husband while he's still in the lobby." With an angry growl, Celina ended the call.

As Ivy hung up the phone, she shook her head. It was wrong to hope there wouldn't even be a wedding Saturday, but she couldn't help it. Celina could do so much better than Harvey Hays. Why couldn't she see that?

"Not my monkey or my zoo," Ivy murmured as worry settled in her stomach.

Shaking the foreboding unease from her mind, she slipped on the new champagne-colored, sequined minidress and matching pale-peach Jimmy Choos she'd purchased hours ago at a boutique downstairs. As she checked out herself in the mirror, Ivy bit her lip. She worried the shimmering, form-hugging designer outfit with its plunging neckline—revealing more cleavage than she'd ever displayed—might be a little over-the-top.

"Go big or go home," she murmured to her reflection.

The only problem with that adage was that Ivy truly wanted to go back home, pack her truck, and start living her new life.

"It'll all be over Sunday morning. You'll have to hang until then," she murmured to herself.

After spritzing on her favorite perfume and tucking her room card into the peach clutch, she headed out the door.

As the latch snicked behind her, she paused and stared at Noble's door. Had he left to meet his friend yet, or was he inside his room getting ready to leave? Visions of his naked body covered in slippery soapsuds—especially his hard, thick cock—filled her mind. God, the dirty things she wanted to do to him, and have him do to her, sent a naughty thrill tingling in her girl parts.

Since she and Celina didn't drink that often, Ivy planned to quickly get her sister shit-faced before rushing back to the hotel to share a night of mind-blowing orgasms with Noble.

In theory her plan seemed spec-fucking-tacular, and no doubt her body was primed for pleasure, but Ivy wasn't sure if she could actually follow through with the sex. Still, she knew if she chickened out, she'd regret it for the rest of her life.

Peering at Noble's door one last time, she swallowed down the lump of lust lodged in her throat and strolled to the elevator. As she descended toward the lobby, Ivy sucked in several deep breaths to try and calm the carnal riot roiling inside her. The doors opened and she started toward the hotel entrance, noticing several men who stopped in their tracks to rake their hungry gazes up and down her body.

When she'd first spied the skimpy dress she was now wearing, in one of the hotel's shops, it'd screamed festive fun. But now she feared it simply yelled hooker. Painting the town draped in bedazzler barf might have been a bad choice. Self-consciously tugging at the hem of the dress, Ivy heard some guy let out a long, low wolf whistle. Suddenly, her insecurities were replaced with feminine pride. She glanced over her shoulder and flashed the older man a cheeky grin before adding a little more sway to her hips. But the second she spotted Celina pacing near the front door, hands clenched into fists and her face pinched in an angry scowl, Ivy's confidence took a nosedive.

*Dammit!*

She'd hoped to spend the night drinking, laughing, and

reminiscing with her sister, not battling Bridezilla. She wanted her fun-loving sister back.

"What's wrong, baby sis?"

"Harvey, that son of a… Do you know where he's going tonight?"

"The strip clubs?"

"Yes," Celine hissed. "I can't believe it."

Ivy bit back a laugh. "Why not? We're going to one. It's what all couples do before they tie the—"

"Yeah, but we're not bringing any of the guys back to the hotel with us."

"Harvey isn't going to bring a stripper back here either."

"How do you know?"

"Oh, come on, Celina. You're a ten. Harvey's a two and a half, maybe a three…at best."

"It's not about looks," Celina spat. "He's beautiful inside."

*Yeah…way down deep inside him.*

Ivy kept that observation to herself and hugged her sister. "Honey, if you don't trust him enough to know he'll keep his dick in his pants then why are you marrying him?"

Big, fat crocodile tears filled Celina's eyes. "Because I love him."

"Okay. But you can love someone and not trust them."

"I *do* trust him," she wailed as she angrily wiped her tears away. "I just don't want him drooling over another woman. He's supposed to drool over *me*. I know you and Mom and Dad think Harvey's a jerk, but he's really not."

"Then stop worrying." Her sister sniffed and nodded. "As long as he treats you like a queen, and he's *your* ten, that's all that matters." *And if he's ever mean to you, I'll hire a hit man who'll make that arrogant pudgy prick suffer.* "Now, let's grab some dinner before we set Las Vegas on fire."

Celina sent her a watery smile and nodded.

# CHAPTER FIVE

After Harvey introduced Celina, Noble struggled to overcome his shock. The woman was drop-dead gorgeous. No, she was stunning…stunning like the sexy, smoking-hot woman staying across the hall from him. Noble didn't understand how a troll like Harvey—friend or not, the man looked like Danny DeVito—had snagged someone as beautiful as Kate Hudson. Celina was so far out of Harvey's league she wasn't even on the same planet.

At least Noble now knew who wore the pants in their relationship, and it wasn't Harvey. The minute Celina had found out they were going to the strip clubs, she blew a damn gasket. Sparks were all but shooting out of the fiery redhead's eyes as she'd railed on her groom-to-be. If looks could kill, Harvey would be in the morgue instead of sitting beside him on the massive party bus, pouting like a little bitch.

"Celina's just gonna have to get over herself. I'm not going to bow down to any damn woman…girlfriend, fiancée or wife!" Harvey stomped his foot. "After the wedding, I'll have her on her knees in the honeymoon suite working her wicked tongue all over my dick."

*Not unless you pucker up and start kissing ass now till Saturday, you won't.*

Noble didn't like drama, anger, or tears. He'd learned how to stay in good graces with the ladies instead of the doghouse. Clearly, Harvey hadn't been schooled on that lesson yet. Based on Celina's rage, the man had bypassed the doghouse and was next in line to be euthanized.

"Yanno," Noble began, "if it's going to upset your bride, we don't have to hit the strip clubs. We could go find a bar and drink till we puke."

"The hell we don't!" Harvey barked indignantly. "No woman is going to tell me what to do. We're going to hit every damn strip club we can find, on principle alone."

*Poor bastard. He doesn't know shit about women.*

Noble inwardly shook his head. Maybe after a dozen drinks, he could drill some basics into Harvey's head. If not, well…there were plenty of divorce lawyers around.

An hour and a half later, they sat in sleazy, dimly lit strip club number four. Like the other clubs they'd visited, the scent of testosterone, pussy, and stale beer hung heavy in the air. Noble tipped back his bottle of brew and glanced at the girl on stage. She ground her crotch on the pole in time with the thumping music reverberating off the walls. The dancer looked as bored as the nearly naked woman straddling Harvey's lap.

He was bored out of his mind, and this wasn't the epic bachelor party Harvey had promised. Noble wished he were back at the hotel exploring Ivy's silky flesh with his tongue.

"That's it…uh-huh…just like that. Daddy's going to treat you real good, baby girl." A hungry glaze infused Harvey's heavy-lidded inebriated, eyes as he tucked a couple of twenties under the corner of the stripper's G-string. "Get bad for me, you naughty little slut, and shove your juicy snatch in my face."

Noble bit back a laugh and drained his beer.

In almost mechanical motion, the women complied. Gripping Harvey's head, she rubbed her crotch in his face as she flashed Noble an inviting smile. "When I'm finished with your friend here, I can take you to a private room and give you a proper lap dance, handsome."

Noble's stomach swirled. The only crotch he wanted in his face was at the hotel. "Nah, I'm good. Harvey there is the man of the hour."

She rolled her eyes and shrugged as his old pal let out a yell and latched his mouth onto the skimpy triangle between her legs. Grinding his nose in her crotch, Harvey grabbed hold of her ass cheeks.

The stripper jerked away and sent him an angry glare. "No touching on the main floor."

"Then take me someplace private so I can eat you up."

The stripper scoffed caustically. "Trust me. There's not enough money on the planet for me to go one on one with you." Harvey was already so toasted the insult didn't even register. With a heavy sigh, the woman backed off his lap. "Time's up. Bathrooms are in the back. There's lotion and towels on the sink. Jack off and come back if you want. I'm sure another girl will give you a dance."

"But I want you," Harvey whined. "You'll give me a repeat customer discount, right?"

The woman wrinkled her nose. "Not on your life."

Frowning, Harvey stood, tossed some bills on the table, and jerked his head toward the door. "Come on, bro. We need to find a club with nicer strippers."

Weaving slightly, Noble followed his stumbling drunk friend out outside.

After Harvey stumbled up the steps of the party bus and plopped down in one of the seats, he flashed Noble a lopsided grin. "This is the shit! You having fun, bro?"

*Not in the slightest.* The alcohol-induced buzz fogging his brain lessened the sting of disappointment. "A blast, man. A blast."

Harvey nodded, pulled a flask out of his suit jacket, and twisted off the top before taking a long pull. "Fuuuuck meeee," he bellowed.

The smell of whatever was in the flask hit Noble's nose, stealing the air from his lungs. "What the fuck are you drinking? Battery acid?"

"Moonshine," Harvey slurred, shoving the flask toward Noble. "Take a drink. It'll melt the hair off your balls."

"I'm good." Noble shook his head, shoving the bottle back toward Harvey.

The man had been shots of Patrón, Absolut, Johnnie Walker, Jägermeister, and now moonshine. He wondered how long before Harvey was puking his guts up or passing the fuck out. While Noble would never break the bro code and abandon his friend, he was definitely ready to head back to the hotel and spend some quality time with Ivy.

The goofy smile on Harvey's face suddenly vanished. "Fuck, man. I'm getting married on Saturday."

"That you are." Noble laughed.

Harvey took another pull of the moonshine, screwed the cap back in place, and tucked it in back inside his jacket. Suddenly, his eyes filled with tears. "I'm one lucky son of a bitch, aren't I?"

"Damn straight you are."

"I have a successful business and a beautiful woman who wants to marry me. Me! Do you know how many fuckers on this planet would fall to their feet and worship her?"

"Probably a ton. She's a beautiful girl."

"Yeah, she is." Harvey's voice quivered. "And Celina picked *me*. Why'd she pick me, man?" A tear tumbled down the man's cheek, followed by another…then a whole stream.

When the man started blubbering like a baby, Noble had no idea what to do. No way was he going to cuddle and whisper reassuring platitudes in Harvey's ear like he did the women back home who came unglued from time to time.

He'd have to try and talk the man down off the ledge. "Clearly she picked you because you're a good man and she—"

"No I'm not. I'm a prick," Harvey bellowed. "But she still loves me…I mean, really, really loves me. I just don't fucking know why."

"'Cause you're a boss."

"But I'm not…I'm nothing but a fraud," Harvey wailed. "Celina was my first."

"Your first what?"

"My first fuck! I was a virgin when I met her."

Noble was glad he was sitting down, because that bombshell rocked him hard. "What about Dee—"

"I never did Dee Ann. I just lied and said I did, 'cause every other guy in town said they'd done her. I didn't want to fuck her… She always smelled like bologna. I hate bologna. I just didn't want anyone to know I was still hauling my cherry around. I'm sorry, Nobe. I never should have lied to you."

Harvey's confession washed away his obnoxious exterior and exposed a butt-load of insecurities. Noble actually felt sorry for the man.

"Don't stress. I never fucked her, either. I was too afraid my dick would rot off."

"You don't hate me, do you?" Harvey sobbed.

"No, man. Never." Noble clapped him on the shoulder.

"Thanks, man." He wiped at his tears. "I did good, didn't I? I did good finding Celina, right?"

"Yeah. You did good…damn good." Noble grabbed onto the seat as the bus made a sharp turn. His head was swimming long after the driver straightened back out. "Damn! I drank more than I thought I did."

Harvey sniffed, wiped his eyes, and raised a fist in the air. "To being fucked up!"

Noble grinned and bumped the man's knuckles. The two of them burst out laughing.

Harvey leaned over and instructed the driver to find another strip club, then slid forward and passed out, face first, on the floor.

Noble bent down and quickly rolled him to his back, checking to make sure he was still breathing. Harvey sucked in a loud snore and Noble grinned.

"Forget the strip club, man. Take us back to the hotel. My friend is baked."

"CAN WE GET four more shots here?" Celina called to the waitress rushing past their table.

Ivy's stomach swirled. She'd been matching her sister, shot for shot, all night long. While she wasn't feeling any pain, she'd definitely had enough to drink. Tomorrow morning her head would be pounding like a million jackhammers and Ivy would be cursing every ounce now blurring her system.

The thundering pipes of a motorcycle blasted through the overhead speakers. All the women in the club went wild as a hunky, bad-assed biker took the stage. He was covered in muscles and tattoos, wearing black leather, with a discernable bulge beneath the black pouch between his legs.

Celina tossed back one of the shots the waitress left at the table before jumping to her feet. "Oh, my god! Look at the hunk! Fuck me! What I wouldn't give to suck the chrome off his tail pipe, stroke his kickstand, and ride his Fat Boy into the sunset."

Ivy laughed as she lifted one of the glasses to her lips and immediately set it back down. Celina let out a whoop and shoved her way to the stage, where she started waving a fist full of bills at the stripper now bumping and grinding on the stage.

"You'd probably have a lot more exciting life with that beefy biker than you will Harvey," Ivy whispered to herself. That sad truth sobered her some.

When the dancer's set was done, Celina returned and grabbed another shot off the table and raised it in the air. "To all the well-hung, skilled men in the world who know how to make women come like freight trains...I will certainly miss you all."

"I'll drink to that." Ivy picked up a shot and tossed it back in one gulp. Memories of Noble's gifted lips and tongue blazed in her head. Warmth that had nothing to do with booze and everything to do with a year and a half of pent-up sexual frustration enveloped her body.

A country tune blasted through the speakers. Ivy turned her head, watching as a tall, broad-shouldered, narrow-waisted cowboy took the stage. He was wearing a black leather vest, chaps, and G-string along with a pair of six-guns slung low on his hips. The black hat he wore hid his identity, but Ivy was already imagining Noble's handsome face in the shadow beneath the brim. As the tempo of the music ramped up, the sexy cowboy began bumping, grinding, and rolling his hips in blatant sexual fashion. Eager women shoved money in his extra-large G-string.

Ivy's attention was fixed on the cowboy's sensual movements while raw and dirty fantasies of Noble unfurled in her mind. Sleeping with the stranger no longer seemed frightening. If spending the night with him, lost in orgasmic splendor made her a whore, so be it. The time had come to end her self-imposed sexual drought.

When the waitress dropped off another four shots, Ivy plucked one up and downed it. Hopefully she'd imbibed enough to make her southern sensibilities pass the hell out. Ivy didn't need her mental moral police patrolling her psyche, making her second-guess her decision.

"What's so wrong about unleashing eighteen months of unbridled lust on a willing man?" Ivy blurted out.

"Not a goddamn thing." Celina pounded her fist on the table. "Wait. Who are we fucking?"

"Nobody." *Yet.* "I was just askin' a question."

"Oh. Not a damn thing," Celina replied, dropping her fist to the table again.

Ivy smiled. She'd missed her zany, impulsive sister. But the Addison siblings were grown women now. Celina was marrying a dipshitiot and going back to Seattle. Ivy was risking every penny from the massive settlement the court had awarded her to open a bakery in a small, quiet town. A town that probably wasn't a Mecca of hot, single men. She might not get another chance to get laid until she was old and gray. One uninhibited night busting up the furniture and exorcizing sexual frustrations with Noble might be the only relief she'd find for a long, long time.

"I wanna go h-home with you…stud."

Celina's slurred plea pulled Ivy from her thoughts. Her sister was all but climbing the biker dude who had been dancing on the stage earlier.

"I'mma wrap my lips round your big ol' pipe and do 'lisciosly naughty things with you all night long."

"Whoa," Ivy blurted out.

She bolted from her chair to stop her sister before the stripper actually took Celina up on the offer. But the heel of her shoe snagged the leg of the table. As the floor came rushing up to meet Ivy's face, she jerked her hands up, and broke her fall. She landed on the cold tile with a bone-jarring thud and cried out as pain screamed up her arms and through her shoulders.

"Ivy!" Celina yelled. "Oh, my god. Are you—"

"Now that's fucking funny as hell." The dancer threw back his head and laughed.

"Shut the fuck up, Sons of Anarchy. It's not funny. Do something… Help her," Celina spat, no longer slurring.

"Not my job to babysit you drunken bitches."

The pain was receding as Ivy slowly hauled herself from the floor. "I've got it. I'm good."

"You're a pig…a motherfucking prick. I hope you get every STD on the planet and your dick rots off, asshole," Celina screamed.

The stripper growled, flipped her off, and walked away.

Ivy couldn't help but laugh at her fuming sister. "I guess you don't want to ride his Fat Boy anymore?"

"I wouldn't touch his Fat Boy if it were the last one on the damn planet. It's probably two inches big anyway. And bet money his G-string's stuffed with socks. Let's get outta here. That bastard's ruined my buzz."

While wobbling on her heels as she dusted herself off, Ivy noticed her sister looking a bit too pale. "You're not going to barf on me, are you?"

"Not unless I drink another shot. Then all bets are off."

Ivy had surpassed her limit as well. Outside the bar, they clung to each other, singing and laughing before flagging down a taxi. Then, they giggled all the way back to the hotel. Once she made sure her sister was safely tucked in bed, Ivy staggered down the hall toward her own room.

She paused at Noble's door and raised her hand to knock but stopped herself. Her sluggish brain wondered if she was sober enough to enjoy all the fun she wanted from him. The thought of passing out in the middle of what was sure to be the wildest sex of her life made her frown. She didn't want to crush the man's ego, especially one as sexually compelling as Noble…whatever his last name might be. No, she wanted to be wide-awake and enjoy every delicious hard inch and thrust. But the urge to tap on his door was like a dark force. She couldn't fight it.

Giving in, Ivy knocked and waited. She stood there for several long minutes, mentally willing the door to open. Teetering on her heels, her heart sank. He'd either changed his mind, fallen asleep, or was still out with his friend. She took two wobbly steps back as disappointment seeped through her and plucked the key card from her purse. Ivy swiped the plastic in and out of the sensor, but it refused to cooperate.

She kicked off her shoes and growled. "Come on, you temperamental sum'bitch," she slurred.

"Looks like you need another lesson."

Noble's deep voice startled her. Ivy spun on the balls of her feet to find him easing in behind her. The alcohol buzz she had going on paled to the intoxicating heat and masculine scent surrounding her. She gazed up into his glassy green eyes and the air around them sizzled.

"Iss broken," she softly slurred.

"I think you might have had a few too many cocktails tonight, didn't you, darlin'?"

"I've had enough."

"Enough for what?"

"Enough to do this." Bolstered by the obscene amount of alcohol she'd consumed, Ivy turned and boldly wrapped her arms around his neck. Lifting onto her toes, she closed her eyes and pressed a soft, inviting kiss to his lips.

Noble welcomed her brazen action by cupping a hand around her nape and feathering his thumb along her jaw. As he took control of the kiss and deepened it, he sank his other hand into her hair, gripping a fistful of her thick curls. She moaned in delight as tingles raced across her scalp. Noble grunted and delved his warm, wet tongue deep inside her mouth.

She clung to him in desperation as their kiss turned raw…urgent.

He swallowed her kitten-like mewls as he pressed his steely body to hers. She was drowning in the passion and promise of his soul-stealing kiss. If Noble hadn't held her pinned to the door, her legs would have given out when he arched his hips and nestled every inch of his thick, hard cock against her dripping folds.

Demand uncoiled low in her belly, then slammed up her spine and sputtered through her limbs like fireworks. Everything this gloriously talented man did to her made her head spin…and they weren't even in bed yet. Ivy wasn't sure she'd survive the magic he was capable of weaving over her once they actually made it to the mattress.

With a whimper of impatience, she lifted her leg and hooked it around the back of his thigh, silently offering herself to him. The fantasies dancing in her head since she'd first laid eyes on him were coming true. The hum of lust and demand roared in her ears as she feasted on his tongue.

With assurance of the primitive pleasure she ached for, Noble rocked his hips, nudging her needy clit. Ivy gasped and ground her sweltering pussy against his massive length. She couldn't wait to drag him into her room and into her blistering body.

Noble eased from her mouth and skimmed his hot lips over her jaw before leaving a trail of fire down her neck. "Tell me what you want, darlin'."

"You," she panted breathlessly. "Every…thick, glorious inch."

"Thank fuck."

Dipping his head, Noble traced the swell of her heavy breasts with his tongue. Her nipples tightened and she arched, wishing he'd draw each pebbled peak into his mouth and assuage the ache there.

"We need to take this inside your room before I lift that pretty dress up over your hips and have my wicked way with you here and now."

His words excited her in a way she hadn't expected. Blaming it on the alcohol, Ivy didn't give a rat's ass if he fucked her in the hall or in the damn lobby.

Silently reminding herself she wasn't an exhibitionist, she nodded. "I vote we take this inside my room."

She felt him smile against her throat. "I do, too."

Easing back, he studied the contours of her face. She could feel the flush of arousal warming her cheeks as she gazed at his glistening and slightly swollen lips. Tendrils of craving flickered in his hooded emerald eyes. His cock lurched against her center. Impatience clawed at her as Ivy handed him her card key.

A wicked grin kicked up the corners of his lips as he slid the plastic into the sensor. The light immediately started flashing green. He twisted the handle and opened the door a couple of inches. "Slow and deep, remember."

"I'm counting on it, cowboy," she purred.

A feral growl rolled from his chest as he claimed her lips again, more urgently than before. Ivy clutched his shoulders, gripping his shirt in her fists.

Noble tore from her mouth, shoved the door open, and plucked her off her feet. Pressing her tightly against his decadent body, he carried her into the room.

His gaze locked onto her lips as he set her down on her feet. "I can't wait to tame your sexy ass, gorgeous."

"We'll see who tames who, cowboy." With a cocky grin, she bounced onto the tips of her toes and climbed his body like a spider monkey.

Ivy locked her legs around his waist and clasped her fingers around the back of his neck before she latched on to his mouth with a fiery kiss of her own.

Noble scooped her ass cheeks up in the palms of his capable hands, then thrust his fat cock against her dripping crotch as the door snicked shut. Their tongues tangled as a symphony of moans floated through the air.

Long minutes later, he tore from her mouth. "Will you let me take control of you, beautiful?"

"Take control?" Ivy repeated. Her mind was jumbled and spinning from the powerful kiss. She didn't understand what he was asking.

"Yes. Control of you…your pleasure."

His words slowly slogged through her alcohol- and lust-soaked brain. A tinge of apprehension rippled over her. Maybe he really was a serial killer. Panic started rising inside her. Ivy swallowed tightly. "You're not going to hurt me, are you?"

The quiver of fear in her voice made Noble blanch. His brows slashed. A serious expression morphed over his handsome face. "No. Hell no. I'd never hurt a woman."

His adamant reply swiftly settled her unease. "Good, because I'm not into pain."

"Neither am I. Besides, I'd much rather drown you in pleasure than pain, darlin'." A mischievous grin played over his lips. "Will you let me do that to you?"

"As long as you don't go getting all kinky on me."

"I'll make sure the clowns are safely locked out in the hallway. How's that?"

A laugh sprang off her lips. "But…clowns turn me on."

He shot her a feigned look of surprise. "In that case, I'll be right back."

"What? Wait. Where are you going? I was just—"

"I need to run down to Circus Circus and rent a clown suit and some of those big floppy shoes. So I can—"

"You're not going anywhere, cowboy. At least not until I'm done with you."

"Is that right?"

"Uh-huh."

Noble teased the corners of her mouth with his lips and tongue. "I can't wait to turn you into a quivering mass of sated bliss."

"I'm certainly not going to stop you."

"I was hoping you'd say that."

Noble clutched her to his chest, melded his mouth to hers, then turned and pressed her against the wall. Caged in his steely arms, her body sang, her cells melted like lava, and Ivy fell deeper under the spell of his hot, silky mouth.

She felt the cold air of the room charge her hot flesh when Noble tugged her dress over her hips. As he worked the material up her body, exposing more of her, goose bumps skittered over her limbs. Noble eased from her mouth just long enough to lift the dress over her head and toss it to the floor. He gazed at her nearly naked body. A decadent promise flickered in his emerald-colored eyes, sending a shiver of excitement to roll over her.

"You're fucking stunning, baby," he murmured with undeniable approval.

Before she could respond, he seized her lips and swept his tongue deep inside her mouth with a hungry growl. Lifting one hand from her ass, Noble gently stroked his calloused fingers up and down her arms. Each fluttering caress amplified the ache throbbing within.

Ivy tried to search for patience, but the freight train of lust filling her veins was chugging downhill and picking up speed…fast. The need to feel his hot flesh melded against hers, to feel his fat cock driving in and out of her annihilated all hope of finding any semblance of restraint.

Pawing at the buttons of his shirt, Ivy whimpered in frustration. His lips, still pressed to hers, kicked up in a knowing smile. He slowly released her mouth.

"Hold on tight to me, darlin'."

She squeezed her legs tighter and locked onto his body before he moved his hands to his shirt. Holding her prisoner with his gaze, Noble pulled several buttons free and drew the shirt over his head. As it floated to the floor, joining her dress, Ivy damn near choked at the expanse of sun-kissed flesh stretched over hard and rippling muscles.

The mere sight of all that man stole her breath. She could only imagine how delicious he'd look when he stripped off his jeans.

"Mercy," she whispered.

"That's exactly what I'm thinking about you, baby."

His lurid gaze slid up and down her body like a stroke of electricity. Ivy's heart thrummed. Cream spilled between her legs. The scent of her feminine musk hung heavy in the air. A second later, Noble's nostrils flared, and she knew he smelled her arousal, too.

Powerless to resist the temptation, she flattened her hand against his abs before tracing her palm over each sculpted ridge. His muscles bunched and flexed beneath her skin. He sucked in a low hiss before gripping her wrist and prying her from his hot flesh.

"Naked, now." His raspy voice was edged in desperation as he gently eased her feet to the floor.

More than ready to comply, Ivy reached behind her back and unfastened her bra. The straps slid down her arms, lifting the lacy cups from her flesh before slipping to the carpet. Noble cupped her breasts in his palms, thumbing her throbbing nipples. Ivy sucked in a gasp as he bent, opened his mouth, and laid siege to one aching peak, then the other. Beneath his talented tongue, lips, and teeth, shards of lightning arced, splintering sanity into fragments. The indescribable friction from every lave, suck, and nibble made her body sing and pulsate in a maddening rhythm.

Short, quivering breaths spilled past her lips as Noble inched his magnificent mouth down her body, leaving an exquisite trail of liquid fire over her already ignited flesh. Ivy moaned and writhed as the flames consumed her.

Moving lower still, Noble swirled the tip of his tongue over her belly, making the muscles there twitch and quake. Ivy sank her fingers into his thick, soft hair and closed her eyes as he peppered kisses from one hipbone to the other.

His moist heat teased the sodden triangle of silk between her thighs and Ivy forced her heavy eyelids open. Noble was now kneeling in front of her. With his lips pressed to her flesh, face tilted up, he watched her. His incinerating gaze singed her soul. Ivy had agreed to give him control, but it took all the willpower she possessed not to shove his face into her weeping center. Gripping his hair tighter, she watched as he hooked a finger beneath the thin string and ripped the silky fabric away. She didn't give two shits that she'd just purchased the thong. She'd buy more tomorrow, if she could walk when they were through.

She eagerly parted for him to put out the fire he'd conjured, but Noble didn't oblige. Instead, he drew the wet silk to his face, inhaled deeply, and stared at the saturated golden curls between her legs.

*Dammit! Why is he moving so slow?*

"Noble," she mewled pitifully.

"I think I'm addicted to the scent of your sweet heat," he murmured, sending his cool breath wafting over her wet center. "I bet you taste like a ripe, juicy apricot."

Every muscle below her navel clutched.

Ivy whimpered.

Clearly, the man was no stranger to seduction.

Capable.

Competent.

She was suddenly worried about two things. One, when he finally stopped dawdling and put his hands and mouth on her, she wouldn't last more than a few seconds. And two, the intensity of the orgasm expanding inside might very well render her unconscious.

*Unconscious nothing…it might kill me.*

Ah, but death by massive O—induced by a living, breathing

man instead of her battery-operated boyfriends—would definitely be the way to go.

As he glided his masterful hands up her thighs, Ivy jolted slightly. He sent her a crooked smile before he flicked the tip of his tongue along her damp yellow curls.

Okay, so she wasn't going to die by orgasm. He was going to tease her to death.

"I'm burning alive here," she groaned.

"Not yet, darlin'…you're simply smokin'. I intend to build a fire so wicked inside your sinful body that the flames will be licking all the way up your spine before I put them out. Starting now."

Noble reached up and gently parted her slippery folds with his thumbs. Ivy held her breath as he leaned forward and inhaled a deep breath. When he extended his wide, wet tongue, every muscle in her body tightened in anticipation.

The first swipe tossed her into a swell of sensation so overwhelming she cried out. Pressing her fingertips to his scalp, she held on as he slowly dragged his tongue over her pulsating clit.

Even before he'd started to drive in and out of her melting center, Ivy was lost, spiraling toward the heavens. But when he eased back and slid his long, thick fingers inside her and began scraping his teeth over her screaming nub, Ivy lost the feeble grip she'd had on her control.

Prisms of colored lights exploded behind her eyes. "Oh, yes. Oh, god…Noble," she screamed.

Her body trembled.

Her heart thrummed in her ears.

Panting, she thrust her hips forward, rocking herself over his mouth and clamped hard around his wicked stroking fingers.

Noble gripped her ass and moaned.

Holding her in place, he dragged his fingers over her G-spot and wrapped his lips around her clit, suckling with a sublime suction that forced her orgasm higher and harder. Grinding against his face, Ivy screamed, loud and long, and dissolved into a million quivering shards of ecstasy.

"Fucking beautiful," Noble murmured, lightly stroking his fingers inside her while brushing his tongue over the throbbing tissue surrounding her clit.

Aftershocks pulsed like strobes, zipping and sputtering through her system as she slowly swayed down to earth. Forcing her heavy lids open, Ivy blinked through the fog permeating her brain, only to be seized by Noble's sharp, hungry stare.

"Again. I've got to watch you and feel that again."

A shiver, elicited not only from his words but also from the feel of him sliding his fingers from her core, rippled through her. The sight of him lapping the nectar from his fingers excited her all over again. Noble then plucked her off her feet and carried her to the bed.

When he placed her in the middle of the mattress, the room started to spin. She wasn't sure if the dizzy sensation was born from too many shots or the lingering aftereffects of the most mind-blowing orgasm of her life. Either way, she closed her eyes before she did something stupid, like barf her guts up and ruin another round of marvelous magic.

Ivy felt the bed dip, then the warmth of Noble's body as he climbed between her thighs. She chanced fate and opened her eyes, watching as he bent his mouth to her pussy and effortlessly coaxed another orgasm—bigger than the last—from her.

Boneless and sated, she soon discovered that Noble wasn't finished with her…not by a long shot.

She was lost in the pulsating, clutching haze of splendor his mouth conjured for the third…no, fourth time when the sound of his zipper releasing sliced through her screams of ecstasy. Ivy's tunnel was still contracting and fluttering as she felt him hovering above her. Claiming her mouth with his wickedly skilled tongue, Noble drove his cock deep inside her.

His thick, heavy shaft stretched her with a fire so exquisite and sublime a sob tore from her throat.

"Relax, darlin'. I'll take the pain away," Noble murmured,

squeezing a hand between them and softly strumming her clit.

Just as he'd promised, relief, like a soothing spring rain, washed over her…softening her walls until she was undulating beneath him.

"That's it, gorgeous," he urged, slowly gliding in and out of her sinful core. "Christ, you feel…like silky…hot, slippery silk. Fucking amazing."

Stroke after deliberate stroke, he dragged his bulbous crest over her electrified nerve endings. Ivy was powerless to do anything but climb the peak as he built her up right along with him. Soon, Noble was gripping her legs, wrapping them around his waist, before he bent and scraped his teeth over her nipples. Arching her shoulders into the mattress, she groaned. Nipping one, then the other between his teeth, Noble then drew each peak into his mouth and laved the sting away with his masterful tongue.

Drowning beneath the cascade of sensation, Ivy moaned and writhed as she helplessly sailed to the stars. He thrust and nipped, laved and plunged for long, superlative minutes before his tempo grew quicker…harsher…more precise. Ivy's whimpers morphed into panting, keening cries of surrender.

Her limbs began to tingle.

Her pussy fluttered and clutched.

"That's it…give it to me…baby. Come…hard for…me," Noble panted in a strained but unyielding tone.

Beneath a tumbling cascade of bliss, Ivy cried out his name.

With a hiss, Noble hoisted her legs against his chest, wrapping her ankles behind his neck, then slammed his glorious cock in and out of her sucking, quaking pussy. The sounds of their whimpers and grunts mixed with their hard, slapping flesh echoed off the walls in a steady staccato.

Blinking past the blur of euphoria filling her mind, she stared at his chiseled face. Saw the tic of his jaw and the sweat drip from his forehead…studied the way his lips pressed in a thin, tight line of determination.

God, he was gorgeous.

But when she dragged her eyes to his, Noble held her prisoner with his penetrating stare. The man wasn't anywhere except right there with her, gaze fixed solely on her. She'd never been with a man who'd watched her like this. But then she'd never been with one as intense and focused on *her* pleasure before, either. Ivy found it unnerving yet erotically empowering.

Noble had unknowingly touched some primitive part sleeping inside her.

Gripping the sheets in her fists, Ivy met his every thrust, slamming and slapping her ass against his thighs. Noble's eyes grew darker. His nostrils flared.

"Again," he roared. "Come for me again." His feral command sent liquid silver spilling through her veins.

While he slammed in and out of her, Ivy slid a hand to her pussy and toyed with her clit. His eyes narrowed as he watched her strumming herself.

"Damn…that's sexy as…fuck," he panted.

Cinching his hands around her legs, Noble pressed them hard against his chest as he thrust deeper and harder. "Give it to me, baby…" he barked, digging his fingertips into her flesh. "Now!"

Ivy closed her eyes as she strained to reach that surging oblivion one more time.

Lifting her hips to meet his driving rhythm, her body bowed as release slammed through her again.

"Noble," she screamed in a harsh, hoarse cry.

"Look at me!" he roared.

Beyond a kaleidoscope of colors exploding behind her eyes, Ivy forced her lids open to find Noble…jaw clenched, brows slashed, and his jade-colored eyes sliding out of focus.

"Shatter hard for me, baby," he panted.

The command had no more left his lips than Ivy exploded with a force that shocked her senseless and rocked her to the soul.

As Noble followed her over, they sang out their rapture in a chorus of screams and grunts. A myriad of mystifying emotions swirled and melted in the throes of pleasure, sending tears spilling from her eyes. Unwilling and unable to decipher their meaning, she quickly blinked them away as Noble collapsed to his elbows and buried his face against her neck.

As night gave way to dawn, Ivy lost count of the orgasms Noble charmed from her body and the ones she'd sucked from him. Sated, spent, and exhausted, she floated off into the darkness, taking with her the realization that the man in her bed had changed her…forever. Fluttering back to the surface, she heard Noble's deep voice spilling over her as a warm, wet cloth gently slid over her sex.

When she opened her eyes again, she discovered that not only was her body throbbing with a delicious ache but also, sadly, she was alone.

Her mouth felt like it was stuffed with cotton, while a nauseating film stained her tongue. She rolled to her side, and Ivy's head began pounding like a gong. The room felt as if it were swaying.

"Shit. I think I'm still drunk," she mumbled as she splayed a palm across her forehead.

Suddenly, an ear-piercing ring came from the phone beside the bed. With a groan, Ivy reached across the nightstand and snatched up the receiver.

"Hello," she croaked, glancing at the clock.

It was nearly noon, but it felt more like four in the morning.

"Rise and shine, sweetheart!" Her mother's chipper voice sent an invisible spike through Ivy's skull. "Daddy and I are heading downstairs for brunch. Would you like to join us?"

"No thanks. I need more sleep." *And aspirin…and water…and to never drink again.*

"You and Celina sound exactly alike. She turned down our offer to eat, as well. By the way you two sound, I presume it was a proper bachelorette party last night?"

*Trust me, Mom, once I got back to my room, there was nothing proper about it!*

Biting her tongue, Ivy peered over her shoulder at the empty bed. All that was left of Noble remained trapped in the sheets...the scent of masculine cologne melded with the earthy scent of sex, imprinted—like her brain—with the memories of the most spectacular night of her life.

"It was...incredible," Ivy replied.

No, she wasn't talking about the bachelorette party, but her mother didn't need to know she'd spent an unforgettable night with a stranger named Noble.

A melancholy emptiness sluiced through Ivy's veins.

The lonely woman inside her wished the man had stayed. She would have given anything to be snuggled up against his warm, rugged body. Logically, she knew it was better this way. There was no awkward morning-after conversation, no fake promises, no worries of any kind. Still, knowing it was called a one-night stand for a reason didn't lessen the emptiness gnawing inside her.

"Well, I hope you two behaved last night and didn't do anything...foolish or tawdry."

Oh, foolish and tawdry was an understatement for what she'd done.

"Neither of us are in a trending video on the Internet this morning, Mom. Don't worry."

Well, not unless Noble had stashed a hidden camera in Ivy's room. But his focus hadn't been on any lights or camera. No, it had been completely settled on nothing but the action.

"That's reassuring, dear. Just make sure you two girls sober up before the rehearsal dinner. Harvey's parents are flying in this afternoon. And you know that first impressions are—"

"They're everything. Yes, Mom. How could I forget?" she drawled. "Celina and I will be on our best behavior. Neither of us wants to be dragged into the fiery depths of bad-impression hell."

Ivy lifted the pillow Noble had rested on last night and pressed it to her face. Closing her eyes, she inhaled his intoxicating scent while memories of the pleasure they'd shared spooled through her brain. The mere smell of him prompted a familiar hunger to blossom deep in her belly.

Her mother's tone turned arctic. "Don't get sassy with me, young lady. I simply don't want Celina's future in-laws thinking I've raised alcoholic or promiscuous daughters. Proper southern ladies do not stay out until the wee hours of the morning, barhopping and getting three sheets to the wind. I'm not particularly proud of the two of you at this moment."

*Are you ever?* The question lay poised on the tip of Ivy's tongue, but she swallowed it down and sighed. "I'm going back to bed, Mom. I'll see you and Daddy at the rehearsal dinner, where Celina and I can try and make it up to you."

"Fine. But just make sure you two don't oversleep. I expect both my girls to be on time. Understood?"

Ivy gritted her teeth. "I'm twenty four, Mom. Not three. We'll be there on time. Bye."

Without waiting for a *proper* goodbye, she hung up the phone.

Her bladder was screaming, and her mouth was sending out an SOS for a toothbrush, toothpaste, and a vat of mouthwash. But most of all, Ivy needed aspirin. Instead of rolling out of bed, she hugged Noble's pillow to her chest and inhaled. She savored his glorious scent for a long moment.

Though she didn't remember everything, thanks to the liquor she'd imbibed, Ivy recalled nearly all of it. The sex with Noble had been the most epic experience of her life. Was it any wonder she felt a bit let down this morning? Honestly, the man had totally ruined her for any other.

The brutal longing not only to enjoy his sexual skills again but to also learn more about him alarmed her. She wasn't supposed to feel anything. Yet knowing she'd never see him again sent emptiness weaving through her system, like an intricate spider web.

She should have spent more time preparing herself for the rush of emotions that were now bombarding her instead of focusing on getting Noble into bed.

With a grunt, Ivy rolled off the mattress and padded across the room. She winced as her sore and swollen folds protested each step. Her sexy sequined dress lay in a heap on the floor by the wall. Right where Noble had first quenched the fire blazing inside her.

Shoving the memories down, she stepped into the bathroom. Before she tended to her bloated bladder and fuzzy tongue, Ivy tossed back several aspirin to quell the pounding in her head. After a long, hot shower, she ordered room service, choked down a bacon cheeseburger and iced tea, then crawled back into bed. The alarm she'd set on her phone woke her at four thirty. Thankfully her headache was gone which made getting ready for the rehearsal dinner a hell of a lot easier.

Wearing the bodice-hugging burgundy lace dress with a wide tulle skirt that her mother had approved back at the bridal shop in Dallas, Ivy hurried outside. As she neared the Venus Garden Chapel next to the massive fountain in front of the hotel, she saw her parents and Celina talking to an older couple. Ivy easily assumed they were Harvey's parents, based on the fact that the older man looked like Celina's narcissist groom-to-be.

*Time to make that all-important proper first impression*, Ivy inwardly groused.

Her mother flashed a wide smile as she extended her hand toward Ivy, welcoming her to the intimate circle. "And this lovely creature is Celina's older sister, Ivy. Dear, I'd like you to meet Harvey's parents, Mr. and Mrs. Hays."

Pulling out all the rigors of southern belle etiquette and charm, Ivy bowed demurely before politely articulating the proper niceties expected.

"What stunning daughters you have," Mrs. Hays gushed.

Both Ivy and Celina flashed the obligatory retiring smiles, while Janice bestowed praises of Harvey's kind and gentle attributes. The lies pouring from her mother's mouth made Ivy's stomach roll. As if reading her mind, her father, Jeff smiled and sent her a knowing wink.

"May I have a moment with you, dear sister?" Celina asked, batting her lashes like a simpering fool.

"Of course, my sweet." Ivy almost choked on her own saccharine-laced reply.

She looped her arm in Celina's and meandered toward a pair of baroque statues, well out of earshot of the posturing parents. "I swear to god, if Harvey doesn't get his ass down here soon, I'm going to march upstairs and drag him out by his dick."

Ivy started to laugh.

"It's not funny," Celina fumed. "His mother has the world's largest sequoia stuck up her ass. She's as warm and welcoming as a barracuda. Do you know what she asked me?"

"No, what?" Ivy asked, still chuckling.

"She wanted to know if I was in a"—she raised her fingers in the air, using them as quotes—"delicate condition. Evidently my expression told her I didn't have a clue what she meant, so she asked me point-blank in a nasty tone if I was pregnant. When I assured her I wasn't, and that Harvey and I were in love, she looked at me like I'd just slapped her with a raw tuna."

"No way."

"Yes way. Thank god they recently retired to Florida. Hopefully I won't have to see them except at Christmas. It's all I can do to be civil to that old cow." Celina clenched her jaw and exhaled mightily through her nose. "Oh, and Daddy Dearest isn't any better. He hugged me and actually squeezed my ass. Harvey's dad is a stereotypical Uncle Bad-Toucher. I'm already trying to figure out how to keep him away from the kids we haven't even had yet."

Ivy peered over her sister's shoulder and studied Mr. Hays. The old fart caught her staring at him, then smiled and sent her a wink. Ivy wanted to retch.

"And for fuck's sake, do not go near that lecherous old fart," Celina warned. "He'll probably try to toss you to the ground and mount you like a damn elk or something."

"Not if he wants to go back to Florida with his dick and balls intact." Ivy smirked. "It takes a special kind of pervert to feel up your future daughter-in-law. I'm just sayin'." Ivy sighed heavily. "Does Harvey know his dad groped you?"

"Not yet. But he will before the night is done. Speaking of nights...how bad was yours?"

"It wasn't bad at all."

*It was fantastic...amazing...life-altering.*

"Ours was. Harvey and I spent all night battling for the crown of Barf King or Barf Queen of Las Vegas. My stomach muscles are killing me. I've never puked so hard or so many times in my life. I'd like to say I won the crown, but Harvey was way more fucked up than me. My poor baby spent most of the night on the bathroom floor."

"Ewww."

"I know one thing. We won't be drinking wine or any other liquor with dinner tonight."

Ivy pressed a hand to her stomach. "Me, either. I'll stick to water."

"Right? We wouldn't want to embarrass Mother, now would we?" Celina rolled her eyes and pinched her lips together to bite back a laugh. She darted a glance over Ivy's shoulder as a look of relief swept her face. "Finally, Harvey made it. Oh, hell...he looks pissed. Now what's wrong?"

Turning, Ivy arched her brows when she saw the groom, red-faced and scowling.

# CHAPTER SIX

NOBLE STRUGGLED TO surface from the inky oblivion holding him prisoner. Fragmented images of Victor LaCroix whistling happily as he brutally severed the limbs off Gina's bound and screaming body had plagued him as he'd slept. Rage and revulsion boiled in his veins, yet he was helpless to kill the bastard. As he forced his eyes open, the late-afternoon sun filtered in through the curtains and the taste of Ivy lay branded on his tongue. His cock turned to stone, but like fire and ice, the anger from his—or rather his twin brother's dream—was warring with flashbacks of driving into Ivy's silky core.

"Dammit, Nate. Get your shit with Gina figured out. I don't want to live your fucking nightmares, man," Noble groused as he sat up and scrubbed a hand over his face.

Shoving his twin's issues aside, he fixated on the spectacular night he'd spent with the wild, willing sex kitten across the hall. In all the years he'd spent seducing and chasing pleasure with women, Noble had never experienced the level of electricity and passion he'd felt with Ivy. It was as if she'd been made for him.

"Shut the fuck up," he railed at the thought.

Reluctant to dissect his sudden fascination with the girl, he paraded to the bathroom, hoping Harvey's stupid rehearsal dinner wouldn't drag on for hours. Noble had his hopes set on spending another night between Ivy's thighs and discovering a million more ways to make her scream his name. And damn if he didn't love to hear her scream.

After taking a long, semi-cold shower, Noble stood in front of the mirror, smoothing a hand over the lapels of his suit coat. He quickly glanced at the clock and cringed. If he didn't get his ass moving, he'd be late, giving Harvey fuel to bitch and whine. On the bus, Noble had glimpsed the insecure man beneath all the bluster and bullshit, but Harvey Hays was still an egotistical pig.

For Noble, this wedding shit couldn't end fast enough. But on the flip side, he wasn't ready to go home just yet. He wanted to spend more time with Ivy. That longing filled him with unease.

"She's different from the girls back in Haven. That's all it is," he mumbled to himself as he snagged his room key and cell phone, and headed toward the door.

Suddenly, an ominous feeling grabbed him by the throat. Stopping in mid-stride, Noble clutched his ribs as an arc of pain careened through the left side of his body. His mouth felt thick and dry and his heart was racing faster than a Bugatti.

"What the fuck?" he groaned as the pain continued hammering into him.

Without warning, the hairs on the back of his neck prickled. All his life he'd dealt with the sensation and instantly knew there wasn't a damn thing wrong with him, but something horribly wrong with…

*Nate.*

As fear clamored through him, Noble plopped down on the bed and tried to lock the onslaught of pain while still focusing on his brother. But the agony only increased, followed by a wave of nausea that caused him to break out in a cold sweat. Whatever was happening to Nate was bad…really bad. His first inclination was that LaCroix had broken out of jail and was exacting revenge, but his twin telepathy told him this was a totally different kind of threat.

As panic chugged, Noble pulled out his cell phone and tapped the screen just as the device buzzed with a text from Sawyer.

*In case your twin thing is going off, Nate was thrown off a horse last night. Just found him a few minutes ago. He's busted up—bad. Flying him to Abilene Regional. Needs emergency surgery. If you're not balls deep in some bimbo, call. I'll fill you in.*

Slack-jawed and shaking like a leaf, Noble read the text again.

How the hell had Nate gotten thrown from a horse? He could outride all of them.

With trembling fingers, he punched in Sawyer's number.

"Don't freak out, all right? Nate is going to be okay." Sawyer didn't even bother to say *hello*. "We're heading to Abilene now. I'm in the Suburban with Dad, Mom, Brea, Ned, and April. Nash, Norris, and Gina are following us in her car. We should be there in about twenty minutes or so."

"How the hell did *Nate* get thrown off a horse?" Noble barked, overwrought with worry and fear.

"He was climbing out of the saddle when a fox spooked the new gelding he was on. The horse reared back and sent Nate airborne straight into a tree."

"Holy shit. What's wrong with him? My whole damn body is screaming."

"He's got some broken bones, but he's getting the medical treatment he needs. So try to block out what he's feeling, take a deep breath, and relax."

"Relax? You're fucking kidding, right? I'm hundreds of miles away, for shit's sake!"

A shuffling sound echoed in his ear as Sawyer complained, "He's losing his shit. I...I can't talk to him when he's like this..."

"Honey, it's Mom. Nate's going to be fine. Please don't worry. There's nothing any of us can do for him right now except pray. He's in the hands of the Lord and the medical professionals."

"How can I not worry, Ma?" Noble groaned. He felt isolated and utterly helpless. "Sawyer's text said he was thrown off yesterday but wasn't found until a little bit ago. Is that right? He was gone all night?"

"Yes, sweetheart. We searched for nearly twenty-four hours. Gina finally found him lying in the scrub way out by the east property line."

"What the hell was he doing way out there?"

"I-I don't know. Oh, Noble…he's broken and bleeding…and…" His mom's voice cracked.

His mother's mournful sobs gripped his heart and squeezed.

After another couple seconds of static, Sawyer's voice came through on the other end again. "He's got two open fractures on the left side of his body. He broke his ulna…that's the arm—"

"I know what the ulna is," Noble barked out impatiently.

"Breathe dammit, because I'm two seconds from hanging up on your hateful ass," Sawyer warned.

"Don't hang up!" Noble yelled. "Look, I'm sorry. I'm just trying to process all of this. The shock is—"

"I know," Sawyer replied sympathetically. "It was hard to see bones and shit sticking out of his body."

"Bones? You mean there's more than one break?" Noble asked bleakly as he scrubbed a hand through his hair.

"He fractured his tibia. Damn thing was shooting straight out of his damn jeans." Sawyer's voice wavered. He paused and sucked in a deep breath. "He has a big gash over his left eye. We know he hit a tree. There was blood on the bark. He lay there unconscious for nearly twenty-four hours, so I'm sure he's got one mother of a concussion."

"Fuck me," Noble murmured, blinking back the tears stinging his eyes. A thousand blades scraped his heart. His mind raced like a cyclone. "I'm gonna pack my bags and head to the airport now. Send Norris or Nash to pick me—"

"No. You don't need to come rushing home. There's nothing you can do for him right now anyway. Stay in Vegas and do the wedding thing. Someone will pick you up in Dallas on Sunday."

"I'm not staying here. Not like this. I'm being stabbed with every fucking twitch, every arc of pain that's blasting through him. I'm coming home!"

"Dude! Listen to me. There's nothing you can do for him," Sawyer bit out in frustration. "Sit tight. As soon as we get to the hospital and find out what's going on with him, I'll call and update. All right?"

"Yeah…okay," Noble lied, placating his insistent older brother as he launched off the bed and began tossing his clothes into the duffle bag.

Sawyer could tell him to stay in Vegas until he was blue in the face. Noble refused to listen. He was leaving, no ifs, ands, or buts about it. Nate had called out to him whether consciously or not and Noble wouldn't find peace of mind until he latched eyes on…and touched his twin.

"Are y'all staying in Abilene with him?"

"Mom and Dad already packed their bags and made a reservation at a hotel near the hospital. They're going to stay until Nate's released from the hospital," Sawyer explained. "After Nate gets out of surgery, the rest of us will head back to the ranch and try to keep things running smoothly for the family."

"Okay. Call me right away when you know more…anything more."

"I will. Promise. Just try to stay cool and calm."

"Not possible." Noble ended the call and raced to the bathroom.

After collecting his shaving kit and tossing it into the duffle, he quickly scanned the room to make sure he hadn't missed anything. Satisfied, he grabbed the bag and raced out into the hallway.

The minute he saw Ivy's door, Noble skidded to a halt. His heart sank.

"Fuck," he muttered.

He'd give anything to listen to her sweet screams again, but his brother needed him. Disappointment warred with worry as he turned and jogged to the elevator. After wasting several interminable minutes checking out at the front desk, Noble raced outside and flagged down a cab. After instructing the driver to get him to the airport…fast, Noble pulled out his cell phone and called Harvey.

When he'd explained the severity of Nate's accident, Noble had expected a modicum of sympathy. But Harvey didn't offer up the slightest morsel. Instead, he blew a fucking gasket. The self-centered prick held zero compassion or concern about Nate's injuries and ripped into Noble, cursing and laying on a guilt trip so thick it paled in comparison to anything his mom could muster, for ruining his *special day*.

There was a part of Noble that wanted to tell the driver to turn around just so he could plant his fist in Harvey's hateful mouth. But he wasn't about to waste another precious minute on the self-centered prick.

Clearly, his apologies were being ignored, and after another thirty seconds of listening to Harvey's verbal insults and assault, Noble lost his shit.

"Listen, you selfish, egotistical prick! My brother…my *twin* brother is hurt…hurt so bad they had to fly his busted body to the fucking hospital. His *life* is a million times more important than your *special day*, so get off my dick and go fuck yourself, you festering asshole!"

With a growl, Noble ended the call.

In the rearview mirror, the cab driver's eyes twinkled in amusement. "Sorry about your brother. Two more minutes and we'll be at the airport."

"Thank you," Noble said, exhaling some of the rage still bubbling inside him.

True to his word, Noble was inside the terminal, bag in hand and forcing an affable smile to the pretty brunette behind the ticket counter. She was eyeing him as if he were a Bomb Pop. Normally, he would be flirting the woman with big brown eyes and ruby-red lips straight out of her panties. But the crushing worry weighing him down sucked all sexual desire from his system.

It didn't take any acting to portray the part of an angst-ridden brother desperate to get home to his injured twin. It oozed from his pores in buckets. Unlike Harvey, the ticket agent showered him with sympathy, and forty minutes later, he handed over a brand-new boarding pass that would take him to Abilene as he strode onto the plane.

A petite blonde flight attendant flashed him an overly welcoming smile. Visions of Ivy flooded his brain. With an inward curse, Noble ignored the woman and found his seat. After stowing his duffle and settling into his seat, he realized—like a kick to the nuts—that he hadn't even gotten Ivy's phone number. He'd never see that wild, beautiful siren again…never touch, taste, or feel her soft, lush body beneath him…on top of him.

*Now I'm waxing poetic like a pussy-whipped bitch.*
And it chafed.

He couldn't explain or rationalize why, after just one night, the fact that he'd lost Ivy filled him with dread. Noble was like silicone when it came to attachment…that shit simply slid right off him. But not with Ivy. She'd left an impression. A disturbing chill rippled through him, making him doubly glad he was leaving Vegas. The strange, unnerving connection he'd felt with her was frighteningly dangerous. God only knew what foolish promises he might have made if he'd stayed.

He inwardly scoffed. Promises only led to disaster.

Noble was eighteen when Sawyer had found out the love of his life, his wife, Sara, was cheating on him. Noble had had a front-row view of the ugly fights that ensued between the two, had heard the whispers in town, seen the looks of pity sent his brother's way by the people in town. But he'd also witnessed the devastating pain, depression, and rage that had seized Sawyer. Helplessly watched his once-happy-go-lucky brother fall into a dark and empty pit of gloom and mistrust.

He'd finally clawed his way back to the surface and eventually found love again with Brea, but Noble never forgot the toll it had taken on his brother. Those brutal memories were the crux, the cement that supported his vow to never get married. Honestly, what rational person would willingly set himself up to take such a ruthless fall?

*Not me.*

Yeah, leaving Vegas was the smartest move he could have ever made. While he wasn't the least bit in love with Ivy, she'd definitely rattled him. Noble had never felt such a bizarre and powerful connection with any woman before.

Unwilling to ponder the meaning of his strange attraction to the woman, Noble shook off the prickly sensations assaulting him and focused on the frightening unknown unfolding back home. While both his mom and Sawyer had assured him that Nate would be fine, their confidence did little to quell the ball-shrinking fear unfurling inside him.

The flight to Dallas and the subsequent hour layover were blessedly uneventful. As promised, Sawyer had left him an update via voice mail. Nate was still in surgery. The fact that they hadn't been able to patch him up quickly only sent the teeth of fear and worry sinking deeper into his soul.

As he finally landed in Abilene, Noble checked his phone, but there was nothing. Not a fucking word. Crawling out of his skin, he grabbed another cab and raced to the hospital.

With duffle bag in hand, he followed the signs to the surgery waiting room. When he turned the corner and saw his grim-faced family and Gina, seated in a semicircle, Noble's gut churned. The tension in the air was strung as tight as a bow and as thick as molasses.

"Is Nate *still* in surgery?" His tone was ripe with fear.

Everyone turned their heads and gaped at him for a split second before his mom, with tears in her eyes, ran straight into his arms and hugged him tight.

"What the hell are you doing here? I told you to stay in Vegas." Instead of anger, Sawyer's voice was slathered in relief.

"I couldn't stay. I had to—" A lump of emotion clogged his throat. Noble swallowed tightly. "Be with my family."

"I'm glad you're here, son." A ghost of a smile slid over his dad's face as he ate up the distance between them.

"Me, too," he replied as his dad enveloped both Noble and Nola in his arms.

"How'd you get out of best man duty?" Ned asked.

He shrugged and took a big bite of crow. "Y'all were right. Harvey *is* an obnoxious little bitch."

Sawyer chuckled as, one by one, his brother's and sisters-in-law lined up to hug and welcome Noble home. All except Gina, who remained in her seat and merely sent Noble a weak smile before dropping her gaze back to the well-worn carpet.

*She's hurting something fierce.*

"Did you get something to eat on the plane?" his mom asked.

"A couple bags of pretzels."

"Oh, dear. That won't do. I'm sure the cafeteria is closed by now, but there's some vending machines down the hall. What can I get you, sweetheart?"

"A soda would be great. Thanks, Ma."

As she left the room, the taut undercurrent of tension dropped about a billion levels. Gina's shoulders slumped as she relaxed and stood before announcing she was going across the hall to the restroom.

"We'll be right here, honey." Norman nodded.

When Gina left the room, his brothers let out a collective sigh, telling Noble what he'd already suspected; the friction was between Gina and his mom.

"Okay, somebody tell me what's going on between those two," he demanded, jerking a nod toward the doorway.

Sawyer shot a furtive look at their dad, who simply nodded.

"When your mom saw Nate on the ground and all his injuries, she freaked out and ripped into Gina," Ned supplied.

"She was nasty, rude, and insulting. It was damn ugly," Sawyer added.

"I'm not defending my wife, but she was caught up in the fright of seeing her child hurt so badly. I don't think she truly harbors any ill—"

"Oh, yes, she does," Sawyer spat. "We all saw how she reacted the other night at dinner."

"Your mom will come around. Just give her some time. She's just worried that Nate will get hurt." Norman heaved a heavy sigh.

"I have no idea what she said, but someone"—Noble stared pointedly at his dad—"needs to make her understand that we're grown men, not little boys. We've lived through scrapes, bruises, and stitches. We're more than capable of surviving a broken heart or two if we have to."

"I know, son…I know."

"I mean it. Gina doesn't need Mom's shit on top of what LaCroix did to her and her worry over Nate. It's got to stop." Noble scrubbed a hand through his hair.

A minute later, Gina returned and sat back down in her chair.

Upset and embarrassed that his mother was being such a shrew, Noble dropped down into the chair beside Gina and draped his arm around her shoulders. "How you holding up, buttercup?"

She answered in a soft scoff. "I've been better. I can't stop thinking about what would have happened if I hadn't found him. He'd still be there…dying on the cold, hard ground." Her voice cracked and her chin quivered.

Noble pulled her in close. Gina dropped her head to his shoulder as he gave her a gentle squeeze and pressed a platonic kiss on the top of her head. "The important thing is that you did find him, and he's getting fixed up. That's all that matters. Right?"

Gina didn't answer, simply jerked her head as her body shook in silent sobs. He didn't shush her or try to turn the tide of her tears. He simply held her as she fell apart and pinned his brothers with a critical glare. None of them had been consoling Gina. They'd left her sitting alone like a piranha.

His mom returned, narrowing her eyes when she saw the woman wrapped in Noble's arms. Fury lined Nola's face and

Noble realized then the reason his brothers had opted to leave Gina alone for fear of getting on their mom's bad side.

*Pussies.*

Nola's lips thinned to a tight line as she shoved the can of soda at him. Noble was damn glad Gina's head was bent, sparing her the disapproval written all over his mom's face.

"I doubt your brother would be happy with you pawing his…*woman.*"

A rage he'd never felt toward his mother before erupted like a geyser inside him.

If she had been a man, fists would be flying.

Noble didn't give two shits about staying on his mom's good side. The woman was totally out of line.

He lifted his chin and sent her an icy smile. "He'd be a whole lot more pissed if he knew his entire family chose to ignore her. It's disgraceful that a family that bestows compassion for a living can't manage to show even an ounce and is forcing Gina to deal with this nightmare alone."

Gina's whole body tensed. "Don't," she whispered so softly he barely heard her.

Ignoring her and letting his tongue fly free, Noble skimmed a scowl over his entire family. "How proud do you think Nate would be of the Grayson clan right now?"

Duly chastised, his brothers lowered their heads. Nola's face burst crimson red and she opened her mouth but quickly snapped it shut. She was dying to lash out at him or take a switch to his backside like she'd done when he was a child. But there wasn't any punishment she could hand down, because he'd only spoken the truth.

Instead, she inhaled a deep breath and turned to his dad, who was wearing a grim expression. Norman opened his arms. "Come and sit beside me, Momma."

"I'm tried of sitting," she snapped like a petulant child. "When is that doctor going to come out and tell us something?"

Norman stepped forward and enveloped her in a hug. "When

they're done fixing him up. Why don't we take a short walk, maybe step outside for a breath of fresh air?"

"No," she barked as she wiggled from his grasp. "I want to be here when the doctor comes out and tells me that I can see my boy. It's this waiting that's driving me crazy."

"Me, too," Gina whispered.

Twenty interminable minutes later, a balding, gray-haired doctor dressed in green scrubs entered the room.

"Y'all must be the Grayson family?" The physician had a thick southern drawl.

"Yes." His dad stood and extended his hand. "Norman Grayson. I'm Nate's father."

"Pleasure to meet you, sir. Ronald Cason," the doctor announced. "I head up the orthopedic team here."

"It's taken so long. Is Nate…?" Nola's voice cracked.

"Yes, ma'am. I'm sorry for your wait. The surgery took longer than we expected. But Nate did just fine all through the lengthy procedure," the doctor began as he sat down and made eye contact with the whole family. "Aside from the visible broken bones I know y'all saw when you found him, X-rays showed he has a couple of fractured ribs as well, but no punctured lungs and no internal bleeding of any kind. We patched up his ulna with a basic bone realignment and sutured up the laceration. But the damage to his tibia was a bit more involved. Somehow Nate managed to break the bone in two places. He's got a few plates and screws in him now, but I was able to connect both breaks. There was some interruption of blood flow to his foot because of the breaks, but when we discovered a weak pulse in his ankle, I quickly called in a consult from the head of our vascular team before we performed any amputation."

"Amputation?" Gina gasped, trembling like a leaf.

Noble's heart sputtered before slamming against his ribs.

"Oh, dear Lord," Norman whispered as he turned a deathly shade of white. He swallowed tightly and cleared his throat. "W- were you able to save my son's foot?"

"Yes. Yes, sir, we did," the doctor assured with an understanding expression. "Dr. Terrell performed an angioplasty. Basically, he inserted several tiny balloons into Nate's blood vessels and opened them up, returning the blood flow to your son's ankle. It's like a Roto-Rooter for veins."

A ripple of soft, relieved chuckles rolled through the room, knocking the oppressive tension down a notch or two.

"Thank god and thank you." Nola sniffed quickly wiping at her tears.

"You're welcome, ma'am." Doctor Carson smiled. "Before I came out to talk to y'all, I checked on Nate. His foot is nice and pink now."

While his mom and dad pelted the doctor with questions, Noble melted back against his chair as fear bled from his veins. When he gave Gina a tight hug, she glanced up at him with a watery smile. He wiped the tears from her cheeks and gave her a wink.

"We're going to keep Nate here with us in recovery with us a few more hours. After that, he'll be moved upstairs to the critical care unit for a couple of days. We stitched up the cut above his eye, but neurology will want to do a full evaluation on him once he wakes up."

"Evaluation for what?" Sawyer asked, worry etching his face.

"Just standard procedure. It's my understanding that Nate was unconscious for quite some time, is that right?"

"Yes," Gina softly replied. "When I told him we'd been looking for him all night and all day, he was shocked. He had no idea he'd been knocked out and lying on the ground for that long."

Dr. Cason nodded. "Well, I'm not an expert when it comes to brains, but I suspect he's got a significant concussion. Lying on the ground, huh? That explains why we had to clean out so much dirt and debris when he first got here. I'll order some additional antibiotics for his IV…"

Noble knew the doctor was referring to an intravenous tube,

but his mere mention of IV sent images of Ivy to hijack his brain. Memories of the vocal and responsive ball-churning strawberry-blonde with soulful eyes, and lush lips charged through his head. Both heads, in fact; his cock began to stir and grow. His hands itched to glide over her silky, smooth flesh...to grip her waist and slide her up and down his dick again. A shiver slid through him and he inwardly cursed his tenacious testosterone before forcing visuals of the sexy vixen aside.

"When can we see him?" Nola anxiously asked.

"Y'all can go back and take a peek at him now if you'd like. But please, only a couple of you at a time, and keep your visits brief."

His parents anxiously followed the doctor out of the waiting room.

"Thank fuck." Sawyer exhaled deeply, snaking a hand to Brea's nape and drawing her to his lips. Instead of sharing a kiss, Ned squeezed his April's hand as a tight smile passed between them.

Noble didn't know what had caused such an awkward chasm to form between the couple, and he sure as hell wasn't going to ask.

"Will you go back with me to see Nate after the rest of family is done?" Gina asked quietly.

"Of course I will, but we're not waiting. You and I are going back next," Noble announced loudly enough for his siblings to hear.

He was prepared for an avalanche of blowback, but none of his brothers even batted an eye. They simply nodded in approval. A grim but grateful smile tugged Noble's mouth.

Several long minutes later, his dad—who looked disturbingly shaken—ushered his sobbing mother back into the waiting room.

"Jesus, is Nate in that bad of shape?" Norris asked in a hushed tone.

"He's hooked up to a bunch of tubes and beeping machines, son. We're not used to Nate being so...fragile." Norman cleared his throat. "He's always been like all the rest of you boys, robust and larger than life."

"As soon as he heals, he'll be that way again, Dad. Don't you worry," Sawyer assured.

Norman nodded. "You and Brea can go back and see him for a minute."

Sawyer shook his head, declining the man's offer. "Gina and Noble are going next."

Nola scowled but kept her mouth shut. Cordoning off his irritation, Noble cupped Gina's elbow and escorted her from the waiting room.

"Gretchen running the bar for you tonight?" Noble asked as they made their way to a set of double doors.

"No. When Nash came running in last night saying Nate's horse had returned but he wasn't on it, I kicked out all the customers, locked up tight, and headed to the ranch to help look for him. I haven't been back since."

The fact that Gina had closed the doors on her only source of income to help find Nate spoke volumes. She loved him…loved him a lot.

"I sure hope my knuckleheaded brother knows how lucky he is."

"I'm the lucky one. I just hope he'll forgive me."

"Forgive you for what?"

"We…we had another fight. I-I told him I needed some space."

Noble's feet came to a stuttering halt. "I'm confused. You don't love him?"

"No. I do," she hastily assured. "I-I'm having a little trouble dealing with everything that happened with LaCroix."

"Then you need to talk to someone, darlin'. Someone who can help you heal from all the shit that prick did to you, so you can put it behind you and live a happy life."

"That's what Nate said I needed to do and…what our fight was about."

"You think you're above talking to a professional about your problems?"

Gina shook her head. A pensive expression lined her face. "It's not that. I-I… It's a long story."

"You'll have to share it with me then." Her eyes grew wide with fear. "Sometime when you're ready."

Her head moved in a barely perceptible nod. "I need to see Nate."

"Me, too," Noble concurred and began walking again.

Though he'd tried to prepare himself, nothing readied him for the sight of Nate hooked up to so many tubes and wires. His strong limbs were covered in heavy white plaster, and his leg was suspended in a sling, attached to a pulley system bolted into the bed.

Noble's gut pitched.

A strangled sob slid from Gina's lips. Tears streamed down her cheeks as she gently combed her fingers through Nate's dark hair. Bending, she pressed her face to the pillow next to his ear. "I'm here, my love."

Noble blinked back the tears stinging his eyes and choked down the lump in his throat. After making his way to the other side of the bed, he threaded his fingers through Nate's undamaged hand.

He didn't bother to use his voice. Instead, Noble relied on their telepathic twin line.

*We're all here with you, Nate. Rest and heal for the family, and for Gina. She loves you, bro…loves you more than you'll ever know. We'll watch over her until you're back on your feet. As always, we've got your back. You just focus on getting well. I love you, man.*

The need to fill Nate with enough strength and encouragement to battle his way back from his injuries outweighed the mystery of whether the drugs they'd given him interfered with their twin bond. Hopefully, Nate had received his message.

"Rest and get well, baby…I love you…love you with all my heart," Gina whispered.

*Told you so,* Noble mentally taunted.

A fragment of a tiny smile curled a corner of Nate's mouth.

"I think he can hear you, darlin'."

He'd barely uttered the words when Nate feebly squeezed Noble's hand.

His heart soared. Grinning, he wiped the tears from his eyes. *I'm glad you can hear me. I heard you all the way out in Vegas. That's why I'm here, brother…here to help you fight your way back to us.*

Gina pressed a gentle kiss to Nate's cheek and nuzzled her face against his neck.

"I love you," Noble choked out in an emotional whisper. Nate exhaled heavily as he squeezed Noble's hand once more. "Rest now. We'll come back to see you as soon as we can."

"I'm sorry, baby. I didn't mean the things I said. I *do* love you, Nate. I'm so sorry. I'll never make you doubt that again." Gina sobbed as she kissed his cheek once more before lifting her head and wiping her tears.

Though his brother was a mess, tendrils of hope melted the icy smoke of worry from Noble's soul.

As he escorted Gina back to the waiting room, he sensed her spirits had lifted as well.

"Are you going back to Haven tonight with the others?"

"No." She shook her head. "I'm not leaving until Nate opens his eyes. I need him to hear my apology and pray I'll have the chance to feel his lips on mine again."

"Don't worry. He'll be all over you like a pair of new boots at a thrift store, darlin'." Noble chuckled. "Sawyer said Mom and Dad have a hotel room already booked. Are you going to be staying at the same place they are?"

A pensive expression crawled across her face. "No offense, but I don't think your mom likes sharing the same planet with me, let alone the same hotel. I'm going to stay here at the hospital. I can curl up on a chair in the waiting room and sleep."

Noble frowned. He aimed to rectify the animosity poisoning

his mother, and soon. Until then, he'd act as a buffer and protect Gina from Nola's venomous wrath. It was the least he could do for his brother.

"I'm staying here, too." He nodded resolutely.

It was nearly three in the morning before Nate was moved from the recovery room to the critical care unit. After helping Gina get situated in yet another waiting room, Noble strolled outside with his family. He waved to his physically and emotionally exhausted parents as they left for their hotel. Then waved again to his brothers and both wives as they started the hour-long drive back to the ranch.

Noble paused and tilted his head back. Staring out at the infinite expanse of sparkling stars, he sent up a silent prayer. He thanked the universe for Nate's successful surgery, for his suddenly dysfunctional family, and for the chance to spend one spectacular night in Ivy's arms.

With a heavy sigh and a strange melancholy pumping through his veins, Noble turned and walked back inside the hospital.

# CHAPTER SEVEN

After pulling the T-shirt on over her head, Ivy plucked up her makeup bag and tossed it to the growing pile on her bed, the same bed she'd shared with Noble.

"Stop thinking about him," she tersely scolded herself.

Not that her self-admonishment would do any good. All Ivy could think about was the man and her burgeoning hormones that refused to go into hibernation again.

Thanks to Celina insisting they get ready for her *big day* together, Ivy didn't have time to keep daydreaming about the hunky, sex-beast. She had to gather up her bridesmaid dress, shoes, makeup, and curling iron, then haul ass up to her sister's suite.

After the temper tantrum Harvey had thrown at yesterday's rehearsal, she was stunned that Celina was actually going to marry the asshole. He'd certainly shown the world his true, ugly colors.

After announcing that his best man's brother had been seriously injured, Harvey then proved he was an insensitive jerk who didn't give two shits about the fate of his friend's brother. He'd cursed, screamed, and pitched a fit like a spoiled brat. The heartless prick railed about how his best man had totally ruined his wedding. If Celina was looking for a compassionate husband, she'd never find it with that immature hot mess.

Unfortunately for everyone, Harvey's initial conniption fit was only the warm-up. When his dad had offered to stand in as best man, hotheaded-Harvey looked as if he was going to beat the shit out of his own father. While it hadn't come to blows, it was downright ugly. Ugly enough that Ivy had wanted to gouge out her own eyes rather than continue watching Harvey's epic, sophomoric meltdown.

Ivy had barely slept a wink last night. She'd tossed and turned, fluctuating between praying Noble would tap on her door and worrying about her sister actually marrying douchebag Harvey.

Ivy was at a loss as to what to do about her hopeless sister.

Even after getting an eyeful of Harvey's hair-trigger temper, Celina was still hell-bent on marrying the prick. Ivy so wanted to smack her sister upside the head and knock some sense into her or kidnap her naïve ass and haul her to some foreign country where Harvey would never find her again.

But there was nothing she could do. Ivy was powerless to save her sister from pending heartbreak. Grasping at straws, Ivy pondered what she could say that would make Celina change her mind.

*I love you, but you're making a terrible mistake.*

*Open your eyes, for fuck's sake...the man's got abusive prick written all over him!*

*Wake up and smell the real coffee, not that soy shit Harvey sells! You deserve so much more than settling for a fuck-wit like him.*

Even if she could come up with the right words to say, Celina would rip Ivy to shreds while defending Harvey with her last breath. And in the end, inciting World War III wouldn't accomplish a damn thing.

Exhaling a heavy sigh, she started gathering her things from the bed when the phone on the nightstand rang. Dropping back onto the bed, Ivy lunged for the receiver.

*Please, be Noble! Please...be Noble.*

Just the thought of his whiskey-soft sexy voice made butterflies dip and swoop in her stomach and her heart sputter and race.

After surviving the high-octane drama at last night's rehearsal, she'd knocked on his door when she'd returned to her room. Either he was already asleep or out with his friend again, because Noble hadn't answered. So she'd returned to her room and mentally relived every orgasm-inducing touch, lick, and nibble he'd drowned her in.

Holding her breath, she lifted the phone to her ear. "Hello?"

The breathless tone of her voice made her sound like a horny nymphomaniac.

*Well…if the shoe fits!*

"Good. I caught you before you leave to join Celina." Her mother exhaled in relief. "Are you sick? You sound funny."

"No. I'm fine…well, as fine as I can be, considering…"

*Considering you're not Noble, who I'd much rather be with, lost in those bone-melting orgasms he so effortlessly steals from me. But no, I'm fine, struggling to deal with my sister's doomed wedding.*

"That's exactly why I'm calling. Ivy, you have to talk some *sense* into your sister."

"Excuse me?"

"Celina will listen to you. She *has* to. If she doesn't, then…then you'll just have to find a way to make her! No daughter of mine is going to marry that…that…beast!" Janice huffed.

"This daughter certainly isn't," Ivy drawled. "And what, may I ask, do you suggest I do or say to stop her, Mother? What words of wisdom will dissuade Celina from walking down the aisle and legally binding herself to that…beast as you called him?"

"I don't know! Bribe her…lie to her if you have to. I honestly don't care. But you've got to stop her from ruining her life. Listen, your father and I have already packed our bags. You need to do the same, because once Celina breaks things off with Harvey, we are getting out of town. After the tantrum he threw last night, I want to be all the way out of this state before he blows up again. That man has a vile, dangerous temper. I'm terrified he'll end up hurting my baby girl."

"I'm worried, too, Mom. But why do I have to be the one to convince her to nix her wedding? Why don't we just send Dad up there? He can toss her over his shoulder and we can all head to the airport."

"Prudence Ivy Addison! I can't believe you'd suggest such a thing. Do you have any idea what kind of scene that would cause?" Her mother's tone was rife with equal parts indignation and exasperation.

"*Do not* call me *Prudence*, Mother. You know how much I loathe that name," Ivy bit out between clenched teeth. "And it wouldn't be any less embarrassing than the scene Harvey displayed last night."

"I could give a damn about how *he* acted. I only care about our actions." Janice exhaled heavily. "Honestly, what on earth does Celina see in that…that…"

"Steaming pile of dickless, pompous pig shit? I have no idea."

"That's enough vulgarity, young lady."

Ivy chuckled. "Right. Like you weren't thinking the same thing?"

"Maybe I was. But a proper southern woman would never allow those words to pass from her lips."

*Right, because her vajajay would shrivel up and fall right off.* Ivy rolled her eyes.

"Please, just do your best to talk Celina out of marrying that barbarian."

"I will. But don't hold your breath, Mom. We both know how stubborn she is."

"Yes, and thankfully, you're equally stubborn. That's why I have faith in you, darling."

Ivy didn't bother reminding her mother that her stubbornness, confidence, and all the other qualities she'd once possessed, along with her Zen, had packed their bags and flown away. All the good traits of her former self were probably now partying their asses off on some tropical island chock full of cabana boys with trays of ice-cold margaritas.

No, Janice was stressed out enough without that tidbit of information.

"Keep me posted, love. Your father and I are ready to make a break for the airport in a moment's notice."

"You got it, Mom." Ivy hung up the phone and rolled onto her back. Staring at the ceiling, she struggled to find a way to accomplish this feat. Long minutes later, her mind was still a blank slate. With a heavy sigh she eased off the bed.

"Guess I'm going to have to wing it."

Filled with dread, Ivy gathered her things, and left her room. In the hallway, the maid's cart was parked next to Noble's room. His door was wide open.

Curious, Ivy poked her head inside to see if he might be there while his room was being cleaned. A middle-aged woman with dark skin, round belly, amd silver streaks in her black hair smiled.

"Help you, miss?" she asked in broken English.

"Oh, no. I was just checking to see if Noble was in the room."

"No. Guest all gone now."

"Gone? You mean he checked out?"

"Checked out. Yes." She smiled, bobbing her head.

Like a physical blow, the air punched from her lungs. Ivy's knees threatened to fold, and her heart felt as if it had just been stabbed. Unsure if she could speak, she swallowed tightly.

"Thank you," she managed to whisper.

As she hurried down the hall to the elevator, tears stung her eyes, magnifying how stupid and foolish she felt. One-night stands didn't come with strings or obligations. But Noble's exodus without even saying goodbye was annihilating her in ways she hadn't expected. Ivy angrily brushed away the tear that slipped down her cheek as she stepped inside the empty elevator.

*I have to stop being so ridiculous right now! There's no time for this melancholy bullshit. He doesn't owe me a damn thing, and I don't owe him a thing, either. I knew what I was getting myself into before I spread my legs for that man. It was a casual fuck. Get over it. Noble has had millions of women, and he'll probably have a million more a month from now. I'm not even on his radar anymore. Why would I be? He got what he wanted. He came. He seduced. He conquered. It's over. Case closed. Now let it go.*

While her internal pep talk dried up her tears, it still chafed that Noble had left without a word. Shaking her sorrow away, she reminded herself that he'd given her exactly what she'd wanted—a mind-bending end to her desolate sexual drought.

Nothing more.

Nothing less.

It shouldn't matter that he'd done it with such skilled precision she'd be basking in erotic, sensual memories of him for the rest of her life…but deep down, though it wasn't supposed to, it *did* matter.

The only solace Ivy could find at that moment was the fact that she was a member at one of the big box stores and could easily buy batteries in bulk.

*Whoop-de-fucking-do!*

Pausing in front of Celina's suite, Ivy shoved thoughts of Noble from her mind and started steeling herself for battle.

As she lifted her hand to knock, the door swung open with enough force to tear it off its hinges. In the portal stood Harvey, red-faced and eyes blazing with rage.

"What the fuck are you doing here?" he viciously barked at Ivy.

"Harvey, stop," Celina pled, racing up behind him. Her eyes were rimmed red and tears streaked her pale cheeks. *Oh, asshole, you've just fucked up big-time. Not only did you yell at me, you made my sister cry.* "I-I invited her here," Celina stammered as she sobbed. "Ivy and I are going to get ready for the wedding together. Please don't be mean to her or send her away."

*Send me away? Fat fucking chance of that!*

The sight and sound of her sister begging the evil bastard filled Ivy's veins with white-hot rage. Harvey's eyes narrowed to ugly slits as he turned his wrath back on Celina. He shot her a mentally unbalanced glare and his lips peeled back in a cold, calculated smile.

McMillian had looked at Ivy that very same way. A shiver raced up Ivy's spine.

"Didn't you hear a fucking word I just said? Are you deaf and dumb? Pay attention this time, idiot," Harvey bellowed in Celina's face. "I let you bust my balls the other night about the strip clubs…let you embarrass the fuck out of me in front of my best man—that pussy momma's boy who had to run home and change his brother's tampon—but never again! Don't ever tell me how to act or what to say. Understood?"

As she watched her sister cower to the demeaning tyrant, Ivy's ghostly fears morphed into a bloodthirsty rage.

"Stop your annoying sniveling and keep your mouth shut unless it's working up and down my cock from now on," Harvey barked. "Put on that goddamn wedding dress that cost me a fortune and wiggle your fat ass down the aisle. I'm the boss now. You won't be leading me around by my balls anymore. Do I make myself clear, you bitch?"

*You bitch!*

*You bitch!*

The hateful words echoed in her ears, not in Harvey's voice but in Eugene McMillian's. He'd used the same insult after she'd kneed him in the balls and run from his office.

Rage, red and blistering, blurred Ivy's vision.

All the items in her arms tumbled to the floor with a soft thud.

Bile burned the back of her throat.

Every raw, festering wound that had taken nine long months to heal ripped wide open.

Indignation.

Disgrace.

Misery.

Humiliation.

And a million other wickedly destructive emotions hemorrhaged from her scars. But she refused to let the caustic flow sweep her back into a chasm of helplessness. No, Ivy had clawed her way out of that vile, emotionally crippling cesspool. No one would ever force her down into that pit again. Clenching her hand into fist, Ivy squared her hips and thrust her shoulders back.

"Hey, Harvey?"

When he snapped his head in her direction, she saw raw and menacing hatred shooting from his dark, beady eyes. "What. Do. You. Want. Cunt?"

Ivy pulled her fist back. Drawing strength from every woman who'd ever been crushed beneath the heel of some insecure, misogynistic, abusive asshole, she plowed her knuckles straight toward Harvey's jaw.

Ivy's day of redemption had arrived.

The paralyzing emotions that had once held her prisoner busted through the sturdy bars. The ghost of her former self—the happy, whole, and secure woman she'd once been—stepped through the rubble, tossed her head back, and shrieked in glorious freedom.

Harvey's eyes widened in shock before they rolled to the back of his head. Then, like a drunken garden gnome, he toppled over backward, landing on the floor with a heavy thud. Pain screamed up her arm and sang through her body as absolution burst from every cell in her soul.

"I want you to shut the fuck up!" Ivy yelled in triumph. "So, who's the *bitch* now, you fat prick? Can't answer, can you? No, you can't... 'cause you just got knocked the fuck out...you vile piece of shit!"

"Oh, my god! Ivy? What...what... Oh, god!" Celina screeched, blinking in disbelief at Harvey's inert body. Abject terror swam in her eyes. "Do you know what you've done?"

"Yeah...the biggest favor of your life," Ivy said, shaking out the pain throbbing in her hand with a hiss.

"But...but..." Celina stammered.

"Go pack your suitcase. We're going home."

"I-I can't... I'm getting married," she wailed.

"Not to that piece of shit, you're not. Go!"

Celina turned and rushed back into the suite.

Ivy pulled out her cell phone. Sucking in a hiss, she punched her mother's number.

"Mom, take your suitcases to my room. I'll meet you there in a few minutes. Tell Dad to grab a security guard and haul ass up to Celina's suite. I don't know what Harvey's going to do once he regains consciousness, but it isn't going to be pretty."

"Regains... What happened?" Janice squeaked.

"You wanted me to stop the wedding? I did. We're leaving...*all* of us," she assured and ended the call.

Cautiously keeping her eyes on Harvey, Ivy bent and plucked up one of the shoes she'd dropped. Gripping the soft designer leather in her hand, she held it like a miniature baseball bat. If doughboy came to before her reinforcements arrived, she'd nail all five inches of that wicked heel into his chauvinistic balls.

"I can't believe you knocked him out," Celina yelled from inside the suite.

"I can't believe you let any man talk to you like that," Ivy countered. "We'll discuss that later. Right now...you need to hurry."

"Just for the record, he's never talked to me like that before. And I am hurrying, dammit. If you think I want to be here when he wakes up, you're crazy."

"*I'm* crazy?" Ivy scoffed. "You were the one who wanted to marry the fuck-nut. I'm just glad you finally saw what he was like before you said *I do* baby sister."

Celina didn't reply, simply raced into the bathroom. "Oh, god, I'm not going to get all this shit packed in time. Get in here and help me."

"No way. I'm not taking my eyes off Cujo. Toss your stuff together. You can fold it and sort it out in my room while I pack."

"Okay." She sniffed as she appeared at the door.

As she struggled to lift the heavy suitcase over the beached whale blocking the door, Ivy caught the sparkle from the diamond on her sister's finger.

"Give me your engagement ring."

"What for?" Celina blinked.

"Just give it to me."

Ivy squatted down next to Harvey. While her sister tugged the ring from her finger, Ivy unzipped his pants.

"What the hell are you doing?" Celina screeched.

"Shhh."

Fighting the revulsion rising inside her, Ivy reached inside the man's boxers and pinched the flaccid flesh with her finger and thumb. After fishing the unimpressive worm out from between the teeth of his zipper, Ivy took the ring and shoved it down over the crest. Admiring the sparkle of the diamond adorning his pathetic little cock, she draped it out over the side of his zipper and stood.

"That's it. You have lost your damn mind," Celine admonished. A short second later, she started to giggle.

Ivy flashed her a mischievous grin. "I have not. I'm simply making a statement."

"A statement?"

"Yeah, this little prick is never going to degraded belittle, or verbally abuse the sister I love."

"Oh, god…I love you, too." A tear spilled down Celina's cheek.

Ivy bent and gathered the rest of her things off the floor. She quickly lifted her head at the sound of footsteps charging down the hall. She smiled and flashed Celina a wink as their dad and a security officer arrived.

Their father took one look at Harvey, passed out on the floor, wearing the expensive cock ring, and burst out laughing. "I've got to give you two props for ingenuity."

He quickly sobered when he took in the shell-shocked expression lining Celina's face. Tucking a finger beneath her chin, Jeff tilted her head back, forcing his younger daughter to meet his worried gaze. "Are you all right, baby girl?"

"I-I don't know yet," she murmured.

"W-what the…" the security guard stammered. "Is that a

wedding ring?"

"Engagement ring," Ivy corrected dryly. "The wedding's off."

"I'd say so. I think this guy needs an ambulance."

"Ask someone else to take care of that, please," Jeff instructed as he plucked Celina's suitcase from her fingers. "I need you to escort us to my daughter Ivy's room. You might think about placing a call to the LVPD. That man is definitely deranged."

The guard nodded and led them down the hall, casting curious glances between Ivy and her sister.

"So, who knocked him out?" Jeff asked.

"I did," Ivy replied without remorse. "He deserved it."

"I don't doubt that for a second. Did you decorate the dick's *dick* as well?"

"Yes, I did. I think he's smart enough to figure out the wedding is off once he wakes up and has to take a pee."

Pride and relief swam in her dad's pale blue eyes. Pausing, Jeff hugged her tightly and pressed a stout kiss to her cheek. "We've missed our little tiger. It's damn good to have you back."

Tears stung her eyes. Ivy quickly blinked them away. She knew protecting her sister had picked the lock on the last cell of her emotional prison, and knocking the verbally abusive bastard out had felt damn liberating. Still, Ivy wasn't quite ready to throw a welcome home party for her bruised and battered psyche.

As they stepped into the elevator, Ivy nibbled her bottom lip. "When you tell Mom what happened, can you maybe skip the part about the engagement ring?"

Jeff frowned. "Why would I do that, pumpkin? It was an epic way to break the engagement, not to mention hilariously funny."

"You know how Mom is. I don't want to have to listen to another lecture about proper southern women and how they never touch a man's private parts." She rolled her eyes.

He waved a hand dismissively. "Ignore her. If she starts in on one of her lectures, I'll simply remind her how often she uses her proper southern hands to touch *my* private parts."

Ivy blanched and pressed a hand to her stomach. "Dad! We

are *not* talking about this anymore."

She wrinkled her nose as Jeff tossed his head back and laughed. Ivy glanced at her sister. Bewilderment and sadness etched Celina's face. She was so lost in her own turmoil she didn't appear to have heard their conversation.

Leaning over, Ivy kissed her cheek. "Hang in there, sweetheart. Everything is going to be fine."

A tear trickled down her sister's cheek. "No it's not."

"Yes it is. You're an Addison. We have your back. I know from experience, in times of crisis, our clan is a force to be reckoned with."

"Damn straight we are," Jeff assured. "The grief you're going through now sucks. There's no way around it, baby girl. You're going to have to drive straight through it, but we're right there with you…all the way. The heart does heal…it just takes time."

*Yes it does and so does the soul. It just takes a long, long time.*

When they reached her room, Janice stood in the hall, wringing her hands—suitcases at her feet. The second she saw Celina's tear-streaked face, Janice wrapped her daughter in a comforting hug. That's when Celina fell completely apart.

As her sobs echoed down the hallway, Ivy retrieved her card key and jammed it into the reader.

The fickle lock didn't disengage.

*Slide it in slowly…then ease it down…all the way down…nice and deep.* Noble's whiskey-smooth voice and sexually charged words coiled through her like a snake. She could still feel the heat of his delicious body rolling over her. Clenching her jaw as emptiness and grief consumed her, Ivy slid the card in as Noble had taught her. The green light flashed as a tear slipped down her cheek. She quickly brushed it away, gripped the handle, and pushed the door open.

As she entered the room, the bed snagged all her attention. Sadness stabbed deep.

*Let it go. It's not helping, and mooning over a man I'm never going to see again is definitely not healthy. It's time I find some semblance of normalcy again…whatever that might be.*

Blinking the images of Noble from her mind, she focused on packing up and getting the hell out of Vegas.

As Ivy threw her belongings into her suitcase while describing the ugly confrontation with Harvey, Janice held Celina and rocked her inconsolably sobbing daughter gently. Jeff was on the phone with the front desk, checking out and securing a shuttle to take them to the airport.

Celina's cell phone chimed. She dragged the device from her purse, but before she could wipe her tears and check the caller ID, Ivy snagged it from her hands.

"Hey," Celina protested.

Ivy ignored her and scowled at the name on the display. "You had your chance, asshole. You blew it. Go fuck yourself."

Janice frowned at her vulgar language but didn't bother with a reprimand.

"I-I need to tell him the wedding is off," Celina sobbed.

"I'm sure he's figured that out already, sister."

"How could he? You knocked him out before she got the chance to tell him, right?" Janice asked.

"Trust me. Harvey knows. We left her engagement ring behind. He'll find it." Ivy avoided telling her mom where she'd left the ring. "Dad will fill you in all about that later."

Jeff shot her a knowing smirk. Celina raised her head, wiped her tears, and sent her a watery smile. Ivy bit the inside of her cheeks to keep from laughing.

Like convicts breaking out of prison, they rushed though the massive lobby, looking over their shoulders. They all exhaled a collective sigh once seated in the shuttle and heading to the airport. By some miracle, Jeff managed to exchange their tickets for a nonstop flight to Dallas, scheduled to leave in thirty minutes.

As the plane taxied down the runway and lifted into the sky, Ivy stared out the window, watching until the grand hotels and casinos were nothing but specks on the distant desert floor.

Closing her eyes, she laid her head back and let the sadness wash through her. Noble was gone forever. And though it had only been one night, she knew she'd carry a part of him with her until the end of time. He might not have said goodbye, but he'd set her free in ways that mattered most. His touch, his kiss, his words...they'd made her feel desirable, alive, and blessedly whole again.

It was after one in the morning when her father pulled into the driveway. Ivy was glad she'd moved back home during the trial. She was too exhausted to spend twenty more minutes driving to her former apartment. After climbing the stairs, she stepped inside her old bedroom, tugged off her clothes, and crawled into bed.

Closing her eyes, Ivy was ready to slide into the oblivion of sleep, but her brain wouldn't shut down. It wasn't so much the heartbreaking sounds of Celina sobbing in the next room that clawed at Ivy's brain. She knew one day her sister would find a man deserving of her sassy, sunny, impulsive spirit. Of course, if he turned out to be Harvey 2.0, Ivy would have no compunction about knocking his punk-ass out, too.

No, Celina's drama wasn't what kept sleep at bay. But it was pointless to waste time dissecting and compartmentalizing the real issue. Still, that didn't stop her from tossing and turning long after Celina had cried herself to sleep. After glancing at the clock for the umpteenth time, Ivy exhaled a heavy sigh. It was after three in the morning and she was no closer to dozing off than she'd been when her head hit the pillow. Yanking the covers off, she got up, slipped on her robe, and quietly padded to the kitchen to fix a cup of tea.

Mug in one hand, Ivy opened the sliding glass door and stepped onto the deck overlooking the expansive backyard. Growing up, she and Celina had hosted dozens of sleepovers on the massive wooden structure. Ivy walked to the smooth stained railing, set her cup down, and tilted her head back. The billions of twinkling stars blanketing the night sky made her feel small and insignificant.

Where did she belong in this grand scheme of life? Or was there an actual scheme to it at all? Those were just two of the millions of thoughts dancing around the periphery inside her head. They were filler…fluff…far from the bull's-eye of what she really needed to be asking herself. But if she ever wanted to sleep again, it was time to come to terms with the aftermath of that mystical, magical one-night stand that had her tied in knots and finally put it all to rest.

She wondered if she'd crossed paths with Noble in Vegas by chance or by fate?

Ivy shook her head. Why was she wasting time obsessing over a man whose last name she didn't even know? A man who was out there somewhere in this vast universe but was forever beyond her reach. She didn't know a damn thing about him, besides the fact that he hated to bale hay in a thong.

A bittersweet smile spread over her lips.

She'd heard it said that life threw you challenges so you could learn and grow from the experiences. Ivy didn't know if she truly believed that, but Noble had definitely reintroduced her to the woman she'd once been. He'd breathed life into her again. Maybe he'd simply been meant to give her an oxygen boost so that she'd be less reluctant to give commitment another try.

She chuckled at her sudden philosophical contemplations.

Bottom line, her time with Noble boiled down to one thing. He'd given her one night of spectacular, life-altering sex. But it was over. The odds of her ever crossing paths with him again were astronomically higher than if one of those twinkling stars in the heavens fell from the sky and landed at her feet.

No, it was time to scrub Noble from her memory banks and quit clinging to furtive fantasies that would never come true.

The man wasn't a regal king who had come to rescue her anymore than she was a rejected maid clinging to a glass slipper.

Fairy tales and happily ever afters were nothing but fiction.

She had to let Noble go.

Ivy took a sip of tea before lifting her eyes to the heavens and the great beyond to acknowledge the gratitude inside her.

"Thanks for letting us rescue Celina from a horrible situation. She's hurting, and it's crushing the rest of us, but we'll prop her up. Help her persevere and grow stronger. I'm grateful that I'm growing bolder, stronger everyday. Packing up tomorrow and moving to a new town to open my own business terrifies me. But staying here, rooted in the safe and predictable, growing stagnant terrifies me even more."

She sucked in a deep breath and closed her eyes. A pang of sorrow pierced deep, but this was the right and only thing she could do.

"Noble…wherever you are out there, I just want you to know I'll never forget, the night we spent together, the things you did to me…made me feel. You're the first man who's ever rocked the foundation out from under me and I'll cherish every spectacular moment. But I can't waste my life obsessing over a ghost. You touched my life in wonderful, thrilling ways, and each breathtaking way is branded to my soul. Goodbye, Noble…whatever your last name might be."

A tear slid down her cheek. Ivy didn't bother brushing it away. She simply drew in a ragged breath and let the rest spill onto the deck beneath her feet.

# CHAPTER EIGHT

NOBLE STOOD ON the driveway along with his brothers, camp employees, and a throng of smiling children, anxiously watching Norman pull his beefy Suburban to a stop next to the barn. Excitement hummed in the air.

Nate was finally home.

While his return didn't change the extra work Noble and his other brothers had been putting in over the past two weeks to keep the camp running smoothly, it was damn good to have Nate home. Damn good that Noble wouldn't have to make the two-hour, round trip, trek to Abilene anymore. *Thank god!* The long drive gave him entirely too much time alone to fixate on Ivy—which he did religiously, whether he wanted to or not. Reliving the astonishing night he'd spent with her, over and over again, was driving him crazy. The fact that he couldn't go a day—hell, couldn't go a fucking hour—without her image popping into his head annoyed the piss out of him. He couldn't forget the feel of her nails digging into his flesh as each orgasm rolled her under, the sensation of her plump lips on his mouth, his cock, his balls, or anything else about the delicious minx.

*For the love of… Stop thinking about her, numb-nuts!*

Noble shook the memories from his brain and watched his dad unload a wheelchair from the rear hatch. His mom and Gina stepped from the car in unison, blatantly ignoring one another but smiling brightly to the group assembled around the driveway. The tension between the two palpably pulsed in the air, like it had each day at the hospital. Thankfully, their animosity hadn't escalated into a scratching, clawing catfight. But Noble knew an unstable powder keg when he saw one. It was probably only a matter of time until one tiny spark incited an explosion of biblical proportions.

The back passenger door opened, and Nate stuck his head out, flashing a sheepish grin. A cacophony of cheers, whistles, and applause burst through the air.

Having Nate back on Grayson land filled Noble with a sense of peace he'd lost the second he'd read Sawyer's text in Vegas. The memory of feeling so gut-twistingly helpless had no more fluttered through his mind when…*bam*…images of Ivy writhing beneath him, whimpering and screaming in ecstasy, plowed him under, like a fucking wrecking ball.

With an inward curse, he pushed the memories down deep and rushed to his twin. Gripping the armrest of the door, he dropped to his haunches alongside Nate. Noble didn't have to see the pain straining across his brother's face; he could feel the spikes of agony screaming along his own extremities.

"Let's make your hello short and sweet so we can get you inside and pump you full of pain meds."

A mixture of relief and gratitude flitted over Nate's face. "Thanks, man."

"Don't thank me yet. I haven't started moving you. Dad's got the wheelchair. Do you want to go up to the house that way, or would you rather I just carry—"

"No. I'm not an invalid. Hoist me out of the car and set me in the damn chair, but first…I need to feel the ranch beneath my feet."

"You got it."

Norman eased the wheelchair in closer.

"Careful…don't move him too fast," Nola cautioned, sliding in behind Noble.

"I've got him, Ma," he replied. "We're doing fine."

Nola nervously nodded and brushed a hand through Nate's hair. "We'll get you into the house and tucked into your own—"

"Actually, Ma," Nate interrupted. "I'm only staying long

enough to grab some clothes. I'm going to recuperate at Gina's place."

Nola reared back as if she'd been slapped.

"In a bar?" She narrowed her eyes, pinning Gina with a hateful glare. "I suppose *you* talked him into this, didn't you?"

"No," Nate barked before Gina could reply. "This was *my* choice...*my* decision."

"Why?" Nola asked, her voice quivering.

Nate's expression softened. "Because you have enough to deal with around here...the camp...the family. I won't add to that. I love you, but I don't want you hovering over me night and—"

"I don't hover." She bristled and quickly softened. "I just want to take care of you. Gina can't do that and serve booze."

Gina cocked her head as if ready to square off with their mom. Nate sent her a subtle shake of his head, warning her off. Crossing her arms over her chest, Gina's lips thinned in an angry, tight line. Nate shot her a wink before turning his attention back to Nola.

"I don't need her waiting on me hand and foot. I'm quite capable of doing a few things for myself. The things I can't, Gina will help with before she opens the bar. If it doesn't work out..." Nate shrugged. "I'll come back home."

Nola almost managed to bank her fury. "Well, you two have certainly worked it all out, haven't you?"

"Yes, we have." Nate nodded firmly. "I love you, Ma, but I'm a grown man, capable of making my own decisions."

"Yes, I know. You reminded me every day you were in the hospital." Her words were clipped in irritation and edged with insult.

"Let's finish this conversation inside, shall we?" Norman's tone was firm but calm as he jerked his head toward the welcoming party.

Embarrassment crawled across Nola's face as she realized everyone was watching the heated exchange. Forcing a tight smile, she nodded. "Forgive me, son. I'm sure she'll take good care of you."

"I know she will." Nate and Gina exchanged loving smiles.

"But how on earth is she going to get you up the stairs to her apartment?" Nola continued in a soft but terse whisper.

Nate glanced up at Noble. No words were necessary.

"I'm going to follow them back to town and get him settled in up there," Noble announced, watching his mother's nostrils flare. No doubt he'd just moved to the top spot on her shit list, but Noble didn't care. His mom was in the wrong and doing wrong by treating Gina so poorly. Locking eyes with Nate, Noble arched his brows. "You ready?"

"Yeah. Let's do this."

Cinching his arm around his brother's waist, Noble waited while Nate pivoted in his seat. He dragged in a deep breath and gripped Noble's arm. Carefully, he eased Nate out of the vehicle. When Nate's feet hit the pavement, he closed his eyes and exhaled the air he'd been holding with a mighty gust. His muscles trembled, and a bead of sweat rolled down his temple as Noble supported his body.

Even while the thumping pain—holding him hostage via their twin bond—pulsed through his body, a surge of peace careened from Nate straight to Noble's heart.

Seconds later, the serenity was wiped from them both as a bitter stab assailed Nate.

"Easy, bro. Just breathe. I've got you," Noble assured.

He gave a jerky nod and sucked in a ragged breath. Norman slid the wheelchair in closer before Noble slowly inched Nate onto the seat. Jaw clenched and sweating profusely, he tucked his heavy casted arm against his chest as another round of applause and cheers went up all around them. Nate smiled tightly and waved again while Norman carefully lifted his injured leg and rested it on top of the elevated calf pad.

"There is no way on god's green earth that Gina can help him in and out of bed. She's not strong enough," Nola hissed.

Fire shot from Gina's eyes. Her patience had obviously come

to a screeching halt. Noble was damn glad her Louisville Slugger, Martha, was tucked safely beneath the bar back in town.

"She's a lot stronger than you think," Nate assured with a scowl.

"She's not strong—"

"Nola. Enough!" Norman chided in a sharp whisper. "They'll get along just fine."

Nate reached out and took Gina's hand. Instantly, her irritation seemed to melt away. She flashed him a megawatt smile and linked fingers with him.

Nola's eyes filled with tears as she watched her son choose the woman he loved over the one who'd brought him into the world. Seeing the devastation crushing her within nearly ripped Noble's heart out. So did watching her turn and run into the house.

He couldn't fault Nate for his decision. After all, their mom was the one who'd started this war. In essence, she'd been the driving force behind Nate having to even choose sides to begin with. Still, Noble didn't understand the crux of his mom's animosity toward the girl.

It was past time to find out.

"I'll run inside and get your suitcase down from the closet," Noble offered before jogging along the same path his mother had just taken.

The minute he stepped inside the house, he could hear her crushing sobs. He hurried into his parents' room to find her on the edge of the bed. She had her hands pressed to her face and was crying her heart out. His mom was always the strong, resilient one who didn't break down easily, and never like this. The sight of her crumbling now eviscerated him.

After striding into the room, Noble sat down beside her and hugged her tight. At first she jolted and tried to wiggle away, but he simply pulled her close against his chest, where she melted against him, crying ever harder.

"What's going on, Mom? You haven't been yourself for weeks. Do you honestly hate Gina so much you're willing to drive a wedge between you and your own son?"

Nola reared back, eyes rimmed red but flashing wide. "Hate her? I don't hate her. Yes, I'm scared she's going to break my baby's heart, but hate? Of course I don't hate… Why would you think such a thing?"

Noble wrinkled his brows in confusion. "Maybe because you treat her like she's a horse apple stuck on the bottom of your boot."

"I do not!"

"You do. You treat April and Brea like queens, but not Gina. You treat her like she's a leper."

"April and Brea are my daughters-in-law."

"And there's a damn good possibility that Gina will be one, too. I've been around you for twenty-five years, and I've never heard you speak to anyone as hatefully as you do Gina."

"Oh, god. Have I really been that horrible to her?" A new wave of tears spilled down her cheeks.

"Talk to me, Ma. What is *really* going on with you?"

"I-I c-can't," she sobbed.

Noble's heart sputtered before hammering in his chest. A million paralyzing questions uncoiled in his head. He swallowed the lump of fear balling up in his throat and peered helplessly into her glistening eyes. "Are you sick? Do you have…c-cancer or something?"

Nola shook her head. "No…worse."

Panic, feral and wild, clawed through him, leaving hemorrhaging gashes. Noble launched off the bed "I'm getting Dad."

His mom reached out and snagged his wrist. "He already knows."

"Knows *what*? Tell me, Ma. Tell me what's wrong with you?"

She raised her head and looked up him. Anguish and fear lined her face. "I-I'm… Oh, honey. Your dad and I wanted to wait until Nate was back home… We wanted everyone here and were going to tell you all tonight at dinner, but—"

"Tell us what?" Noble bellowed, scrubbing a hand through

his hair.

"I-I'm...*pregnant.*"

*Pregnant?*

The air in his lungs and every muscle in his body froze. While his brain was no longer envisioning her imminent death, he still couldn't processes what she'd just told him. But he could see himself, seven years old again, peering into Norris's baby bed and wondering why his parents had decided to bring the peeing, pooping, puking, squalling little nightmare home from the hospital.

"I...I don't know how this happened," Nola cried, tossing her hands into the air.

Noble smirked and quickly started reciting the same words she'd said to him when he'd asked her where babies came from years ago. "Well, when a mommy and a daddy really love each other..."

She glared at him. "Don't be a smartass. I mean, I'm forty-nine years old. My baby factory should be closed...out of business. I-I haven't had a... Oh, never mind. I'm not discussing my menstrual cycle with one of my sons."

Noble sat back down on the bed and hugged her tightly. "Good thing Dad married you all those years ago."

"What do you mean?"

"I'd hate to have to use that shotgun on dad for knocking you up."

"This isn't a joking matter, son," she snapped, face lined in worry. "Because of my age, this pregnancy is classified as high-risk. The chance that this baby will be born without some...*issues* is slim to almost none."

That information shook him hard...at first. Slowly, a knowing smile tugged his lips. "Our whole family dedicates our lives to kids with special needs. You're forever telling us that God doesn't give us more than we can handle. He isn't about to start now."

"Oh, hush." She sniffed as she wiped her eyes. "You don't have to throw all my lectures back in my face." Her shoulders sagged as she exhaled a heavy sigh. "This can't be happening... It just can't be. I'm too old to be a mother again. I don't have the energy to chase after a toddler. For crying out loud, I'm supposed to be rocking and singing songs to my *grandchildren*."

"Well, you won't be getting any of those from me, thank god."

"Oh, yes I will. One day I'll be rocking *your* son or daughter."

*Like hell!*

Steering their conversation away into calmer, less shark-infested waters, Noble chuckled. "So, what's Dad think about being a new poppa again?"

"He's already picked out names." She rolled her eyes and frowned. "Nicholas if it's a boy. Naomi if it's a girl."

"Strong ones. I like them."

"I do, too. But..."

"No buts. That little life growing inside you is a Grayson. Whatever happens, he or she will be surrounded by love and that's all that matters."

She nodded and sent him a watery smile.

"You need to tell the rest of the family your news. But you need to talk to Gina first, in private, so you can apologize to her."

"I've really been that..." A bewildered expression wrinkled her face.

"Nasty? Horrible? Rude?" he supplied. "Yes, and a whole lot more."

"She'll never forgive me. She's going to hate me forever." Nola buried her head in his chest as sobs ripped from the back of her throat again.

Noble held her close and kissed the top of her head. "I know you don't know her yet, but Gina's not like that. She'll understand."

Nodding, his mom sniffed. "Would you please ask her to come back here then?"

"Sure. While you two talk, I'll help Nate pack."

"Will Gina really take care of him as well as I would?"

Noble's heart squeezed at his mom's uncharacteristic insecurity. "No. Because no one could ever take care of any of us the way you do. But Gina will do anything to help him heal… They're head over heels in love."

"I'm glad, really I am. All I've ever wanted is for you boys to find a special woman to love and grow old with." Pausing, she peered up at him. "Even you, my bed-hopping bachelor."

*Not in this lifetime.*

"Sorry, Ma. You're going to have to settle for five out of six storybook endings.

She softly patted a hand against the side of his face the way she used to when he was a child. "When you least expect it, some woman is going to come along and steal your breath, your heart, and your soul, sweet boy."

Like a match to gasoline, her premonition sent images of Ivy to burst in his brain. She had definitely stolen his breath. Thankfully, she hadn't had time to abscond with his heart or soul. But something deep down inside him said she easily could have.

Nate's accident had undoubtedly saved Noble's life. A shiver of relief zipped through him. "I'll go find Gina."

"Thank you, baby."

Noble kissed her on the cheek and strolled out into the hall.

Passing Nate's room, he found Gina all right…straddling his brother's wheelchair. It appeared as if they were trying to suck the other's tonsils out as they fed off each other like rabid dogs on a dead squirrel.

"I'd say get a room, but…" Noble taunted.

Gina jerked her mouth from Nate's and quickly leapt off him. A pink blush stained her cheeks.

"No need to be embarrassed. I've been sucking the lips off women for years."

"Which set?" Gina quipped with a saucy grin.

"Both." Noble chuckled, then quickly sobered. "Mom wants to talk to you. She's in her room."

"Me?" Gina blinked before casting Nate a wary look.

"About what?" His brother's tone was edged in suspicion.

"About the way she's been acting," he explained. Nate still looked skeptical. "I wouldn't send Gina into the lion's den if I thought the beast was going to maul her to death and you know it."

Nate scoffed. "You don't know how ravenous she's been lately."

Noble clapped his twin on the shoulder. *Trust me.* He mentally shoved the command.

"I'll be fine," Gina assured.

"I'm sure you will, but I'm coming with you. We agreed...I would handle her...attitude."

"I'll be fine," she insisted.

"I know you will, but all these weeks you've been biting your tongue. Which I appreciate, but you don't have to put up with shit just to keep the peace. If she starts bitching at you about me staying at your place, or anything else, you push back. Understood?"

"If I need to, I will." Gina gave Nate a quick kiss. She lifted her chin and squared her shoulders, then strolled out of the room.

"What does Mom want to talk to her about?" Nate demanded.

"She wants to apologize and tell her the reason she's been acting so...nasty."

"What is it, menopause or something?"

"She wishes," Noble mumbled.

"I don't get it. Mom never once treated April or Brea like they were crack whores, only Gina."

"It's not Gina, bro."

"Then what the hell is it?"

Noble exhaled a heavy sigh. He hadn't planned to steal his folks' thunder and spill the big news, but the worry plaguing Nate was singeing him as well.

"Mom's pregnant," he whispered.

"Pregnant!" Nate bellowed in disbelief.

Of course, as Murphy's Law would have it, Nash glided into the room at that exact second. A sardonic smile tugged his lips. "You knocked Gina up, huh? Way to go, stud."

"Not Gina, you asswipe," Nate spat. "*Mom.*"

Nash's smug demeanor morphed into shock and horror. "Mom is *pregnant?*"

"Goddamn it! Shut the fuck up, both of you," Noble hissed.

"Noble Franklin Grayson… for the love of…" Nola yelled, barreling into Nate's room. The second she slapped her hands on her hips and unfurled her bitch wings, Noble knew he was toast. "I didn't tell you in private for you to go off and broadcast it to the whole world!"

Gina stepped in behind Nola wearing a smirk.

Seconds later, Sawyer, Brea, Ned, April, and Norris charged into the room, each wearing looks of astonishment.

An awkward silence descended.

Nash's angry tone split the muted air. "You're shitting us, right?"

"I wish I was," Nola whispered, sadly.

"But…but… aren't you and Dad too old to still be…you know, doing it?" Norris stammered as his cheeks grew red.

"We are not *that* old," Nola defied indignantly.

When Norman breached the portal and took in the traumatized expressions of his children, he hurried to Nola's side. Love, sympathy, and understanding etched his face as he hugged his frazzled wife and gave her a tender kiss. "I'll have you know, Norris, I may not the be youngest rooster in the hen house, but I can still get the job done, son."

Gina, April, and Brea giggled, while Noble and his brothers groaned.

"Young or old, you'll always be my stud, baby," Nola cooed with a naughty smile before she sent him an apologetic grimace. "I'm sorry for letting the cat out of the bag, but since Gina and Nate won't be here for dinner, and—"

"I'm not upset, princess," Norman assured.

"Thank you."

She darted a nervous glance over her family and licked her lips. "It's been brought to my attention that I've been acting like a shrew. I blame the hormones, but it doesn't excuse the fact that I've hurt someone very important to this family. Gina has graciously accepted my apology, but I need to tell the rest of you how sorry I am for being so—"

"Bitchy and judgmental?" Sawyer supplied with a crooked grin.

"Yes." Nola nodded contritely. "I'll try and be—"

"Happy," Norman interjected. "That's all we want, is for you to be happy, my love. Having a baby is the most joyous thing on the planet."

While his dad was clearly thrilled, Noble saw the shadows of worry clouding his mom's eyes. She'd likely fret the entire…however long it would be until his new brother or sister was born.

"When are you due?" Brea asked.

"I have no idea." Nola's frowned. "I haven't had a… I thought I was in the throes of menopause. Obviously that wasn't the case. I saw Doc Knight before Nate's accident. He's said he'll take a stab in the dark based on the measurements at my weekly visits."

"Weekly? Why do you have to see him that often?" April asked, clearly concerned.

"Because of my age. This is a high-risk pregnancy."

"High risk for what?" Norris asked, unable to mask his worry.

"Complications. But we'll cross that bridge when and *if* we have to."

"That being said, I expect you boys to pitch in more around the house so Mom can rest." Norman's commanding tone brooked no argument. Then he turned and nodded down at Nate. "All but you. You pack your things and work on getting well. The rest of us will handle the ranch and Mom till you're back on *both* feet."

Nola bent next to Nate's wheelchair. "I'm sorry for hurting you and Gina, baby. Now be a good patient and not a cantankerous pain in her backside, or I'll come to the bar and tan your hide."

Nate chuckled. "I will."

"And Gina, if you need anything, you be sure to call."

"Yes, Mrs. G."

"Good. Now I'm going to the kitchen to start dinner. Who wants to help?"

"I will," Brea offered.

"Me, too," April chimed in before they followed Nola out of the room.

"Norris…Nash, you two go on out there and set the table," Norman directed. "I'll be in to help Mom after Noble and I get Nate loaded up for the ride back to town.

As the rest of the family cleared out, Noble and Gina packed up Nate's things. After loading the patient and things into the truck, they said a lengthy goodbye on the driveway, and headed toward town.

When Noble turned onto Main Street, he noticed several work trucks parked outside the clothing store that had gone belly-up months ago. "Wonder what they're putting in over there?"

"It's a new bakery," Gina replied. "Supposed to open up after Christmas… January or February, I'm not quite sure of the date."

"A bakery, huh?" Nate was probably already salivating. Unlike his sweet-toothed twin, Noble could take or leave most desserts. "Ever had icing licked off your body, baby?"

"Nate!" Gina chided. "We'll discuss that once we're alone, you naughty boy."

"No sex talks until after I'm gone," Noble groaned.

"Sounds like someone needs to get laid." Nate laughed.

"I'll be getting some before you will, gimpy."

"His body might be out of commission, but my mouth works just fine," Gina quipped with a saucy grin.

"Drive faster, man. Much, much faster," Nate urged.

Noble rolled his eyes as he worked to block the memory of Ivy's sinful mouth wrapped around his dick and the most sublime suction he'd ever felt. Biting back a snarl, he stopped the truck in front of the bar and killed the engine.

Thirty minutes later, after much muscle and maneuvering, Noble eased his brother onto Gina's bed and wiped the sweat from his brow. Two seconds later, the woman climbed onto the mattress beside Nate.

Wanting to be long gone before she started drowning his brother in oral pleasure, Noble said goodbye and hurried out of the bar. Once he was alone in his truck, images of Ivy crashed through him, rolling him under in a tsunami of cock-straining memories.

Gripping the steering wheel, he exhaled deeply and surrendered. He let every minute detail about Ivy come out to torture him.

Her sweet, enticing peach scent started inundating his senses.

His fingertips tingled as he remembered the feel of her soft, supple skin.

His cock sprang to life, throbbing and straining as the sweet earthy flavor of her slick nectar sang over his taste buds.

Then out of the clear blue, his mother's words slammed through him, washing every ounce of lust from his system. *When you least expect it, some woman is going to come along and steal your breath, your heart, and your soul, sweet boy.*

An icy, foreboding chill slithered up his spine.

No matter how vehemently he wished he could deny it, Ivy had somehow managed to crawl deep under his skin…branded herself into his psyche, and Noble had no fucking clue how to exorcise her memory.

He unleashed a feral growl, teeming in frustration, and slammed his fist against the steering wheel.

The fact that he'd never see Ivy again should be filling him with relief. Instead, pangs of regret and mourning gnawed at him, like an all-you-can-eat buffet, both night and day. The little vixen had cast some kind of wicked spell on him. Because unlike with any of his usual bed-bunnies, Noble would give his left nut to spend one more night with Ivy, to drag her beneath him and sink balls-deep into her silky cunt. Just thinking about her tight walls sucking at his shaft made him itch like a bad case of poison ivy.

"Poison Ivy." A humorless chuckle slid off his tongue. There wasn't a more fitting name for the sexy, mind-melting siren.

Scrubbing a hand over his face, Noble started the engine and backed out of the parking space. Passing the grocery store, he noticed a flutter of purple. He eased off the accelerator and peered out the driver's-side window.

Wearing a flowing, purple blouse, Trudy clung to a skinny, nerdy-looking geek in thick glasses, wearing a cheap knock-off pair of cowboy boots. She tossed her head back and let out a shrill laugh as they stood beside a sleek, red sports car. When the guy bent to open the door for her, Trudy grabbed him by the back of the neck and slammed a lip lock over his mouth.

"Well, well," Noble mumbled under his breath. "That's got to be the infamous, hair-triggered, little-dicked fiancé, Calvin. You poor, pitiful bastard…if you only knew."

*Not my zoo…and thank god, not my fucking hyena!*

Across the street, the sound of hammers and the scream of a table saw snagged all his attention. Rolling to a stop, he peered past the freshly washed windows of the new bakery. Inside, several workers were hanging drywall and slapping putty on the seams, while a couple others stood on tall ladders, tacking fancy scrolled cornices against the edge of the ceiling. Off to one side of the room, high-dollar rounded-glass stainless steel display cases sat in a row. After mentally adding up the price tag for such lavish upgrades, Noble let out a long, low whistle. Someone was pouring a shit-ton of money into that old building.

His cell chimed, drawing his attention away from the construction. Slowing to the stop sign at the end of Main Street, he plucked the device from his pocket and glanced at the text from a longtime bed-bunny.

> **Bonnie:** *I heard Nate's back home. Hope that means you have time on your hands to play with this…*

Seconds later, a photo that gave a whole new meaning to the term *selfie* filled his screen. Instead of turning the corner toward Bonnie's house and slamming a foot to the gas pedal, Noble cocked his head and studied the image.

"How the hell…?"

She had to have twisted herself into a knot in order to capture such a wide-open, leave-nothing-to-the-imagination shot. But what shocked him more was the fact that the sight of Bonnie's plump, pink pussy didn't even make his cock twitch.

He turned off his phone, dropped it on the seat, and looked down at his snoozing dick.

Tendrils of panic spilled through him.

"You poisoned me real good, didn't you…Poison Ivy?"

With a screech from his tires, Noble gunned the engine and headed back home.

# CHAPTER NINE

*Three months later—*

WAKING WITH A start, Ivy's eyes flew open. It was still pitch-black outside the windows. Rolling over, she whipped her cell phone off the nightstand in her bedroom above the bakery and checked the time—four thirty a.m. Instead of groaning at the ungodly hour, a nervous giggle slid off her tongue.

Anxiety pelted her like tiny hailstones.

*Oh, god, this is it! Opening day!*

In three and a half hours, she would open the doors of Sweet Flours for the very first time. Fear, excitement, and unadulterated joy hummed through her veins. A split second later, her mental to-do list spooled through her brain. Sunrise was still a few hours away, but Ivy needed every second to pull everything together in time. She needed to fill the display cases, prepare and bake the bread, and arrange the trays of samples she planned to give the customers…customers she prayed would come.

Ivy had painstakingly prepared an advertising campaign. She'd run ads for her grand opening the past two weeks in the local newspaper. The fellow business owners along Main Street had allowed her to tape flyers on their doors as well. Thankfully, her efforts had generated plenty of curiosity. If the people stopping to peer in through the plate-glass windows—waving and smiling as she fluttered back and forth from the kitchen, baking her brains out—was any indication of today's turn out, Ivy was going to be a very busy woman.

But first, she needed coffee…lots and lots of coffee.

Tossing back the covers, she climbed out of bed. The minute

her feet hit the floor, her stomach lurched and roiled. Racing to the bathroom, she dropped to her knees and retched in the toilet.

"Not today," she groaned, spitting into the bowl.

Her nerves were getting the best of her. As the grand opening grew near, Ivy was praying to the porcelain gods two or three times a week. Slowly rising to her feet, she gripped the sink and sucked in a deep breath. She closed her eyes, mentally working to calm her anxiety and the acid boiling in her gut.

If it wasn't for the IUD implanted inside her, she might worry that she was pregnant, especially since she couldn't remember if Noble had gloved up before he plowed her lady garden to perfection over and over again. Not knowing if she'd had unprotected sex or not was grossly irresponsible, but in her defense, Ivy's mind had been wholly focused on other things. Like every touch, lick, and thrust Noble bestowed on her. Still, any super-sperm that might have backstroked up to her unsuspecting eggs had been permanently taken out.

Closing her eyes, Ivy allowed the misty memory of Noble to rise to the surface.

Seconds later, she was lost in the guilty pleasure of reliving his calloused hands gliding over her flesh, of his warm, firm lips devouring her like she was the sweetest morsel on the planet. She'd let him lead her down a path of mindless pleasure where he effortlessly dragged earth-shattering orgasms from her over and over again.

Heat coiled and climbed her restless body.

She could still feel the tingles of lightning from his gifted fingers. Remembered her body melting beneath each flick and thrust of his talented tongue. Savored the sweet burn when he finally slid that—*shiver*—fat, hard, exquisite cock deep inside her.

Lifting her heavy lids, Ivy peered at her reflection in the mirror. Her skin glowed in an aroused pink hue. Her pupils were dilated. And between her folds, her clit throbbed with a mournful ache that her battery-operated boyfriends—tucked away in the nightstand—couldn't sate.

Exhaling in frustration, Ivy shoved the memories back down and locked them away. She had too much work to do to allow Noble—whatever his last name was—to occupy her thought process with hours and hours of unmitigated pleasure.

Ivy couldn't afford to let memories of Noble wander free.

It was too risky.

She needed to focus on her business...a business that would either make or break her. After pushing off the sink, Ivy turned on the shower. Thirty minutes later, she was dressed in a pink T-shirt emblazoned with *Sweet Flours* across her chest and a pair of classic black pants. She twisted her hair up in a tight ponytail, the turned and hurried down the stairs to the bakery.

Ivy pushed through the swinging metal doors, flipped on the lights, and stepped into the kitchen...her woman-cave, her solace, her refuge. The scents of cinnamon, nutmeg, various fruits, and buttery rich goodness assaulted her as much as the blinding glare from the stainless steel counters, cooling racks, oversized refrigerator, industrial ovens, and massive double sink.

Focusing on getting all the finishing touches in place, Ivy began pulling trays of goodies she'd prepared late last night off the cooling racks. After carefully peeling back the plastic wrap that had kept them fresh, she trekked to the front of the store and began filling the display cases.

As she passed the coffeemaker, Ivy flipped the switch. While the scent of roasted beans filled the air, she continued loading trays of lemon, blueberry, kiwi, and gooey-butter squares, apple turnovers, cream puffs, shortbread, and several flavors of Danish rolls into the display cases. She stocked the next one with assorted cookies, cupcakes, tarts, cheesecakes, and eight different-flavored multi-tiered cakes covered in buttercream frosting and artfully decorated.

After snagging a large cup of coffee, Ivy returned to the kitchen. She cranked up the tunes on her cell phone and lost herself in the music and the feel of the sticky dough between her fingers. Yeah, it was a cheap marketing ploy, but when the customers entered the store, Ivy wanted the homey scent of warm, buttery bread to permeate the air.

Setting the dough aside to rise, she dipped a flat of plump, ripe strawberries in white, milk, and dark chocolate and drizzled contrasting colors of chocolate over them after they'd cooled. The sun was slowly creeping up over the horizon when she carried the berries up front and slid them into the display case. Her stomach pitched and she pressed a palm against the rioting butterflies dipping and swooping inside.

*I have got to chill out. I don't have time to run to the john and heave my heels every five minutes today.*

She closed her eyes, swallowed the saliva pooling in her mouth, and inhaled several deep breaths. Forcing a calm she didn't feel, Ivy turned and raced back to the kitchen once more.

After quickly kneading the bread dough, she filled several loaf pans and placed them in the oven. As they baked, she arranged the sampler platters and glanced up at the clock.

*Only thirty more minutes!*

"Gahhh," she cried out, unable to ignore the angst-ridden tremble of her hands or the abject fear pinging inside her.

Racing upstairs to her apartment, Ivy hurried to the bathroom. After wiping the smudge of flour from her cheek, she dabbed on a bit more concealer to hide the dark circles under her eyes. She only wished there was a makeup that could hide her surging trepidation or camouflage the fact that her entire future was riding on this one day.

*What if someone recognizes me from that shit show back in Dallas?*

A frightened whimper warbled in the back of her throat.

Ivy scowled at herself. Lifting her chin, she squared her shoulders.

"The past is gone. Today is here. Tomorrow is a gift. No one has control over you but you. Live your life the way *you* want. Be strong. Be happy. And for fuck's sake, be brave!"

Mentally repeating the familiar mantra, she raced back downstairs and skidded to a halt. The scent of baking bread mollified her as she stood, taking in the beauty of the shop with pride and satisfaction.

"Some dreams *really* do come true," she whispered to herself.

A loud tap on the back door nearly made her heart leap from her chest. Ivy scurried through the kitchen and pulled the heavy metal door open to find her mom, dad, and Celina smiling like a trio of loons.

"What are you all doing here?"

"You think we'd miss your grand opening?" Her dad chuckled. "Not a chance in hell."

"Oh, darling. I'm so happy," her mother gushed.

"Congrats, sis," Celina beamed.

Tears filled her eyes, but she quickly blinked them back. They'd come to support her, to help her succeed. But the even more overwhelming delight was seeing Celina smile again. Ivy hugged her tightly and bit back the urge to sob like a baby.

"Welcome back from the dark side, baby sis," she croaked past the emotion clogging her throat.

"Thank you…for everything," Celina whispered.

"All right. Tell us what you need help with," Janice demanded as she peeled off her jacket and rolled up the sleeves of her Neiman Marcus blouse—the woman didn't shop anywhere else. "Something sure smells scrumptious."

"Oh, shit! The bread!" Ivy screeched. She raced to the oven and flung the doors open. After grabbing the hot pads, she pulled out the pans of golden-brown crusted bread.

"We're here to help, pumpkin," Jeff reminded, sending a surge of comfort and warmth to fill her. "Put us to work."

Ivy's brain could barely keep up with the litany of instructions pouring out her mouth.

When all was said and done, Jeff remained in the kitchen, slicing bread. Janice was enlisted to mingle with the customers, offering samples and refilling the platters as needed. Ivy gave Celina a crash course on the pricing structure and how to operate the cash register in the scant fifteen minutes before opening the door.

"I got it. I got it. Don't worry," Celina assured.

Drawing in a calming breath, Ivy lifted her head and glanced at the front door.

Alma Anderson stood front and center, grinning like a lottery winner. Beside her, an older man with a handlebar moustache steadied a hunched-over tiny old lady clutching a cane. Behind the trio was a huge group of others wearing expectant smiles and craning their necks as they stared into the shop.

Ivy's heart rate sputtered. A jagged blast of adrenaline sliced through her system, and the butterflies in her stomach had gone to full-blown riot mode.

"So much for calm," she mumbled under her breath before painting on a faux smile as she hurried to unlock the door.

"Good morning, everyone. It's an honor to have you here to celebrate Sweet Flours' grand opening. Please, come inside."

Alma crossed the threshold first, wearing a beaming smile as Ivy quickly scampered behind the counter. With mouth gaping open, her landlady turned in a slow circle, taking in the renovations with obvious awe. "Oh, my goodness. It's…it's simply gorgeous. If your treats are as remarkable as your eye for design, you're going to make a killing."

"I certainly hope so." Ivy chuckled softly while anxiety began slowly bleeding from her system.

In her usual gracious and polite southern belle style, Janice greeted each customer filing through the door, offering up samples to them.

While boxing up the triple-layer chocolate cake Alma had selected, Ivy craned her neck and glanced out the window and nearly swallowed her tongue. Customers were lined up and down the street, two and three deep in some places. *Oh, my god!*

After Alma paid for her cake, she came back and stood at the end of the display case. "I'll hang out here, out of the way for a bit and introduce you to your new neighbors if you'd like."

Ivy sent up a silent apology for every disparaging thought that had crossed her mind regarding her landlady. "Yes, please and thank you so much. You're a godsend."

True to her word, Alma introduced every person who stepped up to the counter. It didn't take long before names and faces were swirling through Ivy's brain like cake batter. Fortunately, she didn't have time to fixate on her frazzled nerves and the acid churning in her gut.

While more people poured in through the door, Celina effortlessly chatted up the customers while she rang up their purchases. Ivy was doubly glad for the retail experience her sister had gained running her now defunct crystal and herb shop.

At the end of the counter, Alma was lost in conversation with the man she'd earlier introduced as Reverend Thompson when a frail old man stepped up to the counter.

"You got anything in there without nuts?" he barked with an angry scowl. "Doc Knight says I can't have nuts no more 'cause of my diverticulitis. Personally, I think he's nuts, or else in cahoots with those stinkin' money-grubbing drug companies. Costs me an arm and a leg to get my damn pills every month."

Out of all the people Ivy had met so far, this grumpy old codger was hands-down the most colorful.

"I do, Mr...."

"Emmett Hill's the name. Bigfoot huntin's my game," he proudly proclaimed. "You see that big, hairy sum'bitch, you call me. I'll come straight away. Ya'hear missy?"

Ivy couldn't keep from grinning. "I will, Mr. Hill."

"Mr. Hill was my daddy. You can call me Emmett." He flashed what she suspected was a rare smile, then winked as his voice softened. "I like it when the pretty girls call me by my given name."

"All right, Emmett," she said, unable to stop grinning. "You just point to what looks good, and I'll tell you if it has nuts in it."

Without batting an eye, the old fart lifted a gnarly finger and pointed it at her.

A blush heated her cheeks. "Sorry, Emmett. I'm not on the menu."

"That's a darn shame, because you're a pretty, tempting little thing. If I were fifty years younger, I'd be all over you like a huntin' dog on a pheasant." A mischievous grin stretched across his weathered face. "All right…how about that fancy, foo-foo-looking thing with a strawberry on top."

"You picked a winner. There isn't a single nut in that miniature strawberry cheesecake."

"Good enough. I'll take it then, and a large cup of black coffee. And don't go putting any of that flavored crap in it. That stuff tastes like perfume."

"Got it. Cheesecake and large coffee…hold the perfume," she teased.

"Right as rain, missy." Emmett grinned.

Ivy hoped the cantankerous old man would become a regular. Like the town itself, Emmett was strangely unique and oddly calming.

"Quit flirting with that pretty girl, Emmett. You're holding up the line," a tall, handsome man several customers back called out. His arm was slung around the waist of a beautiful and very pregnant woman.

"You could have been in front of me if you hadn't lazed around in bed all morning, molesting your new bride, Colton," Emmett volleyed without even glancing over his shoulder.

"What can I say?" Colton answered with a shrug. "With a wife as pretty as mine, it's a miracle I *ever* get out of bed."

"By the looks of that big ol' bump on her belly, you've already been spending entirely too much time with her between the sheets."

Colton, along with everyone else in line, laughed loud and hard. His wife, whose cheeks were glowing in a bright red blush, simply shook her head.

"Can you blame me?" Colton countered.

"Not one damn bit, son. If I had a filly as pretty as Jade in my bed, I sure as heck wouldn't be standing here."

"No, you'd be trying to remember what the hell to do to her, you old fart," a man wearing grease stained overalls taunted.

"Stick a sock in it, Cletus. Your bed's as empty as mine," Emmett jabbed, again without even turning around. "Stop busting my nuggets and go fix a transmission, boy."

Bagging up Emmett's cheesecake, Ivy couldn't stop grinning as more verbal taunts sailed back and forth through the air. "You come back and see me, ya hear?"

"If this cheesecake thing is as sweet as you are beautiful, you can bet your bottom dollar I'll be back in the morning, missy." He sent her another wink before ambling to a vacant table near the front door.

As he nibbled on his cheesecake, Emmett continued bantering with the people of Haven and filling the shop with raucous laughter.

A smiling woman, with strawberry-blonde hair and pale green eyes stepped up to the counter. "Hi. I'm Gina Scott. I own the bar across the street. I need to warn you now, my boyfriend has a wicked sweet tooth, so you're probably going to get real sick of seeing me."

"No I won't, and that's a promise." Ivy chuckled. "What do you think your boyfriend might like?"

"Uh, two of everything you've got in that damn case." Gina grinned. "But let's start off with a couple of those big, gooey cinnamon rolls and I'll take that butter crumb coffee cake. I don't want him going into a sugar coma until I've had my wicked way with his fine ass."

"Well, they always say, the way to a man's heart is through his stomach."

"What I'm after is below his stomach, sweetheart," Gina quipped with a sassy smile, then lowered her voice. "He's...immensely *gifted*."

Gina's lack of filter instantly charmed Ivy. "Oh, my. Then you'll definitely want to keep him...happy."

"Amen, sister." Gina grinned. "Hey, when you close up shop, come over to the Hangover and I'll buy you a happy grand opening drink."

"Thank you! God knows I need one. I've been a nervous wreck about this grand opening."

The fact that she was openly sharing her insecurities with the feisty bar owner surprised Ivy. But there was a palpable, genuine congeniality humming off Gina that instantly put Ivy at ease.

*It would be nice to have a friend and confidante in Haven.*

"You really turned this old piece of coal into a shimmering diamond, girl," Gina complimented. "You're going to make a killing with this place."

"Thank you. I certainly hope so. And I'll come by for that drink as soon as I can."

"I look forward to it."

Gina clutched her package of sweets and sidled to the cash register as Alma leaned over the display case.

"Honey, you think you'll be okay here?" Concern was stamped over her landlord's face.

"Oh, yes, Alma. I'm fine. Is everything all right?"

"I'm not sure. One of the ladies from my Bible study group isn't feeling well. I want to run by and check on her. Bessie's a hardheaded old mule and refuses to go see Doc Knight."

"By all means, please, go check on your friend and don't give me a second thought. I appreciate you helping break the ice and introducing me to the people of Haven."

"The pleasure was all mine. If you need anything, just give me a call," Alma instructed before hurrying out the door.

After Celina finished ringing up Gina's order, she turned to leave but was quickly wrapped in the arms of an older woman wearing a bright yellow flowing sweater.

"Oh! Good morning, Mrs. G. I didn't see you in line, or I'd have given you cuts," the bar owner exclaimed.

Ivy quickly turned her attention on the young teenaged girl with big hazel eyes and a peaches-and-cream complexion stepping up to the counter.

"Hi. Wow, you sure are busy."

"Yes." Ivy nodded. "It warms my heart that you all came out today to help celebrate the grand opening."

"Are you kidding? Who doesn't like cake?" The young girl grinned. "I'm Megan Butler, by the way."

"It's a pleasure to meet you, Megan. What can I get for you this morning?"

"I'm still trying to decide. Everything looks so…yummy." Her eyes skimmed the goodies behind the glass. "My thighs are going to hate me, but I'll take two of those cheese Danishes."

Ivy eyed the thin wisp and shook her head. "I'd kill to have a body like yours."

A shadow of sadness fluttered over Megan's eyes. "I used to have more curves, but I've lost weight because…well, you'll hear all the juicy details, I'm sure. Gossip grows faster around here than crops in the fields."

"Good thing I don't put stock in gossip." Ivy sent the girl a reassuring smile.

By eleven forty-five, the crowd had dwindled to a steady trickle. The display cases had taken a major hit, while the cash register was overflowing. Ivy's legs felt like rubber and her cheeks burned from smiling so much, but she didn't care. Opening day had exceeded her wildest expectations and she was floating on cloud nine.

If tomorrow proved equally busy, she'd have to forgo the drink Gina had offered, along with sleep, and start baking her buns off again.

It was a little past four when the last customer left with a happy smile and an armload of baked goods.

Inwardly counting to ten, Ivy grinned and let out a triumphant yell.

Her dad rushed from the kitchen with a bottle of champagne and four glasses.

"Now that the work is done, well, everything but the cleanup, it's time to celebrate," he declared, easing the cork from the bottle with a loud pop.

She savored the happiness of her übër-successful first day as they clinked their glasses together after each joyous toast offered up by her mom, dad, and Celina and quickly drained the bottle of bubbly.

Ivy was feeling no pain as they all worked, cleaning and mopping. As she stood tallying the day's sales from the cash register, Celina—who was next to her and munching on a lemon bar—jolted as her cell phone chimed.

Pulling the device from her pocket, she looked at the screen before alarm bloomed over her face. Tears quickly filled her eyes.

Ivy didn't even have to ask. When she was home for Thanksgiving, Celina had confided that Harvey was hounding her for another chance. When she'd returned for Christmas, she'd discovered the prick was still pestering her sister.

*Dammit, Harvey, grow a modicum of pride and leave Celina the fuck alone.*

Setting the money aside, Ivy turned and frowned. "What guilt trip is he trying to send you on this time?"

Anxiety lined Celina's face. "He says life isn't worth living without me."

"You're kidding, right? He's actually threatening suicide?" Ivy scoffed angrily, wishing she could reach through the phone and knock the prick out all over again. "Tell him to call a damn hotline. You're not his therapist, baby."

"I know, but..." Celina sniffed.

"Girl..." Ivy warned, "do *not* buy into his bullshit manipulation. Even if he was serious—which he's not...the man's ego would never allow him to off himself—you are *not* responsible for him or his actions."

"I know, but what if he really does something? I couldn't live with myself."

"If you think he's serious, then call 911. Or better yet, call his parents. Tell his groping father that Harvey is suicidal and to admit him to a mental hospital. But don't you dare even *think* of taking that sack of shit back. You hear me?"

"I hear you. I just feel…"

"Exactly the way he intended to make you feel…guilty!" Ivy exhaled heavily. "Has he ever taken responsibility or hinted at an apologized for the way he treated you in Las Vegas?"

By simply saying the name of the town, Ivy had inadvertently summoned Noble up from the depths from her memory bank. She mentally tried to shove him back down, but it was too late. The damage was done. Like a damn movie premiere, images of the man and all the sinfully wicked sensations he'd immersed her in swirled to life. Goose bumps peppered her flesh. Her nipples drew up tight and hard—throbbing in time with the ache between her legs—as the imagined feel of his hands and mouth blindsided her.

"No," Celina replied, sounding as if she were millions of miles away.

Suddenly, the front door opened with a bang, jerking Ivy from her salacious daydream. She zipped her head toward the noise to see a striking blonde, with colossal boobs, teetering on impossibly tall platform shoes, enter. She'd poured herself into a formfitting, eye-searing, lime-green knit dress that barely covered her cooch.

"Hey, y'all. Welcome to the neighborhood," she called out in a singsong voice, so high-pitched Ivy thought the display glass might crack. "Sorry I didn't get the chance to drop by earlier, but my Calvin was keeping me busy…real busy this morning. I do declare, when he was finally finished, I could barely walk to the shower to get myself together."

*Wow! TMI much, honey?*

"Well…I suppose that's, um…understandable," Ivy stammered.

"Y'all don't know it, but this little bakery, which is just cute as a bug's ear by the way, is going to provide infinite job security for my Calvin."

"Oh?" Celina asked. "How's that?"

"Well, he's the town dentist, don't cha know? I do believe there's enough sugar in this place to rot out half the teeth in Haven. Well, those that haven't already perished from these hayseeds' mouths, that is." She wrinkled her nose in distaste.

"I'm sorry...I'm Ivy. And you are?"

"Oh, bless my heart. Where did my manners go?"

*As if you had any to begin with?* Ivy thought with the plastic smile still poised on her lips.

"I'm Trudy Clarkson...*Mrs.* Calvin Clarkson."

*Holy shit. Some man was actually desperate enough to marry this...thing?*

"There's hope for me yet," Celina murmured under her breath.

Ivy swallowed down the laughter bubbling up inside her and slapped a professional veneer in place. "Well, it's a pleasure to meet you, Mrs. Clarkson. But I'm sorry to say, we're closed for the day. All I have left is some lemon bars back in the kitchen. I'll be glad to—"

"Oh, lord no!" Trudy wrinkled her nose. "I can't eat anything from here. Why, all those sugar- and fat-packed things you sell will make me blimp out like a sow ready to give birth. I'd never do that to this body! And sweet baby Jesus, I can't even think about what havoc those chemicals would wreak on my flawless complexion. No, honey, I just came by to say hey."

"Hey," Janice forced from beneath a brittle smile.

The door of the kitchen swung open and Jeff stepped into the room. "Anymore dirty trays for me to wash?"

The sound of his masculine voice had Trudy snapping her head his direction so fast it was a wonder she didn't give herself whiplash.

"Well. Hello to *you*, handsome," the vixen purred as a calculated, catty smile stretched over her glossy red collagen-injected lips. "Good heavens. Don't tell me this hunk of man-beef is your *dishwasher.*"

"No," Ivy replied flatly. "He's my father."

"What? No way this young stud could possibly be your *father*, sugar. Why, he's not a day over thirty-five."

With an exaggerated roll of her hips, Trudy strutted toward Ivy's shell-shocked-looking dad.

Janice hurried in beside the man and wrapped a possessive arm around his waist.

"Believe it or not, *sugar*..." her mom began in a saccharine-sweet southern belle drawl, "he'll soon be fifty. I should know. We've been *happily* married for twenty-seven years."

Though her mom hid it quite well, Ivy could clearly see the she-tiger rippling beneath the surface. Janice had her fangs exposed, claws extended, and was pacing internally, ready for the slightest provocation to tear the surgically enhanced, husband-stealing slut to shreds.

Ivy discreetly covered a hand over her mouth to keep from howling, while Celina, slack-jawed and wide-eyed, stood mutely watching their mom take on the viper.

"Mercy. Surely you two haven't been faithful to each other all those years, have you?" Trudy asked, eyeing the couple suspiciously.

"Every. Single. Day," Jeff assured, leveling the offensive woman with a glare of warning.

"Why, that's just utterly boring."

As if suddenly aware she'd vocalized her adulterous thoughts, Trudy manufactured an overly bright smile. "Well, bless your hearts. That's...just wonderful. Now, I'd really love to stay and chat, but I'm sure Calvin's last patient has left. It's time for me to drop by his office and inspect his big ol'...um...drill. Toot-a-loo, y'all."

And just as she'd swooped in, Trudy Clarkson, the sexually desperate queen of plastic surgery, sashayed out the door.

"Would someone please tell me *what* the hell that was?" Contempt dripped from each syllable of Celina's words.

"That, my darling daughters, is a lonely, desperate harlot,"

Janice tsked.

"No, sweetheart," Jeff corrected. "That's every man's worst nightmare."

"Married man, you mean?" Ivy asked with a crooked smile.

"Married, single, and bisexual ones, to be sure," he corrected.

"What on earth is she doing in a town like this?" Celina mused. "I mean, aside from the one married dude, Colton, whose wife has a baby on the way, there wasn't a hot guy to be seen."

"The only reason his wife was with him today was to probably keep Trudy from sinking her claws into him," her dad said with a chuckle.

"Well, I'm certainly not letting *you* out of my sight while we're here," Janice vowed.

"You going to be my bodyguard?"

"Darn straight I am."

Ivy watched as her mom lifted to her toes and planted a long, loving kiss on her dad's lips.

Envy sliced deep.

Growing up, Ivy had held the same fantasy most every girl dreamed of—to fall in love with a prince and live happily ever after. Unfortunately, as she'd grown older, it had only taken Ivy a few disappointing dips in the dating pool before discovering that her mother had scooped up the last honest and emotionally available man on the damn planet. Ivy had resigned herself to the fact that she'd never find the kind of unconditional love, respect, or compassion that her parents shared. There'd never be some mystery man to grow old with. She'd have to welcome wrinkles, false teeth, saggy boobs, and Social Security all by herself.

*Nope, I will not flop my happy ass down on the pity pot. If Mr. Right waltzed through the door, I'd have to send him away. I don't have time for a relationship, or the luxury of cultivating one. I have to dedicate every spare moment to making this bakery an actual attainable dream.*

# CHAPTER TEN

AFTER LOADING HAY in the barn all day, Noble stood in the shower, washing the sweat and filth off his body and rolling the ache from his shoulders under the hot spray. He dried off and dressed, ignoring the pangs of hunger gnawing his gut. He strolled into the kitchen, where mouthwatering scents assaulted him as he watched his mom pull a pan of golden-yellow cornbread from the oven. She turned and placed the pan on the opposite counter to cool and Noble crept to the stove like a cat burglar. He lifted the spoon and dipped it inside the stockpot of bubbling chili. As he was lifting the steaming, spicy mixture to his mouth, his mom smacked his arm, sending the spoon back into the pot.

"It isn't time to eat yet."

"But I'm starving." He pressed a hand to his growling stomach, flashed her the most pathetic expression he could muster, and quickly retrieved the spoon and shoved it in his mouth.

"That's what you get for skipping lunch," she chided, jerking the empty spoon from his hand. "I fixed a perfectly good platter of roast beef sandwiches at noon. But *someone* was too busy to stop working and fuel his body. So, now that same someone—*you*—will just have to wait until dinner's on the table."

Yeah, he'd skipped lunch, all right, but not to keep working. The whole time he'd been stacking the heavy bales of hay, the flirty conversation about doing this job in a thong that he and Ivy had shared hammered him. Like a fucking twister, images of the lacy, saturated scrap of silk he'd torn from between her legs had swirled through his brain. He hadn't come in for lunch because his dick had been hard enough to drive railroad spikes through cement.

"I was just trying to pick up the slack. Nate's doing what he can, but until he finishes physical therapy and builds back some muscle mass, the heavy lifting has to fall on the rest of us."

"And it frustrates him something fierce. That's why he's so cranky." Nola scowled. "But you already know that. I just wish you could find a way to block that connection you boys share, because Nate's surly mood is rubbing off on you, too."

Noble nodded. He knew his disposition was shitty of late, but it wasn't a byproduct of his twin's annoyance. He was turning as snarly as a bear with a sore tooth because he hadn't bounced back yet. Noble still hadn't sought comfort with his warren of bed-bunnies since returning from Vegas…three blue-ball-inducing months ago. Oh, he'd thought about sex, thought about it all the damn time. But the only woman he ached to drag beneath him was long gone.

Subconsciously licking his lips, Noble could still taste Ivy's tart cream.

*Dammit! I'm in a no-boner zone.*

Noble quickly redirected his thoughts and willed his thickening cock to take a nap. Still, he knew his efforts were only temporary. He'd jacked off in the shower ten minutes ago, but it hadn't done a damn bit of good. He still burned for Ivy, and it was scaring the fuck out of him.

Noble scrubbed a hand through his still-damp hair and exhaled. "I'll try and sweeten up for you, Ma."

His mom glided across the room and crooked her finger with a conspiratory smile. "I have something that might sweeten you up. Take a peek."

Sidling in beside her, Noble peered down at the pink cake box. "Sweet Flours?"

"The new bakery's grand opening was today. Wait until you see what I brought home for our dessert." She eased back the lid and carefully lifted out an elaborately decorated cake. "It's a chocolate mousse. I saw it in the display case and started salivating."

The second the scent of creamy butter and rich cocoa hit his nose Noble's mouth began to water. Unexpectedly, he wanted to grab a fork and dive into the fancy cake.

"I'll take a slice of that now and eat my chili after."

"I might just have to join you." Nola chuckled. "It's crazy. Like you, I've never been that gung ho for sweets, but I'm craving them all the time now."

"Did you crave them when you were pregnant with any of us?"

Nola shook her head. "No. I only wanted spicy food. Though with you and Nate, I craved ice cream every once in a while." She strummed a hand over the bump camouflaged beneath her shirt. "Guess this little guy is already taking after his big brother."

"Sounds like you're going to be a regular customer of Sweet Flours from now on."

"No way. I'd be as big a house by the time this little guy is born."

"Something smells good in here, Momma." Norman entered the kitchen and strode straight to his wife. He wrapped his arms around her and peered over her shoulder. "What do you have there? Oh, my. That looks delicious."

"I know, right? The new bakery opened," his mom explained. "I couldn't help indulging in a bit of guilty pleasure."

Noble was all about guilty pleasures, but his didn't involve cake. The familiar talons of useless yearning clawed up his spine. As he ambled toward the kitchen table, Nash and Norris raced into the room and plopped down into their chairs.

Noble polished off two heaping bowls of his mom's spicy, thick chili and three slabs of corn bread slathered in butter. When the first bite of the moist, fluffy chocolate cake hit his taste buds, his eyes nearly rolled back in his head. He hadn't tasted anything this sinfully sweet and addicting since he'd latched his mouth to Ivy's pussy.

*You're one masochistic son of a bitch, aren't you?*

Noble bit back a snarl and devoured the moist, rich cake in silence.

Thirty minutes later, he was driving down Main Street toward the Hangover.

The pink awning of Sweet Flours caught his eye, as well as the older gentleman cleaning the glass door front.

*Must be the owner…or one of them.*

Noble tapped his brakes and pushed the button to lower his window so he could welcome the man to Haven and compliment the awesome cake he'd had at dinner. But just as he slowed to a stop, the man tucked a roll of paper towels under his arm and stepped back inside the building.

With a shrug, Noble pulled into an empty parking spot in front of the bar. He strolled inside and handed Gina the bag with chili and corn bread that his mom had asked him to bring the couple. After his mom's massive attitude adjustment and finally cutting Nate from her apron strings, she and Gina had formed a bond of friendship.

Nola didn't even seem to mind that two remained shacked up long after Nate's broken limbs had healed. Of course, their unmarried cohabitation provided plenty of fodder for the gossipmongers in town. The Grayson family ignored the rumors spawned by narrow-minded people with hollow lives.

"Nola didn't have to go to all this trouble." Gina opened the container of chili and inhaled deeply. "Oh, hell! This smells delicious."

"It was, and she's a mom. Taking care of family is what she does."

After setting a mug of beer down on the bar in front of him, Gina quickly glanced over her shoulder. "Nate's probably still in the shower cleaning up from work. I'm going to run back to the kitchen and keep this warm so we can eat when he comes down. I'll be right back."

"Take your time. I'm gonna sit here, drink my beer, and

relax," he announced as she scurried away.

The bell above the door—the one Nate had finally fixed after Gina's abduction—jingled. Glancing toward the sound, Noble felt his blood run cold. Inwardly cursing, he watched Trudy and her sexually inept husband, Calvin, enter the bar. The deceitful tramp was wearing a skimpy red dress. One wrong move and the wardrobe malfunction she'd suffer would be worthy of an arrest for indecent exposure.

Noble didn't remember ever seeing them in the bar before and briefly wondered if Trudy was on reconnaissance, looking for another unsuspecting dick to fuck with.

"Oh, Cal, you naughty boy. Stop."

Her shrill shriek felt like icepicks being shoved in his ears.

Cal, a.k.a. naughty boy, removed his hands from her ass.

"We're in public, lover boy. You keep touching me like that, I might have to find a dark corner so you can put me out of my misery, my big, strapping love machine."

Noble inwardly snorted and took another drink of beer.

"Why, isn't this just the cutest little rustic bar you've ever seen, lover boy?" Calvin issued a noncommittal grunt. "Let's sit at that table over there. I think it might actually have been wiped down in the last decade."

If Gina had been within earshot of the viper's derogatory comment, Trudy would have had an up-close-and-personal introduction to Martha.

"Oh, my stars," Trudy exclaimed. "Mr. Grayson…is that really you?"

Noble briefly closed his eyes and bit back a low, suffering groan. Forcing a tight smile, he turned and gave Trudy a curt nod. "Mrs. Clarkson."

Trudy hurried his way, dragging the *love machine* with her as she flashed Noble a seductive smile. She quickly erased it as her *husband* moved in beside her. "Cal, sugar, this is Mr. Grayson. He's the man I told you about who laid the pipe and fixed that terrible leak of mine."

Oh, she'd been leaking all right...puddling all over the place. Unfortunately, laying his pipe in her was the biggest mistake of Noble's life. Well, the second biggest. His first was leaving Vegas without Ivy's phone number.

When Calvin flashed him a grateful smile and extended his hand, guilt, slick and oily, sluiced through Noble's veins.

"Pleasure to finally meet you, Mr. Grayson. Trudy speaks very highly of the work you did. I can't thank you enough for helping get that mess fixed."

Noble wanted to tell the man that he hadn't fixed a damn thing, and that his wife was still a horny hot mess who took adultery to a whole new level. The polite response should have been *you're welcome* but he couldn't even force those proper words over his lips. The things he'd done to the man's *then* fiancée were morally wrong on every level. Like an evil, living-breathing demon within, remorse came to life. It took all the willpower Noble possessed not to confess his sin and tell the poor schmuck his wife was a first-class slut. If Trudy were a man, he would have already knocked the deceitful bitch on her surgically augmented ass.

Then an idea hit him, one that would completely annihilate Trudy without him lifting a finger. He sent the couple a feigned friendly smile.

"No need to thank me," he assured before pinning Trudy with a blank expression. "To be perfectly honest, laying that pipe was anything but memorable. I'd completely forgotten all about it."

Her eyes grew wide, then quickly narrowed to fiery slits.

The plastic smile adorning her face morphed into a bitter, arctic sneer.

Nostrils flaring, Trudy pinched her collagen-injected face up, like a sun-dried prune.

Noble was having too much fun to stop. "I'm no plumber, mind you, but don't be surprised if that seal eventually stretches so wide anything you shove up in it just falls right out."

"Oh. Right. Right." Calvin nodded, confusion written all over his face. "I'll be sure to keep an eye on it."

"Someone definitely needs to, that's for damn sure."

Trudy's face was a brilliant shade of hellion red. Seething, she squeezed the straps of her designer purse, no doubt wishing her hands were wrapped about Noble's neck. He simply smirked and arched a brow, daring her to say something…anything, so he could bust her lying, cheating ass in front of her husband and save the blissful idiot years of embarrassing gossip.

Then in the blink of an eye, Trudy's rage vanished and a cloying sweet smile spread over her artificially puffy lips.

"Yanno, Cal, baby. I don't really feel much like a cocktail after all. Take me home, toss me into that big o'l bed of ours, and take me hard, daddy."

Noble's stomach pitched.

A lewd grin split Calvin's face. "Let's go, sugar lips."

The poor fucker nearly tripped over his own two feet as he rushed his bitch of a bride out of the bar.

As the door snicked shut, Noble closed his eyes and exhaled a deep breath.

"*Who* or rather *what* the fuck was that?" Gina asked, stationed behind the bar again.

"That's our new dentist, Calvin Clarkson, and his wife, *Trudy*."

"Alrighty then. Does old wifey-pooh know Halloween was almost four damn months ago? Seriously? What the fuck was she wearing?"

"Desperation. And I seriously doubt her peroxide-infused brain cells comprehend anything besides fucking."

Gina narrowed her eyes and studied him before a disapproving frown tugged the corners of her mouth down. Leaning over the bar, she kept her terse tone low and poked her finger to his sore shoulder. "Noble Grayson! I can't believe you fucked the new dentist's—?"

He held up his hand. "Don't! I just ate a fantastic dinner.

Don't say another word or I'm liable to puke it up all over your bar."

"How could you?" Gina hissed. "She's *married.*"

"Not at the time, she wasn't. I didn't even know about Calvin until after the fact. Then I was so pissed I wanted to liposuction all the saline from her body with my fists."

"Ouch!" Gina cringed then smirked. "I know what I'm getting you for your birthday."

"What's that?"

"A fucking blow-up doll. Maybe it'll take the edge off and you won't be so knotted up that you decide to shove your cock into something like that."

"Ha. Ha." Noble rolled his eyes as Gina's sweet laughter flowed over him.

The sound warmed him and confirmed that the problems she'd suffered after her abduction were in the past. Ever since Nate's accident, her mood had done a one-eighty. One night when he was visiting Nate at the hospital, Noble had learned what had precipitated the change in her demeanor.

*"When she found me busted and bleeding in the field, she told me something inside her shifted,"* Nate explained. *"She'd been suffocating under a shit-load of guilt that suddenly took a backseat to what had happened to me."*

"Guilt? What the hell did she have to feel guilty about?"

*"For not fighting Victor off."*

"That's crazy. He's three times her size."

*"I know, but she felt responsible that he'd been able to overpower her so easily. She confessed that she wasn't good enough for me, or couldn't love me the way I deserved, and that she didn't want me wasting my life on a woman who couldn't even give me children—"*

"Wait," Noble interrupted "Why can't she have kids?"

Nate exhaled heavily and closed his eyes for several long seconds. *"She was married once…and pregnant. Her ex was a mean son of a bitch. They fought and he got physical again. She not only lost the baby but had to have a hysterectomy to save her life."*

*Noble's heart sand all the way to his stomach.* "He beat her?"

*Nate nodded.*

"Motherfucker. Do you know who he is…where he lives?"

*Nate nodded grimly.* "When I get out of here and healed—"

"I'm going with you. They'll never find the body, either." *He blew out a big breath and nodded.* "Tell me the rest."

"When Victor had her, Gina said she knew she was going to die before she could tell me how much she loved me. Thankfully, that didn't happen, but she'd still convinced herself that even though she really did love me, we wouldn't be together forever."

"Because of the baby thing?"

"That and our age difference. Her occupation…her unladylike mouth," *Nate said with a crooked grin.*

"But you like her unladylike mouth, don't you, you little perv?"

"No. I love it."

*They shared a good laugh before Nate continued.*

"When they were loading me into the helicopter, she stood in the field and watched it fly away, thinking she'd never see me alive again. It ripped her apart."

"No doubt, but how did that solve the shit with Victor for her?"

"Because when that prick kidnapped her, he mentally tossed her down into the same dark, helpless, and hopeless hellhole that her ex had kept her in. After we rescued her and she was back home, she said she tried to shake off and pull herself out but old tapes kept playing in her head. That and the fact that she knew she'd have to say goodbye to me one day kept dragging her back down. So she did the only thing she knew would protect her. She shut down…wrapped herself up tight in a victim blanket. Instead of talking to me about her fears, she pushed me away…again. That's what started our fight the day I got hurt. Standing in that field not knowing if I was going to live or die was like a slap to the face with a mortality stick. It was her wake-up call. She told me that when the helicopter disappeared from view, she realized that life is short and precious, but love is fragile and the rarest gift in life."

*Noble pondered his brother's words for several long seconds before breaking out into a cold sweat.*

*"When she was finished telling me all the secrets she'd been keeping, I tugged her into this hospital bed, tucked my good arm around her, and told her I was never letting her go."*

As Noble sat on the barstool, drinking in the sound of Gina's laughter, watching her blue eyes twinkling with glee, he was damn grateful that she'd had that life-altering epiphany.

"What's all the racket about down here?" Nate asked, taking the stairs one at a time, like a toddler, munching on a piece of cake.

"Goddammit, Nate!" Gina barked. "That coffee cake was for our breakfast in the morning. Please tell me you didn't eat the whole damn thing."

Grinning, he shrugged. "Okay, I didn't eat the whole damn thing. I'm not a total bastard. I left you a piece."

"A piece? That's all? One lousy piece?"

Noble chuckled at her irritation. "You hit the new bakery, too?"

"Fuck yes, I did." Gina narrowed her eyes on Nate. "But I may not ever hit it again if Mr. Sweet Tooth over there is going to hog all the goodies."

"Hey! I let you have one of the cinnamon rolls this morning."

"Let me! *Let me*?" Slapping on her bitch wings, Gina rounded the bar and stomped straight into Nate's personal space.

"Knock it off, you two," Noble warned. "You know what happens every time you get into a damn fight."

"Oh, this isn't a fight," Gina assured, snatching the piece of coffee cake out of Nate's hand. "This is a discussion that I'm ending right now."

Locking her eyes to Nate's, she shoved the wedge of cake into her mouth. A muffled but satisfied moan rumbled from the back of her throat. "This is…almost better than sex. I'm going to have to buy more tomorrow."

"Now you know why I couldn't stop eating it." Grinning, Nate crossed his arms over his chest. "I rest my case."

"In six months, everyone in Haven is going to need Weight Watchers," Noble scoffed.

"You don't understand," Gina said, pausing to swallow. "One taste of this—"

"Oh, I already know. Mom bought a cake from there this morning. I'm staying far away from that place or I'll end up looking like Harvey Hays, bless his waddling, self-centered, prick-assed heart."

"We tried to tell you he was a—"

"Fuck it. It doesn't matter anymore," Noble interrupted, struggling to thwart memories of Ivy from surfacing. "You wanna play some pool?"

"Sure, but not for money. You're a fucking shark." Nate grinned.

"Pussy."

"He's not a pussy. He's a stud," Gina corrected, wrapping her arms around Nate's waist and aligning their hips.

"Don't worry. I'll save my money so we can eat coffee cake every day. But just remember, you're all the sweetness I need in life." Nate flashed her a sensual smile before claiming Gina's lips in a long, passionate kiss.

Noble looked away before gripping his beer and standing. "I'll meet you in the back when you're done swapping spit."

He hadn't intended his voice to carry an angry growl. He clenched his jaw and asked himself for the umpteenth time how a girl he'd spent *one* fucking night with had sucked the desire for any other woman clean out of him. And oh, god, how that woman could suck! Memories of her soft lips, the blistering, wet heat of her mouth, and the sinful swirl of her tongue as she glided up and down his pulsating cock seared his brain. The feel of her buttery-smooth skin beneath his fingertips…the sound of her kitten-soft moans and keening cries of ecstasy, along with her infectious laughter uncoiled inside him.

Being haunted to this degree by a woman he couldn't call, text, or even find was driving him batshit crazy.

*It's official. I'm losing my goddamn mind.*

With beer in hand, he strode to the back of the bar. After snatching a pool stick off the rack, Noble started taking out his unrelenting frustration and sexual anger on the cluster of colorful resin balls.

# CHAPTER ELEVEN

After slapping her alarm into silent submission, Ivy groaned and snuggled deeper under the covers. "Five more minutes," she whined.

Keeping up the constant pace of long days and short nights was catching up with her. She sat up and scrubbed the gritty sand from her eyes. Averaging four hours of sleep a night, she was finding it harder and harder to dredge up the will to crawl out of bed each morning.

It had been nearly two weeks since her grand opening, and customers were still clamoring for her baked goods. Sales were soaring, putting to rest her initial fear of failure. If only she could put her obsession with Noble to rest, all would be grand in Ivy's world.

So far that hadn't happened. The ghosts of incredible sex past came to haunt her every time there was a lull in customers. Even when she plucked out her credit card to order more supplies, there was Noble, spilling heat down her back and whispering sexual innuendos in her ear as he helped unlock her hotel room door.

The sinful specter was even invading her dreams every damn night, seducing her over and over until she woke in the throes of core-clutching orgasms.

She couldn't escape him.

Thinking about him now filled her with frustration and turned her body into a throbbing, weeping mass of need.

Ignoring her lonely, dripping pussy, she groaned and tossed the covers back.

The minute her feet hit the floor, her stomach began bubbling up the back of her throat...again! Racing to the bathroom, Ivy dropped to her knees and dry-heaved for several long minutes.

"This is crazy," she mumbled.

Her angst about opening the bakery had long passed, yet her morning purge-fest was getting worse. As she stood on shaky legs and rinsed her mouth, Ivy looked down at her stomach. She was visibly bloated.

Like a flashfire, her imagination started running wild. Something was seriously wrong. Could it be an ulcer? What if she had stomach cancer? A blast of fear zipped through her and Ivy quickly shoved it away. Maybe some weird microorganism she'd picked up somewhere was wreaking havoc with her digestive system. She didn't know what was going on, but she knew it was time to see a doctor. Hopefully, she'd only need a round of antibiotics. Taking an entire Monday—the only day the bakery was closed—to drive to her doctor in Dallas was a waste of time. Since she'd planted her roots here in Haven, Ivy decided she'd make an appointment with the local doctor, after she talked to Gina.

Over the past few weeks, the spunky bar owner had grown to be a good friend, one Ivy trusted would tell her if the local physician was competent or not.

After filling the display cases, Ivy unlocked the front door and spied Gina across the street sweeping the sidewalk in front of the bar.

"Hey," Ivy called, leaning out the door. Gina jerked her head up and smiled. "When you get done, can you come over? I'll buy you a cup of java and a chunk of that coffee cake you love so much."

"Will do, but I still owe you a drink."

"I know. I'll come over when I'm not so busy."

Gina scoffed. "Honey, you're a business owner. You're always going to be busy. You gotta make time. All work and no play makes Jane...pent up and bitchy as hell!"

*Don't I know it.*

"I will." Ivy grinned.

"Damn right you will, or I'll drag your skinny ass over here and get you shit-faced myself," Gina threatened, grinning. "Be there in a few."

Ivy waved and was about to close the door when she noticed Emmett Hill plodding past the post office. "Are you coming to see me this morning?"

"You betcha, beautiful. I'm not sure what drug you're putting in my coffee, but I'm mighty addicted."

She laughed. "It's only beans and water. I swear."

The old man grinned before glancing over at her busily sweeping friend. "Heard you jawin' with Gina. She's good people."

"Yes, she is." Ivy nodded, holding the door open for the man.

"Whatcha got good in that case, besides everything?" Grinning, she stepped in beside the man and studied the goodies with him. "Those strawberry cheesecake deelie-bobs you always give me are good, but I'm gonna live dangerous today and try something different."

"How about a cinnamon roll? I can warm it up for you and slather it in butter."

Emmett's rheumy blue eyes widened. "Any chance you'd consider hooking up with an older man?"

Ivy schooled her grin and cocked her head, pretending to ponder his question. "How old are we talking?"

"Ninety-seven next August, if I'm still on the upside of the grass, that is. I might not be a spring chicken, but you wouldn't want for anything. I got a slew of savings accounts, I get a damn good pension, and I have more life insurance than you could spend in three lifetimes." He winked.

"Hrmm. You're giving me a tempting offer, Emmett, but I'm not the kind who likes to hook up. I'm independent, hardheaded, and way too busy to add a man into my life."

He nodded and winked. "Can't blame a guy for holding on

to a pocket full of dreams, can you?"

"Never. Let's let you start living dangerous. I'll fix you that cinnamon roll and a large cup of coffee and hold the perfume."

"You know me too well, pretty missy."

Emmett sat at the table near the window, devouring his breakfast as he watched the customers come and go. A short time later, Gina entered, wearing an expectant smile, and arched a brow at the butter crumb coffee cake in the display case.

"Grab a seat. I'll bring it out to you in a sec."

After carrying over two coffees and a massive wedge of Gina's favorite indulgence, Ivy plopped down in the chair beside her.

"You always get up at the ass crack of dawn to start baking all this stuff?"

"No. I usually stay up past one, *then* I get up at the ass crack of dawn and fill the display cases."

"Jesus. That's some long hours. Makes dealing with drunks almost a vacation. You need to hire some help. You're going to get sick if you keep this pace up."

"Funny you should say that. I've got some kind of stomach thing going on."

"You mean like the flu?"

"No. It's not the flu. I thought it was stress…you know, wigging out about opening up the shop. But it hasn't gone away. In fact, it's getting worse. I'm throwing up almost every morning."

Gina shot her a blank stare. "Any chance you're pregnant?"

"No. I'd actually have to *have sex* in order to get pregnant. Besides, I have an IUD."

Gina frowned. "Sexual dry spells suck donkey balls. I feel for you…been there done that, used to collect the damn T-shirts. I can't fix your gut, but my boyfriend's got a slew of sexy brothers I can fix you up with."

Ivy shook her head. The thought of having sex with any one besides Noble was last place on her bucket list. "Nah, I'm good. But I did want to ask you about the town doctor. What's he like?"

"Doc Knight? Oh, he's one of the kindest souls on the planet. He's always been so gentle with me when...err, when I've gone to see him," Gina stammered, quickly averting her stare as if hiding something.

Ivy wasn't going to press her about it and upset their new friendship. When and if Gina wanted to share, Ivy would be glad to listen.

"Give Doc Knight a call and make an appointment," Gina continued. "He'll figure out what's going on."

Her praise of the doctor sent relief settling over Ivy. "I'll do that. Thank you."

Gina took a bite of her coffee cake and moaned. "This is so good it's sinful. Get your ass over to my place tonight so I can fix you something that will make you dance and lose your pants. We'll find a stud to give your IUD a hell of a workout, sister."

Ivy chuckled. "Don't hold your breath about finding me a stud, but I will come over tonight. Just don't let me get too toasted. I still have to work tonight."

"I'll take good care of you. That's what friends are for...well, that and to help you bury the bodies."

"Thank you."

"There's only one body I want help burying, but that's a discussion for another time," Gina announced before draining her coffee cup. "I need to get back to the bar. Thanks for the goodies. I'll see you tonight."

When four o'clock finally arrived, Ivy locked the door. All she wanted to do was climb upstairs, wash the flour, sugar, and sweat from her body, then crawl into bed. She'd never felt so completely tapped out before, not even after the marathon sex-fest she'd had with Noble. She'd been deliciously sore and spectacularly sated, but nowhere close to the kind of exhaustion screaming through her now.

Maybe Gina had been right. Maybe she did need to hire an assistant.

It was clear that burning the candle at both ends had caught up with her.

Maybe she wasn't seriously sick at all but suffering from exhaustion.

She'd find out Monday morning when she went to her appointment with Doc Knight.

After cleaning the shop, Ivy trudged upstairs and peeled off her clothes before taking a long, hot shower. With her batteries semi-recharged, she took the time to dry and curl her hair before applying a bit of makeup. She dressed in a pair of soft, faded jeans and pulled on a cuddly cashmere sweater that hugged her boobs, just in case a handsome cowboy or two happened to drop into the bar. After grabbing her purse, Ivy headed across the street.

When she entered the bar, she smiled at the rustic ambiance, the dim lights, and the scent of wood and whiskey. But Ivy was taken aback at the lack of customers. How did Gina make a profit from this place?

*It's a Thursday night, barely past six. Later on it'll probably be filled to the rafters with rowdy cowboys, loud music, and raucous laughter.*

"Oh, my god! Somebody *please* call Ripley's. She's here! She actually turned off her fucking ovens and strolled her bony ass across the street. It's a miracle," Gina called out dramatically from behind the bar.

As the three older men seated at a table in the rear of the room peered up at her, Gina burst out laughing, causing Ivy's cheeks to grow hot. She jerked her chin up and sent her a playful grin. "Ha, ha. I told you I was coming over."

"Yeah, well, you've fed me that line for weeks now. Come on up and grab a seat. I'll get you fixed up proper."

Ivy sat down and watched her friend pour several different kinds of liquor together before rimming a crystal flute in sugar and pouring the concoction into the glass.

Gina added a plump cherry and orange slice, then set the light amber-colored drink on the bar. "Voila!" She grinned.

"What exactly is this?"

"I call it the guaranteed hangover."

Immediately, Ivy's mind flipped to the brain-blasting headache she'd woken with the morning after Noble had left her sated and sore. Blocking the memories, she swallowed tightly. "You do remember I have to bake my buns off tonight, right?"

"Aw, you'll be fine," Gina assured, waving her hand absently.

"Easy for you to say. I don't drink very often. This will probably knock me on my ass." Ivy brought the rim to her lips and took a tentative sip. Her taste buds exploded as the sweet and slightly tart liquid slid over her tongue. "Oh, wow! That's...too good."

"I was hoping you'd like it. Go on. Drink up. I'll make you as many as you can handle."

Ivy chuckled. "If I drink more than one, your crumb cake's liable to taste like dirt in the morning."

When she lifted the glass for another drink, movement on the stairs to the left of the bar caught Ivy's attention. She skimmed her gaze up a pair of muscular thighs encased in well-worn denim. Coasting her gaze higher, she swallowed down the liquid in her mouth with an audible gulp. The sight of defined, masculine abs and broad, rugged shoulders outlined beneath a black T-shirt jolted her system. But when she settled on the man's face, shock and disbelief ripped through her like an atomic bomb.

*Noble?*

Her heart sputtered.

Her stomach pitched.

The room began to sway.

Gaping at the man who'd left her in a perpetual state of frustration for months, she wanted to weep. Noble looked as virile and knee-knocking arousing as he had in Vegas.

*What the hell is Noble doing here?* Confusion charged her brain, while fragments of elation and anxiety splintered her soul.

The floodgates holding back her memories ripped open.

Tingles and tremors assaulted her body as every kiss, every touch, every thrust skipped beneath her flesh.

Butterflies dipped and swooped in her stomach.

Each breath she struggled to suck into her lungs felt like sand.

Her body ignited in hunger and longing.

And all the while, the same question circled her brain...

*What the hell is Noble doing here?*

Of all the places on the planet, how had she found him here...in Gina's bar? In Haven?

Ivy didn't have a clue, but she intended to find out.

Nibbling her bottom lip, she felt anticipation spike as she willed him to look her way. Each second ticking by felt like an eternity as she waited for those glorious green eyes to land on her...waited for the first flickers of recognition to morph into shock and disbelief before pure unadulterated happiness lit up his sexy face. She could already see him flash her that toe-curling smile before he plucked her off the barstool and wrapped her in his rugged arms again.

But Noble didn't even realize she was there. His attention was fixed, no, it was riveted on Gina as he swaggered off the last step and strode behind the bar.

Ivy's heartbeat tripled when the seductive grin she knew all too well kicked up one corner of his mouth. But he wasn't granting her a peek at that sexy smile, he lavished it on Gina as he clutched her in a lover's embrace.

Like a bloody, torturous massacre, denial screamed through Ivy as she mutely watched the man who'd drowned her in mindless orgasms press his magically talented mouth to Gina's.

The torrid, passionate kiss they shared sent the walls to close in all around Ivy.

Suffocating beneath a swell of panic, Ivy felt the ground beneath her crumbling away. Her heart sank to the pit of her churning stomach as a barrage of envy, rejection, and bitterness warred with heartbreak, pain, and overwhelming embarrassment.

*I'm such a fucking fool.*

Trembling like a leaf, she mentally begged herself to wake up from this brutal, flesh-peeling nightmare, but Ivy knew in her heart that she wasn't sleeping.

The man who held the staring role in her masturbation fantasies was kissing her new best friend with the same passion and possession he'd branded to Ivy's soul over four long months ago.

In that moment, Ivy realized that Noble was as unattainable now as he'd been when she'd left Las Vegas.

Tears stung the backs of her eyes.

Acid boiled in her belly.

The sweet, citrus remnants of the drink staining her tongue turned toxic.

"Did you enjoy your shower, baby?" Gina asked after Noble finally ended the kiss.

"It was okay. It would have been a hell of a lot more fun if you'd been with me."

Noble's familiar whiskey-smooth voice flowed over Ivy's flesh. But instead of coating her in a balm of reassurance and security, sharp blades sliced deep ribbons to bleed into her soul.

As the bittersweet longing that had fluttered up inside her shattered into a million pieces, an anvil of guilt flattened her to the ground.

*I fucked my best friend's boyfriend.*

Ivy didn't have a clue how long Gina and Noble had been together, but woman's intuition told her their relationship wasn't new. But on the other hand, Haven was a small town. There was no way Noble could have been living across the street from her for very long. Ivy surely would have run into him someplace…the grocery store, the café, the post office…hell, how had she not seen him walking down the sidewalk, for fuck's sake? There was no way he could have been living under nose all this time, was there?

"Baby, there's someone I want you to meet," Gina announced, flashing Ivy a wink and a grin.

When Noble finally turned Ivy's way, time slowed. She held her breath as the listless nanoseconds ticked by. When he finally locked those emerald-green pools on her once again, a shiver slid through her.

But instead of the anticipated look of recognition, shock, or even an awkward grimace, Noble simply sent her a polite, blank totally emotionally void smile.

It was definitely not the kind of greeting she expected him to give the woman who'd taken his thick cock to the back of her throat, sucking him to climax, while filthy, erotic, provoking words rolled off his tongue.

Noble wasn't looking at her but rather looking through her as if he'd never laid eyes on Ivy in his life.

The anxiety singing through her veins immediately bled out, replaced by indignation and fury.

"Do you know who this pretty young thing is?" Gina smiled up at Noble.

"No clue," he replied with such conviction Ivy nearly gasped.

"This is the woman who makes all those goodies I bring home to you from the bakery."

Noble's face lit up and that clit-throbbing grin spread over his mouth...the same mouth that had laved, kissed, and nibbled every inch of her skin as he taunted her with hours and hours of oral bliss. Even now, she could still feel his talented mouth as it laid siege to her weeping pussy.

"Nice to finally meet you. Welcome to Haven. Your butter crumb cake is totally addicting. I'm like a junkie," Noble said with a chuckle.

*Seriously? Welcome to Haven? Nice to finally meet you? Is he fucking kidding?*

Clearly, the prick had missed his true calling. Noble should have been a damn actor, because Ivy had never met a more convincing liar in her entire life.

*So the son of a bitch wants to pretend he's never met me? Fine. I can play that game, too...asshole!*

"Trust me, baby. She already knows." Gina elbowed Noble in the ribs. "I'm over there two or three times a day buying it for you."

"True." Noble grinned. Then he turned his focus on Gina once more. "Sawyer's coming by for a couple of games of pool. I'm gonna head back and grab the table, love."

*Love?*

His declaration of love ripped through Ivy's heart like a well-honed blade, eviscerating all the foolish hope Ivy had clung to all these months.

"Have fun, and try not to take his last penny, baby. You know how grumpy he gets when you do that."

Noble laughed and nodded.

Like a hopeless moron, Ivy's arms broke out in goose bumps at the sound of his laughter.

"I'll try not to," he assured. Pausing an extra second, he sent Ivy a purely platonic smile. "Nice to meet you."

"Same to you," she somehow managed to push past her lips before Noble turned and walked away.

"God, I love that man," Gina gushed. "He owns my whole damn heart. I don't know what I'd do without Nate."

*Nate? Well, that sure as hell wasn't the name he'd used in Vegas. Fucking liar!*

In light of all the revelations that had already unfolded, finding out that Noble...or rather Nate, had used a fictitious name wasn't all that surprising, but it certainly made her feel like a bigger fool. So did seeing the love written all over Gina's face.

"Nate, huh? Nice name," she murmured, biting back a caustic scoff.

"Oh, shit. I'm such an idiot." Gina smacked a hand to her forehead. "I didn't introduce you two properly. Dammit. Well, that's my man...my Nate."

"He's very handsome." *And fucking phenomenal in bed.* "You're a lucky lady."

"Oh, I know it. I count my lucky stars every day. He's not

just great eye candy, he's kind and gentle and loving, too."

Ivy forced a smile. "How long have you two been together?"

*Smooth…real smooth. Dammit!*

She hadn't planned for the question to fall out of her mouth, it'd just…happened.

"Nine months, now," Gina answered dreamily.

*Nine months! Nine fucking months?*

Guilt, like a wrecking ball, slammed every cell in Ivy's body.

*Shit!* How could she have been so stupid…so naïve in Vegas?

The answer was easy… Noble/Nate was hot as hell, had showed interest in her, and her girl parts had been close to shriveling up and dying from lack of use. Still, none of those reasons absolved her guilt and shame. If Gina ever found out Ivy had done the nasty with her *man*, it would crush her and destroy the friendship they'd built thus far.

"Don't go away. I'll be right back. I just need to grab these folks' orders," Gina announced, nodding toward the customers now seated at various tables.

Ivy had been so focused on processing the colossal clusterfuck unfolding around her that she hadn't even noticed others had come into the bar.

As Gina scurried over to take their drink orders, Ivy casually glanced toward the pool table. Nate/Noble didn't even lift a brow. He simply lined up shot after shot with the long pool cue, totally engrossed in his game. Obviously the man was a pro at playing games.

*You prick-assed son of a bitch!*

She was letting her anger get the best of her. Ivy knew she had to leave before she did something even more reckless than she'd done in Vegas. Something like stomping up to the bastard and demanding that he acknowledge her *and* the night they'd spent fucking each other's brains out. While forcing him to confront his sins might give her satisfaction and a whole lot of closure, it would gut Gina. Ivy didn't have the heart to do that to her friend.

Forcing a calm she didn't feel, she tipped her drink back and drained the glass. When Gina returned, busily mixing booze and filling beer mugs, Ivy plastered on a tight smile. The sheer effort of acting as if all was right with her world made her feel like a total fraud…an even bigger one than Noble/Nate was.

But she was out of options.

She needed to get the fuck out of here *now*.

"I'm going to head back over and get to work. Thanks so much for the drink. It was delicious."

"What the fuck? You can't leave now." Gina frowned. "You need to stay so I can introduce you to Nate's brothers. I wasn't kidding when I said I could help end your sexual drought."

Ivy's heart pounded like a drum. She'd rather be waterboarded *and* drown than fuck one of that bastard's brothers. "Maybe next time. I'm still not feeling a hundred percent."

"You make an appointment with Doc Knight, all right?" Gina's concerned tone only made Ivy feel guiltier.

"Already did. I see him on Monday."

"Good. You'll like him. He's a great guy."

Ivy could use a great guy, instead of the lying, cheating pricks she usually hooked up with. Her trust in the male species was at an all-time low. Even if she accepted Emmett Hill's offer, he'd probably end up popping Viagra and banging all the old ladies at the nursing home behind her back.

With the exception of her father, all men were pigs. Since junior high, every guy she'd ever dated had consistently let her down.

*No more! This is the last straw!*

Ivy was through letting pussy-chasing, man-whores sweep her off her feet. Her hormones would surely balk at the long, bleak dry spell ahead, but she'd find ways to cope. She'd simply pour all her pent-up frustrations into baking and making Sweet Flours a success. If that didn't work, she'd buy stock in a battery company and spend the rest of her life burning out vibrators before burying them in a shallow grave behind the shop.

"Thanks again for the referral and the drink. I'll see you in the morning, right?"

"Damn straight you will." Gina smiled and waved.

Ivy headed toward the door, fighting the urge to glance back at Nate/Noble. Logically, she knew self-preservation kept the man from openly confirming he knew her. No way he'd risk trashing his relationship with Gina over a one-night stand with Ivy.

Still, it stung like a bitch.

No, it devastated her.

God, she'd been an idiot spending months obsessing and growing hopelessly infatuated with a man she knew she'd never see again. Now that she'd come face-to-face with him again, the reality that she'd meant dick to him, that she'd been nothing more than a convenient hole to plug his big, fat glorious cock into, annihilated her. Tears stung her eyes. Obviously the amazing sex—*stop calling it amazing, he's nothing but a sexually gifted, lying man-whore*—they'd shared was just an easy way to kill time.

Stepping from the bar as a barrage of embarrassment, hurt, and anger pinged through her. Ivy quickly checked for traffic and darted across the street as tears began to flow.

Once inside the bakery, she ran straight to the kitchen, cursing and swiping at her eyes. Refusing to cry one more tear over that lying sack of shit, Ivy cranked up her music before slamming metal bowls on the counter and vented her anger by measuring, mixing, kneading, and baking.

Like a woman possessed, she raced around the kitchen in banshee mode and shoved all thoughts of Nate/Noble down deep the second they started to surface. At one thirty in the morning, she climbed the stairs and crawled into bed. But the minute she closed her eyes, Noble/Nate was right there…kissing her, touching her, saying all those naughty things that enticed her to scream and shatter for him.

"Stop!" she screamed into the darkness before she fell apart completely.

Mournful sobs tore from her throat. Ivy hugged her pillow and sobbed until sleep finally claimed her.

When her alarm went off, she sat up and rubbed her sore, swollen eyes. Acid, caustic and burning, bubbled low in her belly, but thankfully, when she rolled out of bed, she didn't have to race to the toilet and drop to her knees. She quickly showered, dressed, and hurried downstairs.

As she prepared to open for business, she was already running on fumes. She needed caffeine more than air, so she pumped enough coffee through her system to keep her awake for a week. By the time customers started filing through the door, Ivy almost felt human again.

Several hours later, when Gina rushed through the door, Ivy's heart tripped in her chest, and an inky film of guilt ascended.

"You got time to sit and chat this morning?" Gina asked happily.

"A-ah, I can't this morning. I've got some things in the oven I need to keep an eye on. Sorry." Ivy forced an unhappy frown.

"Oh. Damn. We didn't get to visit last night before you had to leave and I was… Oh, never mind. It's okay." Gina gave a wave of her hand. "I'll just take a couple pieces of coffee cake then, and let you get back at it."

As Ivy filled the order, she could feel Gina's scrutiny. Dammit. She'd have to learn how to be a much better actress, and fast. But it was hard when guilt and shame were pulsating so thickly through her veins.

Over the next three days, Gina visited each and every morning. Their conversations went from uncomfortable to stilted and then awkward. The woman didn't pry or quiz Ivy about the wall she'd erected. Gina simply smiled, waved, and walked out the door, leaving Ivy alone with the elephant in the room. Remorse was eating her alive, but there was nothing she could do or say to pardon her unforgiveable sin.

After finally sleeping in an extra three hours, Ivy sat in Doc Knight's tiny waiting room, mindlessly thumbing through a magazine. None of the articles or pictures even registered in her brain. She was too focused on her worries...worries about her deteriorating relationship with Gina and the unknown medical malady running rampant through her system.

Ivy thought it strange she didn't have to fill out sheets of medical history but shrugged it off as a quirk of a small-town doctor. She figured the man probably didn't want his staff sitting at a computer all day inputting medical records.

"Miss Addison, Doc is ready for you," a gray-haired nurse called from the doorway.

Ivy set the magazine aside and followed the woman down a hall into an exam room. After the nurse took the usual blood pressure, weight, vial of blood, and urine sample, Ivy sat on a paper-covered exam table in a thin, cotton hospital gown.

There was a soft tap on the door before Doc Knight—a balding, late-sixty-something man—entered the room. He wore a crisp, white lab coat and a warm, friendly smile.

"Ivy Addison." He grinned, extending his hand. "Doc Knight. It's a pleasure to meet the woman who's responsible for my expanding waistline."

Ivy softly laughed. "It's a pleasure to meet you, too."

"My wife, Iris, is forever bringing something decadent home from your shop. Not that I mind. You can certainly bake, young lady."

"Thank you. I'm glad you enjoy them."

"So what brings you in to see me today?"

Ivy explained her stomach issues and the stress she'd been under. Doc Knight listened, jotted down several notes on a clipboard in his hand, and nodded until she was through.

"What date was your last menstrual period?"

Ivy strained to remember, but couldn't.

The tiny hum of anxiety singing through her body suddenly roared like a chainsaw.

"I-I don't know... But I'm not pregnant. I have an IUD," she said in a desperate tone.

Doc Knight nodded calmly. "So I take it you are sexually active with your husband or boyfriend?"

"I don't have a husband or a boyfriend. So see? I can't be pregnant. It has to be something else," Ivy explained trying to tamp down the panic rising inside her.

"We'll definitely check everything with a fine-tooth comb after I rule out the more obvious symptoms." His expression was so filled with sympathy that Ivy wanted to weep. "When was the last time you had sex?"

That was the first easy question he'd asked since walking into the exam room. Ivy quickly whipped off the date she and Noble/Nate had all but busted up the furniture in Las Vegas.

"All right. I'm going have my nurse, Harriett, join us while I give you a pelvic exam. I'll be back in a few minutes."

Ivy nodded, fighting the urge to beg him to stay and not leave her alone with the monstrous fears racing inside her head, as she struggled to remember if she'd had a period since returning from Vegas.

Panic had wrapped its icy hands around her throat by the time Doc Knight returned…alone. Where was his nurse? Confusion tore through Ivy's head.

"I asked Harriett to give us a few minutes to talk."

"Okay," Ivy replied softly.

"She's running a blood test to confirm your urine result."

"Urine result? I-I don't know what you mean."

Doc Knight took her hand in his before cupping his other hand over her fingers. "Your urine test came back positive, dear."

*A UTI?*

All the mornings she spent barfing her toenails up were from a urinary tract infection? *Oh, thank god!* All she'd need was a round of antibiotics and she'd be good as new in a few days.

"Thank goodness." She exhaled in relief. "My mind was going everywhere but a UTI."

"A UTI?" he repeated in confusion. Suddenly, his expression softened to one of sympathy. "No, dear. You don't have a urinary tract infection…you're pregnant."

The air froze in her lungs.

The room began to spin.

Black splotches swam behind her eyes.

*Oh, god…my best friend's boyfriend knocked me up.*

Ivy's limbs grew numb. And as the darkness swallowed her up, she heard Doc Knight call out, "Oh, dear. Harriett!"

When Ivy opened her eyes, she was lying flat on the exam table. Both doctor and nurse were leaning over her, concern stamping their faces. Panic swelled with the force of an F-5 tornado.

"Just lie still and take some deep breaths, Ivy," Doc Knight instructed. "I know you're scared and probably a little unsure of what you're going to do. You passed out and I don't want you doing it again. All right?"

She nodded as tears stung her eyes. "I-I'm really pregnant? Are you sure?"

"Yes, dear," he replied in a tone suffused in understanding.

"I don't understand," she said, voice cracking. "I thought the IUD…"

"No form of birth control is one hundred percent. But after you've rested here for a bit, I'll do a pelvic and see what's happened with your IUD. If the device is still inside you, I might need to send you to a specialist over in Abilene or Dallas."

"What do you mean, *if*?"

"Sometimes those devices migrate out, but we'll cross that bridge when we get there. Just try to relax now."

Ivy wasn't focusing on specialists or anything else the doctor said, she was spazzing out with dread and fear. "When…when's the baby due?"

"Based on the information you gave me earlier, you're seventeen, going on eighteen weeks now. So, that'll put your delivery date somewhere around July twenty-sixth."

*Oh, god…Noble/Nate really knocked me up. Oh, Gina…I'm so sorry!*

Her life felt like a bad episode of *Jerry Springer*. Tears filled her eyes. Ivy tried to blink them back but they rolled out as a sob spilled off her lips.

"Oh, honey," Harriett cooed. "Don't cry. It's going to be all right, and don't you worry about what the people in town say about you being pregnant and unmarried. Some just like to talk trash for the sake of having something to say."

*Gossip? Oh, hell…*

The thought hadn't even crossed her mind until now. Once again, scandal was going to surround her, not for being Eugene McMillian's victim but for being an unwed mother. Like she'd done the night she discovered Noble/Nate was in love with Gina, Ivy sobbed, loud and long.

"Harriett," Doc Knight scolded. "She doesn't need to worry about all that now."

"I'm sorry. I-I was only trying to help." The sweet old woman patted Ivy's hand gently. "It's going to be all right, dear. It really is."

"No, it's not!" Ivy wailed. "Oh, god…how could this have happened?"

"Well, when two people love each other—"

"Harriett!" Doc Knight barked. "Why don't you go file some charts for a few minutes. When I get Miss Addison calmed down, I'll call you."

"Fine," Harriett said with a huff before turning and storming out of the room.

Doc Knight shook his head, then inched his backside onto the edge of the examination table and opened his arms. "Come here, dear."

He reminded her so much of her late grandfather that Ivy sat up and threw her arms around his neck, soaking his pristine lab coat in snot and tears. The kind doctor simply held her and patting her gently on the back while he murmured reassuring platitudes.

Twenty minutes later, after Ivy had gained some semblance of control, Harriett entered the room and held her hand while Doc Knight performed a pelvic exam. In the end, there was no trace of her IUD. He explained how the device could have migrated out, either attached to a tampon or simply during urination. If Ivy had known such a thing could have happened, she would have asked her OB-GYN in Dallas to super-glue that damn IUD inside of her.

Numbed by the shock of finding out she was pregnant, she worked to suppress her fear of trying to run the business while caring for a newborn. How the hell was she supposed to handle such a feat? Ivy was already running on so little sleep she could barely function. But adding a newborn who'd be up at all hours of the night into the mix was beyond overwhelming.

When she was dressed and ready to leave her appointment, Doc Knight returned with a sack of prenatal vitamins.

He took her hand once again with a paternal smile. "Professionally, the less stress the better for the little person growing inside you. Personally, I've been alive long enough to know that life has a funny way of working itself out, so don't try to come up with all the answers today. Relax as much as you can, and if you ever need an ear, or a shoulder, I'm here for you, sweet girl."

His kindness was a much-needed balm for her fractured soul. Tears of gratitude swelled in her eyes. She sent him a watery smile. "Thank you."

After making another appointment, as Doc had instructed, Ivy took her vitamins and left the office. The late February sun warmed her skin but didn't touch the icy unrest assaulting her system. Numbly strolling down the sidewalk to the bakery, Ivy found it ironic that she'd chosen Haven to escape attention and find a sense of anonymity. But she'd lived in the south long enough to know those along the Bible Belt didn't lend much sympathy to a girl who'd *gone and gotten herself in trouble*. There was positively no way her out-of-wedlock pregnancy would go unnoticed in a few more weeks.

*Once more, I'm dragging the Addison name through the mud.*

*Priceless.*

She knew she'd have to break the news to her parents, but not today. Ivy wasn't ready to shove another knife of disappointment straight into her mom's or dad's heart. No, today, she simply needed to find a way to come to terms with the curve ball life was throwing her.

Fresh tears stung the backs of her eyes as worries swirled in her head like the leaves fluttering around her feet.

But she continued on, putting one foot in front of the other, just like she'd have to do to survive the changes ahead. Somehow, someway, she'd manage to be a good mom and run her business. And through it all, the only thing she had to do was keep Gina from finding out she was pregnant with Noble/Nate's baby.

That was one secret Ivy vowed to take to her grave.

# CHAPTER TWELVE

After a long day at the ranch, Noble sat inside the Hangover, nursing a beer. On the jukebox a singer wailed out a country song about leaving a pretty girl with the bluest eyes in Texas. A caustic scoff rolled off his tongue. Four and a half months ago, he'd left the prettiest girl with the bluest eyes back in Vegas, along with his fucking libido.

Noble gnashed his teeth and cursed under his breath.

If he didn't find a way to banish Ivy from his brain, he'd have to study Buddhism so he could become a monk. The zero desire to climb between the legs of any woman except Ivy's was starting to worry him.

"That's not what I'm saying, dammit," Gina spat in a tone so angry it pulled Noble out of his internal pity party. Glancing up, he saw the bar owner and his twin scowling at one another. "You're not listening to what I'm saying."

"The hell I'm not," Nate countered exasperatedly. "I'm just wondering why you don't come right out and ask her what's crawled up her ass and clear the air."

"Because she's the only *real* girlfriend I have in this town, besides your mom. I really like her and I'm not willing to risk losing that by getting all up in her face."

"If she was such a *real* friend, she'd tell you what's bothering her."

Noble smirked as Gina bristled. Their conversation was about to get ugly.

"Nate?"

"Yes, my love?"

Nate's voice was low. He reached up to touch her—*fatal mistake, bro*—but Gina slapped his hand away.

"Don't. That's not going to help."

"What is?"

"I don't know." Gina exhaled a heavy sigh.

Noble wasn't sure who or what the drama was all about, and honestly, he really didn't care. "If you two are done fighting, can I have another beer?"

As Gina filled his mug from the spigot, Nate nuzzled in close behind her. "Just go over and talk to her in the morning. All right?"

"I'll try," Gina conceded.

Nate kissed the top of her head and gave a satisfied nod before glancing up at Noble.

"What are you doing here, man? It's Saturday night. You're usually banging a bed-bunny and her headboard right about now."

Noble glanced at the clock on the wall and drained his mug of beer as he purposely blocked the twin connection shared with Nate.

"Funny you should say that. I need to go and…get *busy*," he lied, hoping he'd truly blocked his brother out. "See you two lovebirds later. Oh, and no more arguing. You know what happens when you two fight."

"Don't say that," Gina scolded. "Didn't anyone ever teach you that you never invite negativity into your life by saying shit like that?"

"Nope," Noble said with a wry grin as he lifted off the barstool. "I was too busy learning different ways to make the ladies scream."

"Of course you were, you silly man-whore." Gina chuckled and flashed him a wink.

"Catch y'all later," he called out as he reached the front door.

Noble kept his internal barrier up until he was far outside of town. He hated hiding things from Nate, but he hated lying to the man even more. Life was pretty black-and-white as far as Noble was concerned. He didn't like playing around in shades of gray. It rubbed him the wrong way.

Driving aimlessly toward the ranch, Noble knew if he returned home this early, questions would be asked. Instead of turning into the long gravel drive, he continued along the blacktop a half mile more. Slowing the truck, he turned onto a bumpy dirt road. The access path leading to the creek, cut straight through their property.

When he and his brothers were kids, the whole family would pile into his dad's Suburban and drive down this same dusty path to the creek. While the boys splashed and swam in the cool springwater, his mom would shake out a huge quilt and sit in the shade watching them and laughing, or quietly read a book. Hours later, she'd unpack a picnic basket and they'd all sit on the blanket eating lunch as the warm wind dried their skin.

The memories sent a melancholy smile to tug Noble's lips. Those days had been golden. Carefree. Happy. Growing up, Noble had heard the hushed murmurs and tsks of pity for the couples in town who'd separated or divorced. When he was seven years old, Noble began to worry that his parents might choose to take that same ominous path. When he'd finally gathered the courage to ask his mom about the state of her marriage, Nola simply smiled and hugged him tightly. She'd alleviated all his fears when she told him that she and his father made a vow to one another, and to God, to love, honor, and cherish each other until they died.

Noble spent the next twelve years convincing himself that the Grayson clan was impervious to the embarrassing and life-altering horrors of divorce. Then Sawyer married Sara, and a short time later, the safety bubble Noble had built around him cracked. Fissures had grown into ragged, sharp-edged maws that opened up and shredded his guileless idealism. The taboo curse of infidelity had ripped Sawyer apart, along with his marriage. The seeds of mistrust in monogamy had been sown in Noble's mind.

"So if you're never going to marry anyone, why can't you let Ivy go?" Noble asked out loud. "She was just another partner to chase pleasure with."

Even as those last words left his lips, Noble knew the time he'd spent with Ivy had fulfilled him far more than simply *pleasure*. Still, he didn't want to acknowledge or even let his conscience suggest that the blonde-haired, blue-eyed beauty had ruined him for all others.

But as his grandma Grayson would always say, *the proof is in the pudding.*

"Fuck!" Noble growled.

When he crested the tiny hill, his headlights illuminated the black F-350 truck parked near the edge of the creek. He knew instantly that it was Ned's truck.

As Noble pulled to a stop, his older brother quickly shielded his face until he killed the engine and the headlights. Then Noble climbed out of his truck.

"I'm fine. Go on home. Call April and tell her I'll be home later." Ned's voice was thick with emotion, sending Noble's senses on high alert.

"First of all, I haven't even talked to April. And secondly, you're not fine if you're sitting out here by yourself. What the fuck is going on?"

"I just want some time alone. Go home, Noble," Ned mumbled as he turned and plopped back down on a flattened patch of native sideoats grama grass.

With a shake of his head, Noble strode to where his brother sat and silently eased down beside him.

"I'm not leaving you here to brood alone. You're my brother. If you need—"

"What I need I can't have," Ned interrupted curtly.

"Why not? What is it you need?"

"Because there's no such thing as a crystal ball. No magic beans or pills or any other mystical supernatural shit that'll give me the answers I need."

Noble nodded, pondering how to get the man to open up and talk about what had him so agitated. "I guess the first thing to ask is, what's the question?"

Ned scoffed. "Trust me, Noble. *You* can't help me."

Clearly his statement was meant as an insult, as it stung like a slap to the face. "Why not me?"

"Because you're the poster child for anti-monogamy."

"Just because I'm never saying *I do* doesn't mean I don't know shit about women. I know more about them than probably any other man in a hundred-mile radius."

"Okay, Mr. Estrogen. What I'm about to tell you doesn't leave this creek bank, understood?"

"I'll take the blood brother oath," Noble affirmed. "I'll even get the knife out again like we did when we were young if you want me to."

Ned shook his head and stared out across the prairie for several long minutes before he turned and inhaled a deep breath. "My wife's gone and I don't know where the fuck she went."

A pang of fear slammed Noble's gut. "What do you mean gone? Did you call Jasper?"

"No, I didn't call *Jasper*. April's not missing. She's at the goddamn house…at least physically. But emotionally? Well, I have no fucking clue where that part is hiding."

Immediately, Noble's brain flipped back to the hospital as they all sat in the surgery waiting room. When the doctor finally had come out with the good news about Nate, April and Noble hadn't shared so much as a kiss or a hug. Ned had simply squeezed his wife's hand as she sent him a brittle smile.

"You've been struggling with this for months, haven't you?"

Ned snapped his head up. His brows were slashed and eyes narrowed. "How did you know that?"

"I picked up on it the night of Nate's surgery."

"Yeah, that was a stellar day. April and I were in the middle of World War III when Norris knocked on the door and said Nate was missing." Ned paused before a perturbed scoff rolled off his tongue. "After they found him in the field, April didn't even want to come to the hospital to see if he was okay. She wanted to stay home and study her Bible."

"Her Bible?" Noble echoed in confusion.

"She's gotten real involved with the Ladies' Auxiliary at the church. Every Wednesday she hosts a Bible study group. Reverend Thompson and a whole slew of women invade the living room to read and discuss passages."

"You don't join the discussions?"

"I'm sure Mom would love it if I did, but no, I talk to the man upstairs on my own." Ned picked up a stone and tossed it into the creek with a plop. "I can't even swear in my own house anymore without April taking me to task about it."

Noble simply arched his brows and wrinkled his nose.

"This is way too much TMI, but we don't make love anymore. We just fuck…but only when she thinks she's ovulating so we can *procreate*. It's only with the lights off, and her nightgown can't be raised any higher than her goddamn navel. I haven't seen my own wife's tits for…fuck, I can't even remember. She's turned into a prude. I don't even know who April is anymore. She's definitely not the hot, horny woman I married."

Noble didn't have a clue in hell of what he was supposed to say to that.

"We used to make love on the back porch, under the stars. I loved watching her come in the moonlight. Now, all I can do is pull the memories out of my head and hope she's enjoying what I'm doing to her, 'cause I honestly don't even know if she comes for real anymore or is just faking it so I'll cop a nut and get off her."

Noble shook his head and scowled. "All of this because she got involved in the church?"

"I don't know. All I know is everything between us started changing months ago and I can't seem to put things back the way they were." Ned picked up another stone and tossed it downstream. "So while I appreciate your offer to help, all your knowledge of women isn't going to do shit, baby bro."

"No, this is pretty much out of my wheelhouse. I'm sorry, man. I really am. Maybe you two should sit down with Reverend Thompson and talk about how intimacy is more than repopulating the earth."

Ned shook his head. "No way. I don't want everyone in town knowing my wife's turned into a damn ice queen, or that I can't satisfy her sexually anymore."

"Dude!" Noble gaped. "It's not you. You're a Grayson…a sex machine, for fuck's sake. None of us are lacking in the seduction department. Trust me."

"I used to think so, but now I'm not so sure."

"Have you tried to seduce her…do things to her you used to when you first met?"

A humorless chuckle slid from the back of Ned's throat. "I just told you I haven't seen my wife's tits in eons. I haven't had my mouth anywhere but the lips on her face for even longer than that."

"Shit, man. That's…that's not normal."

"Tell me about it." Ned sighed and shook his head. "So, what the fuck are you doing out here? Can't find any willing women to seduce tonight?"

"Just came out here to think as well."

"About?"

"Nothing important," Noble lied.

"Right. We both know that's bullshit. What's her name?"

"What makes you think it's a woman?" Noble asked trying to deflect his brother's all-too-accurate assessment.

"Why else would we both be out here, man? Someone's fucking with your head just like April is fucking with mine."

Noble considered opening his mouth and spilling his guts…revealing every spine-tingling detail of the unbelievable night he'd spent with Ivy. Ned might be able to offer some sage advice or insight on how to finally exorcise the woman's ghost from his soul. But his brother's plate was already full, overflowing, in fact. The last thing he needed was Noble whining like a pussy-whipped bitch.

"Nah, nobody's fucking with my head except me." Technically, he wasn't lying. But self-preservation dictated he redirect the conversation about women off himself and back on Ned. "So, any idea what you're going to do about April being such a prude?"

"Not a fucking clue."

"Maybe you two should take a vacation, you know, go someplace romantic."

"What was Las Vegas like?"

Noble's heart sputtered.

*Where my wildest, wettest dream came true.*

He swallowed tightly and shook his head. "Nah. Take her to Colorado or someplace up in the mountains, where you two can be completely alone."

"We're alone in the country every damn day, Captain Obvious," Ned taunted with a crooked grin. "It hasn't done a bit of good. Just sayin'."

"True. I don't know, man. Take her to Disneyland. Teach her how to be...young at heart and spontaneous again."

"Hmm," Ned grunted. "You might be on to something there."

"See? I'm more than just a talented sex machine."

Ned actually laughed. "Spare me the details, man."

"Jealous, I know."

"No, man. I don't want to barf listening to you brag about all your sexploits."

"'Cause you'd get jealous."

They both chuckled briefly before Ned turned somber. "Thanks for not leaving when I told you to go."

Noble reached up and slapped his brother on the back. "No need to thank me, man. You need me? I'm always here, no matter what."

"I appreciate that. I guess I'd better get back home." Ned stood and stuck his hat on his head. "You staying?"

"Yeah, for a few. It's peaceful here."

"You sure you're okay?"

"Yeah, man. I'm fine. Don't worry about me. I hope you can find a way to reach April."

"You and me both."

The doubt in Ned's voice made Noble frown. As his brother climbed into his pickup and drove away, he replayed their conversation. Noble couldn't help but wonder if another Grayson divorce was on the horizon.

"Christ," he muttered in disgust.

Life was complicated enough. Why anyone would want to add another person into the mix escaped him.

*Yeah, but you'd love to add Ivy into that mix and you damn well know it,* a little voice in the back of his head taunted.

"Maybe, but I'd never commit my life to her or any other woman," he murmured to himself.

Noble tossed his hat on the ground and gazed up at the stars. Ivy was out there somewhere. He couldn't help but wonder what she was doing. Or who was she with. That thought sent an unexpected spike of red-hot jealousy streaking through him. He scrubbed a hand over his face at the absurdity of his bewildering reaction.

"I need to get a goddamn grip," he scolded himself. "It's a Saturday night and I'm sitting in the dark, still pining for a girl I'll never see again. Christ, I have to be the sorriest bastard on the whole damn planet."

Repulsed by his inability to get his head screwed on straight, Noble plucked the cell phone from his jeans and started scrolling through his contacts.

It was time to put the past where it belonged and climb back into the saddle again.

Names of women who'd eagerly welcome him into their beds and between their thighs slid past his eyes. He imagined their faces…the shapes of their naked bodies…the sounds of their voices as they screamed in pleasure. Yet not a one aroused him in the slightest.

With a heavy sigh, he shoved the phone away and allowed memories of Ivy to flood his mind. Instantly, his cock thickened and grew stiff.

"Figures you'd wake up now…traitor," he groused, looking down at his crotch.

Grabbing his hat off the ground, Noble launched to his feet and stormed to his truck.

When he returned to his house, his dad was sitting in the recliner, thumbing through a hunting magazine. Norman lifted his gaze from the page and shot Noble a quizzical expression. "That sure didn't take long."

"Nope."

"Don't tell me you're losing your stamina," he teased.

"Not hardly." Noble dragged out his cocky attitude and smirked. "Just tired. It's been a long week. I'm heading to bed."

"You feeling okay?"

"Yeah. I'm fine." *Liar.* "Night, Dad."

"Night, son."

Noble strolled down the hall, stripped off his clothes, and climbed into bed. It was nearly three in the morning before he finally gave up, gripped his cock, and stroked himself off to visions of Ivy writhing and screaming.

TWO WEEKS AFTER Doc Knight informed her the rabbit had died, Ivy leaned against the counter in the kitchen. While the scent of butter, cinnamon, and yeasty breads filled her senses, she stared at the screen on her cell phone, struggling to find the courage to call home. She absently caressed her hand over the visible baby bump at her belly. Thankfully, the apron she wore during business hours hid her *delicate condition*, though that wouldn't be the case much longer.

Nibbling her lip, she vacillated on whether or not she could wait another week...or six, before informing her folks they were going to be grandparents. Her damn wonky hormones had her crying at the drop of a hat lately. She didn't want to fall apart over the phone when she heard their startled gasps and disappointed sighs.

"Stop being a wuss and just get it over with," she spat, chiding her procrastinating self. "It's not like you'll be able to hide the truth much longer, from them or anyone."

*Especially Gina.*

Ivy set her phone down and pinched the bridge of her nose.

Every day Gina continued to come into the shop, dissecting her with a stare that grew more and more penetrating, as if trying to probe deep inside Ivy's brain to uncover the reason their easy relationship had suddenly turned so brittle. And every day, heart heavy with guilt, Ivy would paint on a placid smile as she danced around the beastly elephant in the room...that only she could see.

The buzzer on the wall behind her pealed, alerting her that someone was at the front door, and nearly startled her to death. She glanced at the timer before hurrying out of the kitchen and into the main floor of the shop.

Willy, the brown-clothed delivery driver who had started regularly dropping off her orders, stood outside the front door with two large boxes leaning up against his leg.

The baby bed and mattress had arrived. A skitter of excitement rippled through her. Ivy wasn't ready to admit to anyone but herself that she'd fucked up, literally, but she had come to accept her situation...mostly. She'd be damned if she'd be unprepared for the inevitable arrival of the life growing inside her. So she'd started discreetly ordering things for the nursery online.

She was damn glad now for the hindsight to ask Rick Hastings to divide the spacious loft upstairs into two rooms. Baby Addison would have his or her own space to listen to music, do homework, or hide out and brood when teenage angst came calling.

"Hi, Willy." She smiled before signing for the delivery.

"Hey, Ms. Addison. Sorry to bother you on your day off, but…"

"No bother. I'm glad they're finally here."

"This one's pretty heavy," Willy informed, tapping a finger against the shorter box as he dropped his gaze to her belly. "The other one is light but awkward. I'd be happy to carry them in for you."

"That's kind of you, but they need to go upstairs to the second floor."

"Lead the way, ma'am."

She flashed him a grateful smile. "Thank you."

At the top of the stairs, Ivy entered the room she'd fashioned into a nursery. After laying down a base coat of muted mint-green, she'd adorned he walls with colorful hand-painted dragonflies, ladybugs, and flowers.

"Oh, wow. This is awesome!" Willy complimented as he eased the boxes to the polished hardwoods. "Your little tike's going to love this room."

"Thank you." Ivy beamed before a wave of worry crested. "I, um, I know you make a lot of deliveries in town, but I'd really appreciate it if you didn't mention the nursery here to anyone."

"Oh, no, ma'am. I won't say anything."

"Thank you. It's just…well, I'm…" She caressed her stomach. "I like my privacy."

"No need to explain, Ms. Addison. I didn't see a thing here today." Willy gave her a grin and a wink.

"Thank you."

Before Willy left, Ivy handed him a sack of the lemon squares she'd baked an hour ago and walked him to the door. As he drove away, Ivy closed her eyes and tilted her head toward the sun, drinking in its warmth, while the early spring breeze skipped over her skin.

When she opened her eyes and dropped her chin, Gina stepped onto the sidewalk, eyes glued to Ivy's stomach as a look of shock lined her face. "You're fucking preg—"

"Shhh," Ivy cut her off as she nervously checked the sidewalk. Thankfully, the only people around were well out of earshot. "Come inside…we-we'll talk there."

Guilt and dread thundered through her veins.

*Dammit! Why didn't I put on an apron this morning?*

She knew why. It was Monday, the bakery was closed, and she hadn't expected to see anyone…especially Gina.

"Right. Right." Gina hurried inside, murmuring expletives under her breath.

As soon as Ivy shut and locked the door, Gina was in her face. "Why the fuck didn't you tell me?"

"I-I haven't told anyone." Ivy knew her excuse was as flimsy as parchment paper the second it rolled off her tongue.

"Well, it certainly explains why you've been so goddamn moody lately."

"Moody? I haven't been moody." She'd simply been hiding behind walls in hopes that no one would learn her secret, especially Gina.

"Right. And I'm a fucking nun," Gina said with a laugh. "Honey, you've been treating me like a leper for weeks. I've been racking my brain trying to figure out what I did or said that pissed you off."

Like razor blades, that revelation sliced Ivy's shame wide open. Tears filled her eyes and her voice trembled. "Oh, god, Gina. I'm s-sorry. I didn't mean to make you think that you—"

"No. No. Don't start crying. Once you turn on the waterworks, those damn pregnancy hormones make it nearly impossible to stop."

Ivy sniffed and brushed at the tears spilling down her cheeks as she gaped at the woman. "H-how do you know?"

Sorrow, palpable and profound, settled over Gina's face. "I just do."

"You've…you've been preg—"

"Guess we've both been keeping secrets, huh?" Gina announced with a slight shrug.

So it would appear. "You want some coffee?"

"Unless you've got something stronger. But then…you can't drink anymore for a while, can you?" Ivy shook her head. "Sure, I'll take a cup."

While Gina settled in at a table near the kitchen, Ivy prepared a cup of coffee for her friend and hot caffeine-free tea for herself. All the while her mind whirled. What was she going to say? Ivy hated to lie, but she had to. There were no other options.

Donning a mask of protection, Ivy sat down across from her friend and inhaled a deep breath. "I'm sorry if I've been moody. And I'm sorry I didn't tell you sooner. It's just…I've been in a state of shock and—"

"So who's the baby daddy?"

*Your boyfriend.* Ivy swallowed back the words singeing her tongue and waved her hand absently. "Just a guy… It was a one-night-fling thing. We were both kind of drunk and—"

"And your libidos took over," Gina said with a chuckle.

Ivy nodded.

"So I take it the guy…he doesn't know?"

Ivy shook her head.

"You plan on telling him?"

"No. I-I… He's got a life with someone and he's happy." Ivy averted her eyes to the rim of her coffee cup as she stammered. "I-I don't want to ruin that for him."

"Oh, fuck. Do not be a martyr. I know you don't want to rain on his happy little parade because you're a sweet girl, but you need to face the facts. You're going to need help raising this baby…maybe not physically, but financially for sure. And I'm not saying you should let the sperm donor be a part of yours and the baby's lives, but at the very least, he needs to fork over some child support. Raising a kid is damn expensive."

"I don't need his money. I have money."

"Really? You got a hundred thousand or so lying around?"

*Not anymore.* Ivy skimmed a glance around the room, mentally calculating the astronomical amount of money she'd spent on equipment and renovations.

"Because by the time that little bundle of joy graduates high school," Gina continued, "you're going to need that and more to get him or her into a decent college."

Ivy had saved some money from her settlement, but it wasn't nearly enough to fund a college education. She hadn't even thought that far down the road yet. Her sole focus was surviving childbirth. "I'll figure something out. I'll be fine."

"I have no doubt about that. But you still need to make the dipshit who didn't glove up pay."

Ivy adamantly shook her head. "No. I can't tell him about the baby."

"Why not?"

"Because I can't. All right? Just drop it." Ivy slammed her palms onto the table and launched from her chair. Tears streamed down her face before she could try and stop them. "I'm as guilty as he is." *Unfortunately, he won't own up to that fact because he's too busy covering his ass and pretending he doesn't know me.* "I wasn't thinking with anything but my pussy that night. Sure, the sex was mutual, but I'm not going to let my stupidity…or his, ruin his life. So stop badgering me about it!"

Gina rose and eased in beside her. Without warning, she threw her arms around Ivy and hugged her tight. "I'm sorry. I wasn't trying to attack you. I'm worried about you and want what's best for you *and* the baby."

The genuine remorse pouring off the woman, coupled with the soothing hand skimming up and down Ivy's back, ripped her remorse-ridden soul to shreds.

She ached to melt against Gina and drown in the compassion she offered…ached to confess her dirty secret and beg for forgiveness. But like acid, guilt sluiced through her veins—an ever-present reminder that she didn't deserve Gina's absolution.

Ivy tried to compartmentalize the myriad of blistering emotions licking through her but failed…miserably. The dam broke. She clung to the woman she'd betrayed and bawled like a damn baby.

"Shhh, shhh," Gina cooed. "Don't cry. Nate and I have your back. We'll help you through this. Everything is going to be all right. I promise."

The mere mention of Nate's name made Ivy tense like she'd been doused beneath a vat of ice water. She sucked in a ragged breath and pulled from Gina's arms.

"That's kind of you, but I don't need help…not yours and certainly not Nate's." Ivy unintentionally spat his name, then quickly pinched her lips together, inwardly cursing herself for her reckless slip.

Suspicion flared in Gina's eyes before she narrowed her gaze like a scalpel. "What is it you're not telling me?"

"Nothing," Ivy lied.

"Bullshit. There's something more to this. Tell me."

Ivy averted her eyes once more as she shook her head.

Long, awkward seconds passed before Gina exhaled a heavy sigh. "Look, you're not the first woman on the planet who's screwed up. Trust me. I've screwed up plenty of times…badly. But when I took the chance and trusted someone with my secrets, I discovered they weren't nearly as horrible as I'd made them out to be. I'm not one of the town gossips. You can trust me. You really can."

Ivy hadn't grown up having many friends. Her salt circle was small. She'd always been loyal to them, and they to her. But she'd never betrayed any of them the way she had Gina. If Ivy were to spill her secrets, their friendship would be unequivocally annihilated.

"I do trust *you*. That's not the issue."

"Then what *is* the issue, honey?" When Ivy slightly shook her head, Gina's eyes grew wide. "I know the guy who knocked you up, don't I? It's someone here in Haven, isn't it?"

Ivy mutely sat there, unable to refute her claim or push a lie past her lips.

Her deception was like a cancer, spreading inky blackness all through her system, contaminating her soul. Virulent and evil, it sucked the life from the virtues she'd always held dear. Virtues like goodness, truth, and love. Ivy felt empty and hollow. And as the walls began closing in all around her, fresh tears streamed down her face.

"It's Reverend Thompson isn't it?"

The absurdity of question yanked Ivy from her inner self-flagellation. "Reverend Thompson? Hell no! Are you crazy?"

"Probably." Gina giggled. "But you have to admit, he is really hot. It's no surprise that most of the women under the age of sixty suddenly found God the minute he moved to town. Rumor has it, his Bible study group has quadrupled."

"I definitely did not have sex with Reverend Thompson. That's just…wrong on so many levels."

"Why? He's Presbyterian, not a priest. He can suck and fuck any woman he wants. And there's plenty of them who'd jump at the chance to enjoy sinning with him."

"Well, I'm not one of them."

"So, if it's not the good Reverend, who is it?"

"Can we please just drop the subject?" Ivy begged. "The damage is done. There's nothing anyone can do to change that now."

Gina opened her mouth to say something when a knock came from the front door. In unison, they both looked up to see Noble/Nate peering through the glass, wearing a crooked smile. Ivy's heart leapt in her chest as she lurched to her feet, wrapping her arms around her waist in an attempt to hide her stomach.

"Oh, shit. I forgot to tell Nate I was coming over to see you. He must be—" Gina stopped mid-sentence when she caught sight of Ivy. "Are you all right? You're pale as a ghost."

A whimper of panic seeped from between her lips. Her knees began to tremble and she latched on to the back of a chair for support.

"Sit," Gina ordered before sprinting to the front door and ushering Noble/Nate inside.

"What's going on?" His buttery voice was teemed with concern.

"I don't know." Gina anxiously rushed back to Ivy's side. "She was fine a second ago and now...she looks like she's about to pass the fuck out."

Noble/Nate dropped to one knee in front of Ivy and peered up into her eyes.

Like a massive cyclone, the culmination of the truth she'd been hiding, the guilt eating her alive, and the raw pain from mourning the man before her who'd never kiss, touch, or send her to the stars sucked her up into a vortex of chaos. She let out a long, mournful sob as tears slipped down her face.

Noble/Nate turned a look of panic up at Gina. "A little help here, my love?"

"It's all right, baby," Gina softly assured. "She's got a bun in the oven...one she won't be selling to any customers, and whacked-out hormones are getting the best of her right now."

That same crooked smile that had set Ivy's soul on fire back in Vegas kicked up one corner of his mouth. "Well, congratulations, darlin'. Who's the lucky father?"

The dogma of his unwavering façade felt like a knife through Ivy's heart. Anger, caustic and seething, raced through her, decimating every shred of dignity and laying waste to the guilt and shame she harbored.

Ivy balled up her fist and clenched her jaw as she shot him an incredulous stare. Everything in her periphery faded beneath the red haze clouding her vision.

"You're the daddy, you lying sack of shit!" Ivy yelled.

Noble/Nate's smile slid from his mouth. His eyes grew wide and his jaw dropped open in complete and utter shock. His act was more than convincing, but Ivy was putting a halt to his stupid charade.

"Oh, stop playing games and pretending you don't remember me, goddamn it!" Ivy bolted out of her chair and cradled her stomach. "This...this baby is *yours*!"

"Nate? Is that true?" Gina screeched. Ivy blinked through her rage to find her friend's face wrinkled in confusion and pain. Before Noble/Nate could even utter a word, Gina started shaking her head as she darted a look of bewilderment and pain between Ivy and her Noble/Nate. "No. No. There's no fucking way he's your baby's daddy."

The anguish in the woman's voice crushed Ivy's heart. She issued a wail of regret and then softly nodded. "I'm so sorry, Gina. God, I'm so fucking sorry, but he is."

"The hell I am!" Noble/Nate bellowed indignantly. "Listen, lady, I don't know what fucking game you're play—"

"*You're* the one playing games, *Nate*. I'm sorry Gina had to find out like this, but we both know how this happened."

"I don't know shit, lady," Noble/Nate barked. "I also don't know what you hope to gain weaving such destructive lies, but whatever it is, you're not going to succeed."

Ivy let out a watery snort. "I don't want shit from you except for you to finally acknowledge it was me you spent the night with when we fucked each other's brains out."

"You fucked her?" Gina snarled.

"No!"

"Yes!" Ivy countered angrily.

"You son of a bitch," Gina seethed. "When did you fuck her?"

"I didn't. I swear!" Rage, blistering and white-hot, rolled off his rugged frame. His eyes blazed with an indignant fire.

Each ugly second that he denied their one-night stand only served to fuel Ivy's fury.

"Liar! I suppose you're going to try to deny that you ever said"—sneering, Ivy dropped her voice to a masculine timbre—"Christ, you feel like silk…hot, slippery silk. Shatter hard for me baby."

"You motherfucker! You say those exact same words to me." Gina's voice cracked as she started to cry.

Noble/Nate tossed his head back, raised his hands to the

ceiling, and let out an angry roar. The sound was so primal and loud a shiver rolled down Ivy's spine.

"For the last fucking time...I. Did. Not. Fuck. This. Bitch."

*Bitch. Bitch.* Eugene McMillian's demeaning words echoed in Ivy's head. A fury more potent than when she'd knocked Harvey Hay's lights out blossomed within.

"I am not a bitch, you lying prick!" Ivy spat.

"I'm not the one who's a pathological liar, darlin'. You hold that title, hands down."

"Dammit, Noble," Ivy barked. "Cut the innocent act. We both know—"

"*What* did you call me?" Nate interrupted, cocking his head as a slow smile tugged his lips.

"Noble," she spat. "That's the fake name you gave me that night."

His expression instantly softened as he darted an enlightened glance at Gina, who was suddenly scowling. "And where exactly did you and I spend the night fucking each other's brain's out?"

"Don't play dumb," Ivy scolded. "At the hotel in Vegas."

"Ah, got it," Nate answered in a sudden, strangely calm demeanor. He turned to face Gina and nodded. "You and I need to talk."

"Yes, we most definitely do." Gina wiped the tears from her face.

"I-I'm sorry it all had to come out like this. I never meant to hurt you or ruin your relationship. I-I lost my shit...I'm so sorry."

"It's okay. But Nate and I need to talk for a few minutes...alone."

"Of course." Ivy sniffed. "I'll be in the kitchen."

"Thanks." Gina nodded soberly.

Ivy lowered her chin. Overwrought with remorse, she couldn't look at either of them as she turned and left the room. Standing at the industrial metal sink in the kitchen, Ivy splashed cold water on her face. She inwardly berated herself for getting so angry with Noble/Nate that she'd detonated like a bomb and spewed it all in front of Gina. Ivy had let her fury override common sense. But dammit, she couldn't tolerate liars.

At least Nate/Noble had finally tossed his mask of subterfuge away. Hopefully, he and Gina could find a way to salvage their relationship.

Ivy had clung to the fantasy that she might run into the man who'd managed to turn her world on its axis in just one night. But after discovering he was nothing but a lying, cheating pig, she'd unequivocally erased him from the masturbation movies that played in her mind. There'd be no way Noble/Nate could ever redeem himself.

"Bastard!" she muttered.

She wouldn't bother wasting an ounce of pity on the man. He was getting exactly what he deserved. Gina, however, was a different story. The woman projected a rough exterior, but it was brutally obvious she was head-over-heels in love with the man. She deserved so much more than a skeevy player who'd probably been cheating on her all along. While the friendship she'd shared with Gina was irrevocably ruined, Ivy prayed her friend's heart would heal quickly.

With a heavy heart, she silenced the timer that had started chiming and dragged several loaves of bread from the oven. Whenever Ivy needed to soothe away the jagged edges life tossed her way, fresh-baked bread was her go-to comfort food. Right now, she'd give heaven and earth to slice open a steaming loaf, slather it in butter, and eat the whole damn thing. Instead, she simply popped them from their pans and placed them on the cooling racks.

Gina poked her head in the kitchen. "Do you mind coming back out for a few?"

"Of course not." Ivy studied the woman, trying to get a bead on her mood, but couldn't.

When she stepped through the doors, she instantly noticed that Noble/Nate had left. She closed her eyes and exhaled a heartfelt sigh. "I'm so sorry, Gina. Sorry for so, so much. I should have told you what happened between us the first night you introduced us at the bar."

"I wish you would have," Gina said with a soft smile. "It could have saved us both a world of heartache."

Ivy nodded sadly. "I'm sorry. I swear to God, I never meant to hurt you like this."

"You have nothing to be sorry for, sugar. You didn't know."

"No, I didn't, but that's no excuse. If I'd known he was already in a relation—"

"That's not what I meant."

"I'm not following you."

Gina moved in beside Ivy and gently wrapped a hand around her elbow. "I meant, you didn't know about this." Like one of the models on the *Price Is Right* showing off a new car, Gina extended her arm toward the dark hallway that led to the bathrooms.

Noble/Nate stepped from the shadow, grinning like a Cheshire cat. Ivy wrinkled her brow in confusion, but when a *second* Noble/Nate stepped from the blackness and locked eyes growing wide in unadulterated shock on her, Ivy's heart sputtered.

Her body trembled.

A wave of dizziness sent her teetering in her tennis shoes.

Gina gripped her elbow tighter and leaned in close to her ear. "You didn't know Nate had a twin. That one there's your Noble."

*Twin?*

All at once, a parade of mind-numbing emotions charged Ivy's system.

Relief that she hadn't slept with her best friend's man came first, followed by excitement that the *real* Noble was actually standing in front of her again. But the stunned, blank expression now lining his face sent anxiety pinging through her like popcorn. What if he wasn't happy to see her again? She swallowed tightly as she drank in the sight of his broad, strong body and sinfully intoxicating face.

"Ivy?" Noble whispered her name like a reverent prayer.

"Noble." She barely breathed his name, too afraid that if she displaced the air, he might vanish, like smoke.

"Thank fuck you two know each other." Nate grinned. "At least the baby will know its rightful father."

"*Baby?*" Noble spat the word out as if it were poison.

He turned a ghostly white as he slid his shocked gaze from Ivy's face to the slight bump at her belly. Sinking her teeth into her bottom lip, she tried to read the slew of emotions zipping over his gorgeous face.

Suddenly, Noble's eyes fluttered toward the ceiling.

"Oh, shit!" Nate barked.

"Noble!" Ivy screamed. Finding her footing, she rushed forward as Noble toppled to the floor like a giant sequoia.

# CHAPTER THIRTEEN

TRAPPED BENEATH A wall cloud of blackness, Noble registered an annoying hum echoing in his ears. From far off in the distance, he heard someone calling his name. He felt as if he'd been encased in cement. He tried to open his eyes but couldn't lift his heavy lids.

Then, like a lifeline, he heard Nate's voice in his head. *Come on, man. You need to come back to us, bro. You're scaring the shit out of the women. And I'm no poster child for calm myself.*

Hearing and feeling his twin's anxiety, Noble worked to part the inky veil surrounding him.

"Noble, please wake up," begged a sweet and palpably terrified female.

It was the same voice that had been plaguing him night and day for what seemed like a lifetime.

*Ivy.*

A ribbon of light spliced through the gloom, and Noble followed the golden rays like a roadmap to the surface and forced his eyes open.

Ivy was hovering over him with worry marring her angelic face.

The air in his lungs caught and his heart rate tripled.

*It wasn't a dream this time. She's really here.*

Speechless, he gazed into her long-lost pale blue eyes, now rimmed red and filled with concern. Sunlight spilled in behind her, casting her golden curls in an ethereal glow.

*Damn if she isn't the most beautiful woman in the whole world.*

"Noble? Can you hear me?" she asked in a tone thick with

panic.

A bolt of adrenaline zipped through his system, making him want to murder whatever had upset her. But her fear-filled eyes told him the only thing that was scaring her was *him*.

Aiming to erase her fright, Noble sent her a gentle smile. Fuck, she was as stunningly gorgeous as the last time he'd laid eyes on her...exhausted, sated, and sleeping. Charged with the boiling need to drag her beneath him again, Noble reached up to touch her and realized that he was flat on his back in the middle of the bakery.

"What am I doing on the goddamn floor?"

"Y-you fainted," Ivy stammered.

*So that's what passing out feels like.*

"The...the news, shocked you so hard you..." She paused and dropped her lashes.

*Wait! What news?*

His question was internally cresting when the image of Ivy's rounded belly flashed in his brain, sending a tsunami of dread crashing down on him. Sitting upright, probably faster than he should have, Noble ignored the sparks of light behind his eyes as well as his heart thundering against his ribs and zipped his gaze to the tiny swell of Ivy's abdomen.

Well, that certainly hadn't been there when they were in Vegas.

Son of a bitch! She *was* fucking pregnant.

*No. No. No! It's not mine. Can't be mine!* denial shrieked in his brain.

No way could he have knocked her up.

*You sure about that?* a little voice inside him prodded.

Had he gloved up that night? Quickly racking his brain, Noble tried to remember, but like the meaning of life itself, the answer eluded him.

Every cell in his body recoiled as the icy hands of fear gripped both his throat and his balls.

*No way. I am not the one who knocked her up. It's impossible.*

*You sure about that?* Nate wordlessly asked, mimicking Noble's own silent entreaty.

No, he wasn't *sure*, but he damn well better not be the one responsible for...*that!*

As if sensing his repugnance, Ivy slid a protective hand over her stomach.

"Do you feel well enough to get up and sit at one of the tables?" she nervously asked.

Noble lifted his gaze to Ivy's angst-ridden face and his heart sputtered. Christ, he wanted her again...wanted her desperately.

Swallowing tightly to bury his lust, he nodded. Nate offered him a hand. After accepting, Noble stood. On unsteady legs, he shuffled to the nearest chair and plopped down hard on the seat. Gina hurried to the table and set a cup of water down in front of him before sending him a sympathetic smile.

Ivy was as quiet as a church mouse as she took a seat across the table from him. Her posture was rigid—spine straight, hands tightly folded in her lap. The pensive, uneasy woman in front of him was the polar opposite of the uninhibited sex kitten he'd spent that one unforgettable night with.

Noble took a sip of the cool water and cleared his throat. "So, you're...p-pregnant?"

*I'd say that's been well established, Captain Obvious!* he inwardly chided.

"Yes."

Her singular, clipped reply was void of any detail he frantically sought. Namely, whose sperm got loose and impregnated her.

Surely, she wasn't going to try and pin that baby on him, was she?

Noble still couldn't recall gloving up with her, which was pissing him off. He remembered plenty of other things from that night, like the feel of her soft skin yielding beneath his touch, the taste of her warm, tart cream spilling over his tongue, the sound of her keening cries as she erupted on his face and his cock.

The visuals violently running through his head only magnified his ravenous need to strip her bare and devour her right here and now. The only thing stopping him was the prickly panic pumping through his veins.

His heart thundered wildly as he struggled with the sensation of fire and ice consuming him. Part of him was about to spontaneously combust in fiery lust, while another part of him was frozen in a block of unmitigated fear.

Sweat dotted his brow, while his nerves were screaming like an eighties hair-band.

A million questions burned his tongue like a ghost pepper, but Noble couldn't push a single one past his lips. He was too fucking scared.

"We're going to head back over to the bar and give you two kids some time alone to…talk," Nate announced.

Noble soberly nodded, grateful for the brief respite from the guillotine blade pressed against his throat.

Gina leaned in and gave Ivy a quick hug. "If you need *any-thing*, I'm only a phone call away."

"Thanks. I'll be fine," Ivy assured halfheartedly. "I'm sorry again for causing—"

"Nothing to be sorry about," Nate interrupted. "I'm just glad we were able to get you two…reintroduced."

*Leave, dammit.* Noble gave his brother a mental shove.

*We are. But chill out. And don't be a dick to her, all right? Ivy's a hot mess right now. The last thing she needs is you acting like a bobcat with his balls caught in a bear trap.*

*Isn't that Ivy's purpose…to trap me?*

*Not if that baby really* is *yours.* Nate flashed a wolfish grin. *Then it'll be…here comes the bride, gorgeous, pregnant, and wide. Here comes the groom, sweating, swearing, and filled with gloom.*

*Out! Now!* Noble clenched his jaw as his nostrils flared.

Nate simply smirked as he slung an arm around Gina's waist and headed toward the front door.

Noble sat silently cursing Ivy's still, stony posture until the bakery door snicked closed.

"Before we start discussing…the obvious," Noble began, straining to harness his growing contempt, "how the hell did you track me down?"

Ivy's face creased in confusion before she pursed her lips and lifted her chin.

*If my first question has already offended her, this is going to get real ugly.*

"I didn't *track you down*. I…moved here months ago to open Sweet Flours. The fact that you live here too is nothing but a tragic coincidence."

"You gotta be shitting me," Noble scoffed. "How the hell have you been living under my damn nose all this time without me knowing it?"

"I don't know. I wondered the same thing when I first saw you…err, rather, Nate at Gina's bar."

"So where exactly do you live?"

"Upstairs," she replied, pointing to the stairway beyond the cash register.

"You live here alone?"

"Yes."

"Where's your husband?"

Ivy blanched. "My *husband*? I-I don't… I'm *not* married."

"Boyfriend then. Where's the guy I saw outside washing your windows a while back? He sure as hell wasn't from Haven."

Lost in thought, she wrinkled her brow. Long seconds later, she softly laughed. "That was my dad. He was here for my grand opening."

Noble's gut coiled.

By process of elimination, the wicked blade at his neck sank in deeper. Still, he wasn't ready to wave the white flag and give up hope that some other prick had knocked Noble's dream girl up. Immediately, that thought sent a firestorm of jealousy to race deep in his soul. His stomach pitched as images of someone other than him driving in and out of her sweet pussy filled his brain. The brutally disturbing sensation assaulting him made him gnash his teeth and bite back a howl. He knew then he'd fucked up…broken his most coveted cardinal rule—*neverer let a woman worm her way into your heart.*

A rush of heat sailed through his body.

Panic gripped him by the throat, the balls, and the heart.

Noble was thoroughly and unequivocally fucked!

The walls of the bakery barreled in around him.

*Breathe, man.* Nate's calm and reassuring tone reverberated in Noble's head, piercing the angst consuming him. *Just breathe. Whatever is happening, we'll deal with it. Just remember you're not alone.*

*Right,* Noble sent back as he sucked in a ragged breath. *Look, no offense, but I need some privacy. I don't have room in my head for you and all the other shit I'm trying to process here.*

*Reach out if you need me,* Nate mentally sent back, then disappeared.

"Noble," Ivy whispered softly. "I know the shock you're feeling right now. Trust me, when Doc Knight told me I was…pregnant, I passed out just like you did."

"I guess it's time to stop pussy footing around and just come right out and—"

"You're the father," Ivy affirmed barely above a whisper.

Like a lion, rejection roared within.

"How do you know? Show me the blood test that proves it's mine and not someone else's kid." The words, slathered in accusation, were out of his mouth before he could soften them.

Noble immediately wanted to kick his own ass. He'd all but called her a whore. In his heart, he knew she wasn't a slut. She was a good girl…an *amazingly good* girl.

Ivy recoiled. Pain was written all over her face as she mutely gaped at him.

*Fuck!*

"I'm sorry. I didn't mean to insinuate that you were a… It's just, back in Vegas, you were really willing and I don't… You had every right to hook up with someone after I left without… I'm not saying… Aw, shit." Noble shoved a hand through his hair. He was struggling to put his jumbled emotions into words. But the contempt, pain, anger, and insult lining Ivy's face told him he was failing…miserably.

Even though his gut told him she hadn't crawled into someone else's bed after he left her in Vegas, self-preservation and fear had him grasping at straws.

Ivy cleared her throat as her whole body turned to granite. Her lips pressed into a tight, angry line as she lifted her chin defiantly.

"Let me state this as succinctly as possible. You *are* the father. And while I don't *expect* you to believe that," she bit out angrily, "in fact I don't *expect* a damn thing from you, I'm not asking you for a damn thing. I don't want child support, shared visitation, or even your last name—which I still don't know—on the damn birth certificate."

Unwittingly, Noble exhaled a billowing burst of relief.

A flicker of annoyance danced across her still, intoxicating pale blue eyes. "Whether you choose to believe me or not, I've had sex with *one* man in the past thirteen months…*you!*"

*Bullshit!* Noble inwardly scoffed. Her claim was totally impossible. No creature as lusciously gorgeous sensual, kind, and sexually uninhibited as Ivy could have gone thirteen months without some smooth-talking dick-weed seducing her. It wasn't even in the realm of reality. Either she'd been living under a rock, locked away in some impenetrable tower, or she was lying her ass off.

"But no one—not even you—is going to demand a cheek swab or blood test to determine the paternity of *my* child. I know exactly who the father is, and I'm the *only* one who'll matter in this child's life."

Ivy's plan to arbitrarily cut him out of the life of his *potential* child sent a red haze of fury to dim his vision.

"Oh, there will be a damned DNA test, sweetheart. That's not up for debate. You can fucking count on it."

That test was the only way Noble would be able to appease his moral conscience. He had to know if he'd dodged a fatal bullet or had to bite the motherfucking thing and walk Ivy *and* their baby down the aisle.

A new wave of panic slid up his spine.

"That's not your decision to make," Ivy hissed in fury.

A fiery conviction blazed in her eyes. Her lush mouth and pretty face were pinched in determination and Noble couldn't help but grin on the inside. Ivy looked so damn cute when she was all riled up.

"Besides, no one…not even my family knows I'm pregnant. Well, no one but Doc Knight, his nurse, Gina, Nate, and now you. I'll hide my *condition* as long as possible, but when the people of Haven find out, I will not breathe a word to anyone that you are the father."

Her intention of keeping him her dirty little secret pierced him like a pitchfork to the chest.

"My privacy has been sliced, diced, and dissected under a microscope enough for one lifetime. I refuse to let that happen again."

Noble had no idea what she was referring to but made a mental note to find out.

"If the whole town wants to while their days away gossiping about me, I certainly can't stop them, but I won't confirm or deny their speculation. Your identity will be completely concealed."

Noble didn't know why her vow to protect him pissed him off, but it did…royally.

His palms itched something fierce. He wanted to take her over his knee and paddle her ass crimson red.

"You've got it all planned out, don't you?" he asked caustically.

"Yes. I do. I've had weeks to look at this from every possible angle. You've had thirty minutes…tops. I get that you're still trying to process, I truly do. Give it a few days, and you'll see that

I'm right. So, this is how you and I are going to handle this awkward situation. We're going to stand up. You're going to give me a hug, wish me luck, then turn around and *walk away*. I, correction, *we* will be fine on our own," she asserted, strumming her stomach.

Noble finally grasped why Ivy was pissing him off so brutally and bit back a caustic laugh. His mom was the only woman on the planet who had ever issued orders and expected him to obey. But that was years ago when he was child. As an adult, he'd harness the moon for Nola if she *asked*.

Unfortunately, Ivy wasn't, as she put it, *asking you for a damn thing*. No, she was dictating his actions and Noble was already digging in his heels.

Though he was bubbling with rage, a part of him was fascinated. Ivy was showing him a side of herself he'd never known existed. But he knew without a shadow of a doubt if she'd tried pulling rank on him like this out in Vegas, Noble would have tied her sassy ass to the bed and proven beyond a shadow of a doubt who the hell was in charge.

The image of her bound tight and at his mercy made his cock stir.

He'd spent months reliving every ball-churning second with her in Sin City. Now that she was here, sitting across from him, the ache to recreate every magical second was wreaking havoc on his self-control. He balled his hand into a fist to keep from leaning across the table, tugging the elastic band from her ponytail, and sinking his fingers into her silky strawberry curls. Her superior posture, icy façade, and the edict she'd just doled out scraped him raw.

Physically, Ivy was only an arm's length away, but emotionally, she'd locked herself behind a thick, protective barrier…a barrier designed to keep him out. Noble wasn't having it. One way or another, he'd pulverize every single brick as well as melt the fucking rebar supports.

He shot a furtive glance toward the stairs. The demand to

pluck her from the chair, haul her upstairs, and show her exactly how they were...*going to handle this awkward situation* crawled up his spine. His growing erection was totally on board with the idea, but Noble had to think with the head with a brain right now.

Biting back the urge to roar, he worked to keep his voice low and calm. "I appreciate your concern regarding my reputation, but there's no way I'm going along with your...*plan*."

"That's too bad, because it's not up for discussion. I've made up my mind," she bit out defiantly.

"Then you'll just have to change it, because if that baby's mine, he or she *will* carry my last name...carry the Grayson name!"

As soon as the statement left his lips, an icy and foreboding film covered his skin.

*One of these days, you're going to mess up and be forced to say I do to someone you don't even love.* His mother's words rolled through his head with a finality that choked the air from Noble's lungs. When Nola got wind that he'd fucked up and gotten Ivy pregnant—which would be any second in this fucking town—she'd grab her shotgun.

Terror clogged his throat.

His heart felt as if it were going to pound straight out of his chest.

Panic sent a cold sweat to break out over his body.

*Marriage? Hell no!*

Unlike Sawyer, Noble wasn't about to set himself up for disaster. No way would he end up in court listening to a judge rattle off the division of assets, visitation schedule—if the baby Ivy carried was indeed his—then slamming down a gavel dissolving his marriage while Noble stood hemorrhaging failure for the whole world to see.

As if that wasn't bad enough, he'd have to give up his cherished freedom.

*And just how much of that coveted freedom have you enjoyed lately?* the little voice in his head mocked.

None, and it chafed...chafed that the woman sitting across from him had ruined him, forced him into a life of self-imposed celibacy for reasons he still couldn't fucking understand.

But what pissed him off the most was the insistent and voracious demand to touch her, caress her milky soft skin one more time.

"That's crazy. I'm trying to protect you, and you want to go off and announce it to the whole damn world? That's asking for trouble neither of us wants or needs."

The urge to latch his mouth over her ripe lips and kiss some fucking sense into her, feel her writhing breathlessly against him careened through him like a meteorite.

"This baby is yours. But I'll be the one raising him or her *alone*. Addison—which is my last name, by the way, is the one that is going to be printed on the birth certificate."

Ivy's words scored deep gouges in every elemental principle cemented in Noble's core. The foundation beneath him gave way and tossed him into a hot, toxic sludge of fury.

"The hell it will! No child of mine is going to be raised a *bastard*!" he thundered, slamming a fist down on the table.

Ivy flinched. Her eyes grew wide and she reared back in her chair. Fear lined her face as her breathing turned shallow and rapid.

Noble quickly reeled in his fury as he inwardly cursed himself. The last thing he wanted to do was scare her. When he finally harnessed his anger, he sent her an apologetic grimace.

"I'm sorry. I didn't mean to lose my shit." She accepted his apology with a tentative nod, but Noble didn't miss the tinges of doubt and fear still lingering in her wary stare. "I need some time to think...to process all of this. Can we table our discussion until tomorrow night?"

"There's nothing left to discuss." She shrugged slightly and sent him a pained expression. "I meant what I said, Noble. I don't want anything from you. I won't trap you, tie you down, or change your life. All I want is to bring this child into the world and be the best mother possible."

Not bothering to hide his mounting frustration, he pinned her with a steely stare. "Maybe the man who *supposedly* helped create that life inside you wants the chance to be the best father he can be as well."

The look of sorrow mixed with worry lining her face filled him with pain. All he wanted to do was erase it…drag her upstairs and replace the visible tumult with spine-melting pleasure.

But the fragile fate of his future and freedom, or rather, the lack of it, lay in the air, thick and suffocating. He definitely needed time to think, but he couldn't achieve that while his wildest, wickedest wet dream was peering up at him with those intoxicating eyes…the same eyes that haunted every second of his existence.

He stood and sucked in a ragged breath. "I'll come by after work tomorrow night."

Then he turned and started toward the front door.

"Noble," Ivy called out.

Her breathless tone made him pause mid-stride and sent pulses of electricity skipping over his flesh. He planted his feet to keep from turning around. Noble knew if he looked back, he'd take her…take her up against the wall, across the table, and down on the goddamn floor, driving deep inside her sinful pussy all night long.

"Yeah?" he replied in a hoarse, gravelly voice.

Long, silent seconds ticked by before she realized he couldn't face her.

"I'm sorry this is so…complicated. But it's…um, it's really good to…to see you again."

The sound of her cracking voice pounded a massive dent in Noble's heart. He squeezed his eyes shut and swallowed the lump of emotion blocking his throat. "It's good to see you, too, darlin'."

*Good* was a gross understatement.

In that moment, he knew he couldn't just walk out and leave her broken, scared, and resolved to shut him out.

Against his better judgment, Noble turned.

The tears streaming down Ivy's face as she quietly sobbed ripped him in two.

Heart aching, he ate up the distance between them in four long strides. Gripping her by the shoulder, Noble lifted her from the chair.

The instant her soft, warm flesh melted beneath his fingers, he jolted at the sense of rightness that settled over him. The cacophony of shock, uncertainty, anger, and fear screaming through him grew eerily silent.

It was as if he'd found the missing pieces of his soul.

Shoving the terrifying implications aside, Noble slid a hand to her nape, slanted his lips over hers, and laid siege to her soft lips. Urgently, greedily, he ate at her, swallowing every whimper and moan rolling off the back of her throat while he unleashed months of pent-up hunger and passion he'd ached to bestow on her once again.

Splaying his palm to the small of her back, he pulled her in tight, flush against his hips, letting her feel how madly he'd missed her. The second he pushed past her lips and swept his tongue along the familiar silky heat of her mouth, Ivy mewled and melded herself to his chest.

He ate at her like a ravenous animal.

Drank in her life force as if he were a fucking vampire.

But it wasn't enough. It wasn't ever going to be enough. He needed more...not only sexually but emotionally. Noble wanted to own and possess every cell in her soft, lush body. Right. Fucking. Now.

Like a punch to the gut, awareness slammed home, hard.

*No way!*

He wasn't built for the confines of monogamy, marriage, or white picket fences. All he could promise Ivy was a good time, and dammit, she deserved so much more. From left field, the thought of someone else providing all the things he couldn't, filling Ivy's life with love and *commitment*, slammed a spike of jealousy through Noble's system.

The scrape of Ivy's sharp fingernails gliding down his back yanked him from the inky ledge of insecurity and sent sparks of demand crackling down his spine. With a moan, he cupped her scalp, tilted her head back, and delved deep as their tongues danced in urgent desperation.

"Well, goodness sakes. My apologies. I didn't mean to interrupt what looks to be the prequel to a screaming good time any minute now."

The sound of Trudy's familiar drawl scraped his flesh as if he'd been rolled in barbed wire. Noble tore from Ivy's mouth as she abruptly jerked back, blinking the glassy vestiges of lust from her eyes while a bright red blush colored her face.

"I-I'm sorry...." she sputtered breathlessly. "We...err, I'm sorry, the bakery is closed on Mondays."

"Is it? I didn't realize that. Darn." Trudy copped a feigned pout before turning a venomous glare on Noble. "But I must say, it's a relief to know that the rumors about you aren't true."

"Rumors?" He arched a brow, biting back the slew of curses sitting on his tongue.

"You know...that the great Noble Grayson has gone and taken himself right off the market. Why, all the women of Haven are cryin' in their pillows, missing the magical ways you make them scream your name." She lowered her voice as she flashed him a hungry smile. "Me included."

Noble's heart stopped.

*Son. Of. A. Bitch.*

He didn't have to look over at Ivy to gauge her reaction, he could feel the pain exploding off her and singeing his flesh. He'd have to do some serious damage control, but had no clue where to start.

"Speaking of which...Calvin is leaving in the morning to

attend a dental seminar in Houston. He won't be back until late Sunday night. You don't mind me giving you a call if I have another pesky leak that only that big, thick pipe of yours can fix, do you, sugar?" Trudy purred as she inched closer to him.

Noble held up his hand and took a step back. "You're a married woman. You already know the answer to that. Like Ivy said, the bakery's closed. You need to leave...*now*!"

Trudy sent him a caustic smirk before turning a catty stare on Ivy.

She was no longer blushing. Instead, she'd donned an emotionless mask. But Noble couldn't miss the flicker of wounded rejection in her blue eyes.

"So Monday is your day off, sugar? Well, you'll definitely have fun with this big ol' cowboy. He knows the most creative and unique talents guaranteed to get a girl...*off* that I've ever experienced." Trudy chuckled dryly as she lifted her hand and waved. "Toot-a-loo y'all."

Noble briefly closed his eyes and sucked in a ragged breath, picturing the shallow grave he longed to toss the bitch's body in. When the front door snicked shut, Ivy lifted her chin. Noble wanted to howl at the same rigid, closed-off posture she'd worn earlier.

"You need to leave as well. I have work to do," Ivy announced coldly.

Noble wasn't going anywhere. Not until he smoothed over the landmines Trudy had just detonated. "I've never been a choirboy, but you need to know that since I returned from Las Vegas, I haven't been with any other—"

"Don't!" Ivy barked. "I don't care who you have or haven't slept with."

"Dammit! I care. You mean something to..." His words trailed off as he tried to not only identify but also put into words the feelings lashing him.

A blank, empty expression lined Ivy's face. "Take care of yourself, Noble."

Her dismissal stung, but when she turned and walked through a set of steel swinging doors, it gutted him.

Noble knew he could march though those damn doors and force her to listen to him. But the pulsating fear that she would reject him was a dragon he wasn't quite ready to try and slay. He'd been dealt enough ruthless blows for one day. Inviting another was just plain masochistic.

Forcing his feet to move, he left the bakery and stepped out into the fading afternoon sun. Across the street, Nate strolled from the bar and nodded toward his truck. Noble's knee-jerk reaction was to brush his brother off so he could go someplace alone to sort his shit out before getting an ugly drunk on.

*I know.* Nate mentally invaded. *But in your current state of mind, I'm not leaving you unsupervised and to your own devices. God only knows what you'll get yourself into next.*

*Can't be any worse than the mess I'm already in, can it?* Noble wordlessly asked as he jogged across the street.

Nate let out a snort as he pulled a set of keys from the pocket of his jeans. "Sure it can. You could have accidently knocked up Trudy instead."

Nate's stomach pitched and bile bubbled up in the back of his throat. He shook his head and groaned. "*Allegedly.* Did you really have to go and put that cherry on top of my shit sundae?"

"Just trying to help you keep this clusterfuck in perspective." Nate chuckled as they climbed into his truck.

"Get me out of this town for a while."

"Any place in particular?"

"Someplace where I can't give a fuck," he replied.

Neither said another word as Nate turned, drove off, leaving Haven behind.

When he passed the driveway to the ranch, Noble knew then where his brother was taking him. He didn't have the heart to tell his twin that he'd already been to the creek twice this week. It hadn't helped.

## CHAPTER FOURTEEN

IVY CLENCHED HER jaw and gripped the stainless steel counter. The dampness between her throbbing legs coupled with her still-tingling lips bore the unwelcome reminder of how effortlessly Noble Grayson unraveled her.

Less than ten minutes alone with the man and she'd melted against him, let him drown her in desire, and all but handed him an engraved invitation to rape and pillage her fucking heart and soul.

Then, like a scene out of a bad soap opera, that horny, man-grabbing bitch Trudy had waltzed in. It wasn't bad enough that she'd caught them swapping tonsils, but she'd taken immense pleasure informing Ivy that the man in her arms—the same one who'd impregnated her—was Haven's resident man-whore.

Fat tears slid down her cheeks, but Ivy angrily brushed them away. "Just when I think I can't possibly do anything more foolish…"

*I've never claimed to be a choirboy.* Noble's whiskey-smooth voice echoed in her ears.

"No shit. But you could have at least warned me that you were a walking, talking come dispenser, you asshole!"

With a growl, she plucked up a loaf of bread cooling on the rack. Cupping the butter crust in the palm of her hand, Ivy heaved it across the room. With a muffled thud, the bread splattered against the wall before breaking apart and sliding down to the ground. The oily splatter left behind and the broken crumbs littering the floor were sadly reminiscent of her life. Shaking the growing despondency careening through her system, to keep herself from sliding back into that familiar and unforgiving black hole of depression, she clenched her jaw and grabbed a large mixing bowl. As she measured, mixed, baked, and iced, Ivy dragged out the mantras she'd used to mentally and emotionally prop herself up during the trial.

She couldn't escape the fallout of gossip her unwed pregnancy would induce, but she'd keep the promise she'd made to Haven's reputed *sex-god*, and keep his name from being dragged in the mud alongside hers.

The notion that Noble had probably slept with half the town burned Ivy's gut with a jealousy that possessed zero rationale. She couldn't help but wonder how many other women in town were raising Noble's *love child*. From now on, Ivy would be looking at every kid she encountered and wondering if they shared Noble's DNA. The idea of, eighteen to twenty years from now, parents needing a sequence profile before allowing their child to marry anyone local made Ivy shudder.

"That son of a bitch needs a vasectomy so that, five generations down the line, this place isn't teeming with three-eyed, six-toed inbreds," she groused, slapping chocolate cake batter into several round pans.

After she'd placed the pans in the oven and set the timer, Ivy's cell phone chimed. Plucking up the device, she checked the caller ID. A low, suffering moan slid off her tongue when she saw it was her mom.

*Today's already been one giant clusterfuck. I might as well stick a cherry on top of it all and tell Janice she's going to be a grandma.*

Sucking in a deep breath, Ivy answered the call. "Hey, Mom. What's up?"

"Obviously, you haven't heard the news."

The anxiety lacing her mom's words sent Ivy's heart beating faster. "No. I've been in the kitchen baking…" *and sorting out the shit show called Ivy's life.* "What news?"

"Eugene McMillian's wife committed suicide this morning," Janice softly answered.

"Oh, wow. I'm sorry to hear that. That's so—"

"Sad, yes. But speculation and accusations are being lobbed like bombs."

"What speculation and accusations?"

"Oh, honey. I don't know how to tell you this."

"Just open your mouth and say the words, Mom," Ivy urged, growing increasingly nervous.

"Eugene is accusing you of ruining him financially and professionally. He says your lawsuit devastated his life and marriage. He claims *you* caused his wife to take her own life."

Ivy closed her eyes and shook her head. "That's insane. I didn't force him to attack me."

"I know. The man has obviously lost his grip on reality, but he claimed that his lawyer will be filing charges soon against…you."

"Me?" Ivy barked. "What kind of charges, for fuck's sake?"

Janice ignored her improper language for once. "Murder, honey."

Ivy's knees crumpled and she slid to the floor as panic seized her.

"M-murder? B-but…I didn't kill her. She took her own life."

"Don't freak out," Janice instructed sternly. "Dad's been on the phone with Margaret Neill since the interview aired on television a few minutes ago. She's already researching similar cases but wants to meet with you tomorrow. You need to be back here in Dallas by three o'clock."

"Tomorrow?" Ivy screeched as her mind sprinted a mile a minute. "Mom, I can't just leave. I have a business to run. Ask Margaret to call me, because there's no way McMillian can try to sue me for his wife's death. I can't believe any judge in their right mind would clear time on their docket for such a ridiculous and asinine case."

"I know… I know, darling," Janice placated. "I'll talk to your father and ask him to call Margaret again. If you can't come to her, maybe we can all come to you."

"Yes. Please try to make that happen." *That way they can all see my pregnant belly at once. Fuck!* "Mom, there's—"

"Wait a second, darling. There's something more you need to know."

"If you're going to tell me that McMillian's dick fell off and he wants to sue me for that, too, I'm hanging up, packing my bags, and running the hell away."

"At least you're keeping a sense of humor," Janice drawled. "No, dear. But it's obvious that Eugene has been watching you. Either that or he discovered your name on the business license you filed on the bakery. Or he simply hired someone to keep tabs on you, but he knows you're in Haven and that you own Sweet Flours."

*Watching me?* A shiver of fear rippled up Ivy's spine. Refusing to let it pull her under a tide of paranoia, she rationally compartmentalized the information her mother had shared.

"Okay, that's more than a little creepy. But the license is public record. I don't know why this all matters. I moved to—" Then it suddenly dawned on her. "Oh, shit! McMillian mentioned *Haven* and *Sweet Flours* by name during the interview, didn't he?"

"Yes, baby, he did," Janice confirmed in a whisper.

Enveloped in a thick, suffocating blanket of dread, Ivy sprinted from the kitchen straight to the plate-glass window at the front of the shop. With her heart in her throat, she peered out for any sign of the privacy-raping news crews.

"They're not here," she said, exhaling in relief.

"Not *yet*," Janice bid in a foreboding tone. "But by morning… Come home, honey. We'll protect you like we did before from those evil vultures until this whole mess blows over."

Like a soft, cuddly security blanket, her mom's offer was beyond tempting. But Ivy had worked too long and hard to be knocked on her ass and start wallowing in a pit of fear and insecurity again.

"No. Mom, I can't keep hiding every time life throws a left

hook."

"Oh, sweetheart, you've grown so strong. Daddy and I were so worried that we were going to lose you to...the darkness a-again." Her mom's voice cracked.

As her mother's sobs echoed in Ivy's ears, tears spilled from her eyes. She'd been so lost in her own self-loathing, embarrassment, and inability to cope with the upheaval of the trial, she hadn't known the toll her despondency had taken on the ones who loved her most.

Lifting her chin, Ivy wiped her tears and drew in a deep breath. "You're not going to lose me again, Mom. I promise. I'll do what I can to keep the vultures away, but I'm not hiding from them or anyone else ever again."

Janice sniffed. "I'm so proud of you, Ivy...so proud of the woman you are."

A pang of guilt stabbed Ivy's heart.

Janice wasn't going to be proud for much longer.

"Mom, there's something I need to tell you." The flutter in her voice caused Ivy to cringe.

"Yes?"

"While we were in Vegas for Celina's non-wedding... I-I met a man."

"What kind of man?"

"A nice, handsome, incredibly sexy man," *who, ironically, not only lives in Haven but is also the town slut.* Ivy decided to keep that inauspicious tidbit of information to herself. "Mom...I'm..."

"Oh, lord, no! Do. Not. Tell. Me. You're. Pregnant."

Ivy closed her eyes and sighed. She'd hoped that by some miracle of fate, the news might bring her mom a sliver of joy. But the disapproving tone of Janice's voice removed any and all chance of that happening. She lifted her lashes and exhaled a heavy sigh. "Okay, then I won't tell you. Let me know what Margaret says. I'll talk to you—"

"Prudence Ivy Addison! Don't you *dare* hang up on your

mother."

"Call me *Prudence* again and not only will I hang up, I'll stop speaking to you for a year!" Ivy growled.

"Oh, god... You really *are* pregnant. Your hormones have already gone so wonky that you're barking at me," Janice groaned.

*Well, this certainly explains why you've been so goddamn moody lately.* Ivy couldn't help but smirk as Gina's words flowed through her.

"Yes, Mom. I am."

Several long, silent seconds passed. Then Ivy heard her mom sniff again. "I-I don't know what to say, darling. A part of me is jumping up and down, screaming like a five-year-old on Christmas morning. But the sensible, protecting mother in me is a hot mess, worried half out of my mind. What on earth are you going to do? Have you been in contact with this man from Vegas...the father? Does he know you're pregnant? And if so, does he plan to marry you and make an honest woman out of you?"

Her mom's underlying joy of being a grandmother was like a key that unlocked Ivy's soul. For the first time in her life, Ivy saw the woman through a whole new set of eyes.

Yes, Janice was an uptight. She'd been hereditarily conditioned to conform to the rigorous rules of a gentile southern society. And while her moral code was straighter than an arrow, Ivy realized that all the lectures she and Celina had endured about proper behavior weren't to point out their numerous flaws but to try and make her daughters better, stronger, more self-assured women.

Ivy loved her mom more that exact instant than ever before in her whole life.

"Mom," she began, praying she didn't start bawling, "though I didn't show it at the trial, you raised me to be brave and independent. It's the twentieth-first century. I don't need a man to raise this child. I'm quite capable of providing a safe, loving home for him or her on my own."

"Oh, honey," Janice groaned. "You did contact him and tell him about the baby, and that prick told you to kiss off, didn't he?"

Ivy sputtered out a laugh. It was the first time she'd ever heard such an improper word roll off her mother's tongue. "No. He didn't turn into a *prick* and tell me to kiss off. I told him I didn't want a damn thing from him and to take care of himself. So in essence, I'm the prickette who told *him* to kiss off."

"Oh, Ivy," she chided. "If he was good enough to…to rumple the sheets with, he should have been good enough for you to marry."

"Mom—"

"I'm not finished. I'm proud that you're not willing to bind yourself to someone you don't love, but honestly…why didn't you use protection?" Janice paused and sighed softly. "Well, what's done is done. Don't worry about McMillian, the baby, or the deadbeat who got you pregnant. We'll take each day as it comes, like we always do. And Daddy and I will be behind you a hundred and ten percent."

"I love you, Mom."

"I love you, too, sweet baby girl." A tiny squeal escaped her mom. "I'm going to be a gramma. Oh, my…goodness. Daddy or I will be in touch soon."

Ivy silently giggled. "I'll wait for your call."

After saying their goodbyes, Ivy ended the call, and scanned the street again.

Now that the sun was down, Haven resembled a ghost town. Everyone was safely ensconced in their homes, eating dinner, sipping wine, watching television, or maybe already snoring. They were all blissfully unaware that, because of Ivy, a media circus was about to invade their quiet little town.

Remorse and dread consumed her.

Across the street, in the window of the Hangover, a neon sign blinked blue and red, like the lights of a police car. A light bulb went off in Ivy's head as she scurried to the kitchen. While she waited the last three minutes for the cakes to finish baking, she tugged off her apron and donned a jacket that hid her stomach. When the timer beeped, she removed the cakes and turned off the ovens, grabbed her keys, and hurried to the bar.

As she gripped the doorknob of the Hangover, Ivy's pulse quickened. Angst, prickly and warm, swam up from her toes. She wasn't looking forward to facing Noble again this soon, but the clock was ticking, and time was of the essence.

Squaring her shoulders, Ivy lifted her chin and pulled the door open. When she stepped inside, she saw Nate and Gina at the bar, laughing.

"Hey," Gina called out, more subdued than usual. Worry lined her face as she studied Ivy. "You doing okay?"

"Actually? No. Do you have time to talk for a minute?"

"Of course." Gina turned and tilted her face up at Nate. "Baby, you don't mind handling the bar while we have a little girl time, do you?"

"Not at all." Nate sent Ivy a warm smile before daring a glance at the pool table.

Ivy followed his line of sight, and saw Noble tip back a bottle of beer. Butterflies dipped and swooped in her belly as she watched his throat work, draining the bottle in one long gulp. The man beside him holding a pool cue—with matching emerald eyes and dark hair—slapped Noble on the back and handed him another brew.

As if sensing her stare, he lifted his head. Their eyes locked for a long, emotion-filled second before he shook his head and lifted the fresh bottle to his lips and chugged.

"Come on, honey," Gina whispered suddenly at Ivy's side. "He's well on his way to getting seriously fucked up. But don't worry. Sawyer, the one with the pool stick, is his brother. He and Nate are keeping a close eye on him.

Ivy sucked in a ragged breath and followed Gina behind the bar and through a wide doorway that led to a small kitchen. After pausing to grab a couple bottles of water from a large industrial refrigerator, Gina shoved the metal back door open. They stepped out into the alley and walked to a picnic table situated beneath a tall oak tree.

Ivy took a large gulp of water and swallowed tightly. "Earlier, when I accused you of keeping secrets, you reminded me that I'd been keeping them, too."

"I remember," Gina assured solemnly.

"I need your help, but first I need to tell you my secret."

Gina nodded. Her eyes sparkled with unshed tears. "I'm honored that you trust me with them. What you tell me will stay right here," she vowed, laying a hand to her heart.

"Thank you." Ivy choked on the realization that she hadn't lost her best friend after all the crazy chaos earlier. She reached for Gina's other hand and gave it a tight squeeze.

Ivy licked her lips and drew in a deep breath and then proceeded to tell the woman everything. Every detail about Eugene McMillian, the attack, the lawsuit, the paparazzi invading her life, and the depression she'd struggled to overcome. When Ivy was finished, she sat back and let out a heavy sigh.

"Jesus, woman. You've been through the fucking wringer. You're one strong bitch...and I say that with the utmost love and respect." Gina chuckled and sobered. "I get it now. I understand why you told Noble that you didn't want him, and for him to take a hike."

Ivy cringed. "Is that what he said?"

"No, Noble didn't tell me that. Nate did. After Noble left the bakery, he and Nate took a drive. When they came back to the bar, Nate said a few things, but I was able to read between the lines."

"It's not that I don't want him. I'm just not going to trap him or mess up his life. Besides, Trudy came in while we were...um...oh, hell. Noble was kissing my damn lips off," Ivy confessed with a wave of her hand. "She made sure I knew what kind of reputation Noble has around here...how he gets around...*a lot*...like with any woman who'll spread her damn legs."

Gina chuckled and shook her head. "He used to get around...*a lot*. But when he came back from Vegas, no one but Nate knew that Noble had lost all interest in getting nasty with anyone but *you*."

*Huh. So he didn't feed me a line of bullshit after all.* Ivy tucked the information away to dissect later.

"Yeah, well. I'm not looking for a life partner or even a boyfriend, so it'll be a whole lot less complicated if he just goes on with his life."

"God, you two are so much alike it's not fucking funny. Well, it is, but..." Gina winked.

"Yeah, well, life around here is about to get real crazy."

"You having twins?"

"Hush your mouth," Ivy scolded. "No, I just got off the phone with my mom and there's more to the ongoing saga of Eugene McMillian."

She filled Gina in on the newest details and the vultures who'd soon be swooping into Haven and ripping her life open again.

"But if they find out I'm pregnant with Noble's baby, they'll tear his life open and plaster every morsel of information they dig up on him all over the news. I can't let that happen to him. I need you and Nate to help me protect him."

Gina nodded thoughtfully before a sly smile curled her lips. "First of all, Noble...hell, all the Graysons are honest, good, hardworking, and compassionate people. But if you mess with one of 'em, you might as well just slap a hornet's nest with a stick, 'cause they're all gonna come out of the nest, swoop down, and whoop ass. Big-time. Honey, we don't need to worry about Noble. What we need to worry about is keeping those fucking reporters off *your* nipples."

"That's why I came to talk to you. I can handle them, I think. But I need to warn the sheriff and let him know what's about to happen to this quiet town. But I don't know him. I don't know if he'll want or even be able to keep them out or stop them from turning Haven into a three ring circus."

"You haven't met Jasper yet?" Ivy shook her head. "Oh, honey. He'll do everything in his power to keep those bastards away from you and out of Haven. It's my turn to tell you a little story now."

When she was through, Ivy's heart ached for what Gina had endured. Once again, her wimpy baby hormones had tears spilling from Ivy's eyes. She stood and hugged her friend fiercely before they turned and walked back inside the Hangover.

While she sat at the bar, nursing a soda as Gina called Jasper, Ivy could feel Noble's stare raking her flesh. She couldn't let herself even take a peek at him for fear someone might connect them somehow.

Less than three minutes later, the sheriff strolled into the bar. He tipped his hat as Gina made introductions, then he escorted Ivy to an isolated table near the front of the bar.

They'd no more sat down than Noble's loud and angry voice slammed through the air. "What the fuck does she need to talk to Jasper for? What's going on? Is someone fucking with her? Whoever it is, I'll kill 'em…I'll rip their fucking head off and shit down their throat."

Jasper arched his brows at her. "I wasn't aware that Noble was a *friend* of yours?"

"He is…sort of," she ambiguously replied.

"Maybe you ought to go back and try to calm him down before I'm forced to slap a set of cuffs on him and let him sleep it off in a quiet cell."

Ivy blanched. "I'll be right back."

She ran to the back of the bar to find Nate and Sawyer wrapping Noble in a bear hug. Both men were whispering in his ear, trying to calm their irate and extremely inebriated brother down. The minute his blurry eyes fell into focus on Ivy, Noble shrugged his brothers off like a couple of annoying fleas and stormed her way.

"What the hell are you talking to Jasper about?" Noble demanded like an overbearing caveman.

He was so…forceful…so masculine…so fucking barbarian, a shiver of arousal sped through her. Ivy shoved her ill-timed hormonal explosion aside and narrowed her eyes.

"Don't piss me off, Noble. You won't like what happens next," she warned with all the bluster she could feign. "The sheriff and I are having a *private* discussion that doesn't concern you."

"Everything about you concerns me, woman," he growled.

"Lower your voice," she hissed. "We don't need the whole damn town knowing we're *friends*."

"Friends?" A bitter laugh slid from his lips. "Darlin', we're a whole hell of a lot more than *friends*. You honestly think I give a good goddamn what people think…what the fuck they say? Far as I'm concerned, every one of them can kiss my happy ass." Noble's slurred words carried through the air as if they were coming through a public address system, loud and resonating. "All I care about is *you*! Dammit, Ivy, haven't you figured that out yet?"

The sincerity glistening in his emerald-green eyes made her heart clutch. The gooey feelings unfurling inside made her want to wrap him in her arms and haul his *happy ass* across the street and straight to her bed.

"Noble, we'll talk about that later. Right now, I need you to chill out before Jasper hauls your drunken butt to jail. All right?"

When Noble started shaking his head like a petulant two-year-old, Ivy bit her lip to keep from laughing. "Not until you tell me what's going on. Is someone bothering you? If there is, you don't need Jasper. I'll take care of 'em per-mann…permer…permanently."

"Don't go grabbing your shotgun and shovel, Mr. Reaper. I've got—"

"My momma's got a shotgun. And boy howdy…she's gonna

use it on me when she hears what we've gone and done."

Ivy's mouth went dry and her heart rate tripled. "What do you mean when she *hears*? Noble, she's not going to ever find out…no one can *ever* know about…" she said in a whisper.

*Why am I'm trying to reason with a drunk man?*

"Forget it." Ivy shook her head. "Just keep your voice down before the whole town puts two and two together."

"Two and two makes four, but we made one," he said, pressing a hand to her stomach. That and the wicked grin he flashed made her core clutch in need.

This man was her Kryptonite in every way possible.

*I'm so fucked!*

"Shhh. We did, but we don't want people knowing about that, so *please*…just let me go talk to Jasper now and I'll talk—"

"Tomorrow, dammit. I told you we were going to talk again tomorrow. Write that down so you don't forget."

"Okay, I'll write it down," Ivy quickly promised before sending him a pleading stare. "Just be quiet. When I'm done talking to Jasper, I'll come back and talk to you. All right?"

"Only if you let me kiss you again…let me taste those plump, sweet lips of yours." He wobbled slightly as he reached out and stroked a finger down her face. The heat of his touch sent a wall of fire converging over her.

"We'll talk about *that* tomorrow, too. Now, go on back and play pool with your brothers."

"You damn well better let me kiss you again, woman. 'Cause you've got the hottest, softest, most intoxa…intoxilicatling mouth I ever tasted. And on top of that…you're fucking gorgeous, too."

If she had time, Ivy would use his alcohol-saturated brain against him. Use it like a truth serum so he'd spill his guts and tell her how he *truly* felt about her. But dammit, the clock was ticking and the sheriff wasn't going to wait on her forever.

"Okay. I'll kiss you…someplace private."

"My cock's private." Noble's eyes smoldered with promise

and flickered in mischief. He leaned in close to her ear. His moist breath made her clit throb and her nipples draw up like pebbles. "I love the way you kiss my cock, Ivy."

She quickly cast a wary glance around the room. Though all eyes were on her and Noble, only Sawyer and Nate—struggling to keep from laughing—seemed privy to Noble's salacious words.

"Noble, if you don't shut up, I'm never kissing you again."

"Aww, darlin'. Don't go breaking my heart and sayin' things like that. It's not nice."

Losing what little patience she had left, Ivy cupped Noble's face. "Then give me ten minutes to talk to Jasper, and I won't have to break your heart. Got it?"

Noble's body grew taut and she felt a tiny shudder slide through him. His eyes and nostrils flared the way they did when she gripped his beautiful, thick cock. He gently placed his hands over hers and held her palms to his cheeks. "Okay, but if he touches you, I'm gonna have to kill him. Understood?"

"He's not going to touch me."

"That's right. Nobody touches you but *me!*" Noble barked.

A collective gasp went up around the bar. Ivy issued an inward groan. Noble might as well have tattooed his name across her damn forehead. There'd be no way to protect him or their baby now.

Wearing identical concerned expressions, Nate and Sawyer moved in alongside their loud-mouthed brother.

"Come on, man. It's your turn to break so we can get our next game started," Nate said, trying to entice Noble back to the pool table.

"I'm already broken," he murmured before pointing his finger at Ivy and bellowing, "She's the one who ruined me…Ivy…her, right there. That's my poison Ivy. She broke me wide open and is putting me back together. She's fucking amazing. I'm a lucky sum'bitch. Ya hear me? I'm the fucking lucky one."

Ivy prayed a sinkhole would open beneath her feet suck her all the way to China. But no such luck. Instead, Gina sent her a wide grin as Nate and Sawyer led Noble away. When Ivy gathered enough courage to look behind her, every person in the place was grinning like a loon...even the damn sheriff. Doing her best to ignore the increasing buzz of murmurs filling the air, Ivy rushed to join Jasper at the table.

He leaned in and arched his brows. "Fucking amazing indeed if you managed to get under Noble Grayson's skin to the point that he's spilling his soul in public."

Ivy closed her eyes and exhaled. "He's drunk and...it's...complicated."

"It always is, sweetheart." Jasper chuckled. "Now what can I do for you?"

"Gina says you and Nate are the only two men she trusts with her life."

A melancholy smile curled on the man's lips. "If there's something you need to tell me, you have my word it'll stay between us."

Once again, Ivy began spilling her secrets, which, ironically, was much easier the second time around. When she informed him that the news crews were about to turn his town upside down, Jasper leaned back in his chair and grimly nodded.

"Don't you worry about a thing, pretty lady. I can handle the circus coming our way," he announced confidently, then stood and held out his hand.

Ivy thanked him profusely and shook his hand.

He turned to leave, then paused. "I've noticed Emmett Hill likes to visit your bakery every morning. You mind if I park him and his 1945 Browning A5 inside your place during the day?"

Ivy blinked, slightly confused. "No, I don't mind. But is he able to...shoot without killing me or my customers?"

Jasper chuckled. "He shot the shit out of Barbara Rhyme's plate-glass window not long ago. I'll tell him not to load it. That should be enough of a deterrent to keep the reporters back, especially once they see how badly his hands shake."

Ivy chuckled. The sheriff was a warmhearted man.

"Best have Gina brew some strong coffee and start shoving it down Noble's gullet. He's going to want to have his wits about him come morning."

"I'll let her know. Thank you again, Sheriff."

"No. Now that I'm keeping your secret, you have to call me Jasper." He dropped a brief glance at her stomach and smirked. "Guess that's the reason Noble's back there getting his drunk on, huh?"

Ivy felt a blush rush to her cheeks. As promised, she neither confirmed nor denied the sheriff's probing question.

"Don't fret. The Grayson boys were raised right. Loyal as the day is long and a force to be reckoned with if you ever get on their bad side. Noble will figure things out…probably a lot sooner if what you say is coming arrives."

"Oh, they're coming, all right," Ivy resentfully assured.

"Don't fret about that, either. I'll keep that nonsense under control."

There certainly wasn't a shortage of men in Haven who liked to take control.

Jasper shoved his hat back on his head, flashed her a supportive nod, and left as her cell phone chimed. Ivy plucked it from her pocket and read the text message.

> **Mom:** We're coming to you. We'll be in Haven tomorrow, late morning. Oh, and FYI—Daddy doesn't know about the baby. He should hear the news from you. But don't worry; he'll be over the moon like I am! OMG I'M GOING TO BE A GRAMMA! LOL Love you, darling.

Everyone was telling her not to worry, but Ivy couldn't help it. Anxiety and dread chased through her like a cheetah after a gazelle, spiking even higher when she turned toward the pool table.

Noble sat in a chair, sipping a cup of coffee and undressing her with his eyes.

Sucking in a soft gasp, Ivy tried to quiet her hormones and

started in his direction on shaky legs.

"Where's my kiss?" he asked in a low, sensual growl.

His green eyes smoldered.

The heat pouring off him was far more intoxicating than any liquor in the place. Goose bumps exploded over her flesh.

"Not here." There were too many curious stares fixed on them.

"Fine. I'll follow you back over to the bakery, where we can be alone." His voice was surprisingly sober compared to twenty minutes ago. "Then after I kiss you breathless, you're going to tell me what you and Jasper were talking about."

The notion of kissing his warm, firm lips again sent a rush of desire to dampen her folds.

*God help me, what do I do now?*

# CHAPTER FIFTEEN

Noble set his coffee cup down and stood, watching as indecision played across Ivy's face. He steeled himself for her to tell him to go to hell after the suggestion they head over to the bakery to be alone came spilling out of his mouth.

*Suggestion my ass,* Nate scoffed via their private twin link. *That was a fucking order if I've ever heard one. You're lucky she didn't kick you square in the nuts.*

*I need to find out if she's filed a fucking restraining order against me, asshole. Now get outta my head,* Noble mentally demanded without peeling his stare off Ivy's.

She'd been so fucking adamant during their initial conversation at the bakery...adamant and as fucking hardheaded as he was. Noble suspected she'd never asked anyone for help in her whole life.

So the minute Jasper had entered the bar and led her to a quiet table for two, Noble's imagination had gone into overdrive.

If Ivy had gotten some wild hair up her ass and wanted to block him from her life with a damn restraining order, Noble would never be able to prove that she could lean on him. The fear had reached up and grabbed him by the balls with such fury that it extinguished the alcohol buzz anesthetizing his system.

"I don't think it's a good idea for us to be alone again right now," Ivy stated quietly.

"Why not? If you're worried I might knock you up or something...well, too late." He smirked, hoping to break the ice and worm a little smile out of her.

Instead, Ivy dropped her lashes as her cheeks turned a rosy

shade of pink.

*Dammit. That didn't work.*

Noble decided to go with honesty instead of humor. "Look. I need to know what that was all about between you and Jasper or I'm going to lose my damn mind."

"I already told you…it has nothing to do with you."

*Son of a bitch! She is getting a restraining order. No. Fuck. No.*

Tamping down his panic, Noble sucked in a deep breath. "All right. Then that means it has something to do with *you*…that you're in some kind of trouble, which makes it ten times worse. Knowing someone or something is happening to you makes me want to spill blood and mount some asshole's head on a spike and other illegal, crazy caveman shit."

Ivy tensed and nervously flitted a glance around the people in the bar. The fact that she didn't deny his claim or try to placate him set off internal warning bells and buzzers. Unwilling to take no for an answer, Noble stepped in close and cupped her elbow. Little surges of electricity marched up his arm, like they did every fucking time he touched her.

"There's nothing you can do to prevent it, Noble."

She might as well have told him to stop breathing. There wasn't anything he wouldn't do to *prevent* whatever had upset her so badly she needed Jasper's help.

"Oh, yeah? Watch me, little girl." He cinched her elbow tighter. "Come on. We're going for a drive."

"I-I can't," she stammered, trying to pull from his grasp. He reluctantly released her but remained in her personal space. "I have a million things to do before I open for business in the morning. My family is coming up to… I'm sorry. I have to get back to the bakery."

"Then I'll help you…bake stuff."

She blinked up at him and finally graced him with a grin that set him on fire in a whole different way.

"You know how to bake?"

"Well…no, but…I can learn. You can teach me."

"Go back and finish playing pool with your brothers. We'll talk tomorrow."

Noble began shaking his head even before she'd finished dismissing him. "If someone is bothering you enough to get Jasper involved, then I'm going to live up to my name and be your *noble* bodyguard."

She relaxed and softened as the tension slid from her tiny frame. A flicker of gratitude danced in her pale blue eyes. "Fine. As long as you don't kiss me."

"Oh? Why's that?"

"Because it's distracting and I have work to do."

*Liar.*

"That's not the reason."

"No, but it's the only one you're getting from me, right now."

A crooked grin tugged one corner of his mouth as he leaned in close to her ear. "You're afraid I'll kiss you right out of those skintight pants you're wearing, aren't you?"

"You've already done that."

"Oh, I know. I can't ever forget. That's why I'm dying to do it again," he replied in a low, hungry growl.

Ivy's body trembled.

Yeah, she wanted him as badly as he did her. Until he discovered a way to thoroughly annihilate her walls, he'd bide his time…or at least try to. She was his heroin, crack, and any other kind of addictive vice with the potential to totally destroy him, which only made him crave her even more.

When he leaned back, Ivy's eyes were slightly dilated. Her lush, full breasts rose and fell with every shallow breath spilling over her lips. It took all the willpower he possessed to not toss her over his shoulder, sprint across the street, strip her bare, and toss her into bed. He wanted to make every filthy, ball-churning fantasy that he'd stroked his cock to all these months finally come true, over and over again.

He could see the indecision warring with hunger glistening in her eyes. He had to act fast and waved a hand toward the door. "Lead the way, darlin'."

When they stepped outside, Ivy sent a furtive glance up and down the street as if looking for someone to step from the shadows and carry her away. As they crossed the street, Emmett Hill hurried toward them, trusty Browning rifle slung over his shoulder.

"Hunting Bigfoot again tonight, Emmett?" Noble asked while Ivy unlocked the door of the shop.

"Nope. Jasper stopped while I was watering my azaleas and told me trouble was coming Ivy's way. So I grabbed my gun and hurried down here fast as my old feet could take me."

*What the hell?*

Noble narrowed his eyes, pinning her with a barely civil stare. "How come Emmett knows what's happening, but I'm left in the dark?"

Ignoring his question completely, Ivy turned a brittle smile on the old man. "I'm good for tonight, Emmett. Tomorrow I might need reinforcements though."

There was an almost carefree lilt in her voice, which pissed Noble off even more than being left out of the loop.

"Alrighty then. I'll be back first thing in the morning. If trouble does come calling, I'll be ready...with both barrels."

"Thank you. You're a sweet man." Ivy smiled as she unlocked the door to Sweet Flours and stepped inside.

"You keep an eye on her for me, Grayson," Emmett ordered.

"I will," Noble promised.

After nodding somberly, Emmett turned and walked away. With a growing unease, Noble entered the bakery and locked the door behind him.

"You want to tell me what that was all about?"

"I'll explain it all to you while I work."

A sardonic smirk tugged his lips. He loathed the way she took control every time she stepped foot on her home turf. Biting back the smart-assed volley he was dying to lob her way, Noble followed her through the swinging metal doors and into the kitchen.

The room, distinctively designed for business, was large, meticulously clean, and gleaming with massive, high-dollar stainless steel appliances, while the combination of fresh baked bread and cake lent a homey feel.

It wasn't until he saw the look on Ivy's face that Noble finally grasped her need to take charge and direct him. It was the bakery…this kitchen. She was in an environment that made her feel safe…secure.

Realizing that something ominous enough for her to reach out to Jasper might be threatening to destroy her or her safety zone prompted Noble to assert his own control.

"Start talking," he instructed, as Ivy tied a long apron around her waist.

"It's all ancient history, or was until today. About a year ago, my former boss sexually harassed me. I filed a lawsuit against him and won. The courts awarded me a settlement that paid for all this," she said with a wave of her hand. "I found out today that his wife committed suicide and in his twisted mind, he thinks it's my fault."

"You think he's going to come here and try to hurt you?"

"Oh, heavens no." She shook her head. "It's nothing as fiendish as that, but in a news conference he gave earlier today, he named Haven and the bakery in the same ugly breath. I simply wanted to warn Jasper that the town would be inundated with news crews by morning."

Ivy sounded almost dismissive about the sexual assault, and that sent up acres and acres of red flags in his head. He plucked out his phone and leaned against the counter by the sink as Ivy began measuring and stirring something in a bowl. "What's the name of your former boss?"

She glanced over her shoulder and saw the phone in his hand and blanched. "It-it's not important. He wouldn't show his face in town. Trust me. He's too…*important*."

"What's his name?"

"Noble…"

"Name?" he repeated in a tone that brooked no argument.

Her shoulders slumped. "I came here to get away from my past and start a new life…make a new future for myself. Please…just leave it alone. Okay?"

Noble tucked his phone away, temporarily, and pushed off the edge of the counter. Easing in behind her, he wrapped his arms around her, unable to ignore how naturally she fit against him.

"Your past defines who you are. The new life you're seeking and your future are going to involve me if the baby is mine." He placed his palms on her belly. A rush of emotions he'd never felt before came crashing though him.

In his mind's eye, they were both stretched out on a blanket, picnic basket resting on the grass. The summer sun spilled though her long blonde hair and warmed their skin. In the creek a few feet way, three little blonde-haired girls with pale blue eyes splashed and giggled.

*His* girls…all of them.

Noble's heart rate tripled, not from fear but longing.

He'd spent years adamantly denying what his heart had always longed for—a family, the chance to make a lifetime of memories his children could carry into adulthood, just like the ones he had. The fear of finally living out his dreams, then having them ripped away, like Sawyer, had colored his idyllic fantasy so brutally that he'd denied himself the possibility of ever obtaining it in the first place.

Like a waterfall of enlightenment, Noble realized that he wanted that little life growing inside her to be *his*. To carry that stubborn Grayson DNA strand. He wanted to hold that tiny life in his big hands and teach him or her about life, love, and the importance of family. The idea of spending his life with Ivy, of settling down and binding himself to her exclusively sent a flutter of anxiety uncoiling inside him. The implication of monogamy usually sent him running for the nearest exit, but Noble didn't even feel a twinge to flee.

Noble couldn't move…didn't want to.

Splaying his fingers over her slightly protruding belly and holding Ivy in his arms, Noble realized he wanted to spend eternity with her. Wanted to inhale the familiar scent of peaches and sunshine morning, noon, and night. Wanted to move heaven and earth and the seas to keep her safe…protected.

*Christ, could I actually be in love with her?*

Before Noble could begin to process the possibility, Ivy settled her hands over his and issued a heavy sigh. "I know you have your doubts and will demand a DNA test, but I can guarantee you, the baby *is* yours Noble. And I promise that I will raise him or her with enough love for both of us."

Again, her determination to shut him out of her life stung like a slap to the face. But Noble shoved the insult aside. Every cell in his body was screaming that this baby was his, and he felt zero desire to sprint out the front door and run screaming into the night.

He had no idea if he was actually in love with Ivy or if his moral code was so set in stone he couldn't turn his back on his responsibility to her and the baby.

The only thing he knew for certain was that he wouldn't stand to be some faceless, nameless ghost in this child's life.

"I heard you the first time, but you haven't stopped to consider that maybe I want something from you."

Ivy tensed and slid around in his arms until she faced him. "Like what?"

"Like to be a part of your life and our baby's life."

Her eyes grew wide as she blanched. A look of abject terror lined her face. She squirmed from his hold and stepped back, putting a cold, void between them that Noble didn't like.

"What?" She shook her head. "No. I can't do the whole marriage and family thing. If you want white picket fences and minivans, you're going to have to hit up one of the women in town who are…what did Trudy say? Oh, yeah… all cryin' in their pillows, missing the magical ways you make them scream your name."

Noble cringed. He'd suspected one day that his man-whoring ways would come back to bite him in the ass. But why did it have to be *this* day with *this* woman?

"I wasn't blowing smoke up your ass earlier when I said I hadn't been with anyone since you, darlin'. I haven't…" He scrubbed a hand through his hair and laid it all out on the table for her. "Because, try as I might, I can't stop thinking about *you*."

Ivy quickly banked the look of shock dancing over her face and lifted her chin. "Well, you're going to have to learn how, because there's no future for us, Noble."

"And why is that?"

She scoffed. "I won't raise my child in a town teeming with rumors about how his mother and father are both whores. I can deflect their comments and explain their hateful remarks for one parent—*me*—but not two."

Noble loathed the rumor mill maligning either of them.

From either anger or fear, Ivy visibly trembled. He pulled her into his arms. Reaching up, he tucked a couple of strands of hair behind her ear. "We can fix it so they have nothing to talk about."

"There's nothing we can do to stop the gossip, Noble. Not a damn thing."

"You could m-marry me," he stammered.

*What. The. Fuck? Why am I not hauling ass over elbows to get out of here?*

He had no idea where those four life-altering words had come from, but they were out and floating in the air, like a lead balloon now.

Ivy gaped up at him as if he were a space alien who'd just landed in her kitchen.

"Are you out of your fucking mind?" she screeched. "Didn't you hear me? I already told you, I don't do marriage. Hell, I don't even have time to date, let alone have a relationship of any kind."

"Oh, I heard you loud and clear, darlin'. And until a few hours ago, when I saw you standing there in the living, breathing flesh, I swore the very same thing." He dropped his hands to the swell of her soft, warm hips. She met his stare with a beseeching expression. "Please don't shut me out, Ivy."

Her eyes trailed to his mouth and stilled as the plea spilled free. A tiny shudder rippled through her. Memories of her melting and shattering beneath him clawed up his spine.

He could almost taste her sweet kisses.

But fuck if he could live without them ever again.

He dipped his chin and brushed his lips across hers.

When she didn't tense or shove him away, he swept a second time…then a third. As he pressed in slowly and tenderly the next time, Ivy wrapped her arms around his neck and kissed him back.

Relief poured through him, sending bottle rockets and cherry bombs detonating inside him. Though tinges of unease crept under his skin, they were quickly erased by the utter rightness of her in his arms and pressed to his mouth. Noble deepened the kiss and slid his tongue into the soft, warm recesses where he belonged.

*I want her…need her…until the end of fucking time.*

His unspoken conviction was still ringing in his ears when Ivy suddenly pulled from his mouth and his arms.

Breathless, with her chest rising and falling, she shook her head and took a step back. "I-I can't do this with you. Th-there's too much happening. I-I can't divide my head up like this… I just can't."

"Jasper can handle the news crews, darlin'. I'm not asking you to tear yourself in two, I simply want to—"

"It's not just the news crews. My parents…and m-my lawyer are coming to Haven in the morning. I've got to bake so I can open the shop in the morning, and I have to…god, I don't even know what else I need to do, but I'm not ready. I'm not ready for any of this."

The absolute panic in her voice damn near broke his heart.

She was completely falling apart at the seams.

His insistence that she allow him to be a part of her life was only adding to the weight she was trying to carry on her slender shoulders.

Her need for time and space scraped his flesh like knives.

"I have to get busy. You don't need to stay. Watching me work is going to get awfully boring."

Noble shook his head. "I'll keep out of your way, but I'm staying."

She pinched her lips together tightly but ceded with a nod.

As Ivy fluttered around the room, gathering ingredients, mixing bowls, and baking pans, Noble plucked out his cell phone and eased his ass onto the smooth metal counter near the sink.

When she was fully engrossed in her work, he covertly typed her name into a search engine. Immediately, photos and websites filled his screen. He tapped the first image of Ivy. Dozens of microphones were thrust toward her face, which was turned as if she was trying to shield herself. She was wearing the same blank expression she'd donned during Trudy's visit, but the sheer terror Noble saw in Ivy's eyes made him gnash his teeth. She was pressed between the older man that he'd seen, months ago, washing the windows of the bakery—her dad—and a middle-aged woman wearing a tailored suit and a look of determination. Noble didn't know if she was Ivy's mom or her lawyer, but he made a mental note to find out.

As he studied several more disturbing images of Ivy, the sight of what she'd endured made his stomach swirl. Noble tapped a Dallas-based news site and began reading the details of the trial.

Halfway through the article, there was a photo of Eugene McMillian and a paragraph of information about the mid-sixties man. He had the look of a sleazy politician.

Noble studied the image intently, mentally plotting gruesome and painful ways for the prick to die. Finally, he forced himself to continue reading the article. McMillian, the lecherous fuck, had a pattern of soliciting sex from his former female employees. At the end of the trial, Ivy's attorney, Margaret Neill, had given a statement to the reporters.

*Yes, my client and I are satisfied with the guilty verdict and the monetary settlement awarded today. However, the women victimized by Eugene McMillian will always carry the scars he inflicted. Especially my client, Ivy Addison, who had to endure not only his verbal assault but his abhorrent and demeaning physical exploitation, as well.*

A white-hot rage raced through Noble.

Bile bubbled up from his stomach.

The motherfucker McMillian had done more than sexually harass Ivy. He'd physically assaulted her, as well.

Christ. Had the sick fuck raped her? Beat her?

Scrolling back up the article, Noble studied the bastard's photo again, vowing that if the prick ever showed his face in Haven, he'd never get the chance to leave town again. Noble would kill the son of bitch with his bare hands.

Numerous websites touted Ivy's ordeal as: *the trial of the century,* and *unemployed bakery assistant takes down multi-billionaire philanthropist.*

As he skimmed each disturbing article, Noble lost track of time. He glanced at his phone as his stomach growled in hunger.

The buttery-rich aroma permeating the air only made the empty void in his gut harder to ignore. But Noble dismissed his own needs, opting instead to watch Ivy as she squeezed a fat tube of icing, creating perfect red rose petals on top of a tall pink-iced cake.

Watching as she meticulously painted bright green leaves all around the pretty roses, Noble held a new level of respect and pride for his girl. Her life had been dissected and dragged through the mud, yet she'd come out whole on the other side.

Ivy was brave and strong, yet he now knew she was horrifically scarred. Still, she hadn't let Eugene McMillian or the embarrassment of the very public trial break her spirit.

She was tenacious, determined, and as bullheaded as Noble...and the incredible little minx had somehow stolen his heart.

The overwhelming need to protect her and help her fully heal from the vile assault rode him hard. But keeping her in his life was his ultimate goal.

Oh, she'd fight him every step of the way.

Of that Noble was sure, and while he'd never force her in any way, he'd somehow draw her out from behind those infuriating walls and into his arms.

Patience and persistence were his specialties...among his other talents.

As Ivy set the icing down, he eased off the table and moved in close behind her. Unable to stop himself, Noble threaded his fingers through the thick curls spilling from her ponytail. She jolted slightly, but before she could turn around, Noble pressed himself against her back and leaned in close to her ear.

"Are you hungry?" When she shivered beneath him, Noble wanted to send up a fist pump.

"No. I'm fine. Go ahead and get some dinner. I'll be fine here by myself."

"Why are you so eager to get rid of me, sweetheart?"

"I-I'm not," she stammered as she turned her head and met his stare. "It's just...I don't need a babysitter."

"You think that's what I'm doing here...babysitting you?"

Ivy shrugged. "You got your kiss, so..."

"There's still a lot we need to talk about. Why don't you take off that apron and we'll walk down the street and grab some dinner at Toot's Café?"

"I can't. I still need to make a ton of cookies and fill the cream puffs."

"You need to eat something. Not only to fuel your body but the little one growing inside you, darlin'. Come on. It won't take but thirty minutes or so."

A pained expression crawled across her face. "Noble, it's not a good idea for us to be seen together any more than we already have."

"Why? So people don't talk?" he asked, unable to keep from grinning.

"Yes."

"Sweetheart, they're already talking. I'd lay odds that half the town knows I'm here with you now. And not a one of them thinks we're standing in this kitchen baking goodies."

"See? That's what I'm talking about. You shouldn't even be here. It's only going to fuel more nasty rumors. Those news crews that are coming will talk to everyone they can. The second your name comes up, they're going to dissect your whole life like a frog in high school science class. They'll plant their vans in front of your house. You won't be able to step outside to work or go to the grocery store without five or six microphones shoved in your face. That kind of invasion isn't pretty."

"I'm a big boy. I can take care of myself."

Ivy exhaled a frustrated sigh. "Oh, yeah. What if they talk to Trudy? Can you imagine all the stories she'd gladly tell them about you? This bullshit better blow over soon, 'cause if they find out I'm pregnant…"

She let out a long, mournful groan and dropped her head.

He cupped her shoulders and turned her into his arms. Pulling her in against his chest, he dropped a soft kiss on the top of her head. "I think you worry far too much about what other people think."

"Oh, god. I'm turning into my mother," she moaned.

"I don't know, I haven't had the pleasure of meeting her yet, but I will…tomorrow."

"No, you won't."

Noble arched his brows. "And why not?"

"Because she expects the baby daddy to make an honest woman out of me."

"I already tried that, darlin'. You shot me down, remember?"

"You weren't serious and we both know it." Noble frowned. He'd correct her soon, but not now. The tight tone in her voice told him she'd had enough stress for one day. "No. You're not meeting my parents tomorrow. That's nonnegotiable for now."

"So who's going to take care of the bakery while you meet with them and the lawyer you forgot to mention was coming earlier?"

"I'm hoping my sister, Celina, will come with them. She helped me out on opening day. While the shop gets busy, it's nothing like that first day. That was crazy."

"Celina? Your sister is Celina? The same Celina who married Harvey Hays?" Noble barked out in disbelief.

"You know Harvey?" Ivy countered, equally stunned.

"I was in Vegas for his wedding…I was supposed to be his—"

"Oh, my god. You were his best man? You're the guy who took off and made that jackass throw a giant temper tantrum, aren't you?"

Noble chuckled. "He had a little meltdown, did he?"

"Little nothing. The misogynistic prick came un-fucking-glued." She slapped a hand over her mouth and cringed.

"No worries. I refer to him as my ex-best friend, as well. He's an asshole."

Ivy started to laugh. "Yes. And it felt damn good when I knocked him out and hauled Celina out of there before she made the biggest mistake of her life."

"You what?"

She giggled again and Noble's heart melted like a box of crayons in the July sun.

"Fuck what people say or think. Take off that apron so we can go to dinner. I want to hear how you saved your sister."

# CHAPTER SIXTEEN

To Ivy's relief, the café was nearly empty when they arrived. When Noble led her to a booth in the back that virtually hid them from everyone but the waitress, she wanted to throw her arms around his neck and kiss him stupid.

Her ravenous ache to kiss him again, along with a dozen other salacious things, was driving her mad. These stupid pregnancy hormones were going to be the death of her. If she wasn't crying at the drop of a hat, she was wrestling to keep from molesting Noble's fine, sexy ass.

Spending the past few hours in the same room with the man had been murder.

In order to keep her hands off him and her clothes on, Ivy had continuously reminded herself that Noble was the town slut. It didn't help. Every time she whipped up a batch of frosting, she wanted to smear it over his sexy body and lick it off him. Need was humming through her like a live wire in a swimming pool.

Thankfully, she'd been able to gloss over the details about McMillian.

But she'd been at a total loss when it came to dancing around Noble's ridiculous marriage proposal. Thank god he hadn't been serious. She had enough life-altering shit to deal with.

After the waitress brought their drinks and took their dinner order, Noble pinned her with an expectant stare.

"Oh, the story about Harvey, right." Ivy chuckled.

"Yes. And don't skim over anything this time. I want every detail," Noble warned, with a wickedly handsome grin.

As she relayed the events that had unfolded while Noble had

been in the process of returning to Texas, his buttery-rich laughter poured over her like sweet, sticky syrup. Her nipples were as hard as marbles, and Ivy feared when it was time to leave, there'd be a puddle of need on the seat beneath her.

When she got to the part about leaving Celina's engagement ring behind, Noble was howling in laughter and wiping tears from his eyes.

"What amazes me is even after all that, Harvey is still begging Celina to take him back," Ivy said shaking her head in disgust.

"He's desperate. He knows he'll never have a woman as beautiful as Celina again."

"You met my sister?"

"Yes, I did, briefly. Right before Harvey and I were getting ready to… Oh, hell. I should have figured out you two were related then." Noble chuckled. "When Celina found out we were hitting the strip clubs—thankfully he canceled the hookers—"

"Hookers?" Ivy hissed. "Harvey hired…*hookers* for you guys to…"

When Noble told her about the groom's grand plan to make some *kinky memories to think about while plowing* her sister, Ivy lost what little appetite she'd mustered. Of course, during the story, Noble had painted himself the quintessential choirboy, which she didn't buy for a second. He'd never have to pay a woman for sex…they'd easily pay to play with *him*.

She tried to ignore the twinge of needless jealousy slithering through her and counted her blessings that she'd been able to save Celina from marrying such a sick, disgusting prick.

Suddenly, Noble turned somber and reached across the table, threading his fingers through hers. Sadness lined his face. "Look, while you were baking, I read about the trial on my phone. I wish you would have told me more was involved than inappropriate sexual innuendos."

"I never said it was innuendos." Her tone was surprisingly defensive. Ivy tried to pull her hand back, but Noble wouldn't let go.

"No. But you didn't insinuate that he'd gotten physical with you, either. What did he do to you, sweetheart?"

"I'd rather not discuss it. It's over and done and resurrecting the past is a waste of time." She inwardly cringed at her sharp tone.

Noble leaned across the table and lowered his voice. "Fine. But there's one question that's eating me up inside. Did he rape you?"

"No. After he put his hand up my skirt and his fingers under my panties, I kicked him in the balls and ran."

Shoving down the rage of the filthy prick touching Ivy so inappropriately, he worked to paint on a slight smile. "I'll need to keep an eye out for your fists and knees if we ever get into an ugly fight."

"Might be a wise thing to do," she quipped with a sassy smirk.

"What is your lawyer hoping to accomplish tomorrow?"

"I honestly don't know. But I hope she's coming with a game plan for us to put into motion."

"I'll have Nate cover for me at the ranch tomorrow."

"You work on a ranch?"

A little smile tugged the edges of his mouth. "I just realized there's a whole lot we don't know about each other."

*Because it was only supposed to be a one-night stand.*

Ivy had never imagined how that one night would change her whole damn life.

Noble was in the process of telling her about Camp Melody, melting her heart into a massive puddle, when a thunderous boom shook the whole building, rattling the dishes on the shelves.

"What the..." Alarm etched his face as Noble stood and tossed a twenty on the table before heading for the door.

Ivy grabbed her purse and bolted from the booth right behind him as customers rushed to the windows and darted out the door.

"Fire!" a middle-aged man yelled, pointing in the direction of her bakery.

"No. No. No," Ivy whispered as she sped past Noble and sprinted down the sidewalk.

He stayed on her heels, even when Ivy veered off the crowded sidewalk and into the street, until she encountered a wall of heat. Skidding to a halt, she watched flames from the broken windows of Sweet Flours licking up into the night sky. Trembling in shock, she barely felt Noble wrap a protective arm around her waist.

"Son of a bitch," he spat furiously. "Did you leave the ovens on?"

Unable to speak, Ivy shook her head as she numbly watched her dreams literally going up in a crackling inferno. A despondent cry slid past her lips as her knees gave out. Before she could crumple to the ground, Noble pulled her in tight against his rugged body.

*How did this happen?* The question spooled through her head in a constant loop of shock and disbelief. Tears spilled from her eyes, blurring the red, orange, and blue flames into a gut-churning kaleidoscope of heartbreak.

From somewhere behind her, a loud siren wailed. Every muscle in her body tensed as she jerked her head toward the sound.

"It's the alarm...calling out the volunteer fire department," Noble explained. "Come on, let's get out of the middle of the street before we get run over."

"Too late. I'm already roadkill," Ivy mumbled, trapped in a horrific nightmare she couldn't escape.

Noble began leading her from the churning flames and acrid smoke. They'd only made it a couple of feet before Gina and Nate surrounded them.

"Oh, thank god, you're alive." Gina, body shaking and tears flowing freely, wrapped Ivy in a tight hug. "I thought you were inside the bakery when it exploded."

"Exploded?" Ivy repeated numbly.

"Didn't you hear it?" Nate asked incredulously.

"Yeah," Noble confirmed. "We were at Toot's eating dinner."

"Damn glad you weren't inside that, brother." Nate's voice was thick with emotion.

"You and me both," Noble agreed.

When Gina released her, Ivy peered back at the fire, helplessly watching it consume her future. Any hope of providing a comfortable life for her and the baby was gone.

"Oh, god," she wailed. "What am I going to do?"

"You're going to sit down before you fall down, darlin'," Noble instructed in a tone that brooked no argument.

Nate eased in on the other side of her and both men led her inside the Hangover.

"I'll get a little shot of brandy for her," Gina announced as Noble and Nate eased Ivy into a chair near the front window.

"I-I can't drink," she protested.

"A little sip won't hurt you, darlin'. It might keep you from going into shock, which would be twice as bad for you and the baby," Noble whispered gently, kneeling down beside her.

Ivy feared shock already had her in its grip.

She stared out the front window of the bar. Watching the curious and visibly worried crowd clogging the sidewalk growing larger, Ivy felt detached…paralyzed.

With lights flashing and siren blaring, Jasper pulled his cruiser to a halt in the middle of the street. He climbed out of the vehicle, staring at the flames before searching the throng of people with a decidedly worried expression. Megan, the pretty young girl who frequented the bakery, ran up to the sheriff and pointed at the bar. He gave her a grim nod, looked back at the fire, and then jogged toward her place of refuge.

As she heard him enter the bar, Ivy watched several men dressed in bright yellow coats scurrying to unroll thick gray hoses along the street.

"You just scared ten years off my life, Ivy," Jasper announced as he took a seat in the chair across from her. "Any idea what caused that explosion?"

"No." Ivy shook her head. "Noble and I were eating dinner at Toot's. After the explosion, we came out and…" She turned her head and stared at the wicked, destructive flames still shooting from the building.

Gina pressed a tumbler containing a splash of amber liquid into Ivy's hand. She lifted it to her nose and sniffed the strong alcohol. Her stomach pitched and her mouth began to water. She quickly set the glass down. Noble took her hand and held it, absently drawing tiny circles along her knuckles. His touch tamed a bit of the riot within her. Ivy was grateful he was there.

"You warned me things were going to get a little crazy around here, but I wasn't expecting this."

"I wasn't, either," Ivy answered automatically. A split second later a rush of fear consumed her. "Do you think it was intentionally set?"

"Don't know. We'll have to wait for the fire marshal to sift through everything once the boys put the hot spots out."

"Fuck," Noble mumbled under his breath as he moved in closer behind her and placed a wide hand on her shoulder.

The bell above the door tinkled, and a parade of people rushed into the bar. When Ivy spotted Sawyer, she studied the other three young men frantically striding toward them. The resemblance to Noble was almost as uncanny as Nate's.

*Oh, god, his family's here.*

An older woman Ivy recognized from the bakery raced up to Noble and hugged him in a death grip.

"You're all right. Oh, thank you… Thank you, God," she cried out in relief. "When Nate called and said there was an explosion at the bakery and that you might be inside, I nearly had a heart attack."

"I'm fine, Ma," Noble assured after kissing the top of her head.

Noble shot a scowl at Nate. "I told you we weren't in the building."

Ivy didn't remember that exchange between them at all.

"I know. When I tried to call home to let them know you were still alive, no one answered," Nate explained.

"Sorry," Noble apologized sheepishly. "I'm a little rattled."

"Aren't we all?" Ivy mumbled under her breath.

Over the next several minutes, she was introduced to Noble's parents, brothers, and sisters-in-law. Janice would have been proud—for once. Even though Ivy's whole world was literally going up in smoke, she still managed to greet each of them with a polite smile, ignoring the billion ants crawling under her skin.

The Graysons chattered on top of one another as everyone stared out the window, watching black smoke billow from the building as numerous streams of water attacked the flames.

Ivy closed her eyes. All she wanted to do was climb into bed and pull the covers over her head, but she didn't have a bed anymore, or clothes, or shoes, or a computer, or tax receipts... She didn't even have a damn toothbrush.

The reality of everything...literally *everything* that had been taken from her, plowed her under like a ten-ton bulldozer.

Panic and grief spiked, sending her stomach tumbling in a vomitous roll. She clenched her fists and willed herself not to throw up but couldn't contain the pitiful whimper that spilled from her lips.

"Oh, god. I've lost *everything...everything,*" she wailed, hiding her face in her hands and coming completely undone.

As deep, guttural sobs tore from her throat, Noble plucked her up from the chair. Cradling her in his arms like a child, he carried her back behind the bar and into the little kitchen. He eased onto a wooden chair next to a small table. Ivy clutched her stomach as fear of the future overwhelmed her.

Curled up against in Noble's arms, she cried and cried. He held her, caressing her face, and murmuring tender reassurances. Like a badly needed balm, his whiskey-smooth voice smoothed the deathly sharp edges that shredded her soul. He pressed a soft kiss to her forehead before wiping the last of her tears away with the pads of his thumbs.

"You're coming home with us. We've got plenty of room at the ranch. Then tomorrow, we'll focus on doing what's necessary to start rebuilding the bakery. All right?"

Ivy didn't have the energy to fight him and simply nodded.

"Wait." She sniffed. "You said us. You still live at home?"

Noble gave her an embarrassed shrug. "I've been living and working on the ranch my whole life. Until now, I've never had a reason to move out."

"Until now? What's that mean?"

"You're not raising our baby alone. But that's a discussion for another time."

"*Baby?*" His mother stood in the doorway wearing a look of abject horror. She wobbled as if ready to pass out and quickly latched her hand to the doorjamb.

Ivy's heart leapt in her chest. Mortified, she closed her eyes, wishing she really had been turned into roadkill.

"Like I said," Noble began as he stood, lifting Ivy with him, "that's a discussion for another time. But congratulations…Grandma."

"Grandma…" Nola whispered. She lowered her head and smoothed a hand over the flowing blouse hiding her own pregnant belly.

It was Ivy's turn to be stunned. Her eyes grew wide as she glanced up at Noble and wiggled from his arms to stand on her own two feet.

"I should probably warn the rest of the family. We're going to be living with hormones gone wild for a bit," Noble said with a chuckle. "I know you won't mind, but I invited Ivy to come stay with us, Ma."

"Darn right I don't mind. In fact, I insist. The mother of my grandchild needs to be with family. Especially with all this…trauma going on," Nola stated with the same tone of finality Noble often used.

She crossed the room and cupped Ivy's cheek with a sympathetic smile. "Don't you worry about a thing, sweetie. We'll take good care of you. Brea, April, and Gina have tons of clothes. They'll let you borrow until we can get you back on your feet again."

"Thank you, Mrs. Grayson," Ivy whispered, fighting back another round of tears.

"Call me Nola, and no thanks are needed. You're part of the family now...right?" She arched a stern and quizzical look at Noble.

"We're still, ah...working on that," he stammered with a crooked grin.

"Work harder, sweetheart," Nola instructed before she turned and left the room.

"Just a word of warning," Noble started, still smiling. "She's going to wear you down."

"Wear me down?"

"Convince you to say yes to marrying me."

Ivy held up her hand. "Not tonight, Noble. I-I can't handle any more."

"Right." He cringed. "Let's get you home and tucked into bed."

"Whose bed?"

"Mine, of course."

She wondered how many other women he'd taken home to send sailing in ecstasy.

"Isn't that a little awkward?"

"What?"

"Bringing women home...you know...to your *bed*?"

"I don't know. You're the first."

*The first? Oh, wow! Maybe he isn't such a big man-whore after all.*

Even though she doubted Noble would be joining her in his bed, butterflies dipped and swooped low in her belly. When he leaned in and pressed a soft, passionate kiss to her lips and moaned, the butterflies flew away and a wave of tropical heat consumed her.

After rejoining his family, Noble led her out of the bar.

Outside, Ivy forced her gaze to the bakery. Huge spotlights erected on the street shined on the charred, skeletal remains of what was once her pride and joy. Ivy's heart ached. The acrid smoke clinging in the air burned her lungs.

As the rest of the Grayson family spilled from the bar, a buzz of whispers wafted over the crowd. Noble chuckled and slung a purely possessive arm around Ivy's waist.

The familiar scrutiny made her skin crawl. She donned the impassive mask she'd worn during the trial, but the defiant lift of her chin left a bitter taste on her tongue.

"Just a word of warning, darlin'…if you ever hit me with that look, I'll take you over my knee and paddle your ass," Noble whispered in her ear.

Ivy peered up at him, expecting to see mischief dancing in his eyes. Instead, she found irritation. "You don't get to shut me out…ever. Understand?"

Unnerved that he could read her so easily, Ivy swallowed tightly and nodded.

As his family piled into a massive, weathered Suburban, Noble opened the passenger door to a beefy silver pickup truck.

"Buckle up. I'll be right back."

"Where are you—"

"I need to talk to Jasper for a minute. It won't take long," he assured and shut the door.

In the side mirror, Ivy watched him jog up to Jasper, who was standing next to his cruiser. The two exchanged a few words before Noble climbed in behind the wheel and started the engine.

"What was that all about?" she asked as he slowly eased the truck past the smoldering remains of her shop.

"I asked Jasper to check with his sources in Dallas to find out where and what Eugene McMillian was doing tonight."

"You think *he* blew up my shop?"

"I certainly don't believe it was an innocent gas leak, darlin',"

Noble drawled, threading his fingers through hers and resting them on top of his thigh.

"Me, either."

Ivy tried not to fixate on the fact that if she hadn't gone to dinner with Noble, she'd be dead. Was McMillian crazy enough to kill her?

The insane amount of heat radiating off Noble's leg and crawling up her arm, couldn't curtail the ominous chill sluicing through her veins. Paranoia pierced and Ivy's pulse raced as she peered in the side mirror to see if they were being followed. The road behind them was inky black, but her fears continued to mount.

"Me, dad, and my brothers will each take a watch tonight," Noble announced as if reading her mind. "A heavily *armed* perimeter watch. We'll keep you safe, sweetheart."

"Thank you."

His assurance should have calmed her. But knowing that Noble shared her level of paranoia only heightened Ivy's angst.

Focusing on the red taillights of the Suburban in front of them, she mentally tried talking herself off the ledge, but it wasn't working.

"When it comes to business, McMillian is beyond savvy," she stated.

"If he's a multi-billionaire like the article said, he'd have to be," Noble agreed. "But is he cunning and deceptive enough to commit murder? Without leaving any incriminating evidence behind?"

"I doubt it. Outside the boardroom the man's inept as hell. He can't even brew a pot of coffee without his secretary's help." That realization ignited a sliver of hope inside her. "If McMillian is behind the fire, I hope he left a trail so bright the International Space Station can see it."

"Me, too, sweetheart," Noble said as he slowed, turned off the paved two-lane, and followed the Suburban down a bumpy gravel road.

When Noble's home came into view—a massive ranch house surrounded by tall, sturdy oak trees and acres of flat land—a soft smile tugged her lips.

"It's not a mansion, but it's home," Noble announced as he pulled onto a concrete slab and turned off the motor.

"It's beautiful," Ivy whispered, taking in the well-manicured lawn and flowers bursting with color that surrounded the house.

"Sit tight," Noble instructed before launching from the truck and hurrying to her door.

After helping her out, he wrapped his arm around her waist and led her up a slight incline to a huge wooden deck at the back of the house. His family followed them, talking in low, concerned tones. As she stepped through the sliding glass door, Ivy found herself inside a homey, spacious kitchen. The rest of his family gathered there as well, and then Noble's cell phone began to ring.

He glanced at the caller ID and scowled as a hush fell over the room. "It's Jasper."

"Sit and try to relax," Nola instructed, pointing to a chair at the huge wooden dining table. "I'll fix you some hot chocolate."

"Hello," Noble answered, taking a seat beside Ivy. His eyes grew wide as he wordlessly listened. Then smirked and shook his head. "Are you serious? Well, I'll be damned. Hang on a second, Jasper. I'm putting you on speakerphone. Ivy needs to hear this."

"Hear what?"

"The International Space Station just called," Noble said with a soft chuckle. "Ready on this end, Jasper. Can you repeat everything you just told me?"

"Ivy? You there? Can you hear me?" Jasper's voice boomed through the device's speaker.

"Yes. I'm here and can hear you just fine. What's going on?"

"When I started interviewing the owners of the other businesses on your block, I got some interesting information from Ralph Bickermeier. He owns the *Haven Tribune* couple of doors down from your shop. Seems he forgot his lunch box at work today, so he went back to the newspaper office after dinner to pick it up. When he pulled down the alley, he said a fancy forest-green car was sitting in his spot. A fancy green Mercedes Benz with Dallas County license plates."

"Did he write down the license number?" Dad, Norman, asked anxiously.

"He didn't have to. Ralph's one of them fellas that's got a photographic memory. He rattled off the license plate number along with the make and model of the car hogging his parking space."

"You already ran the number, right?" Noble pressed.

"I did."

"And?" he and Ivy asked in unison.

"That fancy green 2018 Mercedes Benz Maybach is registered to one Eugene Caldwell McMillian of Dallas County, Texas."

*Eugene has been watching you.* Janice's words sent a shock wave of terror zipping through Ivy. Her heart thrummed wildly. McMillian really was trying to kill her. She fought the urge to run and hide as the impact of what it meant to find his car at the scene of the crime sparked a flicker of hope.

"If that isn't kismet, I don't know what is," Nola whispered, shaking her head.

"I filed an arrest warrant for Mr. McMillian," Jasper continued, "charging him with one count each of arson and attempted murder. I also faxed it to a close detective friend of mine down at the Dallas PD. As soon as he and his boys serve the warrant, that sum'bitch McMillian is gonna be cuffed and hauled in for questioning. If they can get a confession out of him before he lawyers up, he'll be booked and locked up."

Ivy felt as if the weight of the world had been lifted off her shoulders. Noble jumped up from his chair and swooped her into his arms while his family celebrated with cheers, yells, and fist bumps.

"Guess that means we won't need to take shifts keeping a perimeter watch up all night," Noble murmured in her ear with palpable relief.

When the revelry died down, Ivy plucked up Noble's phone. "Thank you, Jasper. Thank you so much."

"I'm just glad Ralph forgot his damn lunch box and that we now have McMillian by the balls. You can relax now and let the Graysons pamper you. They're damn good at taking care of others."

"It's what we do." Nola chuckled as she placed a steaming mug of hot chocolate on the table for Ivy. "You come on by for dinner one night soon, Sheriff, and we'll take care of you, too. Ya hear?"

"Yes, ma'am. I surely will. Oh, one more thing. Miss Ivy?" Jasper's tone turned suddenly somber.

"Yes?"

"The first of your visitors arrived in Haven about twenty minutes ago. Pulled onto Main Street in one of those fancy vans with big ol' antennas on top."

"Oh, no," she moaned.

"Don't fret. I just wanted to let you know. Oh, and the minute I saw 'em coming, I grabbed my megaphone and told the folks gathered on the sidewalk to zip their lips around those characters, or they'd have to answer to me. By now the whole damn town knows how to say no comment," he said with a chuckle.

"Thanks, Jasper," Ivy said, worry lacing her words.

After ending the call, Noble pulled her tighter to his chest and brushed his lips against her ear. "Don't worry, darlin'. Those vultures are gonna have to go through me to get to you, and they're never gonna get through me. I promise."

A sense of peace settled deep. Ivy hugged him hard and whispered her thanks.

"What do you need us to do for you, honey?" Norman asked, concern wrinkling his sun-kissed face. Ivy reluctantly eased from Noble's arms and took a good look at the older man's face, now illuminated by the bright kitchen lights. There was no doubt who Noble had inherited his striking good looks from.

"I honestly don't know," she replied, still feeling shell-shocked.

"Have you spoken to your family yet? Do they know what's happened tonight?"

"Oh, gosh. No." She slapped a hand to her forehead. "With all the commotion, I-I…" She grabbed her purse off the table and frantically dug out her cell phone.

"Perfectly understandable, honey," Norman assured. "It's been a bit of a wild ride. We'll give you some privacy. Come on, kids let's go see how the Rangers are doing at spring training."

"Even though they've probably already heard the news, I should call Nate and Gina…let them know what's happened," Noble announced.

"I think we're going to head on home, Pa." Ned scowled when his wife, April, turned and walked out the door without uttering a single word. An awkward pall hung in the air. *Something's definitely amiss with that relationship.* "It was nice to finally meet you, Ivy. And I'm sorry about your bakery."

"Nice to meet you as well, and thank you. Luckily, I have insurance," she quipped, hoping to lessen the tension. She sent him a slight smile as Ned walked out the door.

"You should probably make a mental note to call your agent in the morning," Noble suggested as the rest of his family began filtering out of the kitchen.

"Yes. I'd already planned to. I need to call Alma Anderson, too. Let her know I had the business heavily insured."

"I almost forgot." Nola paused in the doorway as Noble talked on his cell. "Alma stopped me as we were walking to the bar. She saw the four of you take refuge inside and wanted me to tell you not to worry. She's got plenty of insurance on the building, as well. You'll be back in business in no time, dear."

"Thank goodness."

"I'll go find you some pajamas and leave them in the bathroom for you, along with some fresh towels and a new toothbrush."

"Thank you, Nola. Thank you so much for…for everything."

The woman simply smiled and winked before disappearing down the hall as Noble finished his call.

Ivy stared at her phone, dreading the call she needed to make.

"You all right?" he asked.

"Yeah, just not thrilled to have to tell my folks about the fire and how McMillian tried to kill me. It's not going to go over well."

Noble slid his hand in hers and squeezed. "Just take a deep breath and make the call."

She nodded, inhaled deeply, and made the call.

The instant Celina answered, the realization that Noble's invitation to dinner was the only reason Ivy could still hear her sister's voice slammed home.

*I could have died tonight.*

Her whole body began to shake.

Like a drum, her heart hammered against her ribs.

A cold sweat broke out over her face.

"L-Leena…it-it's me," Ivy stammered, gasping for breath.

"Easy," Noble murmured as he plucked the phone from her hand and hauled her onto his lap before engaging the speakerphone option.

"Celina, it's Noble Grayson."

"Noble? What the hell…where's Ivy? What have you done to her? Did that asshole Harvey ask you to kidnap her in order to get me—"

"Celina. Stop," Noble growled. "Ivy's fine. She's here with me but is struggling to pull herself together. So I'm talking to you."

"Pull herself together? Why? What the hell is going on?" Celina screeched. "Ivy? Dammit, say something!"

"I-I'm here," she managed to choke out as she clutched Noble's chest and struggled to tamp down the oily fears bubbling up inside. "Just…calm down and l-listen to Noble p-please."

"I'll calm down when someone tells me what the fuck you're

crying about." Celina demanded.

"I'm trying. Take a deep breath and just listen, all right?" Noble instructed in a cool, rational tone. "There was a fire at the bakery tonight. I'm sorry to have to tell you that Sweet Flours is gutted…gone."

"Fire? The bakery is gone? Oh, god, no." Celina's voice conveyed the same level of shock inundating Ivy all night. "Oh, sissy, I'm so sorry. Are you okay? You weren't burned, were you?"

"She's fine. We weren't in the shop when the explosion happened," Noble stated.

"Explosion? There was an explosion? From what? A gas leak?"

"No." Ivy growled. Anger had suddenly replaced the angst from coming face-to-face with her mortality. "McMillian tried to kill me."

"You've got to be fucking kidding me. Hang on…Mom…Dad, pick up the phone. Ivy's on the line and you're not going to believe… Son of a bitch!" Celina spat in the receiver once more. "That man is certifiable. He's even scarier than Harvey! Which leads me to…Noble? What the hell are you doing in Haven with my sister?"

"Ivy? What's wrong, honey?" The sound of her mom's voice was doubly heart crushing.

"Mom…oh, Mom," Ivy moaned, choking on the emotions flooding her system.

"Ivy. Talk to me, baby. What's happened?"

Then, like a ray of sunshine parting dark storm clouds, Noble took over. "Mrs. Addison, my name is Noble Grayson. I'm a, well, I'm a good friend of Ivy's."

"Noble," Janice repeated softly before her voice took on a defensive edge. "Did you meet Ivy in Las Vegas, young man?"

"Yes, ma'am, I did."

"Did something happen to the… Oh, lord, please tell me she's all right."

"She and our baby are both fine," Noble stated proudly, sending Ivy a crooked smile.

"Baby?" Celina screamed. "Ivy's pregnant? Oh. My. God."

"Pregnant? Ivy's p-pregnant?" her father barked.

"Hush, both of you. Let the man talk. I'll explain it all later," Janice scolded. "Go on, Mr. Grayson. Obviously something horrible has happened if you're talking to me instead of Ivy."

"Yes, ma'am. There was a fire...an explosion actually."

While Noble broke the devastating news, Ivy nuzzled her head against his chest and closed her eyes. The reverberation of his deep, soothing voice and steady beat of his heart wrapped around her like a security blanket. Not only did he patiently and respectfully answer every frantic question her family lobbed at him, Noble stretched out his legs, crossed his ankles, and strummed his palm up and down Ivy's back. He wasn't the least bit apprehensive or intimidated talking to the parents of the woman he'd accidentally knocked up.

*Grace and poise under fire*, she thought with a tiny smile.

The more she learned about Noble Grayson and his supportive, gracious family, the more Ivy felt her protective walls chipping away. He might be the town whore, but deep down, Noble was a caring, loving, and fiercely protective man. She could easily become enamored with him.

*Become enamored? Ha. I've been head over heels for months.*

Though she wasn't ready to accept his proposal of marriage, Ivy couldn't help but reevaluate her stance about blocking him from their child's life. As long as it didn't involve anything to do with the birds and the bees, Noble would be a positive influence to be sure.

"Ivy's welcome to stay with my family as long as she needs to, Mr. Addison," Noble assured before pressing a kiss to the top of her head.

"Please let her know we'll be arriving in Haven in the morning," Janice instructed.

"I'm right here, Mom," Ivy finally piped up. "I'm out in the country and perfectly safe with Noble's family, but I'll meet you all in town."

"I'm glad to hear that, honey."

"Thank you for taking care of her, Noble," Celina said with a sniff.

"It's my pleasure." Noble peered down and sent Ivy a devilish smile.

She rolled her eyes and lightly swatted his chest.

After they said their goodbyes, Noble ended the call and cupped her cheeks.

"Let's get you tucked into bed, darlin'. Tomorrow's going to be a long day and you need to get some rest."

"You mean…we're actually going to *sleep*?" she taunted with a sassy grin.

"Eventually." He moaned before claiming her lips in an urgent, passionate kiss.

Ivy was at a crossroads. Did she throw caution to the wind…ignore his reputation with the ladies of Haven, and spend another sweaty, thrusting, screaming night with him? Or did she shut him down and continue holding on to the bittersweet memories for the rest of her life?

Noble's confession swirled through her brain. *I wasn't blowing smoke up your ass earlier when I said I hadn't been with anyone since you, darlin'. I haven't…*

There was still so much they didn't know about each other, but Ivy had spent enough time with Noble as he interacted with his family and the people of Haven to know he wasn't a liar.

Clutching his shirt, she kissed him back with the same level of fire and fury he was unleashing on her. When he traced his tongue along the seam of her lips, Ivy opened for him…opened far more than her mouth for him…she opened her soul.

# CHAPTER SEVENTEEN

Noble lay in his bed waiting for Ivy to finish up in the bathroom and join him. Instead of him fantasizing about her being beside him in his bed, soon she'd be lying beside him in the breathing, living flesh.

His cock, harder and leaking more than he'd ever known possible, pulsed anxiously. Noble's patience was running thin. If she didn't walk through that door in the next ten seconds, he'd streak across the hall and throw her over his shoulder, caveman style.

When the doorknob turned and she entered his room, Noble clenched his jaw and fought the urge to bolt out of bed, drag his mother's cock-softening nightgown off her body, and press Ivy up against the wall before driving balls deep inside her snug, slick pussy.

"Patience, cowboy," Ivy drawled as if reading his mind. "Your parents are right down the hall. I'm not sure we should…you know."

"I'll stick a sock in your mouth if I have to in order to keep you quiet. But trust me, darlin', we *are* going to…you know," he growled.

"A sock? Really?"

"I'd use a clean one," he assured with a lurid grin. "Take that god-awful nightgown off and get your sexy ass over here, woman. I've been waiting an eternity to feel your hot body against mine again."

A pink blush sped from her chest all the way to her cheeks as Ivy tugged the ugly garment off and tossed it to the floor.

With a satisfied sigh, Noble drank in the sight of her lush body.

Her nipples were a darker shade of cranberry and her breasts were fuller, heavier than they'd been before. Skimming his eyes down her naked flesh, he paused and studied the gentle swell along her stomach. *My child is growing healthy and strong inside her.* His heart sputtered and a lump of emotion lodged in his throat. Swallowing tightly, Noble threw back the covers and spread his arms open. "Come here, sweetheart...let me love you."

Ivy's mouth dropped open slightly and a look of shock sailed over her eyes.

It was then that Noble realized what he'd said... *Love? Well, hell.*

He, too, was surprised the four-letter word had slipped off his tongue. He'd never said the *L* word around any other woman, but Noble was quickly learning that his feelings for Ivy were far different from anything he'd felt before.

If she'd let him, he'd love her...now, tomorrow, and for all eternity.

"You can *make* love to me, Noble," Ivy whispered, failing to mask the quiver in her voice.

"I can, but I want more," he replied without fear of digging himself into a grave.

"We already talked about this," she said and sighed heavily.

"Yes. You talked and I listened." He sat up and patted the edge of the bed. She reluctantly made her way across the room and eased onto the mattress beside him. "Now it's my turn to talk while you listen."

"Okay."

He was ready to erase the pensive expression marring her pretty face, starting now.

"When I was eighteen, I made a vow that I'd never get married. I'd convinced myself that love didn't last, and that binding yourself to another person until the end of time was the biggest mistake anyone could ever make." He smiled when she gave him a halfhearted nod. "But I always told myself that if I ever found a woman who filled my life with light, happiness, and challenged me, I'd reconsider my pledge. And if she'd let me, I'd love her with every inch of my heart. Respect and honor her needs and her dreams. I wouldn't take advantage of her, but would treasure the fact that she wanted to share her mind, body, and soul, the same way I'd share mine with her."

"I used to believe in that fairy tale, too," she whispered.

"It doesn't have to be a fairy tale, darlin'." He sent her a soft smile and traced the tip of his finger over her cheek. "Tell me something…when you left Las Vegas, did you ever think of me?"

Ivy issued a tiny scoff. "Do you want the truth?"

"Yes. I don't lie, and I don't *ever* want to be lied to."

"I thought about you every day and every night. You even haunted my dreams."

A slow smile tugged the edges of his mouth. "Same here, and it drove me absolutely crazy. Not to ruin the moment I hope we're gonna be sharing soon, but when I came back home, I could have had a dozen women. I didn't, because the one woman I wanted was *you*."

Ivy shook her head. "One day you'll wake up and want those other women again."

"What makes you so sure?"

"Because monogamy is unrealistic. I mean, the chance of finding one person who'll fulfill all your needs is like winning the lottery a hundred times in a row. It'll never happen because no *one person* can satisfy another, not fully."

"Probably not. But what if you find someone who meets most of your needs? Do you slam the door in their face because they can't meet them all? And what parts are you responsible for filling?"

With a slight scowl, she pondered his words for several long seconds. "I don't know. I've never had anyone want to meet my needs. I'm not sure what I'd do."

"Have you ever let your walls down and opened your heart up

enough to let any of them try?"

A flutter of guilt danced across her face before she banked it. "You missed your calling, cowboy. You should have been a shrink."

"No. The only psyche I want to dissect is yours, darlin'...every nook and cranny." He cupped her cheek. "Sawyer's divorce was the reason I turned against marriage. What turned you against it?"

"I'm a gullible cheater magnet," she announced, as if the title held great esteem.

But the accompanying sadness in her eyes told him she'd earned the label with a shitload of disappointment and heartache. A part of him wanted to kick the shit out of every asshole who'd ever hurt her and forced her to lock herself off from the possibility of love. Because for the first time in his life, Noble wanted to give his love to a woman...this woman.

But would he be enough for her?

"If I could guarantee you eternal love, I'd do it in a New York minute. Unfortunately, I don't have a crystal ball to see into the future. Like I said before, I don't lie. I also don't make promises I can't keep. But I will promise you this—if you'll knock down your walls and let me in, I'll do everything in my power to love you and our child the way you deserve...with all my heart."

Ivy gaped at him as tears shimmered.

"Y-you...love me?" she stammered in disbelief.

"I think so. I mean...dammit, I've never been in love before. I have no idea what it feels like, but I know this...what I feel for you isn't normal."

She pinched her lips together, biting back a snicker.

"Fuck!" He exhaled heavily and scrubbed a hand through his hair. "What I'm trying to say isn't coming out right at all."

Ivy cupped his cheek and brushed a silky kiss across his lips. "I know what you're trying to say. I do. And I don't lie or make promises I can't keep, either. So, how about this... How about we take it a day at a time for a bit? Learn about each other then figure out where we want to go from there. Will that work?"

"No more walls?" he asked, arching his brows.

She shook her head. "No other women?"

"Hell no," he growled. "You're the *only* one I want, sweetheart."

She gazed into his eyes and threaded her fingers through his hair. Prickles of lightning zipped along his scalp as a chill skipped down his spine.

Ivy leaned in close to his ear. "Make love to me, Noble."

His whole body began to shake. He was blindsided by a wild, savage animal buried deep inside him, and the beast was snarling and screaming for him to slam her succulent body to the bed, mount her unmercifully, and mark her with his seed.

*Good Christ! Where did that come from?*

Shoving the ravenous monster down deep, Noble focused on going slow…showing her the tenderness she deserved.

He gently cupped her cheeks before slowly easing her back onto the mattress. As he inhaled her intoxicating scent, he trailed kisses from her lips to her jawline, then down the column of her neck, gently laving and nipping his way south.

Every touch and taste of her silky, soft flesh sent an electrical charge racing through his system as the missing pieces of his soul aligned and snapped into place.

For the first time in his life, Noble felt whole.

Greedily feeding on Ivy's flesh, he laved his way to her berry-hard nipples. She nearly levitated from the bed when he flicked his tongue over her dark, stony peaks. Pregnancy had obviously made them hypersensitive, and he took full advantage of that discovery. Toying with and teasing the tender tips, he reveled in each desperate mewl and moan escaping her writhing body.

She was an uninhibited delight who never failed to amaze him.

They had no need for words. Each touch, each caress and kiss spoke the language blooming from their hearts.

Noble loved her, of that he was now sure.

And even if Ivy wasn't ready or willing to admit it, she loved him right back.

When she gripped his weeping cock, he bit back a howl and grunted. As she slid her soft hand up and down his throbbing length, Noble thrust his hips, driving into her palm with each spine-bending stroke.

Like the ocean tide, they gorged, filling their hunger and demand in a sensual ebb and flow.

Ivy stroked him harder, unfurling ribbons of ecstasy to sail and tangle inside him.

Try as he might, Noble wasn't going to last much longer.

It had been far too long since he'd had…*her*.

Prying Ivy's hand from his shaft, he moved in between her slender legs and gazed at the patch of saturated curls shimmering with her heady, earthy dew. His mouth watered. His cock strained.

"I've been waiting a thousand lifetimes to taste you again, gorgeous."

Ivy purred as she slid a hand to her clit.

Purposely tormenting them both, she slowly rubbed the distended nub and whimpered softly.

"Tease yourself for me, baby…show me how you'd get off all those nights you spent thinking about me." His voice was thick and rusty.

An impish grin curled her lips as she dipped a slender finger into her dripping core.

When she drew her hand away, Noble captured her wrist and drew her finger to his mouth. He groaned as her warm, spicy nectar slid over his taste buds. Memories of the magic they'd made that one incredible night exploded in his brain.

"I've changed my mind," he growled, parting her swollen pink lips and lunging his mouth over her sex.

Ivy gasped and sank her fingers into his scalp as Noble laved her pebbled clit and lapped her silky juices. Panting, she bore down and came all over his face before he'd even had the chance to slide his fingers into her blistering tunnel. Drinking down the deluge spilling from inside her, Noble circled her sensitized clit with this tongue as Ivy gasped for breath.

When she looked down at him with those glassy pale blue eyes, Noble lost the rest of the pieces of his heart to her.

*Mine!*

"Again, gorgeous," he cooed. "You know we're just getting warmed up."

"Oh, god," she whimpered. "I'm glad I didn't die in the bakery. I'd much rather you kill me with orgasms like that."

He chuckled. "I'm not going to let you die, darlin', but I'll make damn sure you sleep hard tonight by the time we're through."

"Mmm," she purred. "I'm glad it's not time to sleep yet."

"Not nearly as glad as I am," he murmured, caressing the insides of her thighs with his cheeks.

Ivy jolted and started to giggle quietly.

"What are you laughing at?"

"Your whiskers…they tickle."

"I've got something else that will tickle…tickle your fancy, sweetheart."

She stopped laughing and gazed down at him with a hungry expression. "Oh, I remember…remember all the fancy things you did to me that night."

"Hey, you could have it every night. All you have to say is…yes."

"One day at a time, remember?"

"No pressure or anything, darlin'. I was just making you another promise."

"Damn," she murmured under her breath.

Noble wasn't opposed to playing dirty. He'd win her over one earth-shattering orgasm at a time. Starting right now.

Feathering his lips and tongue up her thighs, he nudged her clit with his nose. The little gasp she sucked in along with the quivery clasp of her pussy made his pulse quicken.

*Absolutely stunning.*

His cock was screaming for relief by the time he'd brought her to climax two more times. Noble was all but drowning not only on the sweet cream flowing from her but on the sounds of her muffled keening cries. He couldn't wait to take her someplace private, so he could hear her scream his name again as she shattered.

Moving up her glistening body, Noble licked the coating of her pleasure from his fingers and hovered over her. Love and pride swarmed him as he stared at Ivy, sated and panting. Her eyes were smoky and unfocused. A pink blush glowed over her milky flesh, and her hair spilled over his pillow like a halo of gold.

"Christ, you're gorgeous," he murmured as he lowered, supporting his weight on his elbows.

Dipping his head, he claimed her mouth urgently while he aligned his straining crest between her slick, sweltering folds. Inching in slowly, he issued a low groan as her liquid heat engulfed him.

Ivy wantonly thrust her hips upward, impaling herself on him.

Her silky, hot tunnel fluttered, pressing spine-sizzling kisses along his shaft.

Noble's eyes rolled to the back of his head. His balls churned. She was testing his control to the nth degree and he had to fight like hell to keep from spilling inside her too soon.

*Mom's ugly nightgown. Mom's ugly nightgown.*

Mentally repeating the mantra, Noble glided in and out of Ivy's tight core with slow, exacting strokes until the threat of embarrassing himself like an inept virgin passed.

Their tongues tangled, swirling and gliding, dancing in passion and need.

As if trying to reacquaint themselves with every inch of one another's bodies, fingers kneaded, gripped, and caressed warm, supple flesh, branding every lush curve, flat plane, and taut muscle to memory.

Driving in and out of her heavenly core relentlessly now, Noble slowly lifted from her mouth. He gazed down at the gorgeous angel beneath him and lost himself in her beauty. Pleasure played across her face in ripples of delight, giving way briefly to creases of agony as she searched for the elusive bliss of release.

"Open your eyes…look at me, baby," he panted in a commanding plea.

Her lashes fluttered open. Long seconds later, her glassy blue pools focused on him.

"Noble," she purred.

"I-I'm…not gonna last much…longer, darlin'."

A lethargic, sly smile tugged her lips as Ivy thrust a hand to her mound and began strumming her clit.

"Come with me," she begged, causing his cock to grow impossibly harder.

"That's…my…line," he grunted before clenching his jaw.

Her eyes briefly twinkled in mischief before glassing over once again.

She parted her mouth and swiped her pink tongue over her lush bottom lip.

Memories of that ripe mouth wrapped around his cock sent demand slamming down his spine, arcing like lightning deep in his balls. The roar in his ears nearly wiped out Ivy's breathless whimpers.

Unable to hold back the tide, Noble gripped her hips tightly. Shuttling in and out of her tightening core, he surrendered to the blistering swell cresting within.

"Come!" he growled in her ear.

A strangled cry, forcibly muffled, tore from the back of her throat.

Ivy bore down and clamped her heavenly tunnel around him.

Lights exploded behind his eyes.

His driving rhythm faltered.

Ivy arched into him, raking her nails over his back and sinking them into his flesh.

Noble's thrust sputtered into wild, jerky motions as he slammed into her.

As he pinched his lips together, ecstasy charged through him. His muscles turned to stone.

Lightning ricocheted through him as her pussy drew around him, milking his cock in spine-bending kisses.

Biting back a feral roar, Noble captured her mouth as he showered her sucking core in long, thick, and hot ropes of seed.

*Mine…forever!*

DELIRIOUSLY FLOATING SOMEWHERE beyond the stars, Ivy struggled to catch her breath. Noble's head lay nuzzled against her neck as he, too, worked to normalize the bursts of moist air billowing over her flesh.

Sizzling after shocks quivered through her, causing her tunnel to twitch and flutter involuntarily. Noble's embedded cock jerked in mutual indulgence causing him to sporadically moan.

She was boneless and sated, and her limbs felt like sandbags. Still, she clung to his sweat-soaked body, marveling in the inconceivable magic they'd so effortlessly created once again.

*Would it always be like this?* she silently wondered.

No. After time the newness would wear off. Noble would become restless and bored until one day she'd wake up and he'd be gone…sharing a bed with someone else. Oh, he wouldn't mean for it to happen. But men were creatures of habit. And Ivy was already privy to his habits.

He'd seemed to accept her offer to take things day by day. But Ivy knew she couldn't let her guard down. Not completely at least.

Her disheartening thoughts shredded the ethereal splendor she'd been floating in, sending her tumbling back to earth with a reality-jarring thud.

She inhaled a deep breath, wondering what had sent her down such a negative path in the first place. She'd just had the most incredible, mind-blowing sex of her life…for the second time. So why had she allowed Debbie Downer to crash this extraordinary party?

*Because every time you're with Noble, he slices you open, exposing all your insecurities and vulnerabilities. Clearly, you still don't trust him with all the pieces of you. But if you think he'll let you keep him at arm's length, you'd better wise up. Either you're all the way in or out. But you're going to have to make up your mind…and soon,* the little voice in the back of her head offered sympathetically.

Ivy scowled.

Trust took courage. While she'd reclaimed the virtues McMillian had stolen from her, Ivy didn't know if she was strong enough to risk giving Noble the power to crush her. Anxiety wormed its way through her system and she tensed.

Noble lifted his head, peered down at her, and wrinkled his brow. "What's wrong? Did I hurt you?"

*Not yet.*

But there was a ninety-nine-point-nine-nine-nine percent probability he would in the future.

*Stop it!*

She gaped at him, groping for some little white lie to mitigate his concern. Suddenly, his words blared through her head. *I don't lie and I don't* ever *want to be lied to.* Noble had been right by her side, all night, helping her navigate through the shit show McMillian had brought down on her. She owed the man still wrapping her in warmth and compassion the truth.

"I'm just worried that eventually I won't be enough for you."

A sad smile curled over his lips. "A life filled with guarantees would be a wonderful thing, wouldn't it? Unfortunately, we don't have that. All we have is gut feelings, faith, and trust."

She couldn't help but smile. Ivy would have never imagined that inside this sexy-as-sin cowboy lurked such an insightful philosopher.

"My gut tells me you're the one I'm meant to spend the rest of my life with," Noble continued. "So I decided to take that big leap of faith, praying you feel the same about me. I trust you, Ivy Addison. Trust you with my life, because I know in my heart you're a kind and loving soul. But if you're asking if I trust we'll make it till we're old and gray? The only way we'll find the answer to that one is through time, sweetheart."

"How can you be so sure I'm the one?"

He caressed a finger along her cheek. "How can you question the connection we share? Do you trust me, Ivy?"

*Either you're all the way in or out. But you're going to have to make up your mind...now!* the voice in her head vehemently repeated.

The time had come.

Ivy either had to take the plunge or grab her towel and pool noodle and run away.

Did she want to block him from her life, their baby's life, forever? The idea of never spending another night like this, wrapped in his arms, gazing at his handsome face, and openly sharing fears and insecurities ripped a gaping hole in her heart.

Trust took bravery, too.

Ivy had already proven to herself that she was brave. She'd proven that to herself by opening Sweet Flours. Proved it by knocking Harvey—the misogynistic prick from hell—Hays, the fuck out.

Woman's intuition told her she was destined to be with Noble, because no man had ever touched her heart, mind, body, or soul so deeply or profoundly.

Faith was that invisible conviction that sparked hope in those who discovered their own limitations. It took some soul searching, but Ivy possessed that spark, the one Noble had ignited inside her. If five days, five months, or five years from now he walked out of her life, she'd be crushed, without a doubt, but she'd be okay. Ivy was a survivor.

Trust was a fragile, priceless gift. One that time made stronger and sturdier. Noble had already handed her the priceless gift of trust. It was time for her to place hers in his strong, capable hands.

Ivy cupped his face, lifted her head from the pillow, and softly kissed his lips. "Yes, Noble Grayson, I trust you. Trust you with my life."

His nostrils flared.

Tears glistened in his eyes.

He brushed a strand of hair from her cheek and swallowed tightly. "I won't hurt you."

His promise was wrapped in such raw emotion that Ivy knew he'd never made such a vow to anyone else before. Tears sprang out of nowhere.

"Don't cry, love. And please don't be afraid to let me in. I'd rather cut off my arm than ever hurt you. But for now, we'll start out like you said…one day at a time and see where life leads us," he whispered gently.

Holding back her sobs of happiness mixed with fear, Ivy simply nodded.

Noble wrapped his arms around her and slowly eased from her pussy before he rolled to his side, taking her with him. Tucking her in against his chest, he brushed a sweet kiss to her head and sighed.

"Close your eyes, darlin', and go to sleep now. I'll be right here with you, keeping you safe and sound."

With a tiny nod, she let her wet lashes drift shut.

Soothed by the rhythmic beat of his heart, the security of his strong arms, and the delicious heat of his rugged body, Ivy stopped crying and floated away into the inky darkness.

When she woke, sunlight spilled through a gap in the curtains, illuminating an unfamiliar room. Noble lay beside her, snoring softly, with one hand still draped over her hip. Their legs were as tangled as the sheet bunched around them. The familiar ache between her legs, the one she hadn't felt since Vegas, throbbed. It was a sweet pain she could easily become accustomed to. A shiver of anticipation raced up her spine.

As memories of the devastating fire raked her with brutal anguish, Ivy splayed a hand across her stomach. She was alive. The baby was alive. That was all that mattered. She gently stroked her palm over her distended belly and issued a grateful sigh.

*It's the start of a new day, peanut. We might be down, but we're not out. We'll be fine. Mommy…and Daddy will make sure of that.*

*Daddy. Wow!* The word sounded so foreign, but she didn't bother holding back the hopeful smile spreading over her lips.

A light tap came from the bedroom door. Ivy snapped her head toward the sound and quickly tugged the sheet up to her neck.

"Noble, honey? It's Mom. Are you up?"

Ivy glanced over to see the man lying beside her, still sound asleep, snoring contently. She jabbed him with her elbow and hissed, "Noble. Wake up. Your mom's at the door."

"Huh?" He sat up, blinking, clearly disoriented.

"Your mom is at the door," Ivy whispered again.

"Ma?" he called out in a rough, sleepy voice that made her stomach flip-flop.

*Damn hormones.*

"Yes, honey. Can I come in?"

"No," he barked. Noble cleared his throat and launched out of bed, frantically searching the floor. "Hang on a second. Where the fuck are my… What do you need, Ma?"

"I brought Ivy some clean clothes and wanted to let you both know that breakfast will be ready in thirty minutes."

Ivy bit back a grin.

Noble was standing in the middle of the room, buck-assed naked, sporting a most glorious hard-on, and scrubbing a hand over his face.

"Where the hell are my jeans?" he whispered to her.

Ivy shrugged.

"No clue. You were naked, like now, when I climbed into bed

with you," she said, keeping her voice low so Nola wouldn't hear.

"Shit," he hissed. "Just leave 'em outside the door, Ma. We'll get 'em in a minute."

"Fine, but don't make Ivy late for breakfast. That baby needs a well-balanced meal so he or she can grow into the Grayson name."

"I told you so! If Grayson isn't on that birth certificate, she'll skin us both alive," he whispered, flashing Ivy a crooked grin.

"Noble Franklin Grayson, just because I'm getting older doesn't mean I've lost my mother hearing. You're right I'll skin you both if any name but Grayson is given that baby. You hear?"

"We hear, Ma. We'll be out in a few minutes."

"Noble *Franklin*, huh?" Ivy smirked.

"Yes." He puffed up proudly. God, he was so damn gorgeous in all his naked glory. "What's your middle name?"

*Oh, shit. No. No. No.*

"I'll tell your mom the Grayson name is perfectly fine for the birth certificate," Ivy ceded, blatantly changing the subject.

"Good. I like that. So will she. Now what's your middle name?" he pressed, growling and prowling onto the bed like a lion.

She giggled as he hovered over her, boxing her in with his arms and legs. "It's Ivy."

"Oh. Okay, so what's your first name?"

She shook her head vehemently.

"You're not going to tell me?"

"No. I hate my given name."

"Why? Is it Rumpelstiltskin?"

"Close." Ivy groaned.

"Eugenia?"

"What?" She laughed. "Do I look like a Eugenia?"

Noble shrugged. "No, but you don't look like a Rumpelstiltskin either."

"Thank god."

"Twenty minutes," Nola called from outside the door.

"Tell me." Noble cocked his head and gave her a warning glare.

"You're so cute when you do that," she taunted.

"Dammit. That's my intimidating face."

"No it's not, it's cute."

"God help me. What have I gotten myself into?" he said, rolling his eyes and shaking his head.

"You can always back out," she countered with a sassy smile.

"Not on your life, sweetheart." He leaned in, kissing her hard and fast before jumping off the bed. "I'll grab your clothes so you can run across the hall and take a shower before breakfast. Just do me a favor and don't put that damn nightgown on again, okay, Eugenia?"

"You keep calling me Eugenia, and I'll put it on and parade down Main Street in it."

He flashed her a knee-knocking smile that made her toes curl. "God! We're going to have so much fun."

After Noble retrieved her clothes, he peeked his head out of the door, glancing left and right before waving her to him.

"Coast is clear. You can streak to the bathroom."

"Streak?"

"Yeah. Because you're not putting that fucking old-lady nightgown back on while I'm around."

"What if I like that old-lady nightgown?" she asked forcing herself not to smile.

Noble shook his head, snagged her wrist and plopped the stack of clothes into her hands before shoving her bare body out into the hallway.

"Noble!" she yelped.

"What's goin'… Oh, damn. Now that's a wake-up call," Norris exclaimed, coming around the corner and skimming a stare over her naked flesh with a wolfish grin. "This is hella better than a damn alarm clock."

Ivy let out another yelp and quickly hugged her arms over her breasts while slapping a hand to her crotch, dumping the clothes all over the floor.

Noble jumped from his room and blocked Ivy's naked body with *his* naked body.

"Stop looking at her and get the hell out of here!" he bellowed.

Ivy raced to the bathroom, slamming and locking the door behind her before pressing her forehead against the wood. Embarrassment scalded her entire body as she listened to the conversation taking place in the hall.

"She's smokin'-hot, man. She got any sisters… any younger sisters?"

"Go stroke a load in your room and get out of here, you little perv," Noble scolded.

"Bet you're not strokin' it alone anymore, are you?" Norris taunted.

"Next time I'm putting the old granny gown on," Ivy huffed under her breath.

"Go!" Noble barked. Several seconds later, there was a tap on the bathroom door. "Open up, sweetheart. I got your clothes for you."

"Ten minutes," Nola hollered from the opposite end of the hall.

"Better hurry." Noble grinned as he kissed her quickly and shut the door.

After scrubbing the embarrassment from her skin beneath the shower, Ivy quickly dressed and raced through brushing her teeth and hair before rushing to the kitchen.

"Morning, Miss Ivy," Norris greeted with a knowing grin.

Noble stood. As he strode past the youngest Grayson, he smacked his brother on the back of the head before wrapping an arm around Ivy's waist and leading her to the table.

When breakfast was done, sans any additional awkward nudity, Ivy thanked Nola for the delicious spread of orange juice, coffee, bacon, eggs, biscuits, grits, and pancakes. Then she and Noble climbed into his truck and headed toward Haven.

Ivy wasn't sure if she was mentally or emotionally prepared to see the destruction to her bakery in the light of day or deal with the news crews that had arrived last night.

Unfortunately, she didn't have a choice in the matter.

# CHAPTER EIGHTEEN

As the truck ate up the pavement, Ivy's anxiety and fear quadrupled.

"Do you want me to turn around?" He squeezed her thigh with his wide hand.

Every cell in Ivy's body screamed *yes!* But the fact that Noble knew she was an angst-ridden mess and was offering to save her from, well, from herself warmed her soul and melted her heart.

Without a doubt, he was living up to his name. Ivy knew there was never a more gallant or gorgeous knight willing to slay her dragons of insecurity. Still, she wasn't a helpless princess, locked in the tower of some evil queen. She was simply letting her weaknesses overshadow her strengths.

"No. Keep going."

"You sure? Because the worry rolling off you is going to give you an ulcer before we reach town."

"I know. I can't help it. I'm not sure I'm ready to see what McMillian did to my shop or face the reporters. There's so much work to be done and so many outside forces pulling at me, I'm not sure where to start."

"We start with contacting your insurance company. Then we'll hire a structural engineer to come out and see if the structure is sound enough to rebuild. If it is, we'll get a crew in to gut it and start putting it back together. We'll figure out the rest as it comes."

His steady reassurance was like a balm. Ivy laid her head on his shoulder and threaded her fingers through his. "You kept saying *we* through all that."

Noble lifted their entwined hands to his lips and kissed the flesh beneath her knuckles. "We're a team, darlin'. I'm in for the long haul. Don't you ever doubt or forget that. Got it?"

"I won't. Thank you."

Before Noble had turned onto Main Street, the acrid scent of smoke wafted into the cab of the truck. Ivy leaned up and peered past him, catching sight of not one but three news vans parked at the curb in front what used to be Sweet Flours.

A spike of panic pounded through her system. "I'm not ready for this."

"I know. That's why I called Nate while you were in the shower. I'm going to pull into the alley behind the bar. He and Gina are awake and waiting for us."

"No," she blurted out, blindsided by gratitude and fury. She knew Noble's preparations hadn't been contrived maliciously, but the sense that he was stripping control from her thundered through her. "Park in front of the bar and we'll walk in together. I'm through hiding from those people. They're not going to force me to cower in fear anymore."

A slow smile of admiration spread over his lips. "Do you have any idea how strong, brave, and independent you are?"

"I'm trying," she whispered.

"You're succeeding," he said beaming before claiming her mouth in a potent and powerful kiss. "Let's do this."

As Noble turned and eased onto Main Street, Ivy scooched across the bench seat—instantly mourning the loss of his body heat—and peered out the passenger window. Ignoring the news crews lingering next to their trucks, Ivy took in the sight of her gutted and charred business. Tears stung her eyes. But when she spotted Emmett Hill, sitting alone on the wooden bench beside the remnants of Sweet Flours, wearing a lost and forlorn expression, a sob slid off her lips.

Grief, thick and suffocating, pressed in all around her.

"Pull over," she instructed in a voice that sounded like sandpaper.

"Here?" She nodded. "But the news crews..."

"Pull over. I need to talk to Emmett." She pointed, drawing Noble's attention to the old man.

"Aw, hell," he muttered and swung the truck in alongside a big white news van.

Ivy hopped out and rushed to the bench. Emmett lifted his head and sent her a forlorn smile.

"You're a damn good sight for sore eyes, missy." He patted the wood beside him.

"Ivy, what do you have to say about Eugene McMillian's claims that you killed his wife?" a woman yelled out to her.

"Miss Addison, do you know why Eugene McMillian was handcuffed and taken to the Dallas County PD this morning?" another woman shouted.

"Does his arrest have anything to do with the fire at your bakery?" a male reporter yelled.

In a frenzy, the reporters started rapid-firing questions at her.

Ivy ignored them, focusing only on Emmett. "What are you doing here?"

"Back the fuck off...all of you," Noble bellowed from behind her. "Now!"

"Who are you?" another reporter asked him.

"I'm your worst nightmare if you don't get those goddamn cameras and microphones out of my face," Noble snarled.

Ivy smirked and sat down beside Emmett.

Glancing up, she saw that Noble had his back to her. His legs were slightly spread, shoulders thrust back, and arms stretched wide to keep the press back. He reminded her of an impenetrable wall. She could only imagine the intimidating expression chiseled into his handsome face. Over his shoulder she saw Nate and Gina sprinting toward them from across the street.

"Looks like you could use some reinforcements." Nate chuckled, assuming the same stance next to his brother.

"Morning, sugar," Gina called to Ivy with a wink before sidling in next to Nate, twirling the end of her Louisville slugger,

Martha, in her fingers.

Emmett chuckled beside her and slapped his knees. "I was waiting for you to get here. And now that you are, I'm enjoying this here circus somethin' fierce."

As the reporters pelted more questions, Noble, Nate, and Gina lobbed insults and warnings for them to pack up and leave town.

"Yeah, well, it's going to get worse before it gets better." Ivy cringed. "Hang tight. I'm going to go calm the masses."

"Aw, just when it was beginning to get interesting. I wanted to see Gina start doing a little batting practice." Emmett chuckled.

"You're incorrigible." Ivy rolled her eyes, stood, and stepped in beside Noble.

"That's enough!" She glared at the faces of the anxious reporters clamoring in all around her. "I'll say this one time and one time only... No comment."

A collective groan rippled through the news teams before they started calling out questions on top of one another.

"You heard the lady," Noble barked. "Respect Miss Addison's privacy and go on home. You're not welcome here. I'm sure there are bigger news stories that will boost your ratings back in Dall—"

Noble's words were cut off by a short whoop of the siren from Jasper's cruiser as he pulled in behind the news vans. The sheriff stepped out of his vehicle and scowled.

"Great, here comes Barney Fife," a male reporter, wearing a thick layer of camera-ready makeup and hair slicked back, groused.

Jasper's arrival didn't go unnoticed by the citizens of Haven. The door of Toot's Café opened as patrons spilled out onto the sidewalk. Several other business owners and customers exited shops lining Main Street, and like a well-choreographed Labor Day parade, they gathered to watch the chaos unfold.

'Y'all gone and done it now... Not only did you go pokin' the good people of Haven, you went and riled up the po-po, as well," Emmett cackled from the bench.

Gina snorted and Ivy nearly burst out laughing.

"They surely did, Emmett." Jasper smirked before sending Ivy a quizzical look. "Have you given your statement yet, Miss Addison?"

"She did. It was, *no comment*," Noble snarled.

Jasper nodded thoughtfully as he rested a palm on the butt of the gun strapped at his hip. "Then you all got what you came here for. Have a nice trip back to Dallas."

"Or what?" a blonde reporter countered with a smarmy smile.

"Or I'll arrest you for loitering, sweetie," Jasper replied with a feral smile. "We got laws against that here."

"Git'em, Sheriff," Emmett said with a snicker. "Toss 'em in the slammer and throw away the key."

Exasperation rolled over Jasper's face. As he turned toward the old man, Ivy's dad whipped his Audi into the space beside Noble's truck. She glanced up to see Noble's brows slashed in confusion.

"My folks," she whispered.

Noble nodded and grinned as Ivy's dad, mom, sister, and lawyer climbed out of the car and rushed over to join the fray.

"Shit, her lawyer's here," groused one of the reporters.

"Damn right she is," Margaret Neill announced haughtily. "My client has no comment."

"They already know that, ma'am," Jasper said with a thoroughly intrigued grin.

Margaret, equally captivated, skimmed an approving gaze up and down his trim, uniform-clad body and smiled. "Thank you, Sheriff…?"

"Jasper… Jasper Straub."

While her lawyer and the officer briefly undressed each other with their eyes, Janice and Celina rushed over and nearly tackled Ivy in a tight hug. Without thinking, her mom pressed a hand to Ivy's stomach as tears glistened in her eyes.

"Holy shit! She's pregnant!" the blonde reporter screeched.

Like sharks in a feeding frenzy, the news crews charged her, shoving microphones and camera lenses in Ivy's face.

"Oh, god. I-I didn't mean…" Janice whispered in a tone of pure mortification.

Like an avalanche, their questions tumbled over Ivy, suffocating her in a blanket of sheer panic.

"Who's the father?"

"Does McMillian know you're pregnant?"

"Tell us who the father is, Miss Addison."

"Is that McMillian's love child cooking inside you?" the Ken doll wannabe chortled.

"Motherfucker!" Noble snarled as he charged the reporter. In a blur, he pulled his arm back and punched the prick in the jaw. The man's eyes rolled back in his head, just like Harvey's had in Vegas, before he tipped onto the pavement.

"*I'm* the father, you cocksucker!" Noble bellowed.

Like a gong, a collective gasp from the people of Haven reverberated in the air.

"Oh, shit!" Ivy whimpered as a veil of blackness converged behind her eyes.

Her knees began to fold out from under her. And as the inky darkness swallowed her up, Ivy heard her mother scream.

"Open your eyes for me, sweetheart!"

Noble's voice tugged at her from the shadows, but his whiskey-smooth tone was edged in so much desperation and fear that it made her heart hurt.

Like hummingbird wings, soft feminine sobs fluttered in the distance.

"Goddamn it, Ivy! Open your eyes…please, baby…please!" Noble begged unabashedly.

Suddenly, the potent scent of alcohol burned her nose.

"Give her a minute, son. This will help," a familiar voice Ivy couldn't readily place, implored.

When she forced her eyes open Ivy found Noble and Doc Knight hovering over her. She glanced around and recognized the exam room. It was the same one the doctor had delivered the news that she was pregnant.

"There she is," the concerned physician said with a reassuring smile.

"Thank fuck!" Noble said on an explosive exhale. His eyes were brimming with unshed tears as he dropped his head to the crook of her neck. "You scared the ever-loving shit out of me baby."

"Noble," Ivy whispered as she draped her arm around his wide shoulders.

It was then that she noticed her mom and Celina hugging each other, sobbing. Her dad stood beside them wearing a frightened, shell-shocked expression. Nate and Gina clung to one another as worry lined their faces, while in the corner, Margaret Neill's formidable façade had cracked as she stood helplessly wringing her hands.

"What happened?" Ivy asked reflexively. The question had no more left her lips than the memory of Noble knocking out the reporter and his declaration slammed her memory banks. "I passed out again, didn't I?"

"Yes...yes, you did," Doc Knight confirmed. "Isn't any wonder what with all the hullabaloo going on out there."

"She won't be coming back into town until those vultures are gone," Noble vowed, lifting his head.

"It's not them," Ivy pensively began. "It's...you."

"Me?" Noble blanched.

"Y-you just told the whole town that..." She groaned and smoothed a palm over her stomach.

He covered her hand with his as a slow, sexy smile spread over his lips. Keeping his eyes locked on her, Noble softly shook his head. "Y'all mind giving us a couple minutes alone?"

Doc Knight chuckled softly before he stood and quickly ushered everyone from the examination room. When the door snicked shut behind him, Noble eased onto the table beside her and carefully scooped her up into his arms.

"I'm ready to climb to the top of the water tower with a bullhorn and shout for the whole world to hear, sweetheart." He cupped her face and held her prisoner with his fiery gaze. "I lived four long months missing you every empty day and endless night. I'm not spending another five minutes without you...without our child beside me. You told me you were afraid that eventually you wouldn't be enough for me...remember?"

She nodded as his brutally honest words and her tumultuous hormones sent tears spilling down her face.

"Darlin', you're so much more than I could have ever hoped to find." His voice cracked. "I love how brave and strong you are even when you're frightened or unsure. Love the tinkling sound of your laughter. And I definitely love your sinful screams of pleasure. I love that when you're snuggled up next to me, like you are now, that you fit like you were made for me alone. Love the little sizzle of electricity that still shoots up my arm when I touch your soft skin. I love your smart-assed comebacks and the sassy way you're not afraid to tease or confront me."

She could feel the emotions bleeding from Noble's unexpected confession. Each profound and revealing word that rolled off his tongue stripped another layer of uncertainty from her soul.

"I could go on for days, but what I'm really trying to say...what I've never said to any woman before is that...I. Love. You."

He pressed his lips to hers and kissed her...kissed her with a passion and promise she'd never felt before. The walls of denial she'd tried so fiercely to hide behind crumbled to dust at her feet. The lies she'd told herself since Noble had waltzed back into her life swirled like smoke on the wind and blew away.

His declaration split her wide open.

Stripped naked, vulnerable...more exposed than she imagined possible, she drank in Noble's love like a life force.

She'd never felt the sense of rightness that was rising up inside her before.

Ivy knew, without a shred of doubt or fear, that she belonged with him…to him, now and forever.

She kissed him back, trying to fill his soul with the emotions overflowing inside her.

Noble moaned as he clutched her tighter.

Ivy tore away from his mouth and cupped her hands around his face. She gazed into his twinkling emerald eyes and confidently lifted her chin.

"I love you, too," she bravely confessed.

He opened his mouth as if to say something, but no words came out.

She didn't need to hear him…Ivy could see and feel each and every spectacular emotion bursting through him, because they were erupting inside her, too.

A watery laugh slid from her lips. "So when do you want to make an honest woman out of me?"

Noble's eyes grew wide.

His megawatt smile nearly blinded her.

He threw back his head and roared in triumph.

Ivy broke into a blissful fit of giggles.

He kissed her hard, then lifted her into his arms and stood. "We're gonna do this the right way, darlin'."

"What do you mean?" she asked as he strode toward the door.

He didn't answer, simply flashed her a wide grin. As he carried her into the hallway, everyone rushed toward them.

"You stable enough to stand, my love?" Noble asked.

*My love.*

It was the sweetest music she'd ever heard.

Ivy nodded. Noble gently lowered her to the floor and took hold of her hand.

"What was all the yelling about?" Concern laced her mom's words.

"This," Noble cryptically replied before turning to face her father and clearing his throat. "Mr. Addison, I'm sorry for sullying Ivy's reputation and for any embarrassment I've caused your family by getting her pregnant. But sir, I'm deeply…no, I'm hopelessly in love with Ivy. I'm begging permission to marry your daughter."

Her heart damn near exploded out of her chest.

Jeff lifted his chin and studied Noble as if he were a bug under a microscope.

The air around them stilled, becoming so quiet you could have heard a pin drop.

Ivy held her breath.

The muscles in Noble's jaw twitched as he squeezed her hand tighter.

"Under one condition," Jeff announced in a deadly serious tone she'd never heard him use before.

"What condition is that, sir?" Noble bravely asked.

"That you marry her here and not in Las Vegas, for shit's sake," Jeff barked as a wide grin crawled across his face.

She and Noble exhaled in unison.

Laughter filled the hallway as he extended his hand. Jeff latched on to it and the two men shook. "Deal, sir."

Congratulatory hugs, handshakes, and, of course, a few tears were shared.

As Nate busily texted on his phone, Gina put two fingers in her mouth and let loose with an ear-piercing whistle.

"Let's move this celebration over to the Hangover…drinks are on the house!"

Nate looked up from his phone and frowned. "Baby, it's eleven in the morning."

"It's five o'clock somewhere, sweetheart." Her innocent doe-eyed expression didn't sway Nate in the slightest. Gina pouted and let out a heavy sigh. "Oh, fine. I'll make mimosas then."

He sent her a wink and a grin, tucked his phone away, and planted a fiery kiss to her lips.

Leaving Doc Knight to tend to the patients sitting in his waiting room, the rest of them left his office and started for the bar. The minute Jasper caught sight of the entourage, a sour expression settled over his face. Leaving the news crew with a loud warning to stay put, Jasper headed Ivy and Noble's way.

"We've got a problem, Grayson," the sheriff announced.

"Which Grayson?" Nate quipped with a chuckle.

"Noble."

"Let me guess, pretty boy is awake and wants to file assault charges, right?" Noble spat.

"Yep."

"Well, shit! Tell that Ken doll asshat it'll have to wait. We're going to the bar to celebrate."

"Celebrate what?"

"Ivy and I are getting married."

"No shit? Well, congratulations, you two." Jasper grinned.

Margaret stepped up and cleared her throat. "Y'all go on in and get the party started. I'll join you in a minute. I need to have a little conversation with my old friend…the Ken doll, Bart Mannford, a.k.a. Channel Fourteen's wonder boy."

"You know him?" Noble barked.

"A long time ago when I was young, drunk, and stupid, I made a horrible mistake. But old Bart made an even bigger one. I didn't know it at the time, but he was *married*…still is, at least for now." With a devious glint in her eyes, she flashed a wicked smile.

"Oh, my god," Ivy murmured.

"Wow. You must have been really drunk," Celina blurted before slapping a hand over her mouth.

"Oh, I was, sugar," Margaret assured with a smirk.

"I'll escort you over to him," Jasper offered, extending an elbow. As Margaret looped her arm through his, he flashed her a provocative smile. "You know, I've always found cunning women damn…stimulating."

"Git some, sheriff," Emmett, still sitting on the bench, called out with glee.

The celebration was in full swing when Noble's entire family came through the front door, smiling and cheering.

Margaret returned to the group a few minutes later and

announced with a triumphant smile. "All charges have been dropped."

An even louder roar of cheers erupted.

Introductions were extended, glasses were filled, and toasts were made as laughter and love filled the room. Through it all, Noble's steady arm lay wrapped around Ivy's waist.

Nate tossed some money in the jukebox and sent Noble a wink.

When the first lyrics and notes of *"Unchained Melody"* began to play, a melancholy smile curled over Noble's lips.

"Come on, darlin', we gotta dance to this one," he whispered in her ear.

She nibbled her bottom lip and nodded as Noble ushered to the open section of hardwood in front of the jukebox. A flutter twirled in her belly. She hadn't danced since her high school prom. She sent up a silent prayer that she didn't stomp and bruise Noble's feet.

The moment he swept his arms around her and began gliding her across the floor, all her insecurities vanished, like they always did when she was with him.

"My graddaddy Grayson used to listen to this song…used to play it over and over when I was young and visited him every day," Noble explained as their bodies swayed in time to the hauntingly beautiful song.

"I take it he's gone?"

Noble nodded. "Five years ago. God, he would have loved you." A sheepish grin appeared. "One day…I was maybe five or six, I promised him that when I got married I'd play this song at my wedding…b-because it was his favorite."

His voice cracked and he buried his face in the crook of her neck. Ivy choked back a sob and gently stroked the hair at his nape, hugging him tighter. Long seconds later, Noble exhaled and began softly singing along.

Whatever pieces of her heart he hadn't claimed already, Ivy surrendered to him, without an ounce of reservation.

"Thank you," she whispered.

"For what, darlin'?"

"For proving that that fairy tales really do exist."

"Thank you for trusting me and allowing me to be your happily ever after, sweetheart," he drawled before slanting his lips over hers, stealing her soul, and melding it to his.

## THE HOTTIES OF HAVEN SERIES

**Sin On A Stick – Novella**
**Wet Dream – Book One**
**Revenge on the Rocks – Novella**

# ABOUT THE AUTHOR

*USA Today* Bestselling author **Jenna Jacob** paints a canvas of passion, romance, and humor as her alpha men and the feisty women who love them unravel their souls, heal their scars, and find a happy-ever-after kind of love. Heart-tugging, captivating, and steamy, Jenna's books will surely leave you breathless and craving more.

A mom of four grown children, Jenna and her alpha-hunk husband live in Kansas. She loves reading, getting away from the city on the back of a Harley, music, camping, and cooking.

Meet her wild and wicked fictional family in Jenna's sultry series: ***The Doms of Genesis***. Become spellbound by searing triple love connections in her continuing saga: ***The Doms of Her Life*** (co-written with the amazing Shayla Black and Isabella LaPearl). Journey with couples struggling to resolve their pasts and discover true love in her romantic suspense series: ***Passionate Hearts***. Or laugh along as Jenna lets her zany sense of humor and lack of filter run free in her steamy contemporary series: ***Hotties of Haven***.

**Connect with Jenna Online**
Website: www.jennajacob.com
Email: jenna@jennajacob.com
Facebook Fan Page: facebook.com/authorjennajacob
Twitter: @jennajacob3
Instagram: instagram.com/jenna_jacob_author
Amazon Author Page: http://amzn.to/1GvwNnn
Newsletter: www.subscribepage.com/jennajacob

# OTHER TITLES BY JENNA JACOB

## The Doms of Genesis
Embracing My Submission
Masters of My Desire
Master of My Mind
Saving My Submission
Seduced By My Doms
Lured By My Master
Sin City Submission
Bound To Surrender
Resisting My Submission
Craving His Command
Seeking My Destiny

## The Doms of Her Life – Raine Falling
One Dom To Love
The Young and The Submissive
The Bold and The Dominant
The Edge Of Dominance

## The Doms of Her Life – Heavenly Rising
The Choice

## The Passionate Hearts
Sky Of Dreams
**Winds Of Desire** (Coming Soon)

Made in the USA
San Bernardino, CA
07 December 2018